A
BEAUTIFUL
DISGUISE

Books by Roseanna M. White

LADIES OF THE MANOR

The Lost Heiress
The Reluctant Duchess
A Lady Unrivaled

SHADOWS OVER ENGLAND

A Name Unknown
A Song Unheard
An Hour Unspent

THE CODEBREAKERS

The Number of Love
On Wings of Devotion
A Portrait of Loyalty

Dreams of Savannah

THE SECRETS OF THE ISLES

The Nature of a Lady
To Treasure an Heiress
Worthy of Legend

Yesterday's Tides

THE IMPOSTERS

A Beautiful Disguise

THE IMPOSTERS · 1

A

BEAUTIFUL
DISGUISE

ROSEANNA M. WHITE

BETHANYHOUSE
a division of Baker Publishing Group
Minneapolis, Minnesota

Published by Bethany House Publishers
Minneapolis, Minnesota
www.bethanyhouse.com

Bethany House Publishers is a division of
Baker Publishing Group, Grand Rapids, Michigan

Printed in the United States of America

Library of Congress Cataloging-in-Publication Data
Names: White, Roseanna M., author.
Title: A beautiful disguise / Roseanna M. White.
Description: Minneapolis, Minnesota : Bethany House Publishers, a division of Baker Publishing Group, [2023] | Series: The Imposters ; 1
Identifiers: LCCN 2023008949 | ISBN 9780764240928 (paper) | ISBN 9780764241819 (casebound) | ISBN 9781493442126 (ebook)
Subjects: LCSH: Private investigators—England—London—Fiction. | LCGFT: Christian fiction. | Detective and mystery fiction. | Novels.
Classification: LCC PS3623.H578785 B43 2023 | DDC 813/.6—dc23/eng/20230301
LC record available at https://lccn.loc.gov/2023008949

Scripture quotations are from the King James Version of the Bible.

Cover design by Dan Thornberg, Design Source Creative Services
Cover model photography by Ildiko Neer / Trevillion Images

Author is represented by The Steve Laube Agency.

Baker Publishing Group publications use paper produced from sustainable forestry practices and post-consumer waste whenever possible.

23 24 25 26 27 28 29   7 6 5 4 3 2 1

*To the ladies of Patrons & Peers
for the unending encouragement
and support you provide.
This one's for you, girls!*

ONE

April 1909
London, England

*T*he narrow stone ledge beneath her bare toes, cold and sturdy, felt like bliss after three hours of wearing shoes that pinched. Lady Marigold Fairfax might have wiggled her toes in ecstasy if that wouldn't have meant losing her purchase and sending herself plummeting eighty feet down to the street below. No, better to keep her toe wiggles mental. She smiled into the building's façade, moved her fingers to the next hold between stone blocks, and scurried along the ledge toward the corner.

Yates was already there, leaping like a mountain goat to where the ledge continued on the adjacent wall. He glanced at her, the moonlight catching the brows he lifted in challenge. *What's taking you so long?* those arches said.

She stuck her tongue out at her brother and picked up her pace. The wind kicked up just as she was preparing for her own stretch between walls, which sent a shiver coursing through her. But it didn't hinder her confident transfer, nor slow her as she hurried straight into its chilly teeth. Her leotard didn't provide much by way of insulation, but adrenaline warmed her from the inside out.

Yates held up for her at the next corner, just as planned. They navigated around that exposed corner together and then paused, now directly below the window they needed to access. Scaling the wall wouldn't have been a problem had the stone blocks of the other walls continued onto this one, but some genius had decided to go for a smoother look here, eliminating all the fingerholds and toeholds.

Tilting her head back, Marigold took in the window a floor above them. Soft light glowed from the panes, which meant the curtains were open. Not ideal, as they had to avoid crossing in front of the glass, but it was what they had planned for. This high up, and with no building of the same height nearby, the occupants wouldn't be expecting anyone to be able to see into the chamber.

More fools, them.

Marigold executed a quick about-face, putting the wall at her back, as her brother did the same.

"Ready?" Yates's whisper reached her ears even as his hands curled around her waist.

"Ready." She braced her hands on his wrists and coiled her muscles. They bounced together thrice to match rhythms, then he lifted as she jumped. Over, up, her feet finding their familiar places on his shoulders. Once she straightened her knees, arms held out for balance, they did another, slower about-face, putting the wall before them again.

Yates raised his arms, palms flat, and she stepped onto them, gripping the wall with her own palms as he raised his arms inch by inch, lifting her ever closer to the next ledge. After ten seconds that she knew were easier for her than for him—she could feel the quivering of his arms through her feet—her fingers found the ledge. "Got it!" she whispered downward.

Another three bounces, and he gave her a good push—the momentum she needed to swing her body along the wall like a pendulum, hooking both knee and elbow on that other ledge.

Her silk stocking caught on the rough stone, the sound of it making her wince. That was the third pair this month. At this rate, she was going to have to increase her stocking budget. And from where would she borrow the funds? Her feather budget, perhaps. She would just have to make do with more peacock and ostrich feathers and forgo the ones they didn't raise themselves. Or perhaps she could bring lion's mane into vogue, if she could convince old Leonidas to give up a tuft or two of his proud beard.

Marigold grinned as she pulled herself fully onto the ledge and edged her way slowly to the window.

Not only were the curtains open, but the window itself was also cracked a bit too. Excellent. That meant that the voices of those within made their way to her ears without her needing to get any closer.

"I say, Adams, you know that's not the case."

Marigold closed her eyes to better recall the notes she'd studied earlier that evening. The likely players in the room were Lord Adams, Mr. Dormer, and the Swedish ambassador. She'd never heard any of them speak before, except Lord Adams, but the voice sounded far too British for it to belong to the Swede. Probably. Mr. Dormer, then.

"Do I?" Lord Adams, no question. His distinctive whine set her teeth on edge. "I would put nothing past him, Dorm."

Rather typical of him.

FROM THE DOSSIER OF
Lord Thomas Adams, baron

HEIGHT: *5'5"*

WEIGHT: *13 stone*

AGE: *57*

HAIR: *Very little to speak of, and no doubt less still by the time anyone reviews these notes*

EYES: *Brown (and bespectacled)*

STYLE: ~~*None*~~ *Old-fashioned*

PRIMARY RESIDENCE: *Mayfair*

OBSERVANCES: *Lord Adams is a ninny man given to cowardice and suspicion. He is always quick to assume everyone is against him, no matter the circumstances. Despite that, he has a keen mind for business and has been ahead of his competitors and peers in investing in advances such as electricity and automobiles.*

IMPRESSIONS: *If one can avoid his company and simply follow his investment advice, one will be a happy man (or WOMAN, thank you).*

NOTES: *Bought stock in the company I overheard him giving instructions to his broker about. Have already doubled my investment. Must make it a point to listen in on his conversations whenever time permits. At this rate, we could undo Father's damage in a decade or two!*

From inside the room came Mr. Dormer's laborious sigh. "Really, my lord. You have no reason at all to suspect that he's trying to cut *you* out of anything."

The "he" was, she knew, Lord Emory—the one to have employed them—under the guise of their investigative firm, the Imposters, Ltd.—because *he* was convinced that Adams meant to cut *him* out of a deal they'd shaken on.

Adams snorted. "He would. I have no doubt of it, which is why we must act first. I say, where *is* that Swede?"

Shuffling footsteps, a squeaking door, a muffled question to someone in the corridor. Marigold wished they'd had the opportunity to rig up their mirrors so she could see into the room, but alas. The building hadn't permitted it, despite their cousin Graham—architect and Imposter—scouring blueprints and his own hand-drawn schematics looking for any possible ways to mount them without being seen.

But no. Tonight they had only her ears. Praise God that He'd given her excellent hearing.

More squeaking of hinges, more distant footsteps—someone in the corridor?—the sloshing of a beverage being poured into a crystal tumbler. Cognac, if it was Adams. Scotch, if it was Dormer. And then came the sound of hurried footsteps, the door opening again, and then closing amidst a hastily gasped breath.

"Apologies! I fear I took a wrong turn at the top of the stairs." Most definitely the Swedish ambassador.

Finally! Marigold dropped a foot off the ledge and turned it once, clockwise, to let Yates know the meeting was underway.

"Finally!" Adams, with his perpetual whine.

Marigold winced. Sounding like Lord Adams even in her mind was not to be borne. She'd make it a point to think more patient thoughts.

But self-improvement would have to wait. For now, she disengaged any creative parts of her brain and set it to pure memorization. Learning to do so had been a challenge at the start, but after five years of this work, it came naturally.

She soaked in the rest of the conversation, allowed herself a grin as the gentlemen said their farewells, and listened for all sets of feet to exit the room and the chamber door to close behind them. Their client would be impressed with the information they gave him, though heartily put out at Lord Adams.

"Coming down," Marigold whispered.

"Ready for you."

Down was always more difficult than up, in her opinion, but she'd long ago learned to calm the flutter of fear in her stomach. She crouched, gripped the ledge, and walked her feet down the wall, then straightened her arms out. With a stretch of her toes, she found the comfortable expanse of her brother's palms. She settled her weight onto them slowly. "Ready?"

"Ready."

He lowered her much as he'd raised her, widening her stance until she could step onto his shoulders. This time, she climbed down him rather than the about-face maneuver, and soon she was beside him on the ledge.

"Conversation recorded?" he asked as they slid back along the ledge the way they'd come.

"Ready for Gemma's shorthand." She really should have learned it herself before now—and she was working on it— but thus far it had worked best to have her best friend simply transcribe what she dictated.

Two minutes later, they were swinging back into the window of the room they'd staked out as their base. The key still stood in the lock, promising no one had come in and found their discarded evening attire, and the lamp was still burning low where they'd left it. Marigold turned her leg toward the light and clucked her tongue. Her new stockings had a run from knee to ankle—good thing her gown of the night would cover it. And the streaks of dirt too.

Yates shook his head. "We need to increase your stocking budget."

"Feathers, I think."

He made a show of considering. "We have enough peacock and ostrich feathers now, I suppose, with the new additions. And Zelda *did* enjoy dyeing the ostrich plumes."

"Exactly what I was thinking. Time?"

Yates pulled his pocket watch from the slim pajama-style trousers he had on over his own leotard, his wave of dark hair flopping onto his forehead in a way that made her grin. It had been well pomaded at the start of the night, but the wind at great heights had a way of teasing it back into its natural state. He'd grumble about it when he checked his reflection before they rejoined the ball. "Two minutes until Gemma is due."

Enough time to slip back into her gown, then. She hurried over to where she'd left it folded carefully under the cushion of a chair—just in case someone *did* break into the room—and nearly grunted at its weight. So many beads and sequins and pearls! The thing weighed half a ton, and her shoulders twitched at the thought of supporting it again.

There was no help for it, though. She stepped back into it, tugged it into place over her leotard, and did up what buttons she could manage on her own while her brother slid his tuxedo on over his own acrobatic costume.

When the soft tap came on the door, Yates was still at work on his bow tie, so Marigold dashed over to it. She tapped thrice, and when Gemma responded with the appropriate rhythm in response, she turned the key in the lock and swung the door inward.

Gemma, the fourth official member of the Imposters, swept in with a smile. She wore the grey-and-white uniform of the maids, a cap over her golden hair, but her notepad and pencil were in her pocket. "How did it go?"

"Perfectly." Marigold spun for assistance with those last pesky buttons, which her oldest friend did up in a flash. "You?"

"Plenty of tidbits for my next column, and a few items for our general files besides. There. Are we ready to transcribe?"

"I am if you are." Marigold hurried back over to the rest of her things: the ornate headpiece that weighed nearly as much as her gown—or so it seemed as she tried to anchor the thing to her hair—her "jewel"-encrusted slippers, and the oversized ostrich-feather fan, which was perfect for hiding her face behind when she wanted it to remain unseen.

"Just a moment." Gemma sat at the small desk in the room, pulled out her ever-present notebook and pencil, and nodded. "Go on."

It only took a few minutes to parrot back the conversation she'd overheard. She delivered it at a faster volume than the men had used, of course, and Gemma had no trouble keeping up with her shorthand. Yates grunted his opinion of the content as she went, and then grunted again when he looked in the mirror she'd pulled out of her small handbag.

Marigold and Gemma exchanged a grin. Yates was just as predictable as Lord Adams, though not quite as annoying. Most of the time. As younger brothers went, she was rather fond of him.

All right, so she couldn't even begin to imagine life without him. And given that she was at this point destined to spend her life at his side, that was a good thing.

She finished her recitation as she slid the mirror back into her bag. "And that's that. Seems Lord Emory was right to be worried. He is indeed being cut out of the business arrangements."

Yates was trying to comb his hair back into place, using the window as a mirror. "I'll get word to him tomorrow. And collect the balance of our fees when I do so."

Gemma slid her pencil and paper back into her pocket as she stood. "I'll alert James to your need of the confessional," she said of her brother, who was not an official Imposter, but a rather handy supporter, nonetheless. "Eleven o'clock?"

"Presumably." Yates spun back around and graced them with his wide, gleaming smile. "How do I look?"

"As dapper as you did at the start of the evening." Marigold indulged in a straightening of his bow tie, not because it was askew, but because sometimes she just needed to pretend that he still needed her care.

He fussed with one of her curls, and she suspected it was for the same reason. Their eyes met, and they shared a grin, nodded their approval of each other, and turned for the door.

The fun part of the night was finished. Now for the true work: maneuvering through the ball.

Sometimes she envied Gemma for her roles, as she posed as one employee or another to observe those highest of caliber events to which Miss Gemma Parks had never received an invitation, given that she was a steward's daughter. Her alter ego, journalist G. M. Parker, was invited all sorts of places, but Gemma had decided that she learned far more when cloaked in the invisible costume of a servant. Lady Marigold Fairfax always received those invitations too—and Lady Marigold Fairfax had certain expectations she had to meet.

Expectations she had cultivated carefully, yes. But choosing them didn't mean they didn't chafe now and then.

As her brother opened the door, Marigold slipped her fingers back into her satin gloves—the perfect way to cover the chip she'd acquired in one of her fingernails. Together, they exited the room. Gemma slipped away to the right, no doubt to find the servants' stairs. Marigold and Yates strode instead to the left, toward the grand staircase that would lead them back to the ballroom.

The music reached them as they turned the corner, making it easy to slide back into the mask that society knew. Lady Marigold, faceless mannequin whose dress would be written up in the *London Ladies Journal* but whose personality never received a mention. Because—aside from the fact that Gemma was the one who did the write-ups and knew just what to say—no one here knew her. Not really. But they all *thought* they did.

And other people's preconceived notions had proven to be the best disguise.

"Back into the lion's den." Yates offered his elbow at the top of the stairs, along with a wink and a smile.

She snorted a quiet laugh. "Give me Leonidas over this any day."

"Don't worry. You'll be mucking his stall with Franco in a few weeks."

Not nearly soon enough. But for now, she pasted on the vapid little smile she always wore at social events—never full enough to be noteworthy, never serious enough to catch anyone's eye—and walked with her brother down the stairs and into the crowded ballroom once more.

With ostrich feathers waving away the heat and shielding her face, she cast her gaze around the room to catalogue who else may have arrived while they'd ducked out. Lady Abingdon and her sister-in-law. Lord and Lady Ramsey. And—could it be? Marigold's eyes went wide, even as the young lady on whom her gaze had fallen spotted her and lifted a hand, her green eyes going bright.

"Lavinia!" It came out far too happily. Had anyone been paying attention, they certainly would have noticed that it was genuine emotion in her tone, which she never revealed in public. Never.

But it was *Lavinia*. In London! She let go of her brother's arm and rushed forward, not much caring if anyone saw she was actually excited as she met her friend on the edge of the room and embraced her. "Lavinia! You came!"

Lady Lavinia Hemming laughed and clutched her close for a long moment. When she pulled away, it gave Marigold the chance to sweep her gaze over her. Her cheeks looked full again, their color not the too-pink of rouge or the sallow shade they'd been too often over the last five years.

When Marigold had left Northumberland a month ago, Lavinia had been rallying, yes—but her parents hadn't been convinced it would last enough for them to venture to London for any of the early Season. Lavinia had as much as said that they'd likely stay at home instead and continue to rest in the hopes of making the high Season in June.

What joy to see her here despite that prediction.

"Father sent word that he'd like us to come if we could. And I was feeling so well that—well, here we are!" Lavinia's own gaze took in Marigold's extravagant headpiece, the gown, the bag. "I knew you'd be here. And that you'd be easy to spot."

Marigold had little choice but to laugh. "And you've found me!"

"I'm so glad. You must come and call on Mother and me tomorrow." She leaned close, her eyes so bright that Marigold nearly worried she was feverish. "There will be gentlemen calling too—that was why Father sent for us, he wanted to make introductions. Two of them! I can't possibly entertain them myself."

Gentlemen? It took effort to keep her smile in place. If Marigold had learned anything over the last five years, it was that far too many of society's gentlemen had secrets she'd rather not have known. Secrets that made her not at all sad that marriage was out of the question for her. The Imposters had dossiers on at least half of the gentlemen in this very room—perhaps more. None of them filled with things that equaled good husband material.

But she could hardly admit that to Lavinia. What she *could* do was say, "Of course! Eleven o'clock?" and silently promise her friend that whoever these gentlemen were, *they* had better have no secrets that would bring sorrow to Lavinia's eyes.

Because if they did, she'd find out. And she'd make certain they never stepped foot in her friend's drawing room again.

TWO

*L*ieutenant Colonel Sir Merritt Livingstone was no stranger to a club, but the Marlborough, he was quickly discovering, was nothing like the Guards'. Here, the uniform was a suit or tuxedo. Here, the gentlemen were more the sort to be planning their next hunt rather than reminiscing about their last tour of duty.

Here, everyone cared more about who Merritt's uncle was than his most recent promotion.

Just as well, on that score. They may have called it a promotion when they shoved him into a desk, but they all knew it was more a nod to his health over the last six months. Blasted pneumonia—he'd get stronger again. He would. A bit more time, and he'd request a more active duty station.

"Do lighten up a bit, old boy. You look like you're facing down a platoon of enemy combatants instead of looking for a game of whist."

Merritt blinked away the dark thoughts, tried to suppress a cough, and slanted an amused look at Lord Xavier. "That's how one wins at whist, you know. Strategy. Skill."

Xavier gave him the same look he'd been giving him since they were eight. "Yes. But you'll never convince anyone to play with you if you *show* it. Have I taught you nothing?"

He had to laugh, even if it turned into that cough he'd pushed down a moment before. Lord Xavier Hasting—pampered second son of the Duke of Norwich, though Merritt tried not to hold it against him—had certainly taught him much over the years about what a congenial façade could achieve.

But it came about as naturally to him as flying to an elephant.

Xavier's look turned to one of concern as Merritt's cough went deep and racking, and he slapped a hand to his back. "Maybe we shouldn't have come out tonight. You're clearly—"

"Fine." Yes, the word came out choked and raspy as he clamped down on the urge to cough anew, but he was drawing attention he didn't want to draw, and that wouldn't do. He took a few careful, deep breaths, swallowed a few times, and made no argument when Xavier waved down a passing waiter and handed him a small glass of something amber. He didn't know what liquor it was and didn't much care. A sip of it did the same job as the bottle of medicine he had at home, numbing the raw edges of his throat and helping the muscles to calm from their spasm.

Xavier shook his head and planted his hands on his hips. "You should have stayed at home."

"I'm tired of being at home."

"You'll only set your recovery back if you push too hard."

Merritt took another small sip of the drink—cognac, perhaps? He was no expert, rarely partaking of anything stronger than a stiff cup of tea. But when he spotted a pair of wingbacks open with a fair view of the crackling fire, he aimed toward them instead of letting Xavier take him toward the whist tables. "Much as I appreciate the many visits you've paid me, X, I'd have gone mad if I had to spend one more evening staring at my own walls."

With exaggerated drama, Xavier splayed a hand over his

heart and sank into the match of Merritt's chair. "You slice me through. Cut me to the quick. You mean to say my company is not so riveting that it sustains you for months on end?"

What could he do but snort a laugh—and pray it didn't spur another coughing jag? "It has, as it happens. But everything has its limits. At least when paired with a dreadful desk job."

Waving that away, his friend perused the other gents milling about, no doubt searching for familiar faces that he'd better greet to keep from offending anyone. No doubt keeping an eye out for the lord Merritt had told him about too. "You'll be back in the field in no time, slicing down enemies of the Crown. Or at least intimidating small children outside the palace."

Merritt's lips quirked. The Coldstream Guard may be best known for their stone-faced guarding of the royals outside the palaces and the pageantry of each changing of the guard, but they earned that privilege through the best training and exemplary conduct in the field.

He'd done his part in combat. He'd earned his place guarding His Royal Highness. He'd stood there in rain and snow and sleet and pounding sun, ready to be the last line of defense for his sovereign.

And now they'd deemed him unfit.

Promotion, indeed. He'd show them, though. Eventually the cough would fade, his lungs would fully recover, and he'd be ready to train again with his brothers-in-arms. In the meantime, he'd serve at that desk with the same dedication he'd served elsewhere.

Even if it meant sitting here at the Marlborough, pretending he cared about his uncle's connections so that he could observe a certain lord in an environment outside of the office.

As if following his every thought, Xavier leaned closer. "You're certain he'll be here tonight?"

"He said as much."

"But you'll pay a visit to his home tomorrow. If you're not feeling well, we can—"

"*We* will be paying a visit." And not just to Lord Hemming—to his daughter. Which was why he'd procured the invitation for his best friend as well. It was one thing to spy on a chap one suspected of the unthinkable. It was quite another to be tossed into female company by said man, who only saw one as the probable heir to an earl.

If his training had taught him anything, it was that one didn't venture into enemy territory without an ally at one's side to cover one's back. Especially when one would be engaging in completely unfamiliar territory—like social calls made under the guise of courtship.

The very idea was enough to bring thunder to his brow again, if the roll of Xavier's eyes was any indication. But of course his chipper, charming, lighthearted friend wasn't cowed by the thought of introductions to eligible young ladies—he'd undergone countless such things already. And enjoyed them.

Quite possibly a sign of insanity, but since he was an amiable madman, Merritt would forgive it. And be glad to have a reinforcement so proficient in this particular form of combat.

"Oh, I haven't forgotten." Xavier waggled his brows. "I'm rather looking forward to it. Lady Lavinia is a bit of a mystery in society, you know. Sequestered at home in Northumberland for years on end, despite being the heir to Hemming's estate. She's quite the catch. Assuming that she doesn't have eight eyes or ten arms or the wrong opinion of my favorite novels."

Another laugh eased past Merritt's aching ribs. He was nearly certain that last night's coughing fit had cracked something, but he wasn't about to admit it to anyone. He'd merely had his batman wrap a bandage tight around his torso, which was without question all his physician would have been able to do too. "You're welcome to distract the young lady while I survey the household itself."

He, too, looked around at the chaps coming and going. None of them in sight now was Lord Hemming. The man hadn't said what time he planned on being here, only that he would be. Merritt wasn't certain exactly what he hoped to learn about the man in these environs, but it was a situation he'd yet to see him in, so it warranted investigation.

He knew how his lordship behaved within the confines of the War Office Intelligence Division, where Merritt had been assigned with his "promotion." He would soon know how he behaved with his wife and daughter in the comfort of his own home. This, tonight, was another piece of information—how he behaved among his peers and friends.

Perhaps one of those would give him some explanation for the strange wire that had come to Merritt's attention two days ago. *Hemming.* That was all it had said—but it hadn't been *to* Hemming, it had been encoded for Merritt. That much hadn't seemed strange. Merritt was, after all, the officer who had been put in charge of coordinating the reports of the field agents from all the different military branches. He had therefore been in contact with each one, had been setting up regular check-in times. But this particular field agent had been off the grid when he oughtn't to have been, and when Merritt had asked for an explanation, that had been the one-word reply. *Hemming.*

After that, silence. Seven long days of silence, which might not have alarmed him had he not walked into Colonel May's office yesterday when Hemming was there, poised to ask them about the situation, and seen them all too quickly cover up papers on the desk.

Not before Merritt had glimpsed them, though. Not before he'd seen that they were in German.

He took one more sip of the—was it Scotch, actually?—and then set it down on the side table between his and Xavier's chairs. It couldn't mean anything suspicious. It couldn't. But then, why were they behaving suspiciously? They'd all but forced him from the office, even though he'd been given clearance to view absolutely any files. And when he mentioned a too-silent agent, they'd told him not to worry about it.

As if that weren't his entire position now—to worry about their agents. The army's, the navy's, the police's. As the Crown prepared to roll their intelligence efforts under one banner, his job involved nothing *but* worrying over their agents. Why were May and Hemming trying to dissuade him from his one purpose?

An edge of white caught his eye. There, half under the lamp casting a golden glow upon his hand, was a card. A gentleman's card, given the dimensions. No doubt misplaced or dropped—or shoved aside when someone didn't really want it. He tapped a finger to the corner and pulled it out to see whose it might be. One never knew when such a thing could prove useful.

But he frowned again. It wasn't the name of some lord or esquire, nor even a barrister or business acquaintance who a gentleman might require. He wasn't honestly certain *who* it was a card for. Curious now, he pulled the card off the table and squinted at the elegant, elaborately designed text.

The Imposters. Discreet Disclosures for the Most Discerning.

"What in blazes is this?"

"Hmm?" Xavier had been nodding a greeting to a few passing men of his father's generation but turned back to him now. When Merritt flashed the card's face at him, his eyes lit up. "Ah! I haven't seen one of those yet in the wild! Where was it?"

He said it like it was some curiosity to be collected. "There, half under the lamp. You're familiar with this . . . what is it? An investigator?"

"Not *an* investigator. *The* investigator. Or plural, perhaps. Seems they can be in multiple places at once, so there must be more than one of them, though the meetings are only ever with one man." Xavier snatched the card from him, examining it both front and back. "My father has used them twice now." This he said at an unusual-for-him hush. "You remember that Abernathy fellow that Clare fancied before she met Thomas? They're the ones who uncovered his unsavory past for us."

Merritt straightened, more because his ribs were aching and his lungs starting to prickle than because he was surprised that the duke had hired someone to look into the man courting his only daughter. "You never actually mentioned how your father discovered all he had."

"Because it was very hush-hush. These Imposters, whoever they are—they're in high demand and only take on a few select cases for select clients."

The ones with deep pockets, he meant. Probably charged a small fortune.

But then, if it saved Clare from a disastrous marriage, Merritt certainly wouldn't judge the duke for paying any amount. And he must have been truly impressed with their work if he then hired them again.

That, he knew, was saying something. The Duke of Norwich was not easy to impress.

He took the card back, reading the words on the reverse side, though they made him frown. The only thing there was an address, with instructions to send inquiries to it. "But who are they?"

"Well, no one knows. That's the thing—how they're so successful. No one knows who they are, so no one has their guard up around them. Why, they could be anywhere. Anytime." Xavier waved a hand through the air and pointed at a footman. "Could be that fellow there for all we know. Or the cabby who dropped you off. Or that pretty brunette I danced with last night. She *did* seem a bit too amused by my jokes, and I'd never heard of the town she claimed to be from."

Merritt braced his ribs with a hand as he chuckled again. "You're just rubbish at geography. And you're amusing. Add in being the son of a duke—"

"My finest trait, I know." If it bothered him, Xavier had never confessed it to Merritt. He grinned, adding another reason to the list of why pretty brunettes would bat their lashes at him. He may not be the duke's heir, but he was counted as the more handsome of the brothers. "But my point stands. The Imposters seem able to get in anywhere and discover anything, and no one ever has a clue they were there. Given their name, the musing is that they're actors. Actors able to blend in with society for at least short periods of time, with no one ever the wiser."

"Interesting." Merritt stared another minute at the card. It was of the highest quality, the ink a deep tobacco brown, the design eye-catching but easy to read.

The Imposters. Able to get anywhere and discover anything. Talented actors. Chameleons, from the sound of it.

Knowing a few of those could come in handy.

He tapped the card against his palm and then slipped it into his jacket pocket. At his friend's arched brow, he said, "What? You know very well that I never despise a good asset."

"Opportunist."

"Cheers." His smile, however, turned down a notch when he finally spotted Lord Hemming ambling along the corridor—with none other than his own uncle.

It shouldn't surprise him that they knew each other. Uncle Preston knew everyone, or at least everyone "worth knowing." Certainly he knew all the aristocrats who sat with him in the House of Lords. And because he was every bit as charming and amiable as Xavier, he didn't just *know* them. He was friends with them.

It was a blighted impossible standard to live up to, and shoes he couldn't ever hope to fill.

Of course, there was hope. Aunt Josephine could yet produce a son to complement the gaggle of daughters they already had. True, she was closer to fifty than forty now, but if the biblical Sarah and Elizabeth could give their husbands sons when they were well advanced in years, then why not Aunt Josie? Forty-eight wasn't even that advanced.

Perhaps his uncle felt his gaze upon him. He looked their way, and his eyes lit so brightly that Merritt felt the pierce of guilt, and its shaft buried deep in his chest. Uncle Preston had been trying for a year to convince him to swing by the Marlborough one evening, but he never had. Not until today, when it was for work rather than pleasure. He'd never done it for his uncle, only for his own concerns tonight.

He was as rubbish at being a good nephew and heir as Xavier was at geography.

But there was nothing saying he couldn't redeem himself a bit, was there, despite his less-than-selfless motivations? He pushed to his feet, suppressing another cough, and donned a smile. That, at least, was never a hard task in his uncle's company. "Uncle Preston, Lord Hemming, good evening to you both."

His uncle charged forward, shook his proffered hand, and slapped an enthusiastic one to his opposite arm too. "Merritt, my boy, how good to see you here. You must be feeling better."

The ache in his ribs belied the smile he kept beaming.

"Regaining my strength day by day. I'll be back at my usual post in no time."

Lord Hemming snorted at that. "Don't count on it, Sir Merritt. Now that we've got our hooks in you at the office, we won't let you go so easily. Your nephew is a true asset to the Crown, Preston."

"Isn't he just? So like his father, and I've always said that Lawrence was the best of us." For a moment Merritt feared his uncle was going to pat him on the head like he'd done when he was a lad, but thankfully he restrained himself and turned his smile on Xavier instead. "And Lord Xavier! Always so good to see you. How do you do?"

"Couldn't be better." Xavier returned Uncle Preston's enthusiastic handshake and directed his own beaming smile to Lord Hemming. "Especially since Sir Merritt and I will have the pleasure of making the acquaintance of Lord Hemming's wife and daughter tomorrow morning."

Perhaps Hemming hadn't yet made the connection to what friend Merritt had said he was bringing with him, but he certainly did now. His face brightened considerably, and Merritt could practically see the realization taking shape in his mind—not only the presumed heir to an earl, but the second son of a duke, both calling on his daughter. If he'd brought her to London to try to make a match, he'd be congratulating himself on the wisdom of his invitation to Merritt.

Were Mother here and not enjoying the Mediterranean coast, she would chide him for his cynicism. Though if Mother knew he had accepted the invitation not from any desire to become acquainted with Lady Lavinia, but rather to observe her father, she'd do more than chide him. She would be horrified that he would leverage their family's connections and standing to do something as base as *spy* on someone.

Even if it was for the good of the country? Even if it could save lives?

No, she would accuse him of overdramatizing the situation and insist that no one with blood as blue as Lord Hemming's or from a family as upstanding as Colonel May's could *possibly* be guilty of any crime. It didn't bear thinking about.

Which was why, even if Mother were here, he wouldn't have shared such thoughts with her anyway. Why bother when she'd refuse to consider them?

He hadn't shared the thoughts with Uncle Preston either, which meant that he was unknowingly shooting another arrow of guilt into Merritt with his latest beaming smile. "Merritt—making a social call to a young lady? I began to despair ever seeing the day."

Merritt made an effort to keep the smile on his face rather than letting it drop into a frown. He deserved a crumb of credit for that, didn't he? "I'm only seven and twenty, Uncle. Hardly cause to despair my ever settling down." It wasn't that he didn't intend to . . . someday.

"Speaking of my dear Lavinia . . ." Lord Hemming checked his pocket watch. "I promised her mother I'd put in an appearance at the ball they were going to this evening. If you'll excuse me, gentlemen? Sir Merritt, Lord Xavier, I do look forward to welcoming you to my home tomorrow."

They said their farewells, all politeness and well-wishes that Merritt wouldn't have thought, a month ago, could make his stomach go as tight as his ribs. He wanted to like Lord Hemming. He wanted to respect him for all he'd accomplished during his term liaising between the House of Lords and the War Office Intelligence Division. He wanted to be proud to serve there with him.

Which was why he had to put these suspicions to rest, one way or another. Determine why Hemming was reviewing German correspondence that he'd been so quick to hide, and why an agent in Germany had suddenly gone silent after sending his name, encoded, to Merritt. He must find the reasonable explanation so that he could stop looking at both his immediate superior and the liaison to the House of Lords with suspicion.

Uncle Preston watched Hemming disappear out of sight and then turned to Merritt with lifted brows and lips that clearly wanted to grin. "Well well well. Lady Lavinia, is it?"

Merritt sighed and turned back to his chair. "Don't get too excited, Uncle. I accepted Hemming's invitation solely because we work together and it seemed a bad idea to put him off."

Xavier motioned Uncle Preston to take the matching chair. "*I*, on the other hand, accepted because I'm dying for a glimpse of the mysterious young lady."

Uncle chuckled and settled into the proffered chair with a happy sigh. "No great mystery, X. She came down with a nasty something-or-another about five years ago, if I recall, and her parents deemed it best to keep her at home in the country air so she could recuperate."

Merritt's ears perked up, and his brows rose to match. "You know them well?"

"Not especially, for my own part. Though Josie and Lady Hemming were quite good friends there for a while, before said illness struck their house. What *was* it? Not a pox or polio, I don't believe. . . . Can't be consumption, or she wouldn't be improved enough to rejoin us now. Hmm." Uncle Preston tapped a finger to his chin. "I'll ask Josie. But regardless, Lady Lavinia and your cousin Estelle are the same age, so it was a convenient friendship. I believe they were at school together."

That would put Lavinia at about twenty-two. A bit late for her first full Season in society, but Hemming had blamed the illness for that. What, Merritt had to wonder, had this young lady filled her time with in Northumberland all these years? Did she love that northern stretch of country, or was she relieved to finally be able to come to Town?

Questions he could ask tomorrow, which would at least serve as conversation.

Twenty-two. That felt so blasted *young*. When *he* was twenty-two, he'd knelt before the king and accepted a knighthood for his efforts in protecting missionaries during the Boxer Rebellion in China the year before. He hadn't felt particularly young at the time, but it seemed a whole lifetime had passed since then.

Which reminded him that he had a letter from Jonathan awaiting his response, and rereading his friend's latest missive from the Orient and then composing his own would be a far better use of time than staying here now that Hemming had left.

He granted himself one small cough. "Don't get your hopes up, Uncle—and for heaven's sake, don't mention it to Aunt Josie. It's just a courtesy visit. I have no intention of being smitten."

But Uncle Preston just laughed. "We never do, lad. We never do."

THREE

arigold smiled at the servant holding the door open for her at Hemming House and passed him her parasol. It had been ages since she'd had reason to step foot in her friend's London home, but she found it little changed from her last visit five years ago.

Five years—a century. Five years ago, Papa had just died. They'd only just begun to realize what a wretched state he'd left them in. They'd come to Town less for the Season than for meetings with solicitors and accounting firms and banks, and the same message of doom was handed down from them all.

There was no money. None. Nothing left. Papa had spent absolutely everything on the frivolities that had made their childhoods a parade of perpetual delights. Circuses and theater troupes and acrobats and traveling musicians—they had shaped Marigold and Yates in ways few realized but had also left them destitute.

She remembered walking through that same door after meeting with a grim-faced trustee, numb and dumbfounded and desperate for a friend to help her forget it all just for a few minutes. She'd turned to the same drawing room the butler indicated now, and it had been appointed in this same way, with Lady Hemming's favorite pastels and brocades. But Lavinia had been pale and clearly not feeling well.

That, at least, had changed. Her friend sat on the divan with visible excitement, her cheeks a healthy pink and her eyes bright with the adventure of life. Marigold smiled and held out a hand to her. "Lavinia! You look positively enchanting this morning."

Lavinia surged gracefully to her feet and all but skipped to Marigold, bypassing her hand altogether in favor of a quick but enthusiastic embrace. "Can you believe it? It's finally happening. I'm in London for the Season, and I'm entertaining two of the most eligible bachelors!"

"You are indeed." She tried to summon a bit of her friend's excitement, but it was a stretch. Marigold had only been in Town for a month, but already she was dreaming of Fairfax Tower. Ocean breezes, clean air, and all her favorite people—both human and otherwise—there to greet her every morning.

She and Yates planned to take some time between cases and squeeze in a trip home for a fortnight here and there, if for no other reason than to spend some time on the training they couldn't manage in London. True, her muscles were even now aching deliciously from the exercise she'd taken that morning, but the gymnasium they'd outfitted here couldn't compete with all they had at the Tower.

Lavinia clasped her hands together in front of her heart. "I'll be able to see the Flower Shows! The Ascot! I know I've missed a couple of the regattas already, but not all of them. And Father said that I'm certain to like these gentlemen. Oh, but I've forgotten my manners. What would you like to drink? Lemonade, perhaps? Or do you need your second cup of tea yet?"

Marigold's gaze followed Lavinia to the tea cart in the

corner, where someone had set up a pitcher of iced lemon-ade, another of water, and an assortment of little cakes and biscuits. "Lemonade will be perfect. So have you discovered the gentlemen's names?" Lavinia hadn't known them last night at the ball. Apparently, Lord Hemming had only in-dicated that he knew one of them from his service to the Crown.

Lavinia nodded and pressed a hand to her stomach, no doubt to calm anxious flutters. "Sir Merritt Livingstone is the one he invited particularly. The nephew and heir pre-sumed of the Earl of Preston—do you remember Lady Es-telle? Her parents are Lord and Lady Preston, and this is her cousin. She has only sisters."

"Ah yes." Estelle had never been as close a friend of hers as she was of Lavinia's, but she had no objection to her. She'd always been a perfectly likable young lady and was now married to a perfectly likable young gentleman. "Though I confess I'm not acquainted with her cousin. Sir Merritt Livingstone, you say?"

Lavinia nodded. "Do you know nothing about him? I rather hoped you would. You always know *all* the gossip."

Unfortunately true—she made it a point to gather all she could in the drawing rooms of England to add to their files. Women mentioned things about husbands and sons that those men did *not* mention in the clubs. But with Yates observing there and she here, and Gemma and Graham in their respective circles, they had most of society covered from various angles.

This gent, though. She sank to a seat on the cushions and let her face knot up in concentration, trying to remember anything they'd had cause to note about him.

"Let's see . . . the name sounds vaguely familiar. Is he friends with Lord Xavier Hasting, perhaps? A military man?" If she was remembering the correct dossier, then it was slim.

Nothing but a footnote, really, to Lord Xavier's. He hadn't been in country when they'd done their investigation for the duke, so she had merely heard this friend's name mentioned.

Lavinia took the seat beside her, handing her a glass of lemonade. "That's right. In the Coldstream Guard."

She made a mental note. "Impressive." Only the best were permitted in the elite group that served the monarch both at home and abroad. "How did he earn his knighthood, do you know?"

Lavinia shrugged. "Father said something about the Boxer Rebellion, but he didn't mention the specifics. Perhaps we can ask while he's *here*." She said that last word with wide eyes and a new note of awe.

Marigold couldn't help but chuckle. "And the second gentleman?"

"Ah! The very friend you mentioned—Lord Xavier, second son of the Duke of Norwich, which has Mother all aflutter. Do you know *him*?"

Sipping her lemonade, Marigold chuckled. "Everyone in England knows *him*."

FROM THE DOSSIER OF
Lord Xavier Hasting, second son of the Duke of Norwich

HEIGHT: *5'11"*

WEIGHT: *11 stone*

AGE: *27*

HAIR: *Dark brown with a bit of curl*

EYES: *Blue*

STYLE: *Always wears well-cut custom suits, though he doesn't seem to favor any one tailor. Likely to be in whatever new style is seen that Season.*

RESIDENCES: *Grosvenor Square when in London; Castle Wensum near Norwich; stands to inherit Bridewell Manor from his maternal grandfather.*

OBSERVANCES: *Lord Xavier exhibits good humor and is kind to all he meets. No one speaks ill of him. Had good marks in school, keeps company with respectable and reputable people. Devoted to his family.*

IMPRESSIONS: *No one that charming can really be authentic, can he? –M.F. One would think not, but there is no lie to be found in his behavior. –Y.F. Lord X seems to be generally harmless, at least at this point in his happy life. –G.P.*

NOTES: *Most people favor him over his older brother*

"And . . . ?" Lavinia prodded.

How to explain Lord X, as Gemma had styled him for her column? His dossier had also only been completed for the sake of thoroughness in the investigations his father had hired them to do, but Gemma had aptly summed him up with that single word: *harmless.* Which, in the world of the Imposters, was saying something. "He's fun-loving, has a keen sense of humor, is always gracious to anyone he meets, no matter their station, and professes a great love for his family and the Lord. You could do far worse."

Lavinia's fingers knotted in the sheer white overskirt of her day dress. "He won't have a title of his own, but Mother says their family is so well situated that he'll still be inheriting quite an estate from his mother's people. Then there's this Sir Merritt, who is quite likely to become an earl *and* inherit the Preston estates, as they're entailed. Either would be a fine match."

And both would be among the first two gentlemen she was even meeting. Marigold reached over and rested her hand on Lavinia's, feeling ancient as she said, "You needn't pin your hopes on either of them, Lavinia. You've the whole Season yet ahead of you! Who knows who may capture your heart?"

"Of course." But her friend's smile went stiff before it bloomed bright again.

Was it *too* bright? For show? Marigold frowned. And now that she was thinking about it . . . when had her friend begun to call Lord and Lady Hemming *Father* and *Mother* instead of *Papa* and *Mama*? Marigold hadn't noted the change while they were in Northumberland, but had it simply slipped past her?

That wouldn't do. That wouldn't do at all. If she failed to notice small changes in one of her dearest friends, how could she be trusted to note things in the people she was observing for a case?

Lavinia wasn't looking at her, but rather had her eyes focused out the window. "It's just—I'm so excited to finally be here. Able to start the rest of my life. I want to *find* it, as quickly as I can."

"You don't want to rush, though. Not into something as permanent as marriage. These are decisions to make carefully and with much consideration."

That at least reclaimed Lavinia's attention, even if it earned her a dagger of a glance. "Now you sound like Grandmother Hemming. Though it turned out well enough even for her, didn't it? Perhaps there was no great love between her and Grandfather, but they each had their space, and they built a solid life together. They were each happy."

"Just not together. Is that really what you want?"

"If it means marriage and children and a place of my own in society? I'm willing to be reasonable about things like romance and love." The words, so utilitarian and cool, were a sharp contrast to those pink cheeks and dancing eyes.

And didn't sound at all like the Lavinia who Marigold had seen only a month ago. She found herself frowning, and again feeling far older than her five and twenty. "Lavinia—there's no reason at all to think you can't have both. That you can't find a fellow who will adore you *and* give you the station and family you crave. Why settle for less when you yourself have so much to offer?"

Not like Marigold, who had absolutely no dowry and couldn't leave her work with the Imposters, lest her brother plummet into the pits of debt. They couldn't even consider something as demeaning as selling off property to cover their expenses, not given the dear people who depended on them.

Lavinia's look was surprisingly serious. Probing, even. "Is that why you've remained unattached? Are you waiting for love?"

Over the last five years, Marigold had become adept at acting. She ought to have, having studied under the finest tutors, who had set the stage alight for decades. So it was no great task to don an indulgent smile. Nothing strenuous to tilt her head to the side and invite a twinkle into her eyes.

No great thing, except for her heart, which broke a bit at having to do so with Lavinia. One shouldn't have to playact with one's dearest friends.

But there was no choice. No one, not even Lavinia, could know how dire their situation had been. No one, not even Lavinia, could know what they'd resorted to doing to keep them all afloat. Better to be thought an eccentric romantic.

And so she let out a sigh to match the feigned twinkle. "I shall find it someday. And until then, I am perfectly content to torment Yates and wait for it."

Was that pity in Lavinia's expression, or sorrow? "Well, some of us haven't that luxury."

What was *that* supposed to mean? Was it her health she was concerned about or something else? Marigold opened her mouth to press the point, but Lady Hemming chose that moment to rush into the room, arms aflutter. "Oh, the time got away from me!" she proclaimed as she hurried forward, hands outstretched for Marigold. "My dear Lady Marigold, how good of you to come and keep my Lavinia company."

The older woman beamed a smile as she grasped Marigold's hand and kissed the air on either side of her face. A routine they'd undergone enough in the previous years that she knew without a doubt her friend's mother was cataloguing every single aspect of her hat, hair, jewelry, and dress as she did so.

Hat—adorned with peacock feathers and silk that no one would ever know had been harvested from her own mother's trousseau.

Hair—puffed and pinned in the newly popular version of the pompadour, with Gemma's help.

Jewelry—none, save the pendant watch that she always wore, given that time was a far more valuable commodity to her than it was to Lady Hemming.

Dress—modeled after the latest daring haute couture from Paris with its asymmetrical draping, though in fact another remake of a gown decades old, and in a bold emerald green. Unconventional for a day dress, hence why Marigold had chosen it when they were dyeing the fabric. It caught the eye, matched the peacock feathers, and completely eclipsed her face.

She could all but see the lady taking note of each style, each tuck, each bit of ruching, and comforting herself with the very true thought that Lavinia could have pulled it off better and would have looked prettier in the green. She would be concluding—and hence her big smile—that the two gentle-men coming to call any minute would see only Marigold's clothing and not her face, and that her own daughter would shine brighter in comparison.

All by design. Even so, she wished she didn't need to wear the costume here, in her friend's company. She wished that, just for a day, she could forgo the audacious.

But that couldn't happen, not while they were in London. That particular indulgence would have to wait until she was within the concealing walls of Fairfax Tower again.

"Here, dearest, let me get you something to eat. You look absolutely famished."

Lavinia was still on the thin side, to be sure, so Marigold smiled and said yet another prayer for her friend's health. Hopefully now that she was feeling better and stronger, some of the weight she'd lost over the past few years would return.

But it was into Marigold's hands that Lady Hemming thrust a plate of cakes and biscuits, which brought a surprised "Oh!" to her lips, even as her hands closed around the plate. She blinked down at the sweets. She made it a point not to eat much sugar, as she'd found it hindered her training. She'd become an expert at simply declining such treats in company, always claiming to be satiated from her previous meal.

Usually people didn't just force it on her. What was she to do without appearing rude? She muttered a thank-you and slid the plate onto the end table, choosing the smallest biscuit to take a nibble of. "Delicious," she said, even though it tasted like pure sugar to her tongue, unaccustomed as it was to any. "Your cook must be the envy of all your friends."

Lady Hemming preened. "We've hired a pastry chef for the Season, from Paris. We've entertained so little recently that we decided to pull out all the stops this year."

Marigold made an impressed noise, glad when Lavinia jumped to her feet, her eyes focused out the window.

"They're here!"

"Well, don't jump about like a child, Lavinia Rose." Lady Hemming stretched out a stern finger and pointed again at the couch. "Sit like a young lady and wait for Matthews to announce them."

Lavinia sat, but with an excited bounce that made her seem younger than her twenty-two years. Understandable, given that the last five had been a blur for her, had seemed in many ways not to have happened at all. How many times had Marigold had to visit her in her bedchamber at Alnwick Abbey because she was too weak even to come downstairs? She deserved the excitement of gentlemen visitors. She deserved the anticipation of balls and soirees. She deserved the promise of romance and a stellar match.

Which made it ever so curious that she was willing to forgo the first part of that equation if it gained her the second.

Marigold would ponder that more later. For now, she focused on familiar sounds: the knocker sounding on the front door, the wood opening under the hand of Matthews, murmurs of greetings in various masculine tones. She filed away each voice, from the somewhat familiar one of the Hemmings' London house butler to the two younger gentlemen. She'd met Lord Xavier before, yes, but it had been two years ago, and she didn't know his voice well enough to pick it out from this distance.

A moment later, Matthews ushered them into the drawing room, and Lady Hemmings stood to welcome them. Introductions were made all around, how-do-you-dos exchanged, and Marigold given the chance to update her mental files so that she could update their physical ones later.

Lord Xavier looked very much like she remembered—about Yates's height, with the sort of physique that suggested he enjoyed regular sport. He had a head of thick mahogany hair with a curl to it that she suspected he knew well was charming, deep blue eyes twinkling in merriment even now, and an open, engaging smile. Was anyone really so forthright, so cheerful, so perpetually good-humored?

If not, she'd probably get a glimpse of it in the next hour. There were always things to belie one's mask—twitches, movements of shoulder and arm, where one focused one's eyes during certain conversations.

All things she had learned from the theater troupe, who had studied mannerisms extensively in order to give a convincing performance. Marigold and Yates had both soaked in the lessons as children so they could take part in whatever plays were being performed that week at the Tower. Far more useful now was how they'd learned to apply all they studied to their observations.

As the gentlemen accepted the seats Lady Hemming directed them to, Marigold let her attention shift to the unknown quantity. Lieutenant Colonel Sir Merritt Livingstone was as stiff and awkward as his friend was warm and fluid. He sat as though he had a rod lashed to his spine, holding him with rigidity that went well beyond the normal military precision.

His hair was a lovely shade of gold not far from Gemma's, his face chiseled and handsome, lips unsmiling even mere moments after exchanging greetings. His eyes, though, were the most remarkable thing about him—they, too, were blue, but not the deep, comfortable, common shade of Lord Xavier's. No, they were the brightest, lightest, clearest shade of blue she'd ever seen in a face, the sort that gave the impression of looking directly into one's soul.

Not that she'd be putting *that* into her file.

Lord Xavier, clearly the chattier of the two, was saying something about how lovely it was to be finally making the mysterious Lady Lavinia's acquaintance. He turned to include Marigold, obviously too well trained to ignore her completely, as she'd prefer. "And lovely to make your acquaintance, too, Lady Marigold. You are the sister of Lord Fairfax, I believe? I'm amazed we've never been introduced."

Were she interested in displaying any tells of her own, her lips may have twitched at that one. "Oh, but we have," she said in even tones, careful to keep the laughter out of her voice. "Two years ago, I believe, at Lady Quimby's birthday ball. We danced together once."

The fact that he didn't remember was obvious, given the blank, panicked look in his eyes. This was not a man accustomed to forgetting faces, clearly. Another thing worth noting—he took his acquaintanceships seriously.

"Ah . . ." He made an effort to clear the confusion from his face, but it lingered still in his eyes. "Forgive me. I was a bit preoccupied with family affairs that evening, I believe."

Concerned, no doubt, with his sister. That was during their case for his father, hence why they'd made it a point to attend the same ball as the duke's entire family. She kept her smile light and indifferent.

"But yes," he continued. "I remember now." *Lying.* "We spoke of . . . ?"

"You regaled me with tales of your days at Eton. My cousin was a few years behind you."

And why did that make him frown? "I spoke only of myself?" He sounded horrified, which told her far more about him than his stories had then.

She'd kept their conversation focused on him during their dance very deliberately. She hadn't realized doing so would cause him distress—and wouldn't have changed her tactic even if she had. The fewer words exchanged about *her* life, the better. The more likely she was to be forgotten.

It had obviously worked.

But now she would spare him the torment. "I greatly enjoyed your stories, my lord. Having never gone away to school myself, I have always loved others' tales of it."

"She's being quite truthful, I assure you," Lavinia put in with a grin. "Every time I came home on holiday, Marigold insisted I tell her every detail of the term."

Sir Merritt donned a smile, though it looked about as honest as Lord Xavier's claim to remember her. "I believe you attended with my cousin Estelle?"

Lavinia's gaze shifted to her fair-haired guest, her own cheer certainly not feigned. "I did, yes! Ravenscleft Academy for Young Ladies. Estelle and I were very good friends. I've missed her terribly these last few years, but her letters assure me she is enjoying married life."

There, a softening in his countenance, and he even relaxed a degree—though a wince flitted across his face, quickly covered but *there*.

Not stiff with military precision. Stiff with *pain*. Marigold had to keep a frown from marring her brow. It could be anything—an injury from the morning's sport, a sore neck from a strange sleeping position. But whatever it was no doubt accounted for at least some of his reserve.

He recovered quickly, and she doubted the Hemmings even noticed his lapse. "And the two of you?" His gaze flitted Marigold's way, then back to Lavinia. "You do not know each other from school?"

Lavinia shook her head. "Oh no. Marigold would have been ahead of me, had we gone to school together—her brother and I are of an age. But as it stands, we are the closest neighbors, so we grew up together. Our fathers were the dearest of friends."

"Quite right." The art of going unnoticed, she'd learned, was not in holding one's tongue entirely, lest men like Lord Xavier take it upon themselves to exhibit outstanding manners and draw one out. No, the art of going unnoticed involved speaking just the right amount, adding just enough to a conversation to hold up one's end. As expected. That was the key—to do always what was expected and so never earn extra regard. "Fairfax Tower and Alnwick Abbey are but a twenty-minute ride apart."

Lavinia sent her a warm, playful grin. "I practically lived at the Tower as a girl, whenever I could convince Mother to allow me to go. The late Lord Fairfax always had the most engaging entertainments."

Marigold's chuckle may have *felt* bittersweet, but she knew it wouldn't sound it. "He did, at that. Theater troupes, acrobats, circuses . . . My father considered boredom his archnemesis."

"You must have led an enchanted childhood." Lord Xavier's eyes were wide, clearly charmed by the idea of the endless parade of diversions.

Marigold nodded and took a sip of her lemonade, giving herself an excuse not to verbalize a reply. Because the memories were no longer merely sweet, not now that she knew what they had cost her family—quite literally. Even so, the friends they'd made had been priceless. The lessons they'd learned had been beyond compare. The life Papa had made for them had been nothing short of delightful. They'd created a family like none other, turned the Tower into an enchanted kingdom unto itself. The childhood had been enchanted. But the adulthood that resulted from their inherited empty coffers was proving something altogether different.

A kingdom on the brink of bankruptcy, but that dash of cold water had never been able to penetrate Papa's love of *fun*.

Both gentlemen had shifted their focus back to Lavinia, who was telling her favorite story of their time together at the Tower—the day that Leonidas first made an appearance as a cub. The three of them, aged eight and five, had always been terrified and intrigued by the lions in the circus that stayed at the Tower for several months out of the year. Leopold and his mate, Leona, had seemed huge and ferocious to their young eyes. But their cub, Leonidas, had immediately captured their attention upon his birth, and the tamer, Hector, had introduced them early, claiming he was like any other kitten in the stable, except that he couldn't purr.

They'd ended up taking turns bottle-feeding the cub when his mother grew too weak, and had spent one entire glorious summer playing with him daily and turning the terror of the African plains into their own personal pet.

Dangerous. She knew that now and could scarcely fathom that Papa had allowed it. Mama certainly wouldn't have, had she not been spending the summer with her own ailing mother. Because while a lion could be trained, he was never quite *tamed*, no matter what Hector's official title had been. A lion was always wild at heart, and it only took one sound or smell or sight to bring instinct out. They'd learned that the hard way, but she knew Lavinia wouldn't be telling the far more gruesome tale of a hunting dog's demise.

She and Yates and Lavinia, however, being larger than Leonidas for so long, were viewed as part of his tribe—or so said Hector. Marigold had no scientific evidence to back up the claim, but she also had no reason to doubt him. Seventeen years later, and the big cat had never so much as swiped at any of them but in play. His only "attacks" of humans were the coordinated ones he'd once performed for their show, latching onto Hector's arm when he'd "threatened" the damsel-in-distress character, played by Franco's wife, Zelda.

Her fingers flexed against the gold-and-white brocade of the sofa, yearning for the feel of his rough mane between them. When the world felt too overwhelming, she had only to wrap her arms around his shaggy neck to be reminded that it was all merely flashing lights and costumes and choreographed dances, but that deep within them beat the heart

God had placed in each one's chest—primal and passionate and powerful. Just like a lion, they could put on a show of docility and domesticity, but threaten one's family and the roar would spring forth.

That was what she reminded herself of whenever guilt for her work tried to niggle. Did they deceive people? Now and then, perhaps. But mostly they were dedicated to discovering *truth*. And they did so to protect their family.

It was their lion's roar.

FOUR

Merritt may have been tempted to slouch, had his ribs not objected any time his posture relaxed even the slightest bit. Lord Hemming had made a brief appearance to welcome them, but then had begged off, claiming tasks that needed done out of the house—which was more than a little maddening. Why invite him only to disappear?

The suspicious part of him wondered if Hemming would go directly back to the office, if he'd pull out those German letters again when there was no chance of being observed. Have another hush-hush meeting with Colonel May. Had this entire invitation been as much a ruse on Hemming's part as the acceptance had been on Merritt's?

What an utter waste of time. The conversation currently being carried mostly by Lady Lavinia and Xavier had long ago spiraled down into what he considered drivel.

The stories of the circus animals had been entertaining, he would grant that. But then Lady Hemming had interjected, saying how challenging it had been to pry her daughter away from the amusements to be found at the Tower in order to focus on her education, but how she had prevailed—implying none too subtly that it was an oversight on the part of the

Fairfaxes that they hadn't done the same for Lady Marigold, and blaming said oversight on the death of Lady Fairfax when Marigold was twelve.

Pity had stirred then, and he'd looked once more to the overdressed friend of Lady Lavinia. His father had passed away when he was thirteen, and he was ready to empathize with her, if she looked his way.

She didn't. She merely kept that same masking smile on her lips and sipped at her drink and said absolutely nothing to defend herself or even indicate that she noticed the sting of Lady Hemming's barbed comment.

Spineless, oblivious, or mannerly? He didn't know, but either way, it did nothing to endear her to him.

Which was fine. His focus was the Hemmings, not the Fairfaxes. He didn't really expect to discover anything pertinent here in the drawing room with the ladies of the family, but he paid strict attention regardless. If he could redeem the wasted time, he would.

And he did get the answers to a few questions, thanks to Xavier's subtle manipulation of the conversation. He'd asked his friend to mention the trip he and his family had recently taken to the Continent to visit some relatives, which naturally led to asking the others if they had any family abroad. Merritt had volunteered that his mother was even then lounging on the Riviera with her two sisters, but that they had no family who actually lived out of England.

Lady Hemming had claimed the same, saying she'd never even stepped foot out of the United Kingdom. Her husband— here was the ticket—had done a bit more traveling, but he had no foreign family either.

Noted. And grieved a bit, as it dismissed the most probable innocent explanation for his German correspondence.

Of course, then Lady Hemming had to launch into a list of all her daughter's many accomplishments—how proficient she was on both piano and harp, how she had the voice of an angel, and, naturally, how she'd had time to perfect her artistic skill during the last unfortunate years at home when she wasn't yet well enough to join society after a bout of scarlet fever that had left her weak and sickly.

Being surrounded as he was so frequently by his aunt and five female cousins, Merritt was no stranger to—and no admirer of—the long list of so-called accomplishments young ladies felt they must trot out. Not that he was a disparager of actual talent, nor of hard-won skill. But he took offense on his cousins' behalf that these things were named like virtues, which was terribly unfair to one who simply didn't have the God-given talent for some of them. Why not value young ladies for their *actual* virtues? Temperance and prudence and generosity of spirit? Mercy and kindness and patience?

Men ought to be valued for the same.

Xavier, naturally, declared he should love to hear Lady Lavinia play and sing sometime, and then turned to include her friend. "Perhaps a duet?"

The laugh that Lady Hemming released would have sounded mocking and cruel had Lady Marigold's own amused chuckle not joined it. She shook her head. "Oh no, my lord. I am an utter dunce when it comes to anything musical, nor can I claim Lavinia's way with a paintbrush or pencil. I'm afraid I have no accomplishments whatsoever."

Lady Lavinia grasped her friend's hand, eyes wide. "Oh, but of course you have! Why, you were a veritable acrobat as a child."

Was it his imagination, or did Lady Marigold's eyes sparkle under the brim of her enormous hat? "Hardly something to be demonstrated in polite society. Although"—her grin rivaled her frock in brightness—"I can recite nearly all the popular plays in their entirety, from the Bard himself to George Bernard Shaw."

"Plays?" Xavier pursed his lips. "I see them occasionally, but I admit I'm more for novels."

"Oh yes! I adore novels," Lady Lavinia said. "I'm anxious for the next Sherlock Holmes story, aren't you?"

Xavier shook his head. "I quite detest Holmes and am no great fan of Doyle in general."

"You must be joking! How can anyone hate Holmes?"

His friend laughed and declared, "No, I'm quite serious. I have no use at all for Sherlock Holmes. How could I, when Doyle never even gives me the *chance* to see if I'm as intelligent as he? We're never given the information or the opportunity to observe it that his precious Holmes is."

The pretty Lady Lavinia was shaking her head full of dark brown curls, though her consternation seemed more amused than offended. Xavier had that effect on people. "All right, then. If you don't care for Doyle, who is your favorite author?"

Merritt was wincing even before X proclaimed, without the decency to sound apologetic about it, "William Le Queux! There's nothing in the world as grand as a good spy novel."

Perhaps not, but Merritt was personally of the mind that the popular writer's work wasn't exactly *good*. He'd never been a fan, but especially not since joining the intelligence division. It seemed that a full half of their work was assuring people that, no, what Mr. Le Queux wrote was not based on fact, and thanking overzealous citizens for their "reports" of "suspicious activity" that were inspired by the latest serial. Not to mention fending off suggestions from the would-be spymaster himself, who was quite convinced that he understood more about the world of intelligence and espionage than the War Department did.

Well. Merritt's lips settled into the beginnings of a smile. The chap may be onto something there. Not when it came to his own knowledge, but at least as concerned the general ineptitude of the British intelligence machine. Or, as it were, *lack* of a machine.

But they were set to fix that. A unified front would solve any number of issues, including the questions that had brought him here to this drawing room.

Where at least someone else had the good sense to dislike Le Queux.

Lady Marigold's nose had wrinkled in distaste. She said nothing, but that was probably because Lady Lavinia had already leaned forward. "I've yet to read anything of his, honestly. You recommend them? I believe my father has a volume somewhere."

"In our library at the Abbey." Lady Hemming made a show of pouting. "We'll have to pick up a title or two on our next outing. Which do you recommend, Lord Xavier?"

"I've just finished *The Spies of the Kaiser*. I'd be delighted to lend it to you, if you're interested in reading it."

His friend was clever, Merritt had to grant him that, despite his poor taste in fiction. Lending a book meant another visit to drop it off, and at least one more to pick it up again.

The Hemming ladies no doubt realized the same, and no doubt that explained the happy looks they exchanged, more than the promise of a book they could have purchased from any shop in London. "That would be lovely, my lord. Thank you so much for the generous offer." Lady Hemming beamed. "I was just saying to Lord Hemming this morning that I would love to invite you both to dinner as soon as it can be arranged. You could bring it then."

"Perfect. We would be delighted to join you. I'll have to check my family's calendar to be sure they haven't made arrangements for me already, but I daresay we could find a time within the next week. Isn't that right, Sir Merritt?"

Merritt had no need of consulting a calendar. He could simply smile and say, "I am at the disposal of you busier ones. My evenings are all free."

"Not a social butterfly, this one." Xavier gave him a playful—and gentle—cuff on the shoulder. "It was all I could do to drag him to the Marlborough last night."

"I'm afraid I haven't had the chance to spread any butterfly wings yet either." Lady Lavinia gave him a bright smile. "Though I *am* looking forward to meeting more of society. Not that I'll have any hope of aspiring to all of Marigold's connections. She's invited absolutely everywhere!"

It seemed Lady Lavinia was a far more gracious friend than her mother. And for her part, Lady Marigold batted away the observation with a chuckle. "Oh, you'll be much preferred to me soon enough, Lavinia. I assure you, it's not my company anyone desires so much as a peek at my latest hat. Isn't that so, Lady Hemming?"

The eldest lady's cheeks went just a bit pink at being subtly called out on her earlier way of dismissing her. What choice did she have now but to defend her daughter's friend or appear utterly cruel?

Clever girl. Under an absolutely monstrous hat, it must be said. It looked like it weighed half a ton. Didn't her neck tire from supporting it? It so overshadowed her that he couldn't even tell what color hair she had, or what color eyes. All he could see, it seemed, was the bright green of her dress and those waving peacock feathers that swayed every time she moved.

Lady Hemming cleared her throat. "You do yourself a disservice, Lady Marigold. I'm certain everyone appreciates your company, just as my Lavinia always has."

"You're too kind, my lady." She dipped her head, though Merritt couldn't have said whether it was humility, regret at boxing the lady into the comment, or satisfaction that colored her face, given that her hat yet again overwhelmed her expression.

Merritt sneaked a glance at the mantel clock. They had been here for an hour, which was all that would be expected of them on an introductory visit like this. It took only a glance at Xavier for his friend to do that effortless thing of his, promising to send a note round about possible dates and then seamlessly moving into farewells and thanks for the Hemmings' hospitality. Merritt added his own well-wishes and claims to be looking forward to the promised dinner, bowed over each lady's hand in turn, and made his escape with Xavier into the hallway.

The butler was nowhere in sight. No doubt the ladies would be outraged at that, but for his own part, Merritt considered it a stroke of God-given good fortune. He took his hat from the tree where the butler had hung it but slapped it into Xavier's stomach instead of putting it on his own head. "Take this for me, will you? I'll meet you outside in just a few minutes."

Xavier frowned at him, but his fingers nevertheless took hold of the hat. "What are you about? Or do I want to know?"

"Too much lemonade, that's all." He motioned back toward the main hallway, where a lavatory was surely located.

Not that the lavatory was actually his aim, but the excuse sufficed for Xavier, who agreed to wait outside. Merritt wasted no time in stealing along the corridor, rather glad that no loo immediately presented itself, thereby giving him the perfect excuse for wandering about.

The rooms were largely what he would expect—a formal parlor, a small library . . . and, *there*, his actual reason for sneaking about: a study. It took only a glance at the military branch stamps on several of the envelopes littering the top of the desk for him to verify that it was without question where Lord Hemming worked when at home. None had Top

Secret stamps at least. Had he seen *those* just lying about, he would have had something to say about it . . . though he didn't know to whom, exactly, he would have said it.

With a glance over his shoulder to be sure no one was watching, Merritt slipped into the room and, careful to keep his movements silent, eased the door shut behind himself and locked it.

He must be quick, which meant he was unlikely to find anything of real value here today. But he could at least familiarize himself with the earl's system of organization, or lack thereof, so that he could make use of a better-orchestrated visit another time. He surveyed the desk, the filing cabinet, the bookshelves flanking the window, noted the enormous, heavy-framed painting behind the desk that could easily be masking a safe, and—

"Who's in there?"

The voice at the door made him go utterly still, even his breath frozen in his burning chest. A feminine voice, cultured, but he didn't think it was either of the Hemming ladies—Lady Marigold, perhaps? But why would she be hissing that question at the door in a voice more warning than curious or angry?

A soft tap. "Whoever you are, you ought to know that his lordship doesn't approve of anyone in his study, even to tidy up."

Well, that explained not only the mess of papers, but also the layer of dust on the shelves. Though it did rather beg the question of why he left the door hanging open if no one was allowed in.

Though if everyone knew it was off-limits, perhaps that was all the security he deemed necessary for the room itself.

"Though I can't imagine why you would close the door unless you're about something you oughtn't to be." A pause. Merritt had to swallow back the inconvenient urge to cough.

"You had better come out now and explain yourself before I fetch Matthews." The knob jiggled.

Blast. Panic itched his ribs, but he suppressed it just as he did the cough and sent his gaze flying around the room. There were no handy doors connecting this room to the library, which only left the window as an escape route. He padded silently toward it—and threw caution to the wind when he heard a scraping at the door.

Was Lady Marigold so good a friend that she knew where Lord Hemming stashed an extra key to this room? Double blast.

He tossed the sash open, ducked under the pane, and jumped out without wasting any time looking beneath him. They were on the ground floor, thus it wasn't so high a drop that he needed to be concerned.

Except that some fool had placed a concrete bench just under the window, which would have been a gift had he been expecting it. As it was, he tumbled over it, turning his ankle and, worse, cracking his ribs against the seat.

Pain exploded like light before his eyes, and it was all he could do to bite back a groan or shout. Pressing a hand to his protesting torso, he barely managed to pull himself under the bench as the sound of hurried footfalls came toward the window.

Unfortunately, Lady Marigold had not seemed particularly stupid, which meant that she'd noted the open window and made the obvious deduction. He knew she must be leaning out even now, scouring the narrow strip of garden at the side of the house, looking for him. He pulled his knees in a little tighter and prayed he was completely covered by that blighted bench.

A long, long moment dragged by, made all the longer by the searing pain in his rib cage. She didn't call out again, but she also wasn't so foolish that she'd assume he'd vanished.

But what would she do? The bench was a likely hiding place. Would she send someone to investigate? Go around herself? If so, he'd have to make a mad dash for the front while she was gone, ribs be hanged.

He listened for the sound of her hurried steps away, straining to hear it over the thudding of his pulse.

Nothing. Just that interminable silence for another wretched eternity.

Then, finally, a sound . . . but not one he'd expected. It sounded almost like—but no, she wouldn't . . . would she?

Her heels clicked upon the concrete of his prison. Then she leapt lightly to the ground.

Lord, render her blind, if you would. Keep me hidden. You know I have no bad intentions here, I want only the truth, especially if it will clear Lord Hemming of suspicion.

But if she turned and spotted him, if she sounded the alarm, if he was caught in this position—well, he'd likely be sacked from his dreaded desk job. Quite possibly he'd come under scrutiny. He could be court-martialed even.

He could see only her shoes and the hem of her dress as she moved a few steps one direction, then the other.

Estelle and Georgette and Danielle would be envious of the shoes. They'd chattered his ears off just last week about the latest style that Lady M was popularizing and . . . Lady M. Her? Lady Marigold?

His lungs burned for a deep breath, even as they threatened to rebel if he took one. Distracting thoughts of whether the young lady soon to become his captor was the fashion icon his cousins were always raving about at least served to keep him calm, useless as the questions really were.

He would simply tell her a version of the truth when she caught him—that he'd been searching for the lavatory and saw the study, had stepped in out of curiosity. He would say he panicked when he heard her voice.

Perhaps his obvious pain would distract *her* enough that she wouldn't ask why he'd closed the door or leapt out the window.

Her feet returned to their original position, then did an about-face and pointed at the window.

This was it. She *had* to see him now. Any moment she'd crouch down, and that ridiculous hat of hers would wag its peacock-feathered-finger at him and ruin his entire career.

Only . . . it didn't. *She* didn't. Instead, she stepped back up onto the bench, climbed back into the window, and closed the sash. Then, biggest miracle of all, he heard her steps walking back toward the door.

He wasted no time. She *must* be going to fetch assistance, and he wasn't going to be here for them to find when they came round. He rolled out from under the bench, got his feet under him, kept low for a few steps, and then ran as fast as his lungs and ribs would allow toward the front of the house.

Not until he'd plowed, gasping, into Xavier did he stop— and then it was to double over.

"I say! Fire and brimstone, Merritt, where did you come from? And dash it, man, you're about to fall over." Blessedly strong hands gripped his arms and propelled him somewhere or another, all but holding him up.

His vision was blurred with pain, and he didn't honestly know what Xavier was doing until he felt the cushion of the duke's new automobile seat beneath him. He relaxed into it with a groan. "I think . . . I've broken . . . rib."

Xavier muttered something both blistering and concerned before he slammed the door of the auto shut. "You're going to the doctor," he pronounced, voice tight. "And don't bother arguing."

He hadn't the breath to do so, even if he had wanted to. He squeezed his eyes shut and kept his hand pressed to the point of pain on his rib cage, though he could feel nothing through his jacket, waistcoat, shirt, and the bandage his batman had wrapped again this morning.

The other car door slammed. "Do I even want to know what you were doing?"

Merritt shook his head. Kept his eyes closed.

And finally remembered to whisper a mental prayer of thanks heavenward. It was surely only the Lord himself who had blinded Lady Marigold's eyes to him.

A few minutes into the drive, the pain in his ribs had eased up enough that he became aware of the matching throb in his ankle.

A fine predicament he'd made for himself. Now what was he to do? How was he to learn what he needed to learn about the earl?

He couldn't just give up the investigation, not with an agent missing in the field. He *had* to determine why that telegram had given him the lord's name. Otherwise, this could spell the end of their new agency before it even got started. But how could he conduct it if he couldn't move without pain?

As if an answer to prayer, the image of that calling card he'd picked up last night flashed before his mind's eye.

The Imposters.

FIVE

ates walked right by the enormous, heavy front doors of the ancient cathedral and whistled his way into the alley instead as the church bells tolled the hour. Ten o'clock. He tipped his hat to a delivery boy emerging from the side door and entered the cool, dim interior that he knew better than most would assume.

When in London, he and Marigold attended the same church that Fairfaxes had frequented for generations, the one closest to their city home. Most people wouldn't expect him to trek miles across the city to come *here* . . . unless they realized that the serving vicar was James Parks, son of their late steward. Then they'd assume this nothing but a social call.

James greeted him with a warm smile when he poked his head into his office. "Yates! I was wondering if you had any meetings this week."

"I meant to send a note round, but we didn't settle on a day until last night." Leaning into the doorway, Yates cast his gaze around the room, cataloguing each small change since his last visit three days ago, when he'd met with Lord Adams to give his report and collect the remainder of their fee. He made a clucking noise with his tongue and shook his head. "Forgot to tidy up your tea things again, I see."

James's ears flushed red. "You're worse than Aunt Priss."

Yates grinned and nodded toward the book on the table by the chair, whose page marker had moved a good deal. "Looks like you've gotten some reading in. How are you enjoying *Orthodoxy*?"

"Chesterton is his usual clever self, even when writing nonfiction. Do you want to borrow it when I'm through? I know how you enjoyed *The Man Who Was Thursday*."

"Please." He didn't often purchase new books these days. It was difficult to justify when they had an entire library at the Tower and a smaller version here in Town, and he'd yet to read most of the titles in their collection. Even if the newer, popular titles *were* far more alluring than those dusty old tomes that his ever-so-boring ancestors had collected.

It was no wonder Father had overindulged in amusements. When one came from such a staid, boring line, one simply revolted now and then.

Marigold would scowl at him if he ever said as much aloud, so he buttoned up the thought and pulled from his pocket the small book of poetry he'd brought with him this morning. "For now, Browning."

James smiled, and his gaze drifted back to the papers in front of him. "If you see Gemma before I do, tell her Aunt Priss is going to disown her if she doesn't pay her a visit soon."

Yates chuckled, grateful not for the first time that the formidable old bird wasn't *his* aunt. "Always happy to deliver her threats for her."

James's face went serious. "How is Gem? Really? She only ever shows me a smiling face, but I know it for the lie it must be."

At that, Yates had to sigh. "It's all she shows any of us. Marigold says we must give her time."

"Hmm. Your sister is no doubt right. But mine may well cling to this anger for years, if I know Gemma."

"That . . . wouldn't surprise me. But what can we do but pray?" Yates shook his head and shifted, keenly aware of the ticking of time. "Will you be here when I'm through, do you think?"

"Unless I'm called out for an emergency visit, I don't plan to leave until after luncheon."

"Very good." He pushed off the door. "If you're looking for your spare set of spectacles, they're half-hidden on the top shelf behind your ship in a bottle."

James's eyes lit up. "You ought to have come by yesterday. I spent half an hour searching for them."

Smiling, Yates lifted a hand in a temporary farewell and made his way along the familiar corridors of the cathedral. It dated from the time when England was a Catholic country, boasting soaring arches and flying buttresses and the sort of artistry that took decades of work. He always craned his head up to marvel at how anyone had fashioned such impressive architecture with only medieval technology to assist them.

One of his school chums had gotten it in his head that churches like this were a waste of resources better spent on things like helping the poor, but Yates couldn't agree. Not with knowing how much love for the Lord went into each stone and alcove, each window and doorway. Not with knowing how many people through countless generations were taught the story of Christ through the building itself. How many came here for a glimpse of God's beauty in a life otherwise dismal and grueling.

His smile falling from his lips, Yates slipped into the long-abandoned confessional, into the confessor's side. He'd instructed his new potential client, as he did all their clients, to take the penitent's side.

Until five years ago, he'd never understood the trials of the workaday world, the pressure of making ends meet. But he knew now. And it made him appreciate all the more these centuries-old works of beauty and grace.

Proof that things could outlast one man's folly. Legacies could go on, even through upheaval and change. This old building had gone from Catholic to Anglican with each shift in regime, seeing priests and vicars alike behind its pulpits, but its mission had never changed.

Yates's mission couldn't change either. His duty—the only duty he had ever or would ever have—was to care for what was his. His sister, their home, their family, their tenants . . . that was all the earldom really meant. He could finally sit in the sessions of the House of Lords now, yes, and vote on matters that affected the empire—but what *really* counted was whether Franco and Zelda, Hector and Drina and Alafair had a roof over their heads and food on their plates. Whether Marigold was happy. Whether the villagers who relied on him could meet the needs of their families.

He settled onto the hard bench of the booth and closed his eyes for a long moment. As a lad, he'd thought life was all about the next play, the next game, the next adventure. He'd thought the greatest struggle in his life was going to be buckling down to duty when he'd have much preferred touring the country on the stage.

O, young Yates, what a fool you were.

But for all his adolescent idiocy, God had been merciful, hadn't He? He'd led them here, to doing work that let them use all those skills they never should have learned. He provided food for their tables and troughs, friends to protect and shield them. He'd knit Yates and Marigold, Graham and Gemma and James closer than ever.

Well. Graham and Gemma . . . that one may require more prayer than he had time for just now, but he whispered a quick supplication on their behalf and then took a long moment to examine his conscience—something he had decided would be wise when he first put this confessional booth to use.

When one made ends meet by spying on one's peers, it was all too easy to fall into judgment. To let deception become not just a costume one wore but one's very skin. It was all too easy to get caught up in the actions and forget the reasons.

He prayed what he always prayed on this bench. *Lord, help us to seek your truth and justice above the fees we charge. Grant us your discernment. Fill us with your wisdom. And provide for us and all those in our care. Amen.*

After a long, cleansing breath, he pulled out his book of poetry.

By the clock, he still had forty-five minutes before Lieutenant Colonel Sir Merritt Livingstone was due in the booth. But all too often, their clients thought to discover his identity by arriving early and being the first into the confessional, so they could see him approach. Little did they realize that James would have warned him had anyone else been in this section of the cathedral.

Sir Merritt, however, gave Yates ample time to let Browning's poetry roll through his soul. He didn't actively try to memorize the text, but still the words embedded themselves in his mind and heart, as poetry always did. The rhythms, the cadence, the rhyming pattern—ah, bliss. He would recite this one for Marigold and Gemma later. They'd enjoy it.

The sound of the heavy front door opening and then swinging shut again echoed through the quiet cathedral, stirring Yates from his mental recitation. He checked his watch and nodded—a respectable ten minutes early. Given that Livingstone lived a good distance from here and would have had to leave himself time to combat traffic, that was more an indication of good manners than sneakiness, Yates imagined.

Though he frowned as he listened to the footsteps heading his direction. They weren't steady, not as he'd imagined a Coldstream Guard's would be. He had expected quick, clipped steps. Men like that always moved with purpose, didn't they? But this one—this one sounded as though he was limping, and as the steps drew nearer, Yates could also hear rather ragged breathing.

Maybe this wasn't Sir Merritt at all, but someone else who would pass by the confessional on their way to find James. Or perhaps it was even a parishioner who would slip into a pew for a few moments of prayer. That had happened before, though rarely, during his meetings.

But no. The door to the penitent's side opened with a soft *whoosh*, and a moment later, a silhouette settled behind the screen. "'There is nothing either good or bad,'" he said, quoting the line from *Hamlet* that Yates had instructed him to say upon arrival.

Definitely Sir Merritt. Yates finished the quote, careful to pitch his voice into the character's he'd decided on for today—a Welsh sea captain. "'But thinking makes it so.'"

"A rather relativistic thought, isn't it?"

Yates chuckled as he imagined his fictional Captain Ellis would do. "One cannot argue with Shakespeare."

"Of course one can. Shakespeare himself did so all the time within his own works."

"Ah, but most of us are not so great a mind, nor so clever a one as the Bard, I daresay." He injected a smile into his voice. "Good day to you, Sir Merritt. How do you do?"

The man on the other side of the booth tried and failed to stifle a cough. "If I were better, I wouldn't have cause to be here, though I do thank you for asking. And yourself?"

"Fine as a sunny summer day."

"And you are . . . ?"

"Whoever I need to be to help you. But you may call me Mr. A."

"A . . . for Anonymous?"

Impressive. Yates had always thought it rather obvious, but no one had ever made the connection. Or at least announced it. "I see you're an intelligent fellow." He set his Browning down soundlessly on the bench beside him and leaned against the back of the booth so that his own sil-, houette wouldn't be easily seen. "Putting that intelligence together with your limp and clear pulmonary distress, may I assume that you are only seeking the aid of the Imposters because your health requires it? That otherwise you would be pursuing the answers you require on your own?"

A beat of silence, a swallow. "Does my motivation matter?"

"In the utmost." Yates brandished a finger in the air, the shadow of which was likely visible if Sir Merritt was looking through the screen—which he'd have been willing to wager he was, if he were given to wagers for anything larger than a walnut. "But fear not. If you don't want to confess your innermost thoughts here and now, I shall read them for myself through your actions as well as I do the weather over the sea by the clouds and wind."

"And that is to make me feel *better*?"

"It would if you believed me overstating my abilities to discern." Most men did, at least at the start. They had a steady stream of clients because they always delivered results, but many of them arrived in this booth dubious at best.

"Your abilities are not in question. The Duke of Norwich would not have hired you twice if you were not the best investigators in the country."

Interesting. He'd known already that Livingstone was a friend of Lord Xavier Hasting, but they must be close if the duke's son admitted that his father had made use of their services. "I needn't ask who referred you to us, then."

"That was what convinced me you were worth seeking out. Though I found your card as well. At the Marlborough."

"Ah." Good to know. He'd deposited a few of those around the club when last he'd dropped by, in key locations. Graham had questioned the wisdom of the tactic, so he'd be certain to rub it in. "And how can I assist you, sir?"

A shift, a creak of old wood, and the shadow moved closer to the screen. "This discretion your motto boasts—that is more, I trust, than a catchy line?"

"It is our byword." Yates leaned a bit toward the far corner to keep himself shrouded.

"Good. Because it is my hope that you'll prove my suspicions unfounded and ungrounded, and I certainly don't want any aspersions to be cast on the gentleman in question through your search."

They were being hired to prove someone's innocence? That didn't happen often. "I assure you, sir, that I have no interest in defaming anyone's reputation unduly. My investigation will go without notice, and the results will be delivered solely to you, for you to decide what to do with the answers I uncover."

"Good. Good." Another cough, but Sir Merritt didn't retreat from his position close to the screen, no doubt so he could keep his voice pitched to that bare whisper.

Yates didn't bother reassuring him that the booth had been built to absorb sound—privacy for the penitent that proved so very useful for him too. He just sat back and waited for his guest to get to his point. Both reassurance and rushing, he'd discovered, hindered his ability to observe a fellow. Far better to let the client talk at whatever pace he wanted, and at whatever volume.

"All right. I have a packet here that I will leave for you— copies of my own observations and the telegram that has piqued my suspicions. This is of the most sensitive nature, and I must walk the line between what is simply private and what is, in fact, Top Secret. I work, you see, in the War Office

Intelligence Division. I was put in my position specifically to assist the WOID, Naval Intelligence, and the Special Branch as we work toward creating a unified intelligence agency for gathering information abroad."

Spies? Genuine *spies*? Yates had to suppress the urge to clap his hands together in glee. Instead, he granted himself only an understanding hum, meant to encourage Sir Merritt to go on.

"One of my field agents has gone silent when he shouldn't have after sending me a wire with a single word—a name of someone else associated with the collaborative work. At the same time, the man in question began trying to hide information from me, even though I am cleared to read anything that comes into the office. It is my hope these were merely personal correspondence, but . . . they were in German, which makes them suspect in this day and age." A deep breath in, a wheeze out. "Lord Hemming. It is he I need you to investigate, along with, perhaps, my superior, Colonel May. He was discussing whatever these German letters were with Hemming."

Lord Hemming? Yates's veins suddenly pumped fire through his limbs instead of blood. No, no that couldn't be right. Lord Hemming had been one of Father's closest friends. Lord Hemming was Lavinia's father. Lord Hemming was . . . well, he must be innocent. But that was what Sir Merritt wanted him to prove, wasn't it?

Yates cleared his throat. "I will be forthright with you, sir. There is much I will be able to discover, but not within the War Office. I try to avoid stepping on the toes of the Crown itself."

"I will continue keeping my eyes and ears open in the office, and obviously I must withhold anything from you that is Top Secret, including the identity of my agent. That part is my job, no one else's. But it is the work *outside* the office that I find myself incapable of seeing to at present. If Hemming is innocent, as I pray he is, then this connection is personal."

"Then we should make a most excellent team, and I daresay we'll have answered your questions about his lordship within a few weeks. This sort of basic investigation will be seventy-five pounds." Steeper than any other investigator in London, yes—and for good reason. They priced themselves into the jobs they were suited for and out of the ones they weren't.

Livingstone didn't miss a beat. "Very well. How do we communicate?"

"I will send you regular updates via the post. If there is anything that cannot be entrusted to such conventional means, I will send instruction on when to meet me back here or to pick up a packet I have left for you in a secure location elsewhere. And if ever you need me, you have only to leave a note as you did before. That box is monitored round the clock." And the urchins he employed to do so were always more than eager to find him straightaway for the coin he passed them.

"Fair enough. Do you require payment now or upon completion?"

"Forty now, thirty-five when the case is closed. And if it requires expenses that go beyond the basic fees, I will advise you and seek permission beforehand. I never incur any additional expenses without your approval."

"Excellent. Very good indeed." Another pause, long and heavy. "I will consider it money well spent if we can clear Lord Hemming of these suspicions."

From there, it was a simple matter of saying their farewells and promising an update within a week. Sir Merritt left, and Yates waited for the sound of his footsteps to die away and the door to open and close again before leaving his side of the booth and reaching into the penitent's side to gather the file of papers and payment that his new client had left for him.

Marigold wasn't going to like this. Not one bit. He didn't either. But then, better that Sir Merritt had come to them than taking his worries directly to the authorities, wasn't it? Questions like that—questions that hinted at mixed loyalties, if he was guilty of what the man suspected—could ruin a family. Could ruin not only Hemming himself, but his wife and daughter.

He bade a quick good-bye to James and hurried home. He hadn't mentioned to Marigold with whom he was meeting this morning—not yet, not before he knew whether they'd be hired. That was their agreement. He fielded the initial inquiries, only bringing the rest of the team onto the case once they had money in hand.

He didn't relish telling her how this meeting had gone.

Which of course meant that he encountered no traffic and was soon jogging up his own doorstep.

The front door opened, and a ghastly creature in white greasepaint and ragged clothes appeared, making him jump before laughter spilled out. "Rehearsal time, I take it?"

"I was beginning to think you wouldn't return before I had to leave. If I may, my lord?" Neville motioned him inside with the same elegant gesture he used when playing butler rather than the ghost of Hamlet's father.

"Absolutely, Nev. You don't need to ask."

"I wanted to be sure you had no guests coming before I left the door unattended."

Yates waved that away. "No, no. Go on. We can't have you missing a rehearsal this close to opening night."

The actor gave a dramatic bow. "I'll have the tickets in hand this afternoon for you and Lady Marigold."

"And she is . . . ?"

"In the gymnasium, I believe."

He should have expected as much. "Very good. Thanks, old boy. Now get on with you." Yates closed the door behind their old friend, who was good enough to play servant for them when they needed one in exchange for room and board, and then turned toward the gymnasium with a sigh.

Marigold drew in a long breath, took a moment to focus on each limb, each muscle, where her weight was centered. She rolled onto the balls of her feet, bent her knees, and then sprang forward. A forward flip, a second, a twist in midair, and she landed facing the direction from which she'd come, hands in the air and feet firmly planted. Bending backward until her palms touched the floor, she then kicked her legs up and walked a few steps on her hands.

The familiar routine did more to calm her racing thoughts than anything else had managed to do over the last several days. She flipped her legs back down, let her body follow, and slipped down into the splits just as Yates's familiar form appeared in the doorway.

He was still in his regular clothes, which was rather odd. Usually when he came to find her in the gymnasium, he changed first, so he could join her in their routines. Just now, he only stepped inside and leaned against the rack of dumbbells.

Marigold frowned. "What's the matter? Did the meeting not go well?" She tried not to do the maths of how they'd fare if they didn't take on a new case this week. She tried to trust that, as He always did, the Lord would send what work they needed, when they needed it. She tried not to immediately launch into a revised budget, wondering what else they could cut this month.

Her brother's smile was a strange thing. There, but strained.

"It went . . . well enough, I suppose. I have his initial pay-ment."

Which meant she was free to ask, "Who was it?"

Yates cleared his throat and reached for the necktie that he usually shed the very moment he entered the house. "Lieu-tenant Colonel Sir Merritt Livingstone."

Marigold had been bracing her palms on the floor to lever herself back up into her next position, but she paused. *Sir Merritt?* Sir Merritt was hiring them? Her mind spun like Zelda on the trapeze.

She'd said nothing to anyone, not even Yates, after catch-ing him in Lord Hemming's study the other day. What was there to say until she'd managed to make a bit of sense of it? When she'd stood in the side garden and seen him curled into a fetal position under that bench, looking not only ri-diculous but with pain practically radiating from him, she hadn't thought. Hadn't considered. She hadn't had to weigh her decisions.

She'd known exactly what she had to do in that moment, and she'd learned to trust those hard-trained instincts. She'd let him think he'd gone unnoticed and simply climbed back through the window. Because everything she'd learned about him in the preceding hour said he was a man who valued honor above all, and if he was snooping through Lord Hem-ming's private rooms and injuring himself to avoid notice, there was a reason.

But *what* reason was the question—one that kept her every sense engaged through the remainder of her own visit with Lavinia that day, and the two subsequent ones as well. Something was amiss in the Hemming household, she was certain. Something to have lit a barely masked urgency in her friend's demeanor.

What if Lavinia didn't just want to marry to get on with her life—what if she wanted to marry to *escape* her life?

Why? Why would that be?

Marigold moved her legs to a straddle. "He's hired us to investigate Lord Hemming, hasn't he?"

It wasn't often she could surprise Yates so fully, but he looked downright flabbergasted as he slung the hated tie over the dumbbell's bar. "Along with a colonel, yes. But how in heavens do you know that? And here I was dreading telling you!"

Floor exercises were not enough to work through the disquiet blooming in her chest at the thought of the Hemmings. She pushed to her feet and turned to the rings, leapt up to grab hold of them. "What does he suspect him of?"

"At the worst, treason. But first tell me how you knew."

As she swung through her usual routine, she told Yates how Lavinia had seemed just a bit off in their visits, and how she'd caught Sir Merritt in the earl's study. She could only see her brother's face every few seconds as she faced front in her rotation, but even those glimpses were enough to show her that his teeth were clenched.

"And you didn't tell me this before?"

Though she still had several minutes left in her routine, she dismounted with a flip so that she could hold her brother's gaze. "I couldn't be certain it was anything demanding Imposter involvement."

"I'm not just a fellow Imposter, Marigold—I'm your *brother*, and Lavinia is my friend, too, you know."

She did. That was why she'd kept the concern to herself, though she'd learned not to tease him about the crush he'd harbored for their neighbor for at least a decade. The dual blows of their financial ruin and Lavinia's poor health had unraveled all the dreams he'd once had of winning her heart.

What had once been Marigold's favorite way to poke at him had become too cruel then. And shielding him from further heartache had become as engrained as their acrobatic practice. She shook her head. "I know how your emotions get tangled up when it comes to Lavinia." She kept the words quiet, soothing. The voice she'd used with him when he was just a little thing, desperate for the mother who'd been snatched away from them both by the cruel teeth of death. It usually worked just as well now, even when he was a full head taller than she and able to hold her up with one hand.

He practically ripped his suit jacket off—so much for quiet and soothing. "Stop coddling me. I'm a grown man, if you recall, the ninth Earl Fairfax, a member of the House of Lords, and—"

"Still my baby brother. I'm sorry, Yates. I don't mean to coddle, it's just . . . I love you. I don't want you to be hurt, and I saw the look on your face when I mentioned that Lavinia had Lord X and Sir Merritt calling on her."

He shot her a very different look now. "I don't know what look you *imagined*, but it was nothing to warrant not telling me about that suitor clearly trying to snoop through Hemming's study. We don't keep secrets from each other, Marigold. Isn't that the very foundation of all we do?"

It was, and shame welled up inside. Good-intentioned as her silence had been, she had been wrong. "You're right. I should have told you the moment I got home. I'm sorry."

He'd been unbuttoning his shirt, his movements jerky and fast, revealing what she should have suspected all along—he had his leotard on underneath. Always ready to shed the skin of aristocracy and revert to the performer, that was Yates.

Her apology seemed to mollify him only slightly. He tossed his waistcoat, shirt, and trousers to the ground without any of the care he usually gave such movements, picked up two dumbbells, and sat with them on the bench.

He'd turned himself into a veritable circus strongman over the last five years, carving out muscles capable of holding her, tossing her, catching her, and swinging himself into positions no one would ever think to try. He worked his physique as stringently as she did, as stringently as they both worked their minds and memories.

But she still saw that scared, lonely little boy beneath the man too. And loved him all the more for the dichotomy. With a sigh, she moved to his side, draped an arm around his shoulder, and dropped a kiss onto the top of his head. "Forgive me?"

He angled a look up at her—one no doubt meant to be as hard as the iron in his hands, but which twinkled around the edges, as his eyes always did. "You better not shield me from anything else as you do your part."

Her part would be, as it always was, observing their client. A task that would be easier than usual, given that they'd both be calling on Lavinia at the same time. She gave a solemn nod. "You have my word. If Lavinia starts falling in love with either of them, I won't hesitate to tell you."

"Good." It was the complete lack of regret in his eyes that convinced her he may not have been lying for the last three years when he swore he thought of Lavinia only as a friend now.

Funny. Seeing that he really was over his childhood crush made him feel more grown up to her than his height or his training or seeing him drive off to the sessions for the first time last year. She sighed again and mussed some of the pomade out of his carefully styled hair. "All right. Tell me all about your meeting with Sir Merritt. Who were you this time?"

Finally, his grin flashed out. "Captain Ellis," he pronounced, voice deeper than usual and in the accent he'd perfected for the character.

She grinned, too, and turned back to the rings. "One of my favorites. Do go on."

SIX

Two Weeks Later

Marigold flung open the doors to her dressing room and marched inside with all the gusto of Hector entering Leonidas's stall. One could never, he said, show fear to a big cat, and that was the same principle she employed with the terrifying, intimidating towers of hats and gowns and feathers she'd collected and created so deliberately.

Behind her, Gemma was laughing where she'd sprawled on Marigold's bed. "Don't get lost in there, O Valiant Knight. I haven't the time to mount an expedition to save you."

"You tease, but I may have suffocated under all the silk and sequins when that shelf gave way last week, had you not been on hand to save me."

"I would have written you a fitting obituary. I even had my headline all planned out: 'Lady M, Lost to Her Fashions.'"

Marigold chuckled and turned to the shelves full of folded day dresses in the most audacious colors and styles to be seen anywhere in Europe.

She had white ones at home. Simple ones. Comfortable ones. But those were only for Marigold-of-the-Tower. Not Lady M, London's favorite mannequin. She reached out and touched the fabric of one in a bold saffron yellow. She could pair it with the hat that boasted a full rainbow of ostrich plumes, perhaps. "Saffron, do you think? With the rainbow monstrosity?"

"You wore that dress already. If you're thinking rainbow, perhaps the purple."

She frowned. "Haven't I worn that one too?"

"Not as purple. You wore it last year when it was blue, before we added that eyelet lace and altered the hem."

"Right." She picked it up from the shelf.

"You really need to keep a chart."

"But why, when I have you?" She punctuated the too-sweet words by sticking her head back out of her dressing room and batting her eyes at her oldest friend.

Once upon a time, Gemma's parents had been compensated for providing their daughter as Marigold's companion. Once upon a time, they'd all thought she could just continue in that position all their lives, so famously did they get along.

Now Gemma's income from her writing helped support *them*. Well, the whole of them, the family. They all pitched in whatever they could to support the Tower, Gemma with her writing income and Graham with what he earned as an architect—even if Graham hadn't stepped foot in the Tower since last December.

Gemma tossed a pillow toward the door with a laugh that curved her lovely rosebud lips and lit up her lovely blue eyes. *She* was the reason Graham wouldn't come to the Tower these days, but Marigold wasn't about to say a word about that. It would only light the fuse of Gemma's anger—anger that Marigold knew barely covered an endless well of pain.

She ducked back into the closet and pulled out the hat, gloves, and a shawl to finish her outfit, and then returned to her bedroom. If Gemma wanted—needed—to focus on the trivial right now, she would give her that. "The rainbow feathers were genius, Gem. I dare anyone not to notice them."

Her friend took the hat from her and surveyed it with a smug little smile. "Weren't they?" She positioned it over her own hair and turned to the mirror. The wide brim cast her golden hair in shadow so that at a glance, it didn't look so different from Marigold's warm brown. They were the same height, very similar builds, too, though Gemma didn't spend the hours in exercise that Marigold did.

A brilliant hat. Marigold would wear it today in Hyde Park, and then wherever, whenever it next appeared, no one would think to look beneath the feathers to see what face wore it. They would simply assume it was Lady M.

Which meant Marigold would be free to do something else while her hat paraded around London, getting noticed. Something yet to be determined but that would require more stealth . . . and possibly an alibi. Something that would likely involve more scaling of walls or picking of locks or memorizing of conversations.

Something she would do as a faceless Imposter, not as Lady Marigold Fairfax.

Marigold, clad already in her chemise and bloomers and corset, slipped the purple dress over her head and then presented her back to Gemma for help with the row of buttons. "What are you going to be doing today? Do you have a new column to write?"

"As always." Gemma's fingers danced up the buttons with the ease of long practice. "I must write up that musicale we attended last night. I hear Lady M was there in a gown of sparkling gold that put the stars to shame."

Marigold laughed. She, Zelda, and Gemma had spent hours over the winter sewing those sequins and beads onto an older gown in an Egyptian-inspired pattern that Graham had sent them an image of, from his research. It had turned

78

out so well she hadn't even moaned about the weight of all the adornments. She had merely thanked the Lord for something to keep them all occupied and distracted after the tragedy Christmas had turned into.

"And the soprano was amazing too. That aria . . ." Marigold closed her eyes, trying to remember the soaring notes that had filled the room and transported her beyond the confines of London. Back to the wild, heather-strewn countryside, the crashing waves of the North Sea, and the wind whipping through her hair.

She missed the Tower. Missed it from the depths of her soul.

"Very talented. There, all buttoned up." Gemma stepped away and pulled out the dressing table stool. "What are you thinking for your hair today? Chignon? Braided crown?"

Marigold frowned as she sank onto the cushioned seat. She reached for the long, sleep-frazzled braid still dangling down to her waist and untied the end. She really should give in to Gemma's perpetual prods to trim it and remove some of the weight, but she always resisted. Even knowing how much it got in her way, she couldn't disentangle her emotions from the long locks.

It was one of her few memories of Mama that was still vibrant and ever-present. Marigold, sitting on a stool much like this one, Mama behind her with a hairbrush. Stroking through the locks every morning, every night, as she hummed a hymn or a tune from whatever show they'd just seen. Mama, saying how much she loved Marigold's hair. Mama, braiding it, wrapping it around her head, and declaring it her crown. Mama, leaning close with her matching curls framing her face and saying how beautiful she looked.

Marigold shook the braid from the locks now, looked into the mirror, and could still see Mama's face there beside her own and Gemma's. She knew her own features were understated, bordering on plain, easily forgotten—but not Mama's. Mama had been so beautiful that even Papa, ever eager for the newest distraction, never tired of looking at her.

It had been Mama who had taught her all her young life how to make certain her fashions never outshone her. No one had better taste than Lady Fairfax—she knew which styles would complement and which would overpower, when to be bold and daring and when to be simple and elegant. *She*, with her well-chiseled features, could wear the most audacious of styles and still make people look at her face instead of her gown. She'd taught Marigold which of those never to wear, lest they distract from her eyes and smile.

Those were the ones Marigold now wore all the time, to distract from her eyes and smile. To render her face invisible beneath her costume.

Gemma picked up the hairbrush and ran it through the thick weight of Marigold's hair as Marigold said, "Let's go with a braided crown today. It will look better if we end up at Lavinia's house and I take off the hat."

"The two of you are promenading with Lord X and Sir Merritt again, right? I'll make certain I'm home when you return in case you need to dictate conversations."

Marigold had nodded at the first question, but she sighed at the offer. "You're assuming I'll have anything to report. Those two are either the very epitome of upstanding chaps or far too adept at hiding things. I've scarcely anything to add to our files, and we've seen them four times since that initial meeting."

Gemma chuckled and parted Marigold's hair into precise sections for the braids. "Believe it or not, not every gentleman has something to hide. Some truly are just nice men."

Marigold's brows shot up. "Name one, other than them."

"Your brother."

"Ha! He definitely has something to hide." Like the fact that though his pedigree was impeccable, his fortune was lost.

At that, Gemma laughed. "Touché. But he's a nice man, anyway. And I've no doubt there are scores of others like him. It's simply that we don't have occasion to observe that sort very often in our line of work."

"Too true." It would have been enough to make her swear off the risk of marriage, even if she'd had a dime of a dowry to put toward a match. "Have you heard anything more on Lord Hemming from the servant sector?"

The reflection of Gemma in the mirror shook her head. "I plan to meet Claudia at the tea house tomorrow," she said of Lady Hemming's companion—who was also Gemma's second cousin. "If anyone has thought of anything else, I'm certain she'll share it then." She added a dimpled grin. "No doubt more than I really want her to."

A chuckle rumbled its way from her throat. Claudia, ten years their senior, had the most remarkable ability to win the confidences of the domestics of any house she visited. She had always been bursting with more information about every lord and lady she encountered than they'd once wanted . . . and had been happily passing it all along to Gemma in recent years both for the Imposters (unwittingly) and Gemma's columns (quite wittingly).

Ten minutes later, Marigold's hair was pinned in place, the rainbow hat was in her hand, and she and Gemma were laughing their way down the stairs. She had just enough time to check in with Yates before she left to meet Lavinia.

Though Gemma would no doubt soon go and closet herself away in her room with her typewriter, notebooks, pens, and reams of notes on who was wearing what and who had been seen with whom over the last week, for now she remained at Marigold's side. No doubt because they couldn't just leave the reminiscence of Claudia's adventures half-told and chuckled over.

When they stepped into the doorway of Yates's study, her friend froze—and it only took Marigold a glance inside to see why. Graham was here, with Yates. They stood shoulder to shoulder, both of their heads bent over what looked like blueprints.

Gemma backed up a step and was no doubt ready to pivot and run, but Graham looked up at that moment, straightening, his gaze latching onto them. "Gem."

Marigold sucked in a breath. *Let it be different today, Lord.* But a glance at Gemma showed that her chin had ticked up, her eyes cold with masking fury. "Mr. Wharton."

Graham sighed. "I was hoping you would be here today. We need to talk, Gemma."

"We do not. And I bid you good day. I have work to do." She looked every bit the ice princess from one of their favorite storybooks when they were girls as she bestowed a frigid turn of her lips—it would insult the word "smile" to call it such—upon Graham and spun away. "Have a fun promenade, Marigold. Stay out of trouble, Yates. Feel free to throw yourself off a bridge, Mr. Wharton."

Marigold winced on Graham's behalf. Gemma didn't mean that . . . probably. Or at least she would regret it if anything ever *were* to happen to him . . . most likely. How could she not?

When Marigold looked back over at the men, Graham was coiled like Leonidas, ready to pounce. She held up a hand, palm out. "Don't, Graham. If you go after her, it'll just end like it did last time."

He blustered out a breath that left him deflated. Defeated? No, too angry-looking to be defeated. "She can't avoid me forever."

Yates cleared his throat. "She seems to think she can, old boy."

"Just give her time," Marigold implored.

"She's had months!" Graham shoved agitated fingers through his hair. "How long does she need? A year? A decade?"

Marigold shrugged, though the gesture did nothing to soothe the pulsing ache under her breastbone. She hated this, hated the schism in their once-happy foursome. Hated that she knew no acrobatic feat to leap across the gap, had no trapeze capable of closing the distance between them. Certainly had no magical clock to turn back time and undo that disastrous December day. "I don't know, Graham. I know only that her pain is deep."

His nostrils flared. "And she thinks mine isn't?"

Of course Gemma knew he was in pain—she just said it didn't matter. But how could Marigold say *that*?

"We will continue to pray for you both." She advanced into the room so she could see what they were looking at, ignoring the tic in Graham's jaw at her statement. It seemed that with each visit, he grew colder and colder to any mention of God.

Between his new frosty attitude toward God and Gemma's toward *him*, they were like twin ice sculptures. She exchanged a glance with Yates, who had tucked his concern into the corner of his mouth. They'd already talked through the situation over and again. They'd tried all they knew to bring about reconciliation.

They'd declared defeat.

This crack in the foundation of the Imposters would have to be addressed by Gemma and Graham—and God. She and Yates could do nothing to heal it but continue to pray.

She smoothed down the curled edge of the blueprints, beyond the paperweight that anchored it down, and studied the straight lines and intersections with a frown. "The Marlborough?" Her gaze lifted to her brother. "Why do you need these? You're a member, you can just waltz in."

"Being a member doesn't give me unlimited access." He tapped a finger on a section of the building. "Lord Hemming has a meeting scheduled there tonight with Mr. Ballantine."

Marigold's frown only deepened at the mention of their neighbor from Northumberland. "I thought Mr. Ballantine hated London. What's he doing here? And perhaps more to the point—what could it possibly have to do with what Sir Merritt has hired us to do?"

"Don't you recall?" Graham's voice still had an edge to it that she'd once only heard when he was in a heated debate with Yates and James. Usually over something ever so crucial. Like whether dragons would have three claws or four, or which play was the superior, or who had beaten whom in their last game of . . . whatever their last game had been. "Cornelius is in the navy."

Marigold tilted her head. As if she'd forgotten that the son of the Ballantines had bought a commission. "And?"

"We don't know. But the message we intercepted yesterday said that he wished to speak to Hemming about Cornelius." Yates shrugged. "It could be something as simple as hoping Hemming will put in a good word for him. And probably is. But I recalled Mrs. Ballantine saying to Zelda in town before we left that she hadn't had a letter from Cornelius in ages, so it could also be about that."

Neither of those things had anything outright to do with Lord Hemming's loyalties, his relationship with Colonel May—whom they'd also been trailing—or German connections . . . but she'd learned to trust Yates's instincts when it came to which rabbit trails to follow. "Need I even ask if you require my help?"

Her brother shot her a grin. "Might be difficult to sneak you into the Marlborough. But Graham will be playing lookout for me, so I should be all right. I don't think many acrobatics will be required."

She gave them her cheekiest smile. "Good. Because Graham is rubbish at acrobatics."

He may have scowled at her, but it was the playful, light-hearted version that she'd parried all her life—not that too-serious one of the last few months. "Hadn't you better put that ridiculous hat on and go play the part of empty-headed society miss?"

"As a matter of fact." She turned to use the glass of the curio cabinet as a mirror and positioned the hat over her braid, pinning it down with the hat pin she'd slipped into her sash. The way the feathers danced in the draft made her grin. She spun back around and struck a pose to make Zelda proud. "Well? What do you think?"

Graham looked as though he may burst into laughter, but Yates's smile was actually genuine—which either said something about his dubious fashion sense or merely about his approval of her façade. "Beautiful," he declared. "You'll turn heads wherever you go."

She dipped a deep curtsy and came back to his side to present her cheek. "You'll still be here when I return this afternoon?"

"So far as I know." He ducked under the brim of her hat to peck her cheek with the obligatory kiss. "Try to bring up the Ballantines while you're with the Hemmings. See if they react or say anything about hearing from them."

"I will." That part would be easy enough. More challenging would be discovering something useful to add to their file on Sir Merritt. She might have to maneuver her way to his side during the group's outing in the park so that she could control the conversation with him. Otherwise, Lord Xavier and Lavinia kept them all chatting about spy novels and opera the entire time, which had proven rather useless.

Other than to assure her that Sir Merritt appreciated the works of Le Queux no more than she did. Which showed him to be in good taste, but it didn't exactly tell her anything they could use. Except, perhaps, that he wasn't given to the same spy mania that seized so much of the country.

Neville was waiting for her when she made her way to the door, dressed today in his coachman's attire since they wouldn't need his butler skills. His eyes twinkled when he spotted her hat, and if she wasn't mistaken, a chuckle rumbled in his throat too. "Ready then, my lady?"

"As I'm going to be. Thank you for driving me, Nev."

He waved that off and pulled the front door open. "You know I enjoy it, and I haven't any rehearsals until this evening. Although, it must be said. Your father's carriage isn't going to be suitable for long, my lady. More and more of the aristocracy are investing in automobiles, and you two mustn't fall behind the times, not if you're to keep up appearances."

She lifted her brows. "Which is to say, you want to become a chauffeur, not just a coachman."

That twinkle danced. "I'd be willing to learn, let's say. So you could keep up appearances."

Marigold laughed her way out of the house. "Generous of you." She didn't need to point out that the newfangled cars cost nearly a thousand pounds—money they simply didn't have, not to spare on such luxuries. Not with lions and leopards to feed, performers to support, and two houses to maintain. It would take a bit more than borrowing from her clothing budget to afford something like an auto.

But Neville was a dreamer, and she saw no reason to splash reality all over him.

The drive was so short that she could have simply walked if society wouldn't have frowned on her doing so alone. Neville helped her back out of the carriage, and the Hemmings' actual butler opened the door for her. She greeted him with a warm "Good morning, Matthews."

He bowed and closed the door again. "Lady Marigold, welcome. Lady Hemming and Lady Lavinia are awaiting your presence in the drawing room."

She thanked him even as she strode in that direction. What she expected to see was what she always saw—Lavinia and her mother in their favorite chairs, reading or chatting or stitching something, or perhaps positioning hats over their hair for the planned outing. What she saw instead was Lady Hemming going through a list with the housekeeper that sounded suspiciously like items to be packed up, and Lavinia slouched in a chair, arms folded and lips in a definite pout.

Marigold hurried to her friend's side. "Whatever is the matter?"

Lavinia huffed. "We're going *home*. Already! Or will be next week, anyway. And not coming back until June."

All of them? Even his lordship? Yates would certainly be interested in that.

"Lavinia, that is enough. There is more to life than London." Lady Hemming shot her daughter a quelling look, then sent a tight smile to Marigold. "Perhaps you can convince her that this is hardly the end of the world?"

Marigold offered a vague smile. "I can certainly assure her that I would love nothing more than to return to Northumberland. I miss the Tower terribly when we're in London."

Lavinia's eyes lit. "Then come home! It won't be so bad if you're there too."

Ah, a perfect opening. She laughed lightly. "Flattered as I am, there are plenty of other young ladies of good families you could visit—Eugenia Ballantine, Victoria Pence . . ." *There.* Ballantines introduced into the conversation.

Lavinia sighed and shot a look at her mother. "I'm afraid I've drifted apart from both Genie and Tori in recent years, since Tori wed and Genie . . ."

What? Since Genie *what*? Had there been some falling out

between the Ballantine family and the Hemmings? But no, she'd have certainly heard of that. Their neighbors weren't quite on the same social level as either the Hemmings were or the Fairfaxes were assumed to still be, but they were landed, nonetheless. Perfectly acceptable companions, and though Marigold had never known the now-commissioned Cornelius very well, his sister had been a good friend when they were children.

Lady Hemming reached over to tweak the bow tying Lavinia's hat in place. "Never mind Eugenia or Victoria. We should focus on resting while we are in Northumberland so that we'll be in prime form for the height of the Season."

Lavinia didn't look as though she needed to rest, praise the Lord. And she must not have felt she did either, given her sigh. "Perhaps then we could convince Lord Xavier and Sir Merritt to come to the neighborhood for a while. Wouldn't that be lovely, Mother?"

Lady Hemming's smile softened. "It would, and if they had an interest, we could certainly look into houses for them to let. It wouldn't do for them to be our guests for any length of time, as we don't want any assumptions being made about courtships when you still have so many other introductions awaiting you. But they could stay at the Abbey for up to a week, if necessary. I've already suggested your father extend the invitation."

"You did?" Lavinia leapt to her feet. "Why did you not say so?"

"Because, my dear girl, I want you to focus on your attitude when things seem *not* to be going your way, not on simply changing the circumstances that so displease you." The lady frowned. "I have warned your father time and again against spoiling you."

A blush stole over Lavinia's cheeks, and her gloved fingers curled into her palms. She said nothing to that.

She didn't need to. Marigold was saying plenty within her own mind. Lavinia was in no danger of being spoiled, and if her father had indulged her a bit during her long illness, who could blame him? It had not spoiled her by any means. It had simply been an effort to make a dreary, weakened life bearable.

Thankfully, the chiming of the clock interrupted, spurring Lady Hemming into a whirlwind of fluttering hands and exclamations. "Oh, there's so much to do before we leave—and there are the gentlemen, right on time. You two have a lovely promenade with them, and I will see you when you return."

As the door knocker did indeed announce that the men had arrived, Lavinia grabbed Marigold by the elbow and leaned close. "Do tell me you'll be able to come home, too, even if for only a few weeks. It's so dreadfully dull when you're not in the neighborhood."

The idea of a few stolen weeks at home sounded like heaven. Perhaps if Sir Merritt and Lord Hemming both went, she and Yates could too. Marigold grinned. "Even if the gentlemen come? You'll hardly need me then."

Lavinia shook her head, sending her curls bouncing under her hat. "Nonsense—I would need you more than ever. I don't even know if any of the gentlemen I've met thus far are actually interested in a match or just in the curiosity I represent, having been so long absent from Town."

Marigold didn't honestly know either. Lord Xavier certainly gave Lavinia his wholehearted attention when he was here . . . but he did the same with everyone. And Sir Merritt was polite and attentive but far from effusive, which seemed to be *his* usual way . . . but knowing as she did that he was investigating Lavinia's father, did he have any true interest in the daughter, or was calling on her just a convenience? Then there were the other men whom Marigold hadn't seen much.

And since those others weren't the ones currently being

shown in, smiles on their faces, they didn't deserve her attention right now. Careful to position herself half a step behind Lavinia and turn her head just a bit so the plumes on her hat were more on display than was her face, Marigold watched each of them as they greeted her friend and Lady Hemming.

She was looking forward to the walk through Hyde Park . . . and to engaging Sir Merritt in real conversation, if she could.

That empty file with his name on it just couldn't be borne any longer.

SEVEN

*Y*ou're taking a leave."

The words still echoed in Merritt's head as he strode the path before him, mocking and infuriating him as much as the slow pace did. Not because he really would have walked any faster with the ladies here with them, but because even this slow gait felt like a strain on his lungs.

He'd thought he would only be utilizing his lunch break for this meeting, and that he would be in a rush to return to the office. He hadn't expected that the day would begin with Colonel May frowning at him and claiming to have just had a visit from Merritt's physician.

Blast it all. One thing he didn't appreciate about the military was the utter lack of privacy in some things. *Unfit for duty.* Those were the words the blighted Dr. Silverstein had dared to pronounce, the words that had already consigned him to a desk instead of the field. The words that had now "gifted" him with two months of unrequested leave. *"You're no good to us if you let this get the better of you, Livingstone,"* Colonel May had said.

And had he seemed a bit too happy to say it? Was there a reason beyond Merritt's health that he wanted him out of the office? *"Get out of the city for a while. Take some fresh air. A couple months to recuperate, and no doubt you'll be back in peak condition and ready to help us with this new division again."* Those were his words. But had his thoughts been *"Get out of our way and stop poking into things I don't want you to know"*?

A couple months—a couple months. He suppressed a cough and idly watched a duck paddle through the water to his left. What in blazes was he supposed to do with himself for a couple months? And with these questions about Hemming and May still unanswered? He'd received a few updates from the Imposters, which proved them hard at work on peeling back the layers of the esteemed earl and the colonel, but they'd proven neither guilt nor innocence thus far. Only that Colonel May had a penchant for the racetrack and Hemming had no publicly-admitted-to friends in Germany.

A decent amount of information for the time they'd had. But if he would no longer be in the office, keeping a finger on that pulse, then all his hope for answers would rely on them.

It rankled. Irritated like a bur under his cuff. He knew the value of a team, yes, and relied on his brothers-in-arms all the time—but that meant doing his own part as well. Shouldering his portion of the burden. He'd promised Mr. Anonymous—not that he was probably as anonymous as he wanted to seem, given the strong Welsh accent and age in his voice—that he would be on the inside of the War Office, continuing the search there. But now he would have to report that he'd been kicked to the curb, more or less, until he could go a few minutes at a clip without coughing.

He coughed. And may have followed it with a curse if Mother hadn't frowned the instinct out of him eons ago.

"Have those ducks offended you, Sir Merritt, or are you merely put out with the world at large today?"

He blinked his eyes back into focus and looked down, a bit surprised to see a rainbow of feathers before his eyes. He'd been walking by himself a moment ago, X having made a show of taking one lady on each arm, to "spare them from the bear parading as Sir Merritt." When had Lady Marigold disentangled herself and joined him?

And, better question, why had she bothered?

Now he was obliged to relax his features from their comfortable glower and conjure up a smile. "I beg your pardon, my lady. I have just received the news that I'm being forced to take a medical leave." There was no point in hiding it. It was already done, and he'd be expected to obey the orders and decide where to go and recuperate.

He couldn't see the lady's eyes beyond the brim of her hat, but he could hear her hum easily enough. "You are clearly not the sort of man who enjoys idle time."

"Utter torture. Oh, careful." A puddle loomed just ahead of them on the path, but with her face turned toward him, she wouldn't have seen it. He took her arm to direct them both around it, then let her go again.

Though not before frowning anew. Her arm didn't feel like a lady's arm. It was slender enough in her sleeve, but it was . . . hard. Rock hard.

What sort of lady did the kind of exercise required for such toned muscles? None that he knew—not even Georgette, who had become an absolute fiend at tennis this last year, playing nearly every day, despite Aunt Josie lamenting that she was ruining her figure with all the sport.

Not that Lady Marigold's figure would have made Aunt Josie lament. She was trim and slender, the perfect mannequin for whatever bedecked frock she'd chosen this time.

His cousins, upon learning that he'd met her several times now, drilled him relentlessly on everything she was wearing, so he made himself pay half a moment's attention. The hat with those rainbow feathers, a purple linen dress with some kind of lace, white gloves.

There. That would surely appease them.

And really, much as he wanted to label the feathers ridiculous, he almost liked them. The rainbow at least reminded him that God would see him through this storm, just as He had every other.

"Thank you," she said. It took him a moment to realize the words were in reference to his steering around the puddle. She even tilted her hat back enough to meet his gaze for a moment. "I'd have hated to ruin a pair of shoes."

"Mm." He glanced down at her feet too. Fran kept asking him about her shoes, and he kept insisting he hadn't the first clue. Not that he could see much of them, anyway, beyond the hem of her dress. Just the peek of ivory leather with every step she took. "Happy to have spared you. And I do apologize if my mood has clouded the day."

"Oh, it takes more than trying to scare a few ducks into flight to overshadow a day as lovely as this one." She lifted her face up to the spring sunshine, clearly not afraid of freckles or sunburn, as his cousins always were. In the next moment, she looked at him again, and he found himself shifting a bit under her gaze.

In the Hemmings' drawing room, he hadn't even been certain what color her eyes were. Now he could see they were a warm, intelligent brown, and they were regarding him in just the way his commanding officer had surveyed a battlefield before ordering a charge. He found himself glancing down to make certain she had no pistol or bayonet in hand.

"So, Sir Merritt Livingstone despises having to take a few weeks of leave."

"Months." Weeks—as in, the kind that didn't extend into months—wouldn't have been so bad, at any other time. But two months? What was he supposed to do with himself for so long? "Plural. Two of them."

"Detestable. What will you do with yourself?"

94

She sounded genuinely curious, so he let himself sigh. "The very question. I don't know. My physician insists that I need to leave London and find fresh air somewhere. I imagine my uncle and aunt will offer me the use of their home in the Midlands."

"The Midlands." Lady Marigold pursed her lips. "There is plenty of fresh air there, I grant you, and no doubt plenty else to do besides. Though were it me, I'd be looking for a respite with a bit more drama."

A dramatic respite? His lips twitched away a bit of his foul humor. "You'll have to enlighten me. What does that look like?"

"Very much like the seaside, I should think. Crashing waves, crying gulls, storms blowing in and out . . . I can think of nothing better."

"The seaside. I hadn't even considered it." He didn't know anyone who lived near the coast. "I should like to see the chalk cliffs again, and I haven't been to Brighton since I was a boy. Or—no?"

She'd wrinkled her nose. "Oh, I have no doubt the southern coast is charming enough, if you like to be battling other sunbathers for an inch of sand. Personally, I prefer the rugged beauty of the North Sea."

"Ah." His mouth finally relaxed into a full smile. "I'd forgotten you're from Northumberland. Close to the coast, I take it?"

"I can see the ocean from my bedroom. A far cry from my view here in London."

"You miss it." He could hear his surprise in his voice— but who could blame him for that? Lady Lavinia hadn't sounded at all eager to return to Northumberland, as she'd announced they'd be doing; and his cousins never exactly *complained* about the months spent at the manor house, but London was always their goal. He'd have expected that

Lady Marigold, who clearly valued fashion and the chance to be seen in it above all, would revel even more in city life.

But then, he scarcely knew her. A few surprises were to be expected.

She lifted one shoulder in a strangely elegant shrug. "It's home. And what of you, Sir Merritt? What place do you consider home? Your house here in London? Your uncle's? A country estate—in the Midlands, perhaps?"

Each addition she made to her list just made his lips purse a little more, and he had to shake his head at the last. "To be honest, I've traveled so much that I've never really given myself the chance to call any one place home." He certainly had no emotional attachment to the townhouse he let now. His career had seen him stationed all over the empire before earning a post here in London, protecting His Majesty. And even as a child, it had been one rented country house after another, and school in between. Neither of his parents had inherited any land or houses, so they'd simply traveled around wherever the mood or Father's own military postings led them.

Lady Marigold, however, looked aghast, her eyes and mouth both open wide. "You must be joking. Nowhere? There is nowhere you think of in odd moments, that you wish you could get back to? Nowhere you find yourself longing to be?"

"Well." He considered denying it. But why lie about it, just because no one else ever understood? "There's China."

"China." If he'd sounded surprised at her missing Northumberland, she sounded twice as surprised at that, like everyone always was, any time he mentioned the place. But where usually people blinked in confusion or laughed it away or asked—often huffily—*why* he liked that heathen land, Lady Marigold rather lapsed into contemplation for a long moment. He could have sworn that, were his eyesight a bit better, he could have seen her flipping through memories like note cards. "Ah. You served there during the Boxer Rebellion. It was, I believe, where you earned your knighthood?"

He nodded, though those weren't the words he ever would have chosen to describe his time there. Where he met his Lord, he would have said. Where eternity found him. Where the course of his life, of his soul, had been forever changed.

It wasn't the jagged mountain peaks that he missed, or the haunting music, or the graceful pagodas. It was the peace that had found him there, in the middle of a raging war. It was the quiet conversations with the missionaries he'd been sent to save, who had saved him in turn.

"You have friends there. Or perhaps even . . . ?"

Her quiet question pulled him back to the park, and he blinked the yearning from his eyes. "Friends, yes. Jonathan Dilling and his family—missionaries who I helped reach safety during the rebellion. He's one of my dearest friends now. I admit I would love to visit him again someday as a civilian instead of a soldier, to see the country he loves so dearly."

For the space of three steps, she made no response but to look at him. Then she smiled. "You aided missionaries? Is that what earned your knighthood?"

Though he moved his shoulders, it couldn't quite erase the embarrassment that always scratched at him whenever someone brought it up. He hadn't done anything worthy of attention—nothing many of his comrades wouldn't have done, had they been in the same place at that given time. He had simply done his duty. Had he been stationed elsewhere, that duty could have involved burning temples or destroying villages.

But for the grace of God. Instead, his duty had meant helping the Dillings escape, defending them against the enraged mob pursuing them. Learning who this God, this Jesus was that this strange family was willing to die for—a God, a Jesus, who seemed very different from the flat versions he'd been hearing about all his life.

"I'm sorry. I don't mean to embarrass you. You needn't tell me—"

"It's all right." And oddly, it was, solely because she'd noticed his discomfort. "I daresay the knighthood was more a reflection of the king's wish to encourage our missionaries than because he holds *me* in any particular esteem. Though I admit it was treacherous, getting them to safety. We all nearly died, several times over."

He rarely spoke of it, and when he did, people usually leaned in now, eager for the story of bullets and swords and blood and screaming that had haunted him for years.

Lady Marigold, however, tilted her head to the side. "Yet they're back there again? The Dillings?"

He couldn't help but smile. "Nothing could keep them away for long. It is, they say, their purpose—to share the good news of Christ with as many as they can, as long as they have breath. Truly, it is an honor to have played even a small part in enabling them to live another day to do so."

"Your friends sound like people I would like to meet. And you, Sir Merritt, actually seem to be among that rarest of breeds." At his lifted brows, she smiled and said, "A gentleman with a heart actually deserving the name."

Was she flirting with him? He admitted he was unskilled, but it didn't feel *quite* like most flirting he'd seen. Not given the seriousness in her gaze, of her smile.

Even so, his neck warmed beneath his collar. He wasn't about to do anything so obvious as to tug at it, so he merely cleared his throat and mumbled, "Not *so* rare."

Definitely *not* flirting, given the way she stepped away and looked ahead of them, to where Xavier and Lady Lavinia were just coming to where two paths converged and had held up for them. "Sorry to have dominated your time, sir. Though if I have managed to improve your mood a bit before you rejoin Lavinia, as I know you must be eager to do, I shall count it a victory for the day."

Not flirting—but why not? He winced at his own thoughts, which even in his head didn't sound as he meant them. Not that he could blame her or anyone else for not flirting with him, especially when Xavier was right there. But now that he was thinking about it, he realized that she always did that, just that—pointed toward Lavinia. Her every participation in the conversation, each and every time they'd all been together, had been aimed at showing her friend to be the leading lady.

It was odd. Wasn't it? She was an eligible young woman as well. Shouldn't she be vying for Xavier's attention? Or at least seeking to be seen for her own merits?

Maybe she was already spoken for. Though if so, his gossip-loving cousins didn't know of it, and they read each and every column that mentioned Lady M no fewer than a dozen times.

Xavier was sending him a bright grin that didn't quite eclipse the spark in his eyes. "What do you think, Mer? Northumberland for a month or two?"

Had his friend been listening in to his conversation with Lady Marigold? That didn't seem likely, as it would require being quiet enough to overhear, which neither Xavier nor Lady Lavinia seemed to consider a possibility. "Pardon?"

Xavier motioned toward Lady Lavinia. "It seems the Hemmings are returning to their country home until June."

The Hemmings? As in . . . ? "You and your mother, my lady?"

Her smile was easy, bright. Oblivious. "And Father too. It was at his insistence, actually."

Merritt couldn't keep his eyes from snapping back to

Xavier's. *He* knew, though the lady couldn't, that it was his lordship's presence he wanted—no, *needed*—to shadow.

Lavinia went on. "Mother said Father was going to invite you both to visit the neighborhood, if you're interested. She said they know of several houses to let. You could make a holiday of it."

A holiday—medical leave, more like. But he had to take one. And Lord Hemming would be in *that* neighborhood, not this one.

Which meant that, were he to go there, he perhaps *could* keep investigating Hemming, if not May.

No wonder Xavier was grinning. Merritt grinned too. "You know, Lady Marigold *was* just convincing me of what a dramatically beautiful coastline they have up there. If you're game, X."

"Well, I was otherwise planning on making a nuisance of myself with my sister Clare for a while, but I could be convinced to bother you instead."

"Perfect!" Lady Lavinia clasped her hands together, only to reach in the next moment for Lady Marigold. "Say you'll come home, too, Marigold. You can introduce Leonidas and Pardulfo and the others, and we can show them all the fun we had as children at the Tower."

Lady Marigold had reverted to her usual posture, with her hat blocking her face. Though he could hear the smile in her voice as she said, "I daresay Yates and I can be convinced."

That, apparently, was that.

They walked the ladies back to the Hemmings' house, plans and suggestions flying through the air like bullets, and then said their farewells. Xavier soon left him, too, with a clap to the shoulder, a knowing laugh, and a promise to meet him at the Marlborough later. Which meant that Merritt was alone, with no need to return to the office and no other plans for the afternoon.

He ought to go back to his rented house. Pack for a month or two away. Let his landlord know that he'd be vacating the premises for a while and decide if he wanted him to hold it for him or find another place when he returned.

Yet, fifteen minutes later, he found himself walking up the steps to Preston House, like he always did when he had a few spare moments. His uncle may or may not be at home this time of day, but Aunt Josie and the girls likely were.

The butler greeted him with a warm smile and answered the question before he could even ask it. "Ah, Sir Merritt. You'll find your uncle, aunt, and cousins all just sitting down to lunch, and I happen to know Cook has made your favorite soup. Go on in. They were hoping you'd stop by."

"You're all too good to me." He never really *meant* to come here for lunch. But he did, four days out of six. Which made him keenly aware of the fact that he hadn't been entirely truthful with himself when he answered Lady Marigold's question about home. Not that this house meant it to him, really.

But *they* did. The uncle who had stepped in and raised him after Father died. The aunt who treated his mother like her own sister, and him like a son. The cousins who greeted him now like a flock of redhaired sisters.

He didn't deserve this family—or at least, didn't deserve to be the one who stood to inherit everything that was theirs. Didn't deserve for them to love him so fully, given that. Yet there was no shadow in any of their eyes as they greeted him.

"Just in time, my boy!" Uncle Preston.

"Sit by *me* today." The youngest of their five girls, Danielle, who was just twelve.

"No no, your cousin is going to sit there across from me." Aunt Josie, with merriment sparkling in her emerald eyes. "So that he can tell me all about his promenade with Lady Lavinia this morning."

He took his normal seat—across from Josie, sandwiched between the middle two girls, Harriet and Annabeth—but winked at Danielle and smiled at Georgette beside her too. "Did you leave me any of the soup, Geo?"

Georgette—twenty last January—grinned. "Lucky for you. I worked up quite an appetite on the courts this morning."

Harriet leaned toward him, even as he leaned back to make room for the servant to slide a bowl of soup in front of him. "Was Lady M there too? What was she wearing?"

He had the litany prepared. But his cousin would think him truly ill if he just *told* her. He sighed instead and sent the saddest look he could muster at his aunt. "You could have adopted a son or two. Taken in a few orphans. Traded a few of these for a couple of strapping lads."

Harriet huffed. Annabeth laughed and leaned into his arm.

Aunt Josie's eyes just twinkled at him. "You're all the son we need. Now. Tell us all. Did you have a chance to speak to Lady Lavinia, just the two of you?"

"Do you like her?" Annabeth.

"Are you in *love* with her?" Danielle.

"What about Lady M? Did you talk to *her*? What was she *wearing*?" Harriet, of course.

Merritt bowed his head over his soup, ignoring Harriet's insistence that they'd already blessed it, which he would know if he'd shown up on time. He said a prayer. He picked up his spoon. And he prepared to joust and parry.

EIGHT

*Y*ates was beginning to regret his insistence that he didn't need Marigold's help at the Marlborough. He'd suspected he might when he realized that the only way to observe Lord Hemming's meeting with Ballantine would be to position himself in a very small storage room that shared a wall with the chamber the earl had reserved, which was much better suited to his sister's diminutive figure than his own.

But he didn't indulge in more than a moment of silent grumbling as he carved space for himself among the mops, pails, and shelves of assorted whatnot that were *not* very hospitable to their new guest. Marigold wouldn't have been any more comfortable in here, and she'd have had to disguise herself even to get into the building. At least he'd only had to find a moment when no one was looking and disappear, lift the key to this little cupboard from one of the staff, and now drill a small hole through the wall so he could slip the microphone end of his Akouphone into it.

According to the blueprints Graham had brought him, combined with his own reconnaissance an hour ago, the hole would have to be exactly forty-six inches from the corridor-facing wall in order to end up behind a table, where no one was likely to notice the pile of plaster dust he'd just created or the hole soon to be plugged with his tube. Yates had to evict a few cleaning supplies to do his measuring, but then it was a simple matter of folding himself onto the floor, setting his electric torch on the opposite shelf to illuminate the X he drew onto the plaster, and turn his small hand drill until it poked through the other side.

It took a few more minutes to open his bag and pull out all the pieces of his Akouphone—the microphone, amplifier, headphones, and rather unwieldy battery. The device had cost his grandfather a fortune when he'd purchased it in 1899, but they'd all been amazed at how effective it was at helping him hear. Father had been quick to dream up other applications for the technology—just think of what it could do for performers!—but he'd been all ideas. Follow-through had never been his forte.

After Grandpapa died, the Akouphone had been packed away, forgotten . . . until Marigold had complained three years ago about simply not being able to hear quiet conversations during their surveillance. She'd said she finally understood how Grandpapa had felt—and they'd remembered at the same time.

It was too bulky a device to take just anywhere. The thought of juggling it up walls and onto window ledges was ludicrous enough to make him smile at the broom handle threatening to gouge his eye out. But for occasions like this, it was perfect.

There. All in place, and he still had twenty minutes to spare. After double-checking that the door was locked, he settled back into his cross-legged position, slipped on the headphones, and pulled out the volume of Chesterton he needed to return to James soon.

Maybe when he did, they'd have a real, earnest conversation about Gemma, who was going to ruin *everything* if she didn't mend things with Graham soon. Theirs was not a group that could afford even a crack, much less a fissure in their foundations.

Not that either Gemma or Graham would say their problems had anything to do with the Imposters, which was true enough. Their problems were rooted in a tragedy much greater than mere fortune or work. All the more reason for them to work it out rather than turn on each other.

What affected one affected them all, and he couldn't just sit back and watch them implode.

He'd only read four pages when the microphone picked up the opening of the door in the adjoining chamber. Yates put his marker in his book and pressed a hand to the headphones. Footsteps, but no voices. Ah, of course not—the sloshing of fresh water into glasses, the *thunk* of a full decanter being placed on a wooden table. A few other shuffling noises that were harder to identify, and then the footsteps retreated again as the servant left.

Yates knew how the Marlborough worked, so he didn't bother reopening his book. They only prepared the reserved rooms when the patrons were spotted approaching, so that any food or drink put out was at its freshest and best. Hemming would be here any minute.

And soon Yates was picking up the familiar tones of his Northumberland neighbors. They were even swapping stories of home, which would have made him smile if he weren't overhearing it through headphones while folded up in a room he barely fit in.

If this meeting had nothing to do with anything, he'd assign himself an extra ten laps around the courtyard when they got back to the Tower in a few days, with Penelope on his shoulders. Suitable punishment. Whoever had come up with the adage about having a monkey on one's back knew what they were talking about.

Perhaps the gents had dispensed with enough pleasantries on the walk in here, because nearly the moment the door closed, Mr. Ballantine said, "I won't leave you guessing as to my purposes, Hemming. It's Cornelius. We've heard nothing from him since Christmas, and his mother and I are growing alarmed."

A chair squeaked as one of the men settled onto it, then another a moment later. Given the length of squeaking and his knowledge of the size of the two, he'd have wagered that the earl sat first.

FROM THE DOSSIER OF
Mr. Robert Ballantine, owner of Ballantine Shipping

HEIGHT: *5'9"*

WEIGHT: *20 stone*

AGE: *54*

HAIR: *Grey, parted in the middle*

EYES: *Hazel*

STYLE: *Buys his suits from the same tailor in York that his father and grandfather did, but always cut in the latest style*

PRIMARY RESIDENCE: *Denwick Park, Denwick, Northumberland*

OBSERVANCES: *Mr. Ballantine is a pillar of the local community. Though his family made their way to our region from the Highlands, over the generations the hostility they were initially met with grew into acceptance. His grandfather Cornelius established a successful shipping enterprise (pirating!) and he and his wife are both considered good society to keep in the area.*

IMPRESSIONS: *The Ballantines are a congenial family, always happily invited anywhere . . . though be certain your table is well stocked, because the gent can eat.*

NOTES: *Two children, Cornelius and Eugenia. Cornelius bought a commission in 1906. Genie is doing her best to catch the eye of a suitable husband, but pickings are slim in the neighborhood, and they don't believe in wasting money on a Season in London. Beware, Yates. Beware.*

Hemming chuckled. "Now, Bal, you know how young bucks are when they're finally off on their own. No doubt he's enjoying himself on the Continent. Send a note to his commanding—"

"We've done that. You know we wouldn't come to you if it were anything so simple. But, well, with your connections to the War Office—after your long career in the House of Lords and all the many positions you've held—if anyone could find out more, we thought it would be you."

"You know I'm always happy to help a neighbor, though had you sent a wire before you arrived, I could have saved you the trip. We're bound for home next week, and I know how you dislike coming to the city."

"I appreciate your thought of me, my lord, but hearing your plans only makes me gladder that I didn't delay in coming. If you see fit to help, you may require your resources here in London to do so."

Yates frowned into the dark shelf at eye level. What *exactly* did Lord Hemming do for the War Office? He honestly didn't know, and he suspected even his client wouldn't be quick to tell him, other than that he was currently serving in the intelligence division, whatever that entailed. He knew only that Hemming had always been far more serious about his duties to king and country than Father had been, and it had earned him all sorts of positions in the government over the years. Yates had been able to take up his inherited seat in last year's session only, once he was old enough, so he hadn't yet learned much about how the earl behaved in Parliament.

He wouldn't be surprised if he was gunning for Prime Minister. *Watch out, Asquith.*

"This sounds quite serious. Do tell me what has you so concerned."

Mr. Ballantine drew in a long breath. "You're well aware of my son's career aspirations, and we thank you again for your recommendations for him. He was very pleased to be given such prime assignments and speaks quite highly of the other officers he serves with."

Quite the layer of flattery he was laying on—which was unlike him. Ballantine may always be *nice*, but he wasn't usually the type to try to wheedle favors from anyone with too many compliments.

"A deserving young man, that's all. It was nothing."

"But it wasn't. We know that." Ballantine pitched his voice so low that Yates was doubly glad for the microphone. "He made mention . . . he said that he owed his position to you, directly. That were it not for you, he'd not have been enjoying the life he was on the Continent."

Silence gathered two seconds too long. "Now, I distinctly recall instructing him to forget I had anything to do with it and to mention it to no one." The lightness of the tone didn't quite cover over that silence.

"Oh, he didn't say much, my lord! Only that he was grateful, and he instructed his mother and me to wish you a Happy Christmas—that was when he mentioned it, when he sent presents home to us all. If you recall the chocolates we brought to Alnwick Abbey from him?"

"Ah yes. They were delicious. No one makes chocolate like the Germans."

Germans! So Cornelius was stationed somewhere near Germany, if he was able to get German chocolate enough to send home . . . though granted, it was easy to travel around the Continent. That didn't exactly narrow down where he was.

"Yes. But . . . that was the last we heard from him, despite his promise in that letter to write again soon. He's always sent a note every fortnight, three weeks between them at the longest. But it's been months. *Months,* my lord, though from what we can glean, there has been no action to account for his silence. We've tried sending telegrams, letters—which he has always answered very promptly before. But nothing, and his commanding officers will not tell us a thing. Please—is he about some covert business? If so, just say the word, and we'll stop inquiring. We only want to know that he's well."

Covert business—as in intelligence or espionage? Is that what Ballantine suspected? If so, it made sense that he would come to Hemming . . . except, how did he know Hemming worked in the intelligence division? Yates hadn't realized it, until Livingstone had said so. It hadn't *surprised* him, but it wasn't exactly something the earl bragged about at dinner parties.

But Cornelius would have known and must have said something, if Hemming had a hand in assigning him whatever task had him going incommunicado.

Wait. An agent going incommunicado . . . no! Was Cornelius Ballantine the very one who had sent Sir Merritt that telegram with Hemming's name before vanishing?

A knot pulled taut in Yates's stomach, even as he said a silent apology to Penelope, who would *not* be getting a ride on his shoulder during his laps after all.

Hemming cleared his throat. "I'm afraid there's nothing

I can tell you just now, Bal. But I will certainly see what I can discover while I'm still in London and bring any news I find back to you."

"Thank you." Ballantine sounded utterly relieved. "You cannot know how much it sets my mind at ease just knowing you're going to ask a few questions for us."

"I can imagine. I'm a father, too, and I know how I had wished someone could give us answers about our Lavinia's condition." For the first time in the conversation, genuine emotion filled the earl's voice. He had always doted on Lavinia, even more than Lady Hemming did.

"We've prayed for her daily all these years—and it was so encouraging to see her up and about and coming to London. Has her heart strengthened, then?"

"She is flourishing now, yes. It is a great relief. The doctor said that the care we've taken, the years of rest, have allowed her to heal."

"Horrible thing, scarlet fever. I lost a sister to it myself, when I was a child."

Yates kept listening as long as they talked, but the rest of the conversation was only idle chat while they drank a glass of whatever was in the decanter and smoked a cigar—he caught a whiff of it through the hole. He found himself rolling a hand through the air, inviting them to hurry it along before his legs cramped.

At long last, they exited, and he did, too, after giving it a few minutes' buffer. He repacked his gear, rearranged everything in the storage room, slipped into the meeting room to sweep up the plaster dust, and made his way out of the club.

He didn't know if Cornelius was the one who had set this whole investigation in motion with the telegram to Sir Merritt . . . but he could have been. And while he could respect their client's inability to reveal anything Top Secret, he had a feeling he had just stumbled across the information on his own.

Which should certainly convince Sir Merritt, if he retained any doubts, of the abilities of the Imposters.

Now if only he could sort out what the missing chap was about.

NINE

May 1909
Fairfax Tower, near Alnwick, Northumberland

Marigold swung through the upward arc of the trapeze, glorying in the rush of wind, the pull of gravity, the tug of momentum up and up and up. At the apex of the arc, weightlessness caught her for half a breath, one full heartbeat. The cable went slack, and for that eternal, infinitesimal moment, she was suspended there in space.

She loved that moment—the one that had terrified her the first time she experienced it. The moment when gravity and momentum were perfectly equal, when there was nothing to pull her in either direction.

In that moment, anything—*everything*—was possible. In that moment, she could see over the Tower walls, to the sea. All the way to heaven, she liked to think. In that moment, there was nothing but the Lord's arms to hold her.

Then gravity overcame the system, and down she swung again. She knew well her lips were spread wide in a grin aimed at no one but God and the sparrows flitting about the courtyard walls, and she made no attempt at restraining it. Not now, her first morning home again. If only there were a way to mount a trapeze in the London house, she may not miss Fairfax Tower so much when they were away.

Laughter bubbled up and out at that. She missed far more than the trapeze when they were in Town. She missed the crisp ocean air, the sting of its salt, the cry of the birds. She missed Leonidas and Pardulfo and Penelope. She missed the vardo permanently parked beside the wall, with the line of colorful clothes always pinned to it, always drying without ever being fully dry, flapping like standards in the wind. She missed Zelda and Drina, Franco and Hector and Alafair. She missed the freedom to be *herself*.

She jacked her legs upward as she swung, pulled them to her chest, slipped them through the space between her arms, and hooked her knees over the bar so that she could release it with her hands. Dangling upside down, she watched Yates scale the opposite pole's ladder in quick, fluid movements. Once his feet were on the platform, he unhooked the second trapeze and held it in his hands for a long moment, leaning back until the cables were taut.

He would be watching her arc, counting, letting her rhythm become his own pulse. At just the right moment, he swung off his platform, pumping his legs now, letting his momentum carry him next, pumping again.

For a few swings, their arcs were identical, allowing him to warm up, to enjoy the pendulum, the wind. Then he pumped again to change his own rhythm, to speed up, to change his swing slowly until they were opposites. Both at the full outward reach at the same moment, both at the inward apex at the same time too—which put them within arm's reach of each other. He flashed her a grin and, on his way back down, moved his own legs to the bar so that his arms dangled.

On the next swing up, they reached out at the same moment. Fingers found wrists and clasped, Marigold straightened her legs to release the bar, and her body dropped below his.

"Happy to be home?" he asked as they swung together back down, his voice full of a smile.

She laughed her reply.

For a few minutes, they worked through their usual routine—Marigold flipping up onto the bar and standing, Yates switching places with her, then eventually back to their original position so that she could dismount. Three perfectly executed flips through the air, and she landed in the sand of the courtyard with a . . . hop. "Lionfeathers." She could never get the landing right on her first dismount after a few weeks away.

And her brother's loud "Boo! I saw that!" didn't help any.

She spun to face his still-swinging form, hands on her hips. "As if you'll do any better!"

His laugh danced through the air. "You know very well I will." Which she did, dash it all. He may stumble a later one, but *his* first was always impeccable. "Want to go again?"

She did, but she'd already decided that she'd pay a visit to the Ballantine ladies this morning, and she had better bathe before she went. Complete with a washing of her hair, though it then wouldn't be dry before she left. That took hours. But if she didn't smell fresh as a rose when she arrived, Genie would wrinkle her nose and accuse her of reeking of the barnyard.

Not that she was going to shout all of that up to Yates. She simply said, "I can't. I'm going to visit Genie, remember?"

Yates had pulled himself up to standing on the bar, and his gaze was locked on something beyond the Tower walls. "No, you're not."

"What? Why not?" Though even as she asked, she paused to listen. At first she heard only the *whoosh* and creak of the trapeze, the muted crash of the waves, the call of Peabody and snuff of Leonidas. But once she filtered those familiar noises from her perception, she could hear what he must have seen—a motor puttering along the seaside road.

114

There were only two people in the neighborhood with cars—Lord Hemming and Mr. Ballantine. And no one from the Abbey would be coming from that direction, most likely. "Lionfeathers," she said again, just for the fun of feeling the syllables against her lips. Louder, she called up, "Is it Genie?"

"Unless her mother has shrunk."

There was no way she'd have time to fully bathe and wash her hair, not unless she wanted to keep her neighbor waiting for an hour—which would elicit an even stronger chiding than a faint smell of animals. "I don't suppose you want to join me?"

"Not on your life, big sister."

Traitor. But with the way Genie sighed over him, she couldn't blame him. "Well, you'd better get down. If she sees you up there dressed like that, she'll make such a show of swooning at the memory, I won't be able to drag any other information out of her."

Yates visibly winced—and he also promptly folded over and dropped himself out of sight, guaranteeing it by dismounting on the next upswing. And, of course, nailing his landing a few feet from her. Feet together, knees bent, arms out in a perfect Y.

"Always showing off." But she grinned, and grinned all the more when Franco emerged from the stable with Penelope on his shoulder. The capuchin monkey let out a happy shriek the moment she spotted Yates, abandoned Franco with a leap, and was soon clambering up Marigold's brother, in search of her favorite spot in all the world—on his left shoulder, with one arm curled around his head.

Yates laughed and tickled the monkey's belly. "Good morning, Penelope. Do you want to go with Marigold this morning? Say hello to Genie? She loves you *so much*."

Penelope rested her head against Yates's, all but declaring, "I'm staying with you."

Smart monkey. Marigold reached out to shake her little paw and then angled herself toward the house. "I'd better hurry." She greeted Franco as she went, and the old ring-master gave her a gap-toothed smile on his way to the vardo he and Zelda still lived in, even though they'd offered them rooms in the house time and again. Only on the coldest winter nights did they abandon their wagon.

She paused in the little room between the courtyard and the kitchen that they'd outfitted with an old wooden bench and racks to hold their muddy—and worse—shoes. As she sat, she unwound from her head the scarf she'd had con-straining her thick braid and pulled out the basin of luke-warm water from beneath the bench for her bare feet.

At least she hadn't visited the animal pens yet today, so it was only sand she was rinsing off. With a quick pat of the towel, she was dashing into the kitchen, where Drina was belting out a ballad in Romani and twirling a wooden spoon through a pot.

She paused her song when Marigold ran through. "You want a baking lesson again today, my golden one?"

Marigold smiled at the old nickname. "Want, yes. But Eugenia Ballantine is on her way up the drive."

Drina's eyes went wide, and she smacked the spoon down onto the workbench. "What are you dallying about for, then? Hurry! Go and tidy up. I'll put water on to boil for tea, she always wants tea. And biscuits. We have a few left from your welcome-home dinner last night, I think. . . ."

Leaving her to it, Marigold dashed up the back stairs, taking them two at a time. As she burst into her room, she found herself wishing she hadn't assured Gemma that she'd be perfectly fine at home without her for a few weeks, that she should feel free to stay in London for as long as she'd like, where it was easier to write her columns. Marigold could have used the extra set of hands now, as she had no other maid. Drina or Zelda would step in when she had an occasion to prepare for, but she never wanted to pull them away from their tasks in the morning.

With a staff of five trying to maintain a house that had once employed ninety, no one ever exactly had spare time. And it was especially difficult when guests showed up.

Thank heavens it happened but rarely in the last five years. Genie came once in a while, but that was about it, since Lavinia had been so unwell. And Genie never wanted to venture beyond the drawing room, so keeping up appearances was simple.

Someone had left warm water in her pitcher for her. She added a bit of fragrance to it, stripped out of her leotard, gave herself a quick wash, and flew toward the day's clothing she had set out and waiting. A simpler dress than she'd have chosen in London, but not without its embellishments, given that Lavinia's note had promised that she, Lord Xavier, and Sir Merritt would be by this afternoon.

Things were going to get more complicated over the next few weeks with these new guests, but she would simply tell them, if it came up, that they'd already given the staff time off for the Season, since they'd expected to be in London.

The bell rang through the house. She slipped into her clothes and dashed to the mirror, praying her braid wouldn't be too frazzled and that she could just repin it.

One look at her reflection, and she breathed again. Though the trapeze whipped it into a frenzy if she wasn't careful, the scarf had done its job well this morning. Other than a few wisps around her face that she decided to label charming and not fuss with, her braid was still tight and smooth. A few twists around her head, ample pins, and the weight of it was secured.

All that remained was finding her shoes, which had wandered off when her back was turned. Where *were* they? Ah—

there. Her favorite leather ballet flats, which she'd never dare wear out of the house. She slid them on and then ran back out of her room, along the corridor, and to the front stairs.

Alafair—formerly an acrobatics master and now their butler, footman, and anything else they needed—was just coming out of the drawing room. The expression on his face was pure relief when he spotted her.

Marigold jumped onto the polished railing, slid down, and hopped off at the bottom. "How long has she been waiting?"

"Only a few minutes," he whispered back. "Drina met her with a tray of treats, and then Genie had to deliver her lecture about not letting the animals near her father's car, so she's only just sitting down."

"Good. Thank you." Finally pausing long enough to suck in a long breath, Marigold took a moment to smooth her dress and square her shoulders. "Am I all in one piece?"

"Lovely as the morning dew." Her old friend patted her arm and moved out of her way.

Well then. One more fortifying breath, and she strode into the drawing room.

Miss Eugenia Ballantine wore this spring's latest fashions, a neat little hat perched atop her white-blond hair, and white lace gloves encasing her fingers. She sat primly on Mother's favorite wingback chair, her legs in that perfect *Z* all the finishing schools taught, crossed at the ankle, knees angled. She sipped from her teacup with her pinky extended, holding the saucer evenly underneath it.

But her hands trembled. Her blue eyes were bloodshot. And she looked as though she'd lost half a stone. In fact, the biscuits Drina had brought her were still untouched.

Unusual indeed. Marigold came forward, hands extended. "Genie! I was going to call on you this morning, but it seems you've beaten me to it."

"Oh, Marigold, thank God. I was beginning to think you wouldn't see me." Genie slid her cup onto the table with a clatter as odd as her lack of appetite and surged to her feet.

It had only been a few minutes. But that was Genie. Marigold kept her smile in place as Genie grasped her hands, squeezing them tight, and leaned in to kiss her cheek. "Of course I would see you. Though you look troubled. Is there anything I can help with?"

"I hope so. I truly do." When Genie pulled away, her eyes were glassy. "You scarcely smell like manure this morning at all—have you heard about Cornelius?"

Queen of the non sequitur, as always. Marigold's nostrils wanted to flare at the observation about her smell, but she fought to keep her expression placid.

Genie hadn't used to be this way, not until after she came home from finishing school. Marigold missed the old Genie. "I daresay not. What is it? Last I heard was what you shared at Christmas."

Genie fluttered her hands. "That's the last *we've* heard. Officially, anyway. He's gone utterly silent, which is so very unlike him. He—gracious, Marigold, could you not even deign to put on real shoes?—he hasn't responded to any of our wires or letters, and his crew doesn't seem to know where he is."

"That's very strange. I know your brother has always taken care to write to you regularly." Marigold curled her toes in their supple leather, then made herself straighten them again. Told herself it didn't matter if her childhood friend disapproved of her now. She led her guest to the sofa that matched Mother's wingback.

"We're so very close. As close as you and . . . *Yates.*" As always, she sounded like his given name was a secret thing that she scarcely dared to utter, even though they'd all known one another as children and so had *always* used given names.

119

She even pressed a hand to the hollow of her throat before shaking off the awe he inspired. "You have to help me. Something's dreadfully wrong, I just know it. Two weeks ago, I awoke from the most horrific dream—he was lost, imprisoned, someone was holding a gun to his head—and I just *knew*. I knew something terrible had happened."

Marigold frowned and sank onto the cushion. She wasn't one to put much stock in her *own* dreams, random as they always were. But she wasn't one to discount another's so easily, especially since Genie had told her of several over the years that had been startlingly true to reality.

Including when they were twelve, and she'd dreamed of Mother's death two days before it happened. Genie had her faults—didn't they all?—but she had her gifts too.

"I'm so sorry, Genie." When her friend took the seat beside her on the sofa instead of returning to the chair, Marigold reached for her hand. "I'll help in any way I can, but . . . how?"

For the space of two heartbeats, Genie stared at her in a way she never had before. Completely frank, that gaze, without any guile or hidden intents—and demanding. A gaze that offered no quarter. "The Imposters."

It took every ounce of the years of theater training Neville and Drina had given her to keep Marigold from jolting in shock, to blink in confusion. "Who?"

Genie let out an exasperated breath. "Oh, come now, surely you've heard of them! Papa said all the aristocrats in London know of them."

Know *of* them. She dared to breathe normally, furrowing her brow as if in thought. "Jog my memory."

"They're investigators! The best of the best. Papa is hesitating to contact them, unsure if they do any work on the Continent, but I am convinced they're our best chance, and I need you—or perhaps *Yates*—to help me with that part.

I can't exactly go flitting off to London like *some* people can."

As if every flit to London and back didn't mean a day's worth of food for the animals. But she daren't defend her "flitting," no matter how necessary it was. "So you want us to go to London and inquire of them for you?"

"Money is no object." Genie lifted her chin. "I will cover all your expenses, and theirs too. I assume they charge enormous fees, but there is no price too great if it gets us answers about Cornelius."

Money. She'd always been aghast at how eagerly the Ballantines talked of it. It was of the utmost concern to everyone, the aristocracy included. But no gentry she knew spoke of it so openly. It always startled her to hear Genie doing so. "Oh, I was not concerned . . . that is—"

"We pay our own way. We can afford to. I'll have you know that Ballantine Shipping is one of the premier companies on the North Sea. Even Lord Hemming covets our operations!"

"I—beg your pardon?" Though Marigold had been about to assure her that she knew their company was in demand, the mention of the earl gave her pause. "Lord Hemming?"

Genie's chin raised another notch. "I overheard him and Papa last autumn. He wanted to purchase our entire operations to merge with his own, but Papa refused. It's our family legacy, after all."

"Merge with his *own*?" Marigold hated feeling like a dunce—but since when did Lord Hemming have shipping enterprises?

"Really, Marigold, don't you ever think of anything but your ridiculous fashions?" She waved a dismissive hand at Marigold's dress, which wasn't even *that* ridiculous today. "You ought to give up all that nonsense. It certainly hasn't caught you a husband, and I daresay it never will."

She wanted to snap back that she had no interest in catching a husband. But that would send the conversation tumbling down a too-familiar tunnel of bickering and tweaked pride, since she knew Genie *did* want one and hadn't yet succeeded in finding one. "What have I missed about Lord Hemming? I knew their family has a diversified array of investments"—something she certainly wished *her* father had seen fit to arrange for himself—"but I didn't realize any were shipping."

Genie snorted a mocking little laugh. "Oh, you oblivious dear. He's going to be building *dreadnoughts*. That's his goal, anyway, if the contract comes through."

Battleships? Lord Hemming owned a shipyard that would be building *battleships*? She at once wondered if Yates knew that and decided he couldn't, or it would have appeared in his notes by now. "I didn't realize. I thought the *Dreadnought* was built in Portsmouth."

"It was, at HM Dockyard—but his lordship told my father he means to outperform them in both speed and efficiency, and he believes that his dockyard up here in Northumberland will make it much easier to avoid the prying eyes they have to protect against down on the southern coast, at least if he could expand to include *ours* as well." Genie's eyes glinted with the victory of knowing more than Marigold, though the fire banked a moment later. "So you see, we are no one to be ignored simply because we have no title. Simply because my great-grandfather came from Scotland. There is no reason for these Imposters to turn us down."

"I never thought there was." But her mind was spinning like Drina on her silks. Ever since the HMS *Dreadnought* was launched in 1906, tensions with Germany had been mounting, and their two countries had been racing to outgun each other on the naval front. After Germany's naval bill passed last year, everyone had been shouting that England had better pass one as well, so they could keep up.

She'd known *that*. She simply hadn't known that Hemming had a proverbial dog in this proverbial hunt—standing to profit greatly from any bill that passed, if he could secure that contract.

The aristocracy might not *speak* of money often, but that didn't mean they didn't pursue it.

"You'll do it, then? Inquire of the Imposters for me?"

"Oh." Back to that. Yates had needed to parry such questions a time or two, when acquaintances asked him if he'd heard of them, but this was a first for her. "I—"

"I thought you said you wanted to help." A thunderhead overtook Genie's features. "Why is this so much to ask? I've told you it'll cost you nothing but a bit of time."

And why did Genie always, always assume the worst of her? Had Marigold been such a terrible friend? Maybe she had. Maybe she'd been too caught up in their own woes these last few years.

And maybe she'd make it that much worse by over-examining it now and taking too long to answer. She gave Genie's fingers another squeeze and offered the calmest, most encouraging smile she could muster. "Of *course* I will help however I can. It's only that I don't know how to go about getting in touch with these Imposter people. Do you have any information on—oh."

Genie had unclasped the small handbag looped over her wrist and pulled out a card. *Their* card. The one she and Yates and Gemma had agonized over the wording of, and which Graham had used his artistic skills to draw for them. The ones they'd printed up with some of their last remaining money, praying they would prove a worthwhile investment of the precious funds.

They had.

Still, it was strange to see one appear now, here, in her own drawing room, in Eugenia Ballantine's hand. Refreshing her smile, Marigold reached for it and made a show of reading each word, front and back. "Where did you get this?"

Yet again, Genie's chin came up. "Papa picked it up at the Marlborough."

The second client in a row to come from those strategically placed cards. Yates would be rubbing in that *his* plants had been yielding more fruit this month than the similar ones she'd dropped around all the ladies' clubs and societies.

She nodded, knowing better than to let on that she knew Mr. Ballantine had only been granted entry to the club as a guest of Lord Hemming. "So we write up an inquiry and send it here? Do you have something—written?"

Of course she had. She pulled a folded sheet from her handbag, too, and handed it over as well.

Marigold unfolded it and scanned it. It was a more detailed and chronological version of what Genie had said, very much like what Yates had recorded overhearing at the Marlborough. "Perfect. We shall see to this for you, Genie, either Yates or me. It is an honor to be able to help—and we'll be praying too."

"Thank you." For one more moment, her shoulders remained square, her spine straight, her chin up—then it was as if she were a puppet whose strings were snipped, and she sagged against the sofa's back, her eyes welling with tears. "I don't know what we'll do, Marigold. I just don't know what we'll do if he's . . . if he's . . ."

"Don't think the worst." She set the paper and card aside, wondering if they'd even be able to help—never mind the job they were already working, they truly *didn't* have the sort of contacts on the Continent that they had here, and . . .

Wait. Actually, they did. Zelda, Drina, Hector, Franco, Alafair—they were Romani. Wanderers, nomads. They'd traveled all over Europe before retiring here, and they still had family in other circuses and troupes, all throughout

England, yes, but also on the Continent. Hadn't they told countless stories about their travels through France, Belgium, Germany, Italy, Spain? The Imposters had never had to call on those connections before, but they could.

They *could*.

She gave her friend a bolstering smile. "I'm certain these people will find the answers for you. But I shall pray that, before they can even get started, you'll receive word from your brother."

"Excuse me, my lady, Miss Ballantine."

At Alafair's voice, Marigold looked up, surprised to see him standing there with a silver salver in hand, cards upon it. "Lord Xavier Hasting, Lieutenant Colonel Sir Merritt Livingstone, Lady Lavinia Hemming, and Miss Claudia Hamilton have arrived. I've shown them to the parlor."

Now? What happened to this afternoon? At least Alafair had the good sense not to show them right in. Genie would obviously want to make an escape. She wouldn't want strange gentlemen to see her with red-rimmed eyes.

Or perhaps she would.

"Lord Who and Sir What?" Eyes going wide, Genie leaned close—her distress neatly buttoned away behind obvious excitement.

"Xavier and Merritt. The Hemmings invited them to stay in the neighborhood for a few weeks while Sir Merritt is recovering from a bout of pneumonia. Would you like to meet them now, Genie, or—"

"Well, of course I do! You wouldn't keep me from them, would you?" Her moods shifting like clouds over the North Sea, Genie's fair brows slammed down. "That's petty of you."

Marigold didn't bother stifling her sigh. "I am happy to make introductions at whatever time you feel is best—now, or when you're feeling more composed."

"I am perfectly composed." Apparently the signature lift of her chin was meant to prove it.

So be it. If Genie wanted to chase thoughts of a missing brother with thoughts of potential beaux, who was Marigold to judge? She sent a tight smile Alafair's way. "Do show them in, if you would."

Though to be honest, she felt bad for the two gents. They were already outnumbered, with Gemma's cousin Claudia—Lady Hemming's companion—coming to act as chaperone, and Genie's presence would skew the numbers still more. Perhaps not a tragedy in general, but her neighbor's personality *could* be a bit overwhelming for the uninitiated.

The guests weren't the only ones to file into the room a moment later. Yates slipped in, too, dressed in a pale grey morning suit, his hair still damp. As he moved stealthily to her side, she couldn't deny the relief that filled her, lighting a spark of a smile on her lips. "I thought you were going to stay outside," she whispered.

"I decided to take pity on the new arrivals when I spotted the earl's car coming this way. Balance the odds a bit." He flashed a glance Genie's way, his lips twitching. "Plus, I wanted to meet them."

As himself, he meant. Good. Having her little brother at her side reminded her of who she was like nothing else could.

A reminder she found she needed after time spent in Eugenia Ballantine's company.

TEN

$\mathcal{M}$erritt let himself fall to the rear of the group. It wasn't that he hadn't enjoyed the last hour in the drawing room of Fairfax Tower— mostly. Nor was it that he was so eager for a moment of quiet that he would accept even that two-second version that came when the others stepped out of doors ahead of him—much.

It was that the longer he sat there, listening to Miss Hamilton's gossip and Miss Ballantine's flirtation and Lady Lavinia's laughter, the more he wanted to shout at them all to drop the pretense that everything was normal, that there was nothing more important than *this*.

The more he wanted to ask Miss Ballantine outright what she thought had happened to her brother. To ask Lady Lavinia why her father had *not* asked anyone in the War Office about Cornelius before leaving London, even though Mr. A had reported that he'd promised to do so—and had asked Merritt to simply either verify that Ballantine was his already-missing agent or let him know if they now had *two* missing sailors to investigate.

He hadn't realized, when he hired the Imposters, that there was a personal connection between his agent and Hemming, which they would be able to observe. They were certainly proving their capabilities.

And the Fairfax siblings—he'd like to ask *them* to explain what those truly bizarre noises were that kept coming through the windows. The growling sounded less like the ocean than some sort of wild animal, but that was absurd. No one else seemed alarmed by the rumbles, other than Xavier, who kept shooting him startled glances, so perhaps the ocean *did* just have a strange music here.

A dark-haired, olive-skinned domestic who spoke with an accent he couldn't quite place had wheeled in a cart loaded with refreshments about half an hour ago, so they'd all had to have some of the lemonade and sweets, but he'd certainly put up no fuss when Lady Lavinia had suggested—somewhat giddily, it seemed to him—that the Fairfaxes give their guests the grand tour of the estate.

He wasn't generally all that keen on house tours. But then, the Fairfaxes weren't leading them through the house, but rather outside into an enormous inner courtyard that he never would have guessed was hidden behind the ancient stone walls. He oughtn't to have been surprised, he supposed. Alnwick Abbey, where the Hemmings had been hosting him and X for the last two days while they secured more permanent lodgings a few miles away, was a medieval fortress of a house, so it was reasonable to think Fairfax Tower dated from a similar era. They certainly had the same honeyed stone walls.

Xavier's booming laugh drew Merritt's feet out the door a few seconds after the rest of them, and his brows didn't know whether to lift up or pull together. He drew up beside his best friend and surveyed the space before him. "Is there a . . . circus? Here?"

It certainly looked like it. A ring circled the center of the courtyard, filled with dirt or sand or some combination thereof. Two towering platforms and poles stood sentinel on each end, a highwire stretched between them and trapezes suspended from each one. There was even a Gypsy wagon parked along the far wall, its faded lettering proclaiming CAESAR'S MENAGERIE & CIRCUS.

Lady Lavinia laughed and spun in a circle, arms outstretched, as if she were an act in the circus herself. "There's *always* a circus here! The Caesar family have retired here—isn't it charming? You should see Zelda and Franco on the trapeze!"

Not having any idea how he was supposed to respond to that, Merritt let his gaze drift to Lady Marigold and her brother. Neither had struck him as particularly prone to flights of fancy during their conversations. If anything, they had come off as the more grounded of the bunch. But to have invited circus performers—Gypsies, no less—to reside here permanently? Wasn't that inviting theft and other unsavory behavior? That's what his own father had always said, on the few occasions that they went to a circus or menagerie during Merritt's childhood. *"Enjoy the show, but watch your pockets."*

Neither of the Fairfaxes looked particularly concerned about their tenants, nor apologetic. Both were, in fact, grinning. The master of the house motioned toward an opening in the wall opposite. "The human members of the family are all about their work, I know, but come. Let us introduce you to the *other* members of the family."

Miss Ballantine made a distressed noise. "Not the animals, my lord. We'll make a mess of our shoes and smell for days afterward."

Was it his imagination, or did Lady Lavinia actually roll her eyes? "Feel free to stay right here in the nice, clean courtyard, Genie, if it causes you such distress. I, however, haven't paid a visit to Leonidas in far too long. I cannot believe it's been five years since I've been here!" Perhaps to spite Miss Ballantine, who had been making moon eyes at Lord Fairfax all morning, she linked her arm through his and smiled up at him. "Lead the way, my lord."

"With pleasure, my lady." With a twirl of his hand worthy of one of the circus performers, Fairfax led Lady Lavinia forward with a bouncing, skipping pace that had her laughing but matching him step for step.

An interesting chap, the young earl. During the last hour he'd quoted poetry, a variety of lines that Merritt *thought* were from Shakespeare—though it had been far too long since his schooldays for him to be certain—offered rather keen spiritual insight of the value of prayer, and issued an open invitation for Merritt and Xavier to join him any time they'd like for a ride, a bout of tennis or squash, or whatever sport they fancied.

Xavier was never one to let an offer of hospitality go unaccepted, so they now had a standing engagement with him each morning at nine, here at the Tower. Merritt hadn't pointed out that he was supposed to be resting. He would be careful, but he needed to regain his strength at some point.

His ribs were feeling better after he'd nearly been caught by the gent's sister in Lord Hemming's study, and his ankle had only been twisted, not sprained or broken, but the bruise to his ego still smarted. He was supposed to be among the best of England's best, with keen instincts and the most rigorous training. Worthy of defending the king himself. Yet he'd been cornered under a bench by a slip of a young lady whose only training was in fashion.

Xavier was even now offering their hostess his arm and leading her out behind her brother, which gave Merritt the opportunity to note that her dress wasn't half as ostentatious as usual, and she hadn't put on a hat at all, nor even one of the headpieces she usually wore otherwise. The only thing on her head was a braid that wound round and round enough times to make him wonder how long her hair was—and how much it must weigh.

Then he realized he had better offer his own arm to one of the two remaining females. He smiled first at Miss Ballantine, since she was guest rather than chaperone. "Will you be joining us, miss, or staying in the courtyard?"

Miss Ballantine's smile looked genuine as paste, though she took his proffered arm. "I suppose I'll come. Thank you, sir."

Good. When they'd all been introduced an hour ago and he realized this was the daughter of the family spoken of in his last report from the Imposters, Merritt had prayed he would have the chance to engage her in conversation. And here it was, handily delivered to him by Fairfax and Xavier's quick manners.

He wasn't half so deft at conversation as Xavier was, but he'd already considered how best to manage this one, and he began with a smile. "You are a neighbor, correct? Are you by chance one of the Ballantines of Ballantine Shipping?"

There. He wasn't a total dunce.

Her eyes lit up. "I am, yes—my father is the current owner, my great-grandfather the founder. You've heard of us?"

"Certainly I have. I believe I even met your brother once, if he is in the Royal Navy."

"He is." A flash of pride, but it was followed quickly by a throb of pain. She turned her face away, but not before he saw it. "When did you meet him?"

"Oh, just in passing, about six months ago." In the new office, but he wasn't about to share that. It had been his first week at his new assignment, and he'd been given an introduction to a few of the intelligence officers from the various divisions he would be overseeing—the ones who were in London at the time. "He seemed an amiable chap, the sort I'd have liked to get to know more. I imagine you miss him terribly."

Her face fell. "So much. It's been . . . it's been far too long since we've heard from him." No doubt that was all she'd say on the matter with him, stranger that he was.

He couldn't blame her for that, nor could he assure her that he could help her. He couldn't do nearly as much as he wanted now. Had he not been barred from the office for this medical leave . . . not that he had left work behind quite as much as Colonel May might hope. But now his every inquiry had to be carefully shielded under the guise of "trying to fend off boredom."

He'd gone into the office before he left Town to fetch something he'd left at his desk, and he'd convinced one of his colleagues to keep him apprised of some of the work he'd been forced to hand over to him, via the post. Lieutenant Gaines had been happy enough to agree *"so long as you don't overexert yourself."*

As if he could, here, with only a few letters to look forward to.

But he had asked Gaines outright if anyone had heard from Ballantine lately, saying truthfully that he was overdue to get in touch. He'd confirmed that no one had. Merritt had then asked if someone hadn't looked into his silence— Hemming, maybe?

Gaines had had to check up on that, but the answer had just come via letter this morning. *No one has thought to question the silence of the party about whom you inquired.*

No one, meaning Hemming. Not even after Ballantine had specifically asked him to do so. To Merritt's mind, that meant one of two things—either Hemming already knew where the young man was and so knew his father had nothing to worry about . . . or he knew where he was and that he *did*, but he didn't want anyone else to know.

They passed through a stone archway and into the open area beyond the Tower's back walls. From the front, there had been a profusion of gardens just beginning to bloom but very little else to detract from the startling beauty of the manor house itself. Back here, however, he caught his first glimpse of a veritable village of outbuildings, all in matching stone. He'd guess the one connected to the drive was the carriage house, and the long one Lord Fairfax was aimed for had the look of stables.

As for the others . . . "It seems we're too far back for me to hear the tour. Do you know what all these buildings are?"

"Oh yes. The late Lord Fairfax was all the time entertaining the neighborhood." Miss Ballantine pointed to the southernmost building and worked her way north. "That's the theater. The gymnasium with the indoor training facilities, for when weather doesn't permit practicing in the courtyard. That next one is the stadium, where they work the animals and stage any shows that require them. And then the stables and carriage house."

Merritt didn't know how to reply to all of that. Theaters, stadiums, gymnasiums? He shook his head. "You clearly know the place well."

She tilted her head a bit. "Not as well as Lady Lavinia—I wasn't the favorite of Marigold that she was when we were all children." And her affront came through loud and clear. "But well enough. We were here nearly once a week, I think, while the late earl was alive and entertaining. Sadly, Lady Marigold and her brother haven't proven themselves quite so hospitable. They haven't had a single show since their father's death, nor even a dinner or ball. I've scarcely been here at all in the last five years."

He decided to ignore the complaint portion of her speech. "Good neighbors are certainly a blessing. I imagine your three families, being the leading ones in the area, all saw one another often when you were children."

Xavier would have been proud, had he heard that bit of

flattery. He honestly didn't know if the Ballantines were considered a leading family, but it seemed reasonable—and Miss Ballantine clearly appreciated the sentiment. She preened a bit like that peacock strutting in front of the stables there.

"Yes, we did—and still do, both here and in London. Just a week ago, my father and Lord Hemming dined together at the Marlborough."

He almost wished he didn't know the circumstances of that particular meeting. It made sorrow fill his heart for her—both because of the reason for it, and because she clearly wanted to claim connections that were dubious at best. "Indeed? My uncle and I are members, but I'm afraid I've only gone twice now. I'm more often at the Guards' Club."

A roar sounded again—a roar that was definitely *not* the ocean. His gait hitched, and then his eyes landed on the colorfully painted row of wheeled cages parked at one end of the stables. Painted with tigers and leopards and lions, elephants and giraffes and zebras, monkeys and kangaroos.

He suddenly suspected it wasn't horses that claimed the stalls in that stable.

Before he could open his mouth to ask, a small brown something streaked from the interior, hooting and crying and making a mad dash for Lord Fairfax. The earl's laughter convinced him the creature posed no threat, but it wasn't until it landed on his shoulder that Merritt realized it was a monkey.

Miss Ballantine came to a halt and sniffed her opinion of their greeter.

Fairfax turned, his face alight with a smile, and said, "Well, here's the first, gents. Allow me to introduce Penelope. Penny, greet our guests."

The monkey—the same sort he'd seen with organ grinders in the city—was wearing a *skirt*. Which she now gripped in both hands and held out while she bobbed her knees.

Laughter tickled Merritt's throat. "How do you do, Penelope?" he said in tandem with Xavier.

Her answer was a series of hoots that sounded friendly enough. Xavier stepped forward, releasing Lady Marigold's arm in favor of taking the little monkey's hand. She bobbed another curtsy, patted Xavier's cheek, and then climbed onto the top of Fairfax's head.

Another chuckle won a place in Merritt's chest. "A gracious welcome." His smile froze when a bulky, low form first filled and then passed through the wide stable doors. The lion, tawny and rippling with muscles, was enormous, its mane declaring it a him.

But why was it—he—*free*? Just wandering about? Perhaps he'd escaped from his cage or stall or pen or whatever they kept him in. Surely a tamer or trainer would come running out any moment, wouldn't they? With a whip or a three-legged stool, ready to push the monstrous creature back inside.

"Leonidas!" Lavinia called out, waving a hand. Was she calling for the trainer? Or—no. The lion. Of course it was the lion called Leonidas—Lady Lavinia had told them a story about the day of his birth during their first visit. But he hadn't realized the lion was still around and, blast her, now it was coming toward *them*.

He felt himself go stiff and taut, muscles coiled, ready to spring into whatever action was needed even as his lungs burned just from the walk. Even as he also noted that all the locals were far from alarmed, and Lady Marigold even stepped away from the others, hand out and whistle on her lips as if it were a dog sauntering their way instead of the king of the blasted jungle.

The saunter turned into a lope, and the fool girl actually laughed and leaned forward, arms out. Merritt moved a step toward them without knowing exactly why—clearly she didn't feel she was in any danger—but he paused when a man in dusty trousers, shirt, and waistcoat stepped out of the stables.

He had the look of a trainer. And he was smiling. So apparently it was perfectly fine that an enormous African lion was charging for the earl's sister, strange low rumbles coming from his throat.

A moment later, he was upon her, big paws trying to plant themselves on her legs and knocking her over—still laughing—in the process. Her hands buried themselves in his mane, tousling it with obvious affection as he butted his head against hers.

Lady Lavinia and Xavier had both moved to his side, and his friend, let it be noted, was gaping just as he was. "A pet *lion?*" he said.

The lady grinned. "Not a *pet*, exactly. Hector—that's him there—will be the first to say that there's no such thing as a tame lion, only a well-trained one. But Leonidas was born right here, and the Fairfaxes and Caesars are his pride. Or so Hector says, and we don't dare to argue."

He certainly seemed to be behaving like an oversized house cat, rolling now onto his side so Lady Marigold could rub his chest. Though he'd managed to knock her hair from its pins, so that a long, thick braid dangled to her waist.

It made something shift as he watched her. The lion, the contented smile on her face, the hair a-tumble, the fact that she was rolling around in the grass in her beaded and bedecked dress—he'd had the wrong of her. He'd thought her concerned with nothing but fashion, nothing but a mannequin.

He'd been mistaken. He could admit that.

She eventually got back on her feet, though she kept one hand fisted in Leonidas's mane as she turned to the rest of them. "Lavinia first, please. He'll remember you best."

Lavinia moved toward her, not hesitating but also not throwing herself toward the big cat as Marigold had done. She held out a hand. The lion didn't do anything so obvious as sniff it like a pup, but Merritt would have sworn the beast nodded his approval of her after a moment. At Lady Marigold's word, she then moved slowly forward, until she'd rubbed a hand down his neck.

Lady Marigold looked to the rest of them after her friend had stepped away. "If anyone else would like an introduction, come up one at a time, hand extended. I promise you he won't bite it off. Probably." This she delivered with a grin the likes of which he'd yet to see from her—deep, dimpled, and utterly mischievous.

Either she never wore that grin in London, or her hats had hidden it in their shadow. But Merritt couldn't deny its effect. He found himself stepping away from Miss Ballantine and Xavier—whose breath of laughter sounded incredulous— and toward the lady and her lion.

He stretched out his hand and moved with careful, even steps. It wasn't, he decided, so very different from the approach he'd been taught in the military. Plan each step, show no fear, never hesitate, never rush.

The lion watched him with considerably more wariness than he had Lady Lavinia. He shifted from paw to paw, leaning into Lady Marigold's side and rumbling again. Without releasing the handful of mane she held in one fist, she stroked his nose with the other hand, murmuring something to the big cat. Something not in English, though he couldn't have said what language it *was*.

When Merritt was a step away, Leonidas gave a small shake of his head, sat down, and lifted a front paw.

The lady chuckled. "You've been accepted. Go ahead and shake hands."

He'd trained his mastiff to shake when he was a lad and

tried to tell himself that the lion wasn't *that* much bigger—though he didn't really believe himself. Still, he offered the king a smile and enclosed the furry, golden paw in both his hands, moving it up and down once. "How do you do, Leonidas?"

Perhaps he'd been trained to reply to the greeting, because the lion let out a noise he decided to call an overgrown meow before reclaiming his paw.

Well. He'd have a story to tell the girls when he next saw the Prestons, wouldn't he? And for that matter, the chaps in the office, when he returned to duty. His gaze moved to Lady Marigold. "Lady Lavinia said he was born here?"

The lady nodded, scratching the beast behind his ears. "Seventeen years ago. He's an old man now—aren't you, Leonidas? Older than he ever would have lived to be in the wild. But he's seen all of England and even part of Europe in his day, traveling with the menagerie."

"Amazing." He'd never really thought to wonder about the circus animals he'd seen as a child, but now he did. "If he traveled so much, how is it that he knows you so well?"

Lady Marigold gave that free, unfettered grin again. "Caesar's Circus always wintered here, so we had months of every year together—and being around him so much when he was so young, he came to think of us as his own. Every time they returned, it was like a family reunion. Wasn't it, boy?"

Leonidas leaned into her, gave a mighty yawn, and then turned back toward the stable.

She chuckled. "And that's enough excitement for him for one day, the lazy thing. Lord Xavier, I'm afraid if you want your turn at a shake, it will have to wait until another day."

"Shame, that. Perhaps you can just introduce me to the peacock instead."

He clearly meant it as a joke, but Lord Fairfax said, "Peabody? He's a bit standoffish, I'm afraid."

Xavier's face drew into the most amusing, startled frown. "You named your peacocks?"

Fairfax turned the confusion right back around on him. "Don't you?"

A laugh from X. "I don't have any."

"Wise of you—noisy things, and they refuse to make friends. Peabody is constantly squawking at us all. And don't get me started on the ostriches."

"On the . . ." Xavier blinked at him, then at Lady Marigold, and finally settled his bemused gaze on Merritt. "And here I'd given Clare a hard time for having three cats."

"Leonidas has a pet cat." Fairfax motioned them forward again, his grin not unlike his sister's. "It's rather hilarious. She'll curl up on his back and sleep there, and he always saves a few bites of his meat for her. Though she won't let us humans near her."

"What a bizarre turn this day has taken," his friend muttered to him as they continued toward the stable. "When you woke up this morning, did you have any idea you'd be shaking hands with a lion?"

Merritt chuckled, only coughing a little at its end. "I didn't, at that. It never once crossed my mind."

But it had certainly taught him a lesson on a day he thought would be filled with brooding over the missing Ballantine son—that nothing was ever quite what it seemed.

ELEVEN

Marigold stood in front of the carriage house, her umbrella held in her folded arms. It did nothing to protect her legs from the rain-bejeweled wind, but she wouldn't let that dampen her smile.

The situation had done a fine enough job of that otherwise. "Are you certain you don't want me to come with you?"

Yates sent her a *we've-been-through-this* look. Which they had, at least half a dozen times. But still. It was one thing to decide that the best way to tackle their multiple jobs was for Yates to make a quick trip back to London while she attended the country dance that the Hemmings were hosting tonight at the Abbey. It was another to bid him farewell when they'd only been home for a week. To think ahead to the night to come and realize she'd have no one watching her back while she attempted to slip away and do a bit of snooping through the family wing while all the family were at the ball.

To know that when she entered Alnwick Abbey this afternoon, it wouldn't be in the way she'd entered it a thousand times before. This time, she wasn't just coming as Marigold, Lavinia's dearest friend.

She was coming as an Imposter, hired to ferret out information about the earl's dealings. Perhaps his very loyalties.

The rain drummed on her umbrella in a rhythm that may have been happy if she didn't have this silly band of anxiety around her chest.

They'd been separated before. Countless times.

She'd visited Lavinia's home by herself before. Countless times.

Even Hector and the rest of the Caesars had left them before. Countless times.

But *that* was gnawing at her, too, watching their old friend hitch up not only the horses to the Fairfax carriage, which Franco would use to deliver Yates to the train station, but also Zig, one of their three zebras, to one of the wagons that hadn't rolled farther than Longhouton in the last five years.

It would travel considerably farther over the next few days, all the way to Leeds. There, Hector would meet up with a few cousins about to depart from their own winter lodgings and take their circus to Europe for the summer. He'd already made arrangements to travel with them this year.

To gather information for Yates and Marigold. To try to find Cornelius Ballantine.

"You are fretting. What do I tell you about this?"

At the familiar chiding, Marigold sighed and turned to where Drina had come up with her own umbrella, ready to send her own brother off. "It isn't fair of us to ask this of him. You are all supposed to be enjoying your retirement, not dashing off to the Continent to chase wild geese for us."

Drina's lips pulled up into a sparkling smile. "Ah, but you know Hector. He needs to chase a goose now and then, yes? To keep things interesting. Too much relaxing and enjoyment make him cranky."

Marigold chuckled. Hector, the youngest of the Caesar

crew, *had* jumped at the chance to become an Imposter-at-Large in Germany or Austria or Belgium or wherever else he had to go to follow leads for them.

Even so. She liked him *here*. She liked Yates here, at least when she was. She liked Gemma and Graham here, and neither of them were, and in a few hours she wouldn't be either, if only for a night.

A second sigh skipped after the first. "I'll be back as early as I can manage tomorrow, to help with the animals. And the baking. And the cleaning, if—"

"My golden one—stop." Drina reached over with her long-fingered hand and took Marigold by the chin. "You are a lady. You go, you dance with the other ladies and gentlemen, and you have a good time. Maybe flirt a little, yes? Laugh. Forget, for an hour or two, everything else and let your inner light outshine your gown. It will do you good."

"Well." Yates hefted one more bag into the carriage and angled a look at them. "She could forgo the flirting bit. I grant that Lord X and Sir Merritt both seem like decent enough chaps, but let's not get ahead of ourselves."

"There will be no flirting. Not by me, anyway. That is for Lavinia and Genie and whoever else comes." Likely the baronet and his two daughters, from Rothbury. Miss Shields, from Amble. Perhaps even the Alstons from Bamburgh, if they weren't in London already. "I'll have other things to occupy my thoughts, thank you."

Drina shook her head and mumbled something in Romani that sounded suspiciously like "foolish girl."

Marigold may have defended herself, but Yates had loaded the last of his things into the carriage and turned to her with that smile of his. "Drina's greater point *is* a good one, sister mine. Try to enjoy yourself. You'll have plenty of time both for a bit of fun *and* snooping through Hemming's things."

She found a smile of her own for him. "Shall I give Genie

your heartfelt regrets for missing the dances you promised her?"

Amusement lit his eyes, undarkened by regret. "If she complains, just remind her that I'm going to London for *her*. Or so she's welcome to think."

It still felt odd, having Ballantine money in their pockets. They'd refused the reimbursement of Yates's train fare, insisting it was their pleasure to help their neighbor, but they couldn't exactly refuse the fee for the Imposters that Genie had pressed into her hands three days ago.

"I don't know how much it may cost," she'd said, *"so just take all of this. It's the pin money Mother and I have been saving for years. It ought to suffice."*

It would *more* than suffice, and Marigold had tried to say so without sounding like she knew what she was talking about—but gracious, how much pin money did Mr. Ballantine provide them? They obviously spent plenty of it on the new clothes and hats and shoes they bought, but they still had a small fortune tucked away in that handkerchief.

Genie had simply met her gaze and said she fully trusted them to return whatever wasn't used, but she wasn't going to lose any sleep over it. "Don't take no for an answer. Offer them more, if you must. If this isn't enough, we can get more quite easily."

It would feed them all for months—that was a blessing, not something that should make her feel so guilty. And they'd already been hired to investigate another of their closest neighbors. Why should this exchange have made her feel so strange? So duplicitous?

Because it wasn't an old friend who had hired them for the Hemming case, probably—and she hadn't been the one negotiating. Even so, she wished she could have just volunteered their assistance without destroying their anonymity.

They couldn't, though. Nor could they afford to refuse

143

another case. So Yates had used the money to purchase Hector's fare to the Continent and handed much of the remainder over to him to use while there. The rest they'd added to their household funds.

Yates ducked under Marigold's umbrella now to give her a quick embrace. "If you need anything, you know how to reach me. If you don't hear otherwise, look for me on the Friday afternoon train."

"I will." She kept her smile pinned to her cheeks and waved as he and Franco soon rolled down the drive, through the steady spring rain. Once she was fairly certain he wouldn't still be watching her, she let both umbrella and smile sag.

"There now." Drina's arm came around her shoulders. "We'll help the Ballantine girl sort out what's happened to her brother. And we'll have answers soon too about his lordship, no doubt. All a misunderstanding, that one, I wager."

Though Marigold nodded, it was more a prayer than an agreement. According to the information Sir Merritt had left for them, which Graham had forwarded, not only had Lord Hemming not done any checking on Cornelius Ballantine, but Cornelius was indeed the one who had sent the one-word telegram with Hemming's name.

Why? What had Cornelius known or suspected—or perhaps, *please, God,* wanted to convey to the earl?

Perhaps she'd find something at Alnwick Abbey while she was there, some clue to help them. At the very least, perhaps she would end up with some good time with Lavinia, just the two of them.

The day away from home would be totally worthwhile if she could at least sort out why her friend was suddenly so eager to marry and leave her family.

"It's no great mystery, Marigold." Lavinia held up a be-jeweled pin to her elaborate hairstyle and pursed her lips at her reflection. "Here, do you think?"

Marigold moved her friend's hand three inches up. "So you say. But I haven't been able to sort out the answer."

Laughing, Lavinia accepted her suggestion on location and slid the pin into her dark curls, then reached for another. "I *do* realize he's your brother, but even you have to admit that Yates is quite unlike the other gentlemen we know. I admit I did a bit of admiring of his form when I last saw him on the rings myself." Unlike Genie, whose preoccupation with *Yates* they'd been discussing, Lavinia didn't flush at the mere mention of his name.

Marigold took the next pin from Lavinia's fingers and pushed it into the perfect place near the back of her mass of curls. Then wiggled her fingers for the next one. "I will be the first to sing my brother's praises—never think for a moment that I'm not his loudest encourager. But *no* man is deserving of all her flushing and cooing and whispers."

Lavinia dropped five more jeweled pins into Marigold's palm and watched in the mirror to see where she put them. "I don't entirely disagree there. Maybe your primary objection is more to the thought of ending up with Genie as a sister-in-law."

With anyone else, Marigold would have made an effort to control the wince. With Lavinia, she let herself be genuine. "I like Genie. Just . . ."

"In smaller doses than you'd get if she lived with you?" Lavinia chuckled. "You'll hear no argument from me. I'm rather glad I don't have a brother for her to have set her sights on."

"It isn't . . . well, it's just . . ." Marigold sighed and slid the other pins into the best places to catch the light and shimmer. "She always makes me feel as though I should apologize for simply *being*."

It seemed like a petty objection to her friend, in light of what the Ballantines were currently worrying over. Cornelius was missing, and Marigold was complaining about Genie pointing it out when she smelled like the stables? That surely made *her* the petty one, not her friend.

She never should have brought it up. Here she was seeking solace in the face of their neighbors' arrival, even though it amounted to gossiping about her—something Marigold made a point never to do, being so keenly aware of how often gossip filled out their files.

She may learn from it. But she wouldn't participate in it. The rule she'd just broken, for no reason other than her own nerves.

Lavinia tilted her head to see a few of the pin placements and then spun on her stool. "I think you're a saint for simply taking all the insults she dishes out without ever once returning them. If she spoke to me as she does to you . . ."

"But she doesn't. No one could have any reason to insult you."

"Don't be silly. Everyone has just felt sorry for me for so long, they got out of the habit." Lavinia winced at the observation and pushed to her feet, a hand splayed over her chest. "My heart may have been weakened from that dratted fever, but it isn't as delicate as all that. I can handle hearing people's true opinions."

"Of course you can. But why would anyone have a negative one?" Marigold smiled at the figure she cut—perfect elegance, from the bejeweled hair to the understated gown of rose, to the matching slippers.

A far cry from the overdone getup Marigold had chosen for the night. G. M. Parker may not be attending their little country ball to write it up for her column, but Marigold still had to maintain the reputation she'd built.

And truth be told, she did rather fancy all the flowers

they'd sewn onto tonight's ensemble. It may have suited Mother—or even Lavinia—better than Marigold, but the dress itself was gorgeous.

Lavinia's look was so pointed, it bordered on patronizing. "If I didn't know you were simply biased, I'd accuse you of flattery. I am hardly without my faults, and people are allowed to notice them."

Her throat tickled with laughter. "Well, *this* is a strange argument." But also the perfect introduction to what she *really* wanted to talk about, and since the lady's maid had gone to assist Lady Hemming, now was as perfect a time as any. "Our gentlemen guests certainly don't seem to notice any faults in you. They've been all attentiveness, haven't they?"

She expected a sparkle in Lavinia's eyes, a grin to overtake her lips. Certainly not for a frown to furrow her brow. "They're polite. Well, and Lord Xavier is simply over-charming." Lavinia lifted one shoulder. "I don't anticipate either of them declaring their desire for a courtship at the end of their visit. Certainly not Sir Merritt—he's a bit standoffish, isn't he? And there's just no telling if Lord Xavier means a thing he says. Or rather, that he doesn't mean everything he says to absolutely everyone and is incapable of feeling any preference."

They sounded to Marigold's ears more like Lady Hemming's observations than Lavinia's. "That's unfair. To both of them. Lord Xavier, I think, is quite genuine, and to call him *incapable* of feeling a preference is certainly unearned. The fact that he hasn't yet declared a preference doesn't mean he never will—and you're a more likely recipient than any, if you ask me."

Lavinia rolled her eyes. "And will you defend Sir Merritt too? You cannot possibly argue that that rock-hard shell of his is hiding a soft heart just bursting with love for me. He's a veritable statue! Utterly without expression."

Not true. Granted, he'd at first kept that mask firmly in

place, but Marigold was convinced it had been to cover physical pain when they first met. In the weeks since, and especially since coming here, he'd relaxed degree by degree. "Are you quite serious? He smiles and laughs and frequently jokes with Lord X."

"It hardly matters." Lavinia stalked to her jewelry armoire and opened one of its doors, revealing a row of delicate dangling necklaces. Her mother had already told her which one to wear, and Marigold knew she'd obey the dictate of pearls, but it didn't stop her from pulling out a half dozen other options and holding them up to her neck before the mirror. "I am unconvinced that he would be a good match. His aunt is still young enough to surprise the family with another babe, which could yet provide his uncle with an heir. Or, God forbid, she could pass away before he does, and he could remarry. There is no guarantee that Sir Merritt will inherit anything at all."

Who *was* this creature parading around in Lavinia's skin? Marigold sank onto the foot of the bed, wrapping one satin glove-clad arm around the tall post. "And that is how you'll measure him? By his aunt's fertility and his uncle's likelihood to remarry if she dies?" It sounded harsh. It *was* harsh. And the very idea made a strange anger simmer in her veins. "You won't even consider his bravery in rescuing missionaries in China, or his dedication to that family that could yet disinherit him, or your father's own recommendation?"

"Oh, I considered *that* part." She considered the effect of a diamond-and-pearl pendant and then slid it back into its place in the armoire. "Frankly, I think Father invited him more to size him up in a professional capacity than to present him as a potential spouse for me. I was just his excuse."

That gave Marigold pause. Not because of the blasé tone that hinted at this new cynicism she wanted to root out, but because she may well be right. Sir Merritt had shared his con-

148

cern that Colonel May had wanted him out of the office. . . . What if he was truly in the crosshairs of him or Hemming?

It made her pulse skitter like a flock of startled ostriches— loud and dangerous in her ears. Sir Merritt had already tried to go through Lord Hemming's London study. What if someone else had caught him at it instead of her?

What if he'd been snooping about *here*, at the Abbey? Being seen? His actions noted?

It took her several blinks to refocus on her friend, who had tried and discarded a choker with a gold flower motif as well. "I don't dare to guess at your father's motives. Though I wonder at your eagerness in inviting the two of them to join us here if you're so disinterested in them both."

"Well, it takes more than an hour in the park to really understand someone, doesn't it?"

She'd learned quite a bit about Sir Merritt during that walk in Hyde Park, actually. Certainly that he was more than a stiff uniform and a statue beneath it. "Of course it does."

"And I *do* enjoy their company—quite a bit. Lord Xavier is endlessly entertaining, and I am not immune to the appeal of a man in uniform." There, finally, a smile that looked like *Lavinia*. "Seeing the two of them and Yates running about the lawn the other day in their shirtsleeves was no hardship, I confess."

Marigold chuckled. "Chasing escaped cassowary chicks is destined to become the next sport of the royals, I daresay."

Laughter won out as they remembered the spectacle— three grown men running all about the lawn, lunging periodically at those quick-footed chicks, Franco chasing behind them with a cage, the angry, enormous parent birds threatening to break through their pen to come to the rescue of their little ones.

Ordinarily, she would have been the one chasing chicks with Yates. But watching on the sidelines with Lavinia and

Claudia had proven far more entertaining. And she'd been happy to note that Sir Merritt had only paused to cough once and hadn't seemed much more winded than the others after the last runaway had been captured.

Perhaps his physicians had been right about the healing property of country air. One week here, and he was already markedly improved.

Once their laughter died down, Marigold sent her friend a warm smile. "I do hope you come to admire someone—be it one of them or not—for more than their estates or title, Lavinia. I want every happiness for you."

"I know you do." Lavinia turned back to her jewelry. "But honestly, Marigold, if my heart directed me to one particular gentleman, I'd likely run the other way. It hasn't exactly proven itself a trustworthy organ."

Marigold's fingers curled around the bedpost. "You know very well that your physical organ and the center of your emotions, hopes, and dreams are not *really* the same."

"Do I?" She slid all the necklaces back, drew the strand of white pearls from its protective velvet bag, but then laid it on the armoire's top. She spun to face Marigold. "What I know is that when my heart was weak, *I* was weak. All the way down to those emotions and hopes and dreams you talk about. I couldn't hope, Marigold. I couldn't dream. Some days I could scarcely even sense the love I knew I felt for my family, for you. It was only pain. Pain and that dreadful weakness, all the time."

She reached back in the armoire, drew out a necklace that Marigold had given her for Christmas—a bold statement piece made of rhinestones and some alloy sure to tarnish—and fastened it around her neck. "I swore to myself that if I lived, if I improved, I wouldn't be the prisoner of my heart anymore. I wouldn't let it rule me—and I won't. I won't be like—"

Marigold waited, but Lavinia said no more. She leaned closer. "Like who?"

Lavinia shook her head and focused her attention on her reflection. "Nothing. No one in particular, just . . . everyone, really. When does romance ever last? What couple do you know who still feels that love after a decade or two of marriage?"

"Mine did. And yours do." But Marigold frowned and moved closer to her friend, reaching over to center the sparkling paste gems between Lavinia's clavicles. "Why do you doubt that?" Lord Hemming lavished Lady Hemming with affection—with gifts, with attention, with regard. Until Lavinia's sickness, the two had never been separated. When his lordship had to be in London for the sessions or other responsibilities, the lady was with him, even if it meant leaving Lavinia in the care of a nurse or governess here in Northumberland.

Lavinia averted her gaze. "I don't." She said it too quickly. "Or . . . maybe I just feel guilty. My illness came between them. They were apart so much these last years. And . . ."

And? And *what*?

There was no time to ponder the question. The bedroom door swung open even as a perfunctory knock tapped out, and Lady Hemming swept into the room. Her gown was a deep blue, accented with black beading. Lovely . . . in a safe way. Nothing daring, nothing unusual. Perfectly acceptable for a small country dance.

Marigold had to stifle the urge to recommend she put on the Hemming sapphires instead of the understated jet necklace she'd chosen. Perhaps her persona was getting the better of her. But suddenly, she wasn't sorry she'd chosen the garden of a gown she had, nor that she'd piled her hair and woven a garland of ribbon, rhinestones, and roses through the tresses.

151

She may be overstated, but at least she wasn't boring. And if she was going to have to listen to Genie's insults regardless, she might as well have earned them.

Lady Hemming shot a hard look at her daughter. "I said the pearls."

"I know." Lavinia didn't look cowed as she touched the rhinestones. "I wasn't in the mood."

For a moment, the pair squared off, gazes locked in a silent battle of wills. Marigold had no idea who would win.

Apparently, the clock. It chimed, and the lady of the house spun away with hands in the air. "It hardly matters, given the limited company who will be here. Downstairs with you."

Marigold went with Lavinia, trailing behind her mother. She greeted the guests as they arrived, keeping her smile polite rather than bright, her face always turned down just a bit. She played the role she'd learned so well, the one she'd written for herself, and she wondered if that was what Lavinia was doing, too, in a way.

Trying to write the role she wanted to play. That of a strong, unaffected young lady. The sort ruled by reason, who would be master of her own circumstances.

Dear Lord, catch her, if so. Because that is a net full of holes. She knew that far too well.

For an hour, she moved about the room with practiced skill, dancing now and then—neither well enough to be a favorite nor poorly enough to be ignored. Noting everyone who came. Avoiding Genie for all but a few minutes during which she'd been informed that she looked like an overgrown bower and then grilled on why *Yates* wasn't in attendance.

Oh, how she missed the Genie who would laugh with her.

At the hour mark, she moved to the fringes of the room—stage two of the plan. Blend into the ornate wallpaper. Be forgotten.

At an hour forty-five, she slipped out of the ballroom,

into the corridor, and stole through the shadows until the music receded and the quiet of the family wing overtook her.

As she turned the corner that would take her to the rooms she knew least well—and hence wanted to investigate, as it was where Lavinia's parents kept all their accounts and files—she sucked in a breath.

Another figure moved along the corridor ahead of her, also dancing with the shadows. But when he crossed before a window, the moonlight showed his coat to be Coldstream red.

It seemed she wasn't the only one determined to do a little sleuthing while all the household was engaged with the ball.

TWELVE

omorrow, Merritt and Xavier would be taking temporary possession of a small, timeworn manor house five miles away—which meant that tonight was his last in Alnwick Abbey, at least that he could count on.

Merritt rolled his feet to make his steps quiet and even on the stone floor, keeping to the edges of the corridor, where the shadows were deepest. No one would miss him at the ball. He'd danced once already with each of the young ladies present and had been careful to make a show of coughing now and then and appearing a bit more worn after each round.

All right, so only part of that was feigned—but that was improvement, really. In London, it wouldn't have been feigned at all. Much as it pained him to admit it, his physician had been right about the fresh sea air.

Regardless, no one would think anything of him disappearing for a while to rest and recuperate. He would be back before the supper was served. In the meantime, he meant to make use of the preoccupation of absolutely every member of both staff and family and do the last bit of exploring he'd had on his agenda.

The rest of the house he'd already explored over the course

of the week. Every time a maid or footman noticed him in a new place and asked if perhaps he was lost, he'd given a vague smile and said he was only trying to get some exercise, to strengthen his lungs again—and then asked if it was all right for him to be in each particular section. Courteous, that's how he would appear if anyone reported his behavior.

Inquisitive, really. Because there'd been one section that the servants had told him he'd better not go. The family wing.

Understandable. Bachelor guests were certainly not to be permitted in the wing where the family—particularly their unmarried daughter—resided. But the family wing could also be where Lord Hemming kept records and correspondence that he wanted no one else to see. So to the family wing he went now.

Last night, he'd sneaked his way into Hemming's main study in the central part of the house—the one where he met with staff and other visitors. He'd found nothing of interest there, which meant this was his last hope.

Hope. A strange word to apply, since what he truly hoped was that there was nothing to be found. How difficult it was to prove a negative. To prove a man innocent. Especially when one wasn't entirely certain of the charges.

A moment after he turned the final corner, he paused, ears straining. Had those been footsteps behind him? He pressed his back to the wall and looked, but nothing met his gaze aside from the expected painting frames and alcoves with vases and artwork. Must have been his imagination. He continued, bypassing any door that was open, peeking quickly into the ones that were closed. Bedrooms, an old nursery, sitting rooms.

At the very end of the corridor, the knob to the last door refused to engage the tumbler, and he smiled into the night. Locked was a good sign.

He reached into his pocket and pulled out a ring of keys.

They were technically the keys to the weary abode called Hawkhill House, and the man who'd let it to them had handed the whole set over with a shrug and instructions to learn for themselves which fit which door. *"Only so many locks and so many keys,"* he'd said. *"Something's bound to fit."*

He had a point. There were only so many lock designs in the whole world, and only so many keys to turn them. One of these could well turn *this* knob, as well as a random one at Hawkhill. With another glance over his shoulder to guarantee he was alone, he started trying them, one by one.

On key number eleven, he struck gold. A *click* sounded, and the door opened for him when he turned the knob. A single glance told him he'd found a study or office of some kind, exactly as he'd been looking for. He slipped inside, eased the door shut again, and relocked it.

Not like the time he'd done the same in London—this wouldn't be like that at all. That had been reckless, foolish. How had he even had the gall to sneak into a room in broad daylight, with an entire household at the ready? Tonight was different.

His brows furrowed as he flashed his torch over the furniture. It smelled of mildew in here, of must and disuse. A thick coating of dust covered nearly everything. Clearly, this was *not* a well-used room.

A waste of time. He had better slip back out and . . . then what? Where else could he look? The earl's *bedroom*? That thought didn't sit well.

Then something caught his eye on the desk. Or rather, a lack of something. There were clean streaks, spots in the dust. He moved over to the desk to investigate and shone the light across the surface.

A ring of clean space, as if someone had set a cup down. A place where it was disturbed in a less-distinct fashion—

perhaps from papers? Two smudges on either side of that one, exactly where someone would have placed elbows had they been sitting in that old chair there.

So someone had sat here, probably for a while, if they'd come with sustenance. Reading something, perhaps. Why? There were many better places in the house to read—unless they hadn't wanted anyone else to know *what* they were reading. In which case, could that something still be in this room?

Did he even dare to look? Another would see evidence of him as surely as he was seeing it of them. But . . . ah. The handles of some of the drawers of the desk were already clean. He could simply walk in their footprints, so to speak, and see what they had seen.

He slid the slender, central drawer out first and found a collection of dry-rotted rubber bands, pens whose ink had probably turned to a crust long ago, and a wax seal with the letter *H* on it, along with a half-used stick of sealing wax. Nothing unusual or interesting there. Moving to one of the deep side drawers, there was more to sift through. Stacks of stationery and envelopes—all unused—a box of blank Christmas cards, a lined notebook without a single word in it.

Just desk things. Normal, ordinary desk things. Heaving a sigh, he stepped back and looked at the desk itself. It reminded him a bit of one of Uncle Preston's desks in its design and—yes! It even had the mark of the popular woodshop of a century past. A woodshop popularized in part because of the clever mechanisms they'd worked into many of their pieces. Drawers and sliders and even things like letter openers that would pop out when you pressed just the right way on just the right ornament.

He didn't go pressing willy-nilly. He moved his beam of light slowly over each of the swirls and flourishes in the wood, looking for any that were abnormally clean. Two possibilities met his eye, but the first, on the desktop, looked as though it was one of the letter-opener compartments, too small to hold anything more. He pressed the other instead, smiling when he heard a release of a metal clasp. He had to open the righthand drawer again and feel up above it, but his fingers met with a lowered piece of wood now instead of a smooth plane. He pulled another, smaller drawer out.

His breath caught when he saw the crisp white paper folded inside it. Unlike all that stationery and such, this looked new. He pulled it out, then paused when his light hit on something else, flat but glossy.

A photograph. He pulled it out, too, looking at it before he unfolded the white paper. A group of people standing before a half wall of stone, water behind them. There were no fewer than a dozen of them, men and women, their ages varied. All dressed in styles from decades ago.

His eyes snagged on one, a woman who bore a remarkable resemblance to Lady Lavinia. Or perhaps not so remarkable—it must be her mother. She was young, probably not yet married. The earl was certainly nowhere in the image.

He scanned the other faces, frowning. Was that King George? Not that he'd have been king at the time, but . . . no. The fellow looked very much like him, but not quite. No, he looked more like . . . like . . .

Merritt drew in a long, quiet breath. Not George—but his first cousin, William. Or rather, as his own people knew him, Wilhelm. Now *Kaiser* Wilhelm.

And that was no English lake or seacoast behind them. The towering columns of Mediterranean cypress trees said this photograph was taken somewhere in Europe—France or Italy, he'd have bet.

His teeth clenched. Hadn't the lady said on their first meeting that she'd never stepped foot out of England? She was clearly lying. But why? Nearly every nobleman he knew had traveled abroad at some point or another for holidays. Why would Lady Hemming insist she hadn't?

He flipped open the paper and discovered it to be a letter dated January of this year. It was short, only taking up half the sheet, and the signature read simply *CB*.

CB. Cornelius Ballantine, perhaps? Merritt returned to the top.

Dear Lord Hemming,

First allow me once more to extend my most sincere and heartfelt gratitude for all you have done for me in my career. It is my most fervent prayer that I can serve you and the Crown in a way befitting your faith in me, and it has been an honor to pursue the answers to the questions you put to me. I am proud to be so trusted.

To that end, I have applied myself most diligently to the tasks assigned to me and have made considerable inroads. I happened across the enclosed photograph while operating in the line of said duties. I am certain, knowing you and her ladyship as I do, that there is a simple and innocent explanation for this image, which contradicts all she has said about her history. I took the image from its home and send it to you in hopes that it provides a few of the answers that you need, despite the fact that I have not uncovered what in particular they may be.

I have also omitted mention of this in my official reports thus far. Please advise in how I ought to proceed on this matter before my next report at the end of the month, if possible.

That was it, other than the signature. But it hefted a new stone into Merritt's chest with each word. It certainly sounded like it was from Ballantine. And that the claim to have no foreign ties was not just a passing one made to Merritt but was a story Lady Hemming seemingly spread far and wide and perhaps even expounded upon, if their neighbor spoke of it in such terms.

But whatever business Ballantine had been about on Hemming's behalf, he had *not* made any mention of it in his last report. Perhaps Hemming had asked him not to. And if it was of a personal nature, this request for information, that might make sense, but . . . what had the nature of the investigation been? Something to do with Lady Hemming? With her appearance in this photo with German nobility and royalty?

Merritt's breath blustered out. With the way tensions had been rising between Germany and England for the last two decades, it wasn't exactly odd that she—or even they— would want to downplay or hide any past associations like that. It was possible she had made no mention of them to her husband, but he had somehow found out and was displeased, given his own role in anti-German politics.

Was it as simple as that? A lord concerned that his wife's past friendships could rear up and bite him?

Lord, may it be so simple. Though it wouldn't explain why Ballantine had gone missing. Maybe there was some clue in his previous reports that would make sense of it, with this new context. Though blast it all, he hadn't access to everything now. He would have to ask Gaines to make him copies, to sift through every report Ballantine had ever filed, every request for funds, every pound sent his way. There *must* be a clue somewhere.

Merritt read through the letter again, wishing he'd thought to bring pencil and paper of his own along so he could copy it word for word. He'd have had to be careful not to disturb any intact dust, but—

A noise at the door. He froze, switching off his light. A clattering at the knob sent his pulse skittering. Swiftly but silently, he replaced the photo and letter, eyes casting about in the darkness for a hiding place, lips moving in breathless prayer.

Before he could even get the hidden compartment reset, the door swung open, and another torch flashed on—which made no sense. Why didn't his captor simply turn on the lights proper? The beam struck him square in the eyes, making him wince and raise an arm.

"Lord Hemming is coming." The voice was barely a whisper, feminine and familiar. Lady Marigold? "Speaking to someone about 'fetching it,' and he bypassed his own room already. Quickly, quickly. Come."

He hadn't time to wonder why she was there, why she was helping. He had time only to return the compartment and follow her waving hand as she led him to the marble fireplace on the opposite wall.

What, did she think him St. Nicholas? That was no hiding place.

But she put her hand in a crevice he'd never have seen and pulled the whole fireplace out from the wall by a foot or so, just enough for him to slip into whatever space she'd opened. She squeezed in behind him and closed the fireplace again.

The light from her torch was just enough for him to see they were in some kind of tiny room, nothing in here but a bench, an empty pottery jar that looked old and dirt-caked, and a rusted metal can.

Lady Marigold set her torch on a brick shelf built into the wall, so that its light diffused through the small space, and pressed a finger to her lips.

He frowned, though he didn't dare to so much as breathe when he heard the study's door squeak open again, and the earl's voice, muffled through stone and brick, saying, "Find him first. If the wrong people get their hands on him and he spills the truth—"

"I know, my lord." The second voice was just as familiar, even the sympathy in its tone. Colonel May—speaking to Hemming in the selfsame way he'd spoken to Merritt when he delivered the news about his medical leave. "We'll find him."

Ballantine? Someone else? What truth was Hemming so afraid of?

Neither of them spoke again, and Merritt was forced to imagine any number of horrors—that the earl was noting disturbances in the room, that he was even now looking for them. Had the drawer's hinge and hook re-engaged properly? Had he—or Lady Marigold—left telltale footprints on the dusty floor? Could their light be seen through some crack?

He reached for the torch, but she shook her head, pointing to the seam in the wall. Leather strips were cleverly mounted on the inside, creating a perfect seal around the door. No danger, then, of the earl seeing their light. He wouldn't know they were here unless Merritt did something stupid, like cough.

Naturally, his throat tickled and his chest burned at the very thought. He swallowed it down, took a couple deep, slow breaths, and prayed for relief.

A priest hole. That's what this must be. He'd heard of such things, places where priests could escape to evade arrest when Catholicism was outlawed by Queen Elizabeth. Plenty of recusant families still practiced their faith in secret. Many had built hides for the priests who served them and other Catholic families. But he'd never seen such a place for himself.

It made sense, in a house with *Abbey* in its name. And it equally made sense that Lady Marigold, who'd no doubt spent countless hours here as a child, knew of it.

He just didn't know why she'd used such knowledge to save him from discovery.

The burning in his chest finally eased, and his throat relaxed.

Lady Marigold was paying him no mind. Her attention was on the door, as if staring at it would make what was happening on the other side visible to her. Sounds filtered through, though he couldn't quite place what they were. A drawer opening and closing, perhaps? Was Hemming reclaiming that photo and letter?

No—a jingle, like of coins. "There. This should cover the expenses and won't be linked to the office. Take care nothing enters the books, do you hear me? No records."

Lady Marigold glanced over at him, the lift of her brows saying, *Well, that sounds suspicious.* Or perhaps it was his own thoughts he was reading into her expression. Regardless, he could only incline his head in acknowledgment.

Footsteps. One set at first, then a few drawers sliding and thumping, then the second set of feet, presumably the earl's, going out the door, which slammed shut behind him.

Merritt held still for a full fifteen seconds and then indulged in a quiet cough.

Lady Marigold let out a long breath. "That was a bit too close."

And would have been far closer—as in, he'd have been discovered, most likely—if she hadn't come to his rescue. "Why did you help me?"

Her gaze shifted, the light in her eyes changing from the flat, society-lady look she usually wore to the glimpse he'd seen of her first in the park and then at the Tower, when she was with her lion. "Because you are clearly in need of a lookout, Sir Merritt. This is the second time I've caught you sneaking in Lord Hemming's private rooms, and what would happen had someone *else* come along first? I didn't fancy seeing you hiding under a chair with your eyes squeezed shut again."

All his air leaked out of him. "I thought you hadn't seen me." Which was ludicrous. "I'd prayed for a miracle."

Was that amusement sparkling in her eyes? It was hard to say, given the low light. "And you received one. I decided not to say anything, didn't I?"

Not exactly the miracle he'd expected, but a certain adage about beggars and choosers sprang to mind, so he would thank the Lord for it regardless. "Why?"

"Because you're clearly a man of principles, and I decided there must be a reason for you to have done such a foolish thing. And it must be a good one for you to have tried it again." She nodded toward the movable fireplace. "That certainly sounded questionable, I'll grant you that. What is it, do you think, that has him so afraid, and that he doesn't want any record of?"

"I don't know. But I've yet to come up with an innocent explanation." He glanced again at the small room scarcely big enough to hold them both. "Is this a priest hole?"

She nodded. "One of two hides we know about, though Lord Hemming is convinced there are more in the house yet to be rediscovered. This one bears the marks of Nicholas Owen. Have you heard of him?"

It sounded vaguely familiar, but that was likely just because it was a common enough combination of names. He shook his head.

"He was a master hide builder operating in the late 1500s up until his own capture and execution in the early 1600s. He worked closely with the Jesuits, who snuck priests into the country after Catholicism was made illegal."

"Fascinating." And it was. Or would be, had they not currently been hiding in one such hide. "As long as we can get out as easily as we got in."

The lady chuckled and felt around for a moment before pressing or pulling on something that created a soft *click*. She pushed on the wall, and it glided open again. "Lavinia and I used to love to play in here—until her parents caught us at it. I've never seen the two of them so furious! We'd apparently been eavesdropping on a sensitive conversation, though I couldn't for the life of me tell you what it had been about. We weren't truly listening; we were simply playing that we were hiding from rampaging Vikings."

"Let me guess—when your imagined Vikings forced open the door, you screamed, thereby being discovered."

"You can imagine our surprise when the door actually opened—our screams redoubled." She smiled at the memory, snatched her torch off the shelf, and led the way back out into the main chamber.

Merritt frowned at her back. "Lady Marigold . . . Why did you have an electric torch with you at a ball?"

She scarcely spared him a glance, looking instead at the desk she'd caught him at. "A lady never knows when she might be in need of light. I always keep one in my handbag." She held up the small beaded bag looped over one wrist.

He blinked at her. Many ladies carried such a reticule at all times, yes—he'd been thumped with several of them while dancing. But he'd assumed they kept . . . honestly, he'd never given a moment's thought to what they kept in there. Powder for their noses? A few coins? A needle and thread in case of a ripped seam?

Not torches. Definitely not torches. "What else do you have in there? Anything with which I can make a copy of a letter—assuming he didn't take it out with him again?"

"Of course, if we need it. Though I could probably memorize it faster than you could copy it."

"You're kidding." He'd done his fair share of memorization, first in school and then in the line of duty. It took considerable concentration and hours rather than minutes, reciting it over and again until it stuck.

"Circus folk aren't the only ones with whom I spent my childhood, if you recall. I was schooled by actors, too, who had me drill lines with them. I won't remember it forever, but long enough to get to safety before we stop to record. Where was this letter?"

He returned to the desk, his breath catching in relief when both the photo and the letter were still there. He handed them to Lady Marigold.

She looked at the photo first, just as he'd done, and frowned. "I thought she said she'd never left the country. Why would she lie?"

"The question of the hour." And it seemed he now had a co-conspirator to help him sort through it.

He hadn't thought to pray for such a thing. Certainly wouldn't have considered her a likely candidate. Yet the realization of it, that she was here, helping him, made an invisible weight lift from his shoulders. Xavier knew a bit and helped where he could without risk, but that *without risk* had always been an understood caveat. Merritt never would have asked him to go sneaking about with him.

She set the photo back in its place, exactly where it had been, and turned to the letter. She didn't read it as he'd done, but rather looked at it for a few seconds, then up at the ceiling. Back to the page, then up again. Paper, ceiling, paper, ceiling.

He didn't dare breathe another word lest he upset whatever process she was using. He simply waited for her to finish and refold the paper, put it back in its spot, and then he returned the desk to its original condition.

They slipped silently out of the room, and as he relocked the door with lucky key number eleven, he wondered how *she* had gotten in. In the London house, he'd assumed she knew where a key was stashed, but here too?

He'd ask her when it didn't feel dangerous to even whisper. The moment they started down the corridor, she took the lead, darting along at a pace faster than he'd have set. In a few minutes, they were back in the main part of the house, where the music from the ball provided what he deemed a nice security. "My lady—"

"Not yet. In here." She led him into the library, which was well lit and clearly an acceptable place for guests to come. In fact, a foursome was laughing in the corner over a game of cards, but their presence didn't seem to deter Lady Marigold. She waved a hello at them and kept on marching toward another table in the opposite corner.

Here she found paper and a pen in one of the table's drawers. She sat down and quickly scratched words onto the page, arranged just as the original letter had been. Only once she'd signed the *CB* did she look up again, that dull smile back on her lips. The one she never wore at her own house, where cassowaries and peacocks and ostriches strutted about and lions jumped on her.

Why did she don it here?

"There. All finished. Here you go, sir."

Merritt accepted the sheet she held out, held it to the light to see if the ink was dry enough, and then folded it. "Thank you, my lady." What now? He wanted to ask her a thousand things, but they could hardly have a conversation with that duo of couples right there.

"Shall we return to the ball?" She stood, clearly intending to do just that.

He nodded, though the moment they were out of the library, he said, "I'd like to talk to you before we go back in."

"You can talk to me *after*. Where the noise will drown out anything you say." She stayed a full step away from him rather than taking the arm he offered by rote. And moved in front of him as they approached the ballroom doors, so that she entered a full three steps ahead of him.

All right, then. They weren't to be seen as coming in together. That was fine. He simply followed in her wake as

167

she skirted the room, gliding around the edges of groups, even though he thought for sure it would result in her being hailed a dozen times.

But no. People looked at her, but never *at* her. Or rather, never at *her*. They looked at her headpiece. They looked at her gown. They offered smiles even vaguer than hers, nodded, perhaps lifted a hand in greeting. But no one spoke to her. No one, so far as he could see, even met her gaze.

He felt his brows go knotted and low. She outranked nearly every one of those ladies. She ought to be one of the most sought-after matches for any of the bachelors. Why did everyone look straight through her?

She was a perfectly nice girl. Not at all unpleasant to look at or speak to. Granted, one had to dig a bit to get beneath the plethora of feathers or flowers or sequins or whatever her decoration of choice was on a given day, but he'd found it to be worth the excavation. Why had none of her neighbors?

Chairs were set up all about the edges of the room in clusters of two, three, and four. She chose one on the end of an empty triad and looked out at the gathering, boredom on her face.

Merritt hesitated a moment and then moved to sit beside her. She shot him a look that had him taking the other end instead, leaving an empty chair between them. "Really?" he breathed.

"Appearances, good sir. Unless you want to find yourself engaged to me by morning." She delivered the words without even looking over at him, no tease on her face even though he'd heard it in her tone.

Well. He could look casual too. He leaned against the chair back, as relaxed as he ever was in his dress uniform. "How did you get into those rooms? Are there keys hidden?"

"I'm inclined to ask you the same thing. I saw the ring of keys you carried, but where did you get them?"

"They're for Hawkhill House." He let his gaze drift over the assembly. "I thought I'd see if any of them worked."

She breathed a laugh. "Decent chance, given the number you had on the ring, I suppose. There are only about a hundred locks in all the world, and seventy percent of them can be opened with the same master key." She opened her bag, drew out a key, and flashed it in her palm for a second before closing it back into the satin and beads again.

He would have liked to gape at her but didn't dare. "How . . . why . . . ?"

"Did you by chance see Harry Houdini when he was in London a few years ago? He'd enlisted the services of a few of the Caesar cousins for some of his shows. He shared the most amazing facts with them about locksmithing. For their own acts, you see."

That was how the famous escape artist got out of all the locks and chains? With *keys*? Didn't seem quite sporting. Though really, what else would it have been? Magic? "So you just carry around a master key?"

"Why not? A lady never knows when she may need entrance into a room."

She seemed to have a very different list of what a lady might need than his aunt and cousins did. "I suppose. Can we talk about that letter?"

She pressed her lips together for a moment, though her countenance reverted to unperturbed a moment later. "Ballantine was investigating something for the earl—something about Lady Hemming? Or at the very least, that's what he found. That she has contacts and history on the Continent that she's lied about."

"And now Ballantine is missing." He didn't know if she knew already, but if it was news to her, she didn't show it.

"That's what Genie said. But you can't think . . . ?"

"I don't want to think it. But I don't know what the

alternative is." He sighed and watched the dancers on the floor. Xavier had Lady Lavinia in his arms again, and they were both laughing their way through a waltz.

For a moment, only the notes of "The Blue Danube" spoke. Then Lady Marigold opened her fan and set it moving before her face. "You aren't actually interested in Lavinia, are you?"

He went stiff against the chair. "She's a lovely young lady."

"But?"

"But . . . no." Being in her company was no hardship, but he never found himself craving it when they were apart. She certainly didn't distract him from his true purpose in spending time with the Hemmings.

Lady Marigold simply tilted her head a bit to the side. "The letter, then. What do you intend to do about it?"

"Nothing, exactly. Not yet. I simply have some inquiries to make. And I'll send a copy of it to my investigators."

"Your investigators?" She glanced at him, somehow putting question in her fleeting gaze.

"Mm. Have you ever heard of the Imposters, Ltd.?"

A tilt to the other side, and one more look. "Funny you should ask. Genie just sent my brother to London to enlist their aid."

That's why Fairfax had returned so soon to the city? Interesting. He'd assumed something was up for vote in the House of Lords that he hadn't wanted to miss.

Well. The Imposters would be laughing over their good fortune with this one—hired to solve the same case by two different people. He would pray they'd find the answers for them all.

THIRTEEN

*Y*ates tossed the last pitchfork-full of dirty hay into the wheelbarrow, pausing to wipe the sweat from his forehead with his sleeve before he moved to the pile of fresh bedding waiting to fill Pardulfo's stall. "And you say he sent all this to us in London?"

His sister sat in Leonidas's stall across the aisle, the lion's enormous head in her lap, his eyes closed. She hadn't bothered pinning her braid up yet, so it hung over her shoulder and vanished into the mane through which her fingers stroked. "Three days ago, yes. It didn't arrive before you left, I take it."

"No." Which made him far more irritable than mucking a leopard's stall ever did. He tossed fresh hay into its place but then just leaned onto the pitchfork, thinking. "This is a new sort of wrinkle, isn't it? Both working for him anonymously as the Imposters, but also as his known ally? We're going to have to tread carefully. It would be too easy to slip up and reference something we oughtn't to have had time to receive yet as the Imposters, or mention as us something only they should know."

Marigold arched her brows, a smile playing on her lips. "Would you have preferred I let the earl catch him?"

He made a show of considering, even though it wasn't really a question. "Well, he *did* trounce me at racquetball last week before I left. I may carry a grudge."

"Challenge him to a highwire competition."

Yates snorted a laugh at the very thought and exited the leopard's stall. Franco had Pardulfo outside for his exercise at the moment, but they'd be finishing up any time now. "Better still—a stall-mucking race. I daresay I could whip both him *and* the duke's son at that. Put together, even."

Her chuckle sent a few of the parrots roosting in the rafters to squawking. "I daresay you could. One of your many surprising skills, your lordship."

He tipped an invisible hat to her. "You have a few yourself, my lady."

Usually such an observation made dimples wink to life in her cheek. Today it earned a sigh. Which made him frown. "Is something the matter? I mean, other than the Hemming questions? Or is it perhaps that?"

She shrugged and eased out from under Leonidas's head. The lazy lion's breathing didn't even hitch as she crawled over him and exited the stall, latching it behind her. "Partly that, no doubt. And partly . . . just worry. That I tipped my hand too much with him. Let him see too many of our cards."

Yates returned the pitchfork to its hook on the wall and returned to the wheelbarrow, taking its handles in his hands. When he was a boy, there'd been stable hands to do these jobs. Lads no older than he was, paid to do the lowliest, dirtiest work on the estate.

He'd helped then, too, because that meant he could lure Milo and Jax away from their work more quickly, and they could go and seek whatever entertainment awaited them that day. Watch the jugglers or the fire-breathers or the sword-swallowers.

And Mother would fuss and fret at him and tell him future earls shouldn't behave so.

Poor Mother. Her lessons never stood a chance against the allure of Father's diversions. But at least it meant that he knew how to do the very un-earl-like chores necessary to keep things running around here. Fairfax Tower wouldn't thrive, after all, on pedigree alone.

He considered his sister's concern as he wheeled the hay and manure out the door. "I would probably agree, had you done such a thing in London, where he knew you as nothing more than Lavinia's overdressed friend. But here?" He paused just outside the stables to toss a grin over his shoulder and motion with his head toward their rather unusual estate. "It isn't exactly a secret to him now that you're a little, shall we say . . . eccentric."

She lifted her chin in that way Genie always did and imitated her intonations as she said, "Whatever do you mean, *Yates*?"

He laughed and continued toward the compost pile. "Still. I *am* surprised you trusted him enough to reveal *anything* to him."

"You think I shouldn't?"

"Did I say that?" He upended the wheelbarrow and rolled it to the back wall of the stables and left it there, then took off the soiled gloves he'd been wearing and slapped them onto the stone window ledge. "From all we've learned of him, I can't see any reason *not* to trust him. I wouldn't unfold the intricacies of our limited liability company just yet, but, Marigold." He turned to face her, to look deep into her eyes.

She looked worried. Tired. As if, in his absence, she'd tried to hold the whole of Fairfax Tower on her shoulders, like she always did. He sighed and reached to slip an arm around her shoulders. Sometimes he wished he'd been born the elder. Perhaps then she wouldn't feel as though her entire life's work was to take care of him, of this, of theirs. "If you want to show someone a glimpse of who you truly are, then you absolutely should. I never liked that you've hidden yourself so fully behind this façade of yours—no matter how entertaining that façade may be. You still need to be *you*."

"I am." At his lifted brow, she said, "I *am*! Just not with everyone."

"Not with *anyone* who hasn't known you all your life—and even with those who have, like Lavinia, you insist on at least part of the façade. Maintaining appearances, offering excuses." He understood, he had agreed to it. But even so, he hated that they could never share their true concerns—and hence their true selves—with anyone but Gemma and Graham and the Caesars.

He tugged her against his side and pulled them both into a walk, back toward the house. Their guests would soon be arriving for luncheon, and he'd better wash the smell of barnyard off himself first.

And give some thought to the fact that the first and only person she'd ever *wanted* to be so honest with was a man, not another young lady her age. He did like Sir Merritt—and despite all their best investigating, they'd turned up absolutely nothing objectionable about him. If one were to list his virtues and faults in their files, his would be a most sterling dossier.

Even so, he'd have to watch him through different eyes from now on. Not as a client, not as a case. As a friend. As his *sister's* friend.

It made a world of difference, that lens.

"Now, back to all this new information the two of you gleaned, and which we as the Imposters will not now be privy to for days yet. That just won't do. The information itself—what we ought or oughtn't to know—we can sort through easily enough. But the timing. That's going to get frustrating."

174

"I was thinking about that. Why not write to him and say that Mr. A has traveled into the neighborhood for his own investigation? It would make sense—and you could provide him with a local address to which he can send his updates. We won't then be waiting for things to go all the way to London and back."

"Good idea. I can send him a note directly from here, saying Mr. A has just arrived in the neighborhood." He turned his head toward where the sea crashed its way onto the shore. "I do believe our client's health has improved already, don't you think?"

"He's been coughing a great deal less." Marigold pulled her shawl tight around her arms when a gust of air twirled around them and looked to the sea too. "What if his suspicions are right, Yates? What if Hemming is involved in something underhanded? I keep trying to tell myself that this thing with which he wanted no one to associate him is nothing *bad*. Nothing more than an old friend of the lady's that he wants to be kept secret for political reasons, but I don't know if I believe that." She turned troubled eyes on him. "Why don't I? I *should*, shouldn't I? He's one of Father's closest, oldest friends. We've known him quite literally our whole lives. I ought to trust him implicitly, by default."

"You worry this business has tainted us." He worried it, too, at least about her. His sister—his tightrope-walking, trapeze-swinging, Shakespeare-quoting sister—had once been all golden light and endless laughter. She'd been costumes and playacting and a mad whirl of colors and song.

But since Father died, since their reality collapsed about them like papier-mâché left out in the rain, Marigold had changed. All the pieces were still there, but rearranged. Only what served a purpose was kept. Anything that didn't was cut from her life, from her heart, from her personality.

Tightropes and trapezes—only for the stunts they must

pull in their work. Shakespeare and song—only if she needed to trot out a quotation or a lyric at a dinner party. Costumes and playacting—only to convince the world that she was this figment whom Gemma had dubbed Lady M.

She drew in a long breath and pulled away from his arm. "I worry that I don't know how to believe the best of anyone anymore. That soon I'll start doubting Lavinia and her mother and Genie . . . and then what? Will I even wonder if I can trust Gemma and Graham? James?"

"Me?" He met her gaze with a wink. "Just pointing out that you'd done a regular *reductio ad absurdum* there, sister mine. You'll never question those of us you love most dearly. But the others—specifically Hemming—maybe you *should* question. Maybe we'd all be wiser, maybe fewer people would be hurt, if we questioned more. If we didn't think that closing our eyes to darkness meant it didn't exist. As if by closing them, we didn't just create more darkness."

She shivered, but he suspected it wasn't due to the wind. "Sometimes when I look back on our childhood—our charmed, picturesque, ridiculous childhood—I can't believe we've come to this. Spying on our neighbors. The people who should have been our friends, our peers. But then other times, I look at all this, and I wonder where else it possibly could have led." She shifted, squaring her shoulders, turning to meet his gaze. "We're doing good, aren't we? We're seeking justice and truth. Finding answers for people who otherwise have nowhere to turn."

"And feeding a few big cats and Romani vagabonds and ourselves in the process." Yates gave a decisive nod. "The truth isn't always pretty. But I like to think it's always beautiful."

Her lips twitched up. "Should I stitch that onto a sampler and hang it on our wall?"

"Would you? I *would* love to see my own wisdom dangling there before me day in and day out." He chuckled and bumped their shoulders together. "Whatever the truth is about Hemming, it doesn't change who *we* are. Who Father was."

"I don't know. I think the truth *always* changes us. I think it always should." She leaned in for one long moment and then turned again toward the house. "I'm glad you convinced Gemma to come home with you."

He chuckled. "Oh, it didn't take any convincing. Graham kept 'just stopping by because he was in the neighborhood' and to update me on what he'd learned by trailing Colonel May. I tried to be conveniently absent a few times, hoping they would talk, but that didn't work so well. I think she decided a tactical retreat was the only way to avoid him."

Sorrow overtook her face. "I wish she wouldn't. I wish they would work things out—heal, together. I wish we could all sit down like we used to, the four of us. The Imposters— would-be circus troupe turned private investigators." She chuckled, no doubt remembering their brazen plans to pretend to be commoners so they could enjoy the life they wanted. Imposters indeed. Just not in the usual sense.

"We'll have those days again. They can't stay like this forever." Her look said she doubted it, but it was a concern they'd given up voicing.

And they had concerns enough for today.

Marigold didn't mean to pay more attention to the gentlemen at their sport than the ladies' conversation. It was simply that the ladies' conversation was absolutely dull and the gentlemen were engaged in a rather competitive game of football on the back lawn. Yates and Sir Merritt had teamed up against Lord Xavier and Franco, and they turned out to be rather evenly matched.

Poor Penelope was at loose ends, with both her favorite people darting around so crazily. She'd resorted to jumping between Marigold's shoulder and the tea table—empty of tea, thankfully—as she watched the game.

Lavinia pulled her chair a bit closer to Marigold's. "You seem awfully intent on the game. Are you wishing you were out there with them? Or perhaps simply . . . admiring a certain view?"

The tease in her friend's voice had a new note to it, one that said she was speaking of something far more novel than Marigold's inclination toward physical activity. "I don't know what you mean."

The look Lavinia sent her said she *should*. "I saw you two at the ball the other night, you know. Sitting together. Talking. I believe you were even spotted writing something for him in the library—what was that? A love note?"

It took no great acting skills to roll her eyes at that one. "Yes, Lavinia, I was penning him a love note in your library while he watched."

Lavinia laughed. "Well, what then?"

She shrugged. "I was only copying something I'd just read for him."

"Boring. Utterly boring." Lavinia made to lean toward the table, but when Penelope jumped on it again, hooting over whatever she perceived to be happening on the pitch, her friend adjusted and leaned back instead. "At least tell me it was some obscure Shakespearean sonnet that spoke of love and hearts and souls."

"It was some obscure Shakespearean sonnet that spoke of love and hearts and souls," she recited, voice flat and even. Though a smile won at least the corners of her lips when Lavinia laughed. "I don't know why you're so set on reading into my very limited exchanges with Sir Merritt when you're convinced that love and romance are for the weak of heart."

"No, no. I said only that *I* have no desire to be ruled any longer by my heart. I have absolutely no problem at all with *you* falling prey to the whims of affections."

A snort of laughter sneaked out. "My, when you put it like *that* . . ."

On the pitch, Sir Merritt executed a rather spectacular dodge of Franco, the ball seeming to obey his will as much as his feet, and then passed it to Yates, who with one mighty kick sent it hurtling toward the goal. Lord Xavier made a flying lunge for it and missed. Yates and Sir Merritt both whooped, while Franco offered a hand to pull Lord X back to his feet. The side of his once-cream-colored clothing was streaked with green.

Lavinia chuckled. "It's a good color on him."

Marigold certainly didn't envy his valet—or whatever village laundress his valet hired—the task of getting those stains out. She did *not* point out that her friend's gaze followed Lord Xavier a bit more than it should if she was as disinterested as she claimed.

She was only glad Lavinia didn't seem fascinated with Sir Merritt—since his court was no court at all, merely investigation. Not because of any interest on *her* part.

He was becoming a friend, yes. But that was all. All she could allow, and certainly all he would be interested in anyway.

Apparently growing bored of watching the game, Lavinia let out a gusty exhale and glanced over at where Gemma and Claudia were talking and laughing together on the other side of the monkey-filled tea table. "Did you not invite Genie today, or could she not join us?"

Claudia answered before Marigold could. "Have you forgotten, my lady? Mr. Ballantine's birthday garden party is three days hence. Miss Ballantine will be helping her mother with all the preparations, given that the entire county will be in attendance."

Lavinia wrinkled her nose. "*We* won't be."

"You won't?" Marigold frowned. True, Lavinia hadn't attended the Ballantines' annual party in recent years, but she'd assumed it was because of her health, and that her parents had begged off to care for her. The look on her friend's face said otherwise.

"Of course not. That horrible thing is packed with riffraff, you know. They invite *everyone*."

By *riffraff* she meant merchants and teachers, solicitors and bankers. Perfectly respectable people, just without title or estate. Marigold's blood warmed in her veins. "Are you afraid there will be Gypsies and vagabonds there to steal you away?"

She didn't, obviously—the Ballantines would never invite as guests people who most of society deemed true riffraff. But it did rather beg the question of how Lavinia viewed the Caesars if she sneered so at the middle classes.

At least her friend had the grace to flush. "That's not what I mean. But you needn't take that high moral tone with me, Marigold. The Caesars were hired entertainment and are now hired help. Domestics. Servants. They are not *guests*."

No. They were far more. They were family.

"And I don't know why you're looking at me like that. It isn't as though *you* ever go to the Ballantines' party."

True, but only because they were usually already in London this time of year, for the Season. "Well, I'm going this year."

When Lavinia got that particular tilt to her chin, she was very nearly as insufferable as Genie. "You needn't act as though you'll be doing them any favors. It isn't as though G. M. Parker will be there to report on it and make them famous."

Marigold was careful to keep her gaze from flicking to Gemma. Claudia may know that her cousin was the columnist, but the Hemmings didn't—and wouldn't. "One never knows. I do believe she was issued an invitation."

"As if she'd leave London for *that*. A tiresome all-day affair in the remotest part of the country."

"Stranger things have happened," Gemma said, her tone offhanded but her eyes glinting. No doubt because she knew that Lavinia deemed *her* "riffraff," too, and Claudia as well. Acceptable as paid companions, yes. As guests, no.

Lavinia directed her gaze back to the pitch. "Regardless, I'm not going. I have no doubt that Genie will have invited all her pretentious friends from that awful finishing school she went to, and I can't abide the lot of them."

Marigold exchanged an amused look with the cousins. "There is nothing wrong with her finishing school, Lavinia, other than that it is the rival of your own."

Lavinia's eyes still glinted, but at least with a touch of fun now. "They are *hardly* our rivals. They admit anyone with coin enough and have wretchedly low standards. Ravenscleft, however, is one of the best schools outside of Switzerland, and certainly the best in the north."

Claudia rolled her eyes, the same color blue she shared with Gemma. "I seem to recall you crying when your mother informed you that would you be attending Ravenscleft instead of one of the Swiss châteaus, my lady."

"Only because I didn't understand the choice at the time. All I knew was that the other young ladies of my station went abroad. But in retrospect, I'm glad they made the choice for me that they did. I don't know how they knew it would be superior to a Swiss education, but it certainly was."

Or at the very least, Lavinia was certainly biased. Marigold buried a smile and let her gaze wander back to the football game when the shouts from Franco and Lord Xavier signaled they'd yet again tied the score.

Claudia, being Claudia, took that "I don't know how"

as an invitation to solve the mystery. "Oh, but there was some sort of personal or family connection, wasn't there? Your mother knows the headmistress. What was it? Are they cousins? Third or fourth? Or perhaps they went to school together."

Lavinia's look of patience was exaggerated. And annoyed. "Don't be ridiculous. Mother has no German relatives; she's never been abroad. And Miss Feuerstein didn't attend school in England. Her credentials were on the wall of her office for all to see."

Claudia frowned. "I am quite certain I heard your mother refer to the headmistress in familiar terms."

Lavinia blinked. "You're mistaken."

Claudia opened her mouth again, poised to argue the point—Claudia not only loved to be the source of information, but she also *hated* having it contradicted—but Gemma silenced her cousin with wide eyes and a shake of her head.

It wasn't always enough to make Claudia button her lips, but this time she obeyed and pasted a flat smile to her lips. "As you say. I must be misremembering."

She wouldn't be. Claudia remembered gossip and society connections like Marigold remembered lines from plays. If she said there was a personal connection between Lady Hemming and Miss Feuerstein, then there was.

A personal connection to a woman with a very German-sounding name. Her gaze tangled with Gemma's. Perhaps this was the connection they'd been searching for.

FOURTEEN

"*A*h-ha! Here it is. I *knew* the name sounded familiar."

Marigold lowered the newspaper she'd been hunting through and turned to where Gemma had pulled out a box of magazines. Specifically, the most recent issues of the *London Ladies Journal*, from the looks of it. Not surprising that she had those, given that each edition would have a column of hers in there. "What have you found?"

"An advert. Ravenscleft always has one in here. See?" She flipped the magazine around on the library's table so that Marigold could see the colorized drawing of a beautiful old manor house surrounded by lush greenery.

Ravenscleft. The premiere school for young ladies, wherein they shall learn etiquette and deportment, French and Latin and German, and the basics of mathematics, science, and literature, so as to be able to uphold their end of any conversation with today's leading gentlemen.

Not exactly a catchy motto, but they couldn't *all* have quips like "Discreet Disclosures for the Most Discerning." Marigold tapped one of the words. "They teach German—that's unusual, isn't it? Don't finishing schools in England usually focus solely on Latin and French?"

"One of the things that sets it apart, I suppose." Gemma was flipping through another of the magazines. "Though I didn't realize Lavinia spoke German."

"She's rather rubbish at any foreign language." Marigold grinned. "Not unlike you. I daresay she learned enough to pass her exams and then promptly forgot it all."

Gemma stuck her tongue out at the barb to her own lack of linguistical prowess. "Some of us focus on mastering the *English* language. If I can turn a phrase in my mother tongue to stick with my readers, then I am a happy writer, my dear Lady M."

Marigold chuckled and turned back to the advert, which had several lists of classes and a few endorsements from families of graduates. *"I can imagine having sent my darling daughter nowhere else. Now she is truly fit for her new title of Lady L—!"*

Funny, that. "How to Catch a Titled Husband" wasn't listed as one of the classes, yet everyone knew that was the primary goal of these sorts of schools.

"Here!" Gemma smacked the issue she'd been flipping through onto the table overtop the other she'd shown Marigold and jabbed a finger at a smaller black-and-white advert. "I *knew* I'd seen something else from them in last week's edition."

"Well, move your finger and let me see." She brushed her friend's hand aside and read the words that had garnered such enthusiasm.

Miss Feuerstein of Ravenscleft Academy for Young Ladies was holding a series of interviews for the position of French teacher. Qualified individuals could apply in person, with references, on this coming Friday; those who passed the first round of interviews would be invited to stay overnight at the academy and participate in the final interview with the headmistress on Saturday. Final decisions would be made

Saturday afternoon, and the new tutor would be invited to take up residence at once.

Gemma's fingers did a jig on the tabletop. "How perfect is that? I can go and do a bit of snooping under the guise of applying for the position. I don't know how else we'd ever get inside. The place is a fortress."

Marigold sent her a long look. "You. Apply for the position of *French* teacher?"

Gemma lifted her brows. "I only need to get on the grounds."

"No, you need to be able to pass those first interviews so that you'd be there overnight to poke about when everyone is abed. Which means *I* need to go. *You* need to attend the Ballantine's birthday bash as me and report it in the next *Journal*."

Gemma sighed, but the purse of her lips said she knew it was the better plan. "Dratted French. Aunt Priss warned me that I would regret my inattention. Now *you* get to have all the fun, simply because Zelda taught you so well."

It did come in handy, having a Romani here who had spent her childhood in Paris before she married into the Caesar family. Marigold grinned. "If it makes you feel better, you get to compose a few falsified references for me."

Gemma's eyes lit. "That *will* be fun. And we'll plan your wardrobe. A bit less daring than usual, though *I* may just wear the rainbow hat to the Ballantines'." She frowned. "It's a bit risky, that. People around here know us both."

"And if anyone looks closely and sees it's you, they'll just laugh that you've borrowed my hat. But no one will." She'd proven that well enough at the Hemmings' ball, hadn't she? Other than Lavinia herself, no one paid her a stitch of attention. No one spoke to her, no one even met her gaze. And since Lavinia wouldn't be at the birthday party, that meant the only true danger would be Genie. "We'll just have to enlist Yates's help with Genie."

"Cruel sister." Gemma winced on Yates's behalf. And chuckled. "I can do it. I've been practicing my Lady M walk, you know." She turned from the table and glided about the room with the posture she'd first helped Marigold perfect—a walking mannequin, every movement elegant but specifically geared toward drawing attention to her gown instead of her face.

A bit more of a challenge for Gemma, whose face was far more striking than Marigold's, but supply her with a hat with a wide enough brim and she'd be set. "Beautifully done."

Gemma curtsied her thanks.

Commotion from the front doors inspired Marigold to sweep all of the *Journals* back into their box and nudge it under the table. She would share their thoughts and work through the details of the plan with Yates later, but she certainly didn't need Lord Xavier or, even worse, Sir Merritt wondering at her sudden interest in Ravenscleft Academy for Young Ladies.

Tritone laughter drew her from the library and toward the foyer. She heard Yates laugh often, yes. But usually with Hector and Franco, or James and Graham. He didn't really have any more true friends among the aristocracy than she did, so it was striking to walk into view and see him getting on so famously with a duke's son and an earl's presumed heir.

It made an odd little something *thwang* through her heart like an arrow.

It had been one thing for *her* to decide never to show her true self to society, to relegate herself to having no true friends outside of the ones she grew up with here. She'd made the choice when she was already grown, when she had already tasted a bit of society and realized she never quite fit, that she was relegated to the sidelines and overlooked by one and all.

Why not, then, do something different? Why not shock with her clothing and keep her personality cloaked?

Yates, though . . . Yates had the potential to be well loved by all. She ought to encourage him more to seek that out. To make friends. There was no reason he couldn't. They'd never tried to secure the same anonymity for him that they did for her. It would have been useless, given his responsibilities in the House of Lords.

And these two were a good place to start. Sir Merritt and Lord Xavier both genuinely seemed to like her little brother—proving they had excellent taste. And now that they had their own residence, they were staying longer at the Tower than they had when they arrived with Lavinia, it seemed. This was the third day in a row they were still here hours after Lavinia and Claudia had returned to Alnwick Abbey.

For a moment, her stomach turned at the financial ramifications of all these guests. They'd been serving tea and luncheons and dinners to far more people than usual since they came home. And even though no one batted an eye at country fare being simpler than what fine houses would be expected to serve in London during the Season, she knew it would be stretching Drina's culinary abilities. But she'd been rising to the challenge. And the food budget wasn't completely depleted yet.

Praise God for the fees from Genie.

Sir Merritt looked up, spotted her, and smiled. Which made her stomach turn in a whole different way. Less a turn. More a . . . flip. Not unpleasant, exactly, but not precisely welcome either. *Friends* shouldn't make one's stomach flip.

But it wasn't *him* so much as his attention. That must be it. She wasn't accustomed to anyone but her brother really noticing her. The fashions that earned her the vague regard of the ladies tended to put off the gentlemen, which was fine by her.

But she wasn't wearing so many of them here at Fairfax Tower. Maybe that was why Sir Merritt slid her way with no reservations, those startlingly blue eyes of his shining a greeting. "How was your morning, my lady?"

She let herself smile. "Considerably less grass-stained than yours." For a moment, she debated mentioning the lead about the finishing school . . . but no. Much as she found herself wondering what his thoughts would be, that was something that she'd be investigating as an Imposter, which meant Marigold couldn't well talk about it yet. Not until the Imposters reported whatever she discovered to him, and he then chose to share it with her.

Yates was right—this was convoluted and could easily get confusing.

"My condolences to you on that." He grinned, which he didn't do nearly often enough. It turned his face from chiseled to boyish.

Lionfeathers. Her stomach flipped again.

"Dare I ask what you ladies spent your morning talking about? Feathers and lace? The latest shoes from Paris?"

"Don't be silly. We were far too busy talking about *you*."

She couldn't have said why, but seeing his neck and ears go red made her feel as though she'd gotten even for the stomach-flipping he'd caused. She laughed. "Well, not *only* you, if that makes you feel better."

He glanced over at Lord Xavier and seemed to calm a bit. "Not even primarily, I daresay. Not with those two about."

"You seem to take comfort in that notion, so I won't disabuse you of it." Sensing Gemma coming up behind her—and definitely sensing the finger she poked into Marigold's back—she cleared her throat and said, "I don't believe you've met my companion yet, have you? She only just returned from London."

Sir Merritt shifted his gaze to Gemma. Though not, interestingly, until Gemma held out a hand and said, "Miss Gemma Parks. How do you do, Sir Merritt?"

He took her hand, gave a cursory bow over it. "Very well, thank you, Miss Parks. And yourself?"

"Happy to be back in Northumberland for a few weeks."

"I find I'm quite enjoying it here myself." At which he directed his smile to *Marigold*.

Lionfeathers. And leopard stripes too.

She was more than a little grateful when Drina saved the day by stealing their guests' attention. She obviously wasn't paying any mind to the fact that they had guests, or she would have come down the stairs like a normal person. But her eyes were glued to the small book in her hands, and so she defaulted to her not-normal-person way of getting downstairs. She hooked an arm around the two-story-high silk suspended from the ceiling, hopped onto and off of the railing on the first-floor landing, wrapped one ankle around the silk, too, and slid down to the ground floor.

Of course, it didn't *look* as simple as all that. It looked graceful and beautiful and gravity-defying, and both Lord Xavier and Sir Merritt fell silent and just gaped at her.

Marigold had reacted similarly the first time she saw such a feat. "That would be Drina, sister to Hector and Franco. Amazing, isn't she?"

Sir Merritt blinked and shook himself, angling a half smile down at her. "Can you do that?"

He was joking. And would no doubt think she was, too, as she replied, "Why, can't you?"

He chuckled. "Yours has to be the most interesting manor house in all of England, my lady."

The man knew how to pay a compliment. "I daresay you're right about that."

His smile held as Yates declared it time for lunch and led the way to the dining room—not apparently thinking to offer his guests rooms to tidy up in after their football match—and Sir Merritt offered Marigold his arm.

She'd refused it the other night at the Hemmings' ball, as much for her own peace of mind as for appearances. But it seemed entirely different to refuse it now, in her own home, when there were no appearances to be preserved.

Peace of mind was overrated anyway. She rested her hand on his forearm and smiled.

He leaned down a bit as they walked. "I've been meaning to tell you—I heard from my investigator. The Imposters. It appears that his own research has led him into the area as well. He was quite glad to have the information we sent him."

We. Was he really thinking of her as so fully involved in his own search? And should that make her chest swell? She kept her own voice as quiet as his. "I'm glad of that. Did he have anything else to report to you yet?"

"He has dispatched someone to the Continent, it seems." He sounded impressed. "I will be curious what he uncovers. In the meantime, I hope to hear from a colleague soon."

She frowned now as she had when he'd told her the day after the ball that he meant to have a friend look more deeply into Ballantine's past activities and reports. "You're certain you can trust this fellow not to mention anything to Lord Hemming or Colonel May?"

"Quite. He's never seen eye to eye with his lordship, and he and May have butted heads a few times—Lieutenant Gaines is navy. But he's a good chap."

Lieutenant Gaines. She didn't *mean* to dig through her mental files to try to put an identity to the name. It had simply become natural.

FROM THE DOSSIER OF
Lieutenant Ronald Gaines, Royal Navy

HEIGHT: *5′11″*

WEIGHT: *12 stone*

AGE: *31*

HAIR: *Middling brown, military cut*

STYLE: *Rarely seen out of uniform, and even if so, his clothes have military precision*

PRIMARY RESIDENCE: *Hammersmith, London*

OBSERVANCES: *Lt. Gaines is generally devoted to his wife and two small children, though he has a weakness for gambling. No great debts; he seems to enter the hells with a budget and sticks to it, amazingly enough. But he plays every Monday and Thursday and loses as much as he wins. His wife thinks he spends those hours with his brother and cousin, discussing books.*

IMPRESSIONS: *His discipline is rather astounding, given his vice. Perhaps because he doesn't pair it with the other vice of drinking.*

NOTES: *His wife has her own little secrets, and she carries them in a sterling silver pill case. Does he never wonder at why she's glassy eyed so often? Fortunately, she employs a nanny to see to the children.*

It had been, if she recalled correctly, one of his gaming companions they'd actually been investigating, but they'd ended up following the Gaines couple about for a few days to verify they weren't involved in the embezzlement scheme.

She was willing to believe that Lieutenant Gaines was as trustworthy as Merritt said. And she had no desire to reveal the family's secrets to him—that would forever change how he looked at his colleague, as Marigold knew firsthand.

But she'd also mention his source to Yates so that the Gaineses' weaknesses couldn't be used against them.

To Merritt now, she simply nodded.

He led her around to her usual chair and pulled it out for her. "Please feel free to say no, but . . . have you by chance learned anything from your friend or perhaps her chaperone that could explain any of this away?"

It was that *away* that sealed it. Had he just said "explained it," then loyalty to Lavinia would have forbidden her, as Lady Marigold, from saying a thing.

But he clearly *wanted* to find an innocent explanation. And there could yet be one. Foreign connections did not equal treason, after all. Hiding them could simply be for political reasons. She looked up into his eyes, using the cover of the others' laughter to say, "Perhaps. Claudia mentioned this morning that she thought she'd heard mention at one point of Lady Hemming having a German cousin. Lavinia thinks her mistaken. Perhaps you could pass it along to your Imposters."

His eyes lit. "I shall. Thank you." Those eyes softened again. "And I don't mean to ask you to betray your friend's trust."

"I know. And I wouldn't."

But if Lavinia's parents were lying, and if the reason *wasn't* innocent, then Marigold needed to know. She needed to be able to protect Lavinia. She needed to give her time to recognize that her heart wasn't her enemy, to help her dare to trust it.

Especially since that heart wasn't, for some reason, inclining toward *him*.

Lionfeathers. Marigold reclaimed her gaze and sat. She wasn't nearly so not interested in Sir Merritt as she wished.

FIFTEEN

When Merritt had first chugged his way into the Alnwick train station on his way up from London, he hadn't been particularly impressed. It had been a drizzly, chilly day that had made him question the wisdom of coming so far north. Today, the sun beamed its splendid smile onto the earth, and the half-century-old stone building struck him as charming and cheery.

He glanced to the clock and tried to calculate how much longer it would be before the train from London chuffed into the station. It should have been here by now, but clearly it wasn't running with the same discipline of at least one of its passengers.

Gaines was taking the family into Scotland for a few days' holiday and had wired Merritt that they'd pass through Alnwick on his way to Edinburgh so that he could hand off some information.

Only convenience? Possibly. Or it could well be that it was information he didn't trust to the post or, even worse, the telegraph wires, and so wanted to hand-deliver it.

Merritt did hope the train would hurry. The daylong party at the Ballantines' estate was already in full swing, and he was eager to get to it. According to Lady Lavinia's rather snobbish commentary, none of the Hemmings would be going, but "Lady Marigold *insists* she will, probably out of pity for what the family is suffering with their questions about Cornelius."

Xavier had begged off, more because he'd pulled a muscle in his back yesterday during their too-enthusiastic exploration of the Fairfax gymnasium than because of Lady Lavinia's absence—probably. But Merritt intended to be there. To learn more about the Ballantines and their connection to Lord Hemming, if possible.

And to spend a bit more time at Lady Marigold's side, regardless.

Not that he'd declared *that* intention to anyone. Not to X—though the look his friend had sent him said he suspected the motivation—and certainly not to Marigold herself. That would be akin to announcing he was courting her. Which he wasn't. Because he was fairly certain she'd have refused him if he tried. More than once in their conversations with the group, she'd intimated that she meant to spend the rest of her life at Fairfax Tower, "annoying her brother and keeping the circus running." By which she meant caring for the performers-turned-staff and the menagerie of animals.

He shouldn't find that so blasted alluring, should he? He'd never even thought of himself as an animal person, particularly. A few dogs when he was a lad, but not since he'd bought a commission. Yet he found himself looking forward to his near-daily visits to the lion's den. Or stall, as it were.

A train huffed and puffed its way into the depot, but not the right one. This train was coming from the north, not the south. He sighed and checked his own watch against the station's clock. Both agreed—Gaines's train was nearly an hour late.

Only a few passengers trickled off the southbound. Two elderly women, one middle-aged man, a young mother with a sleepy toddler and a maid in tow. Even fewer people had emerged from the building or stood from the benches to board. Two adult women who he'd guess to be mother and daughter, a brown-habited friar, and a slender young woman dressed in serviceable grey.

He looked away, then back again, narrowing his eyes. That girl in the grey—was that . . . ? No, it couldn't be Lady Marigold. Lady Marigold would never be caught in public in a plain dress more suited to a maid or governess than an earl's sister. Nor a hat without a single feather or flower or ribbon. And Lady Marigold certainly wouldn't be boarding a southbound train when she was scheduled to attend a birthday party for a neighbor.

Except that it *was* Lady Marigold. She didn't move like her, and she didn't wear her clothes, but it was without question the very face that he'd been studying more than he was ready to admit beneath that boring straw hat—and disappearing now into the train.

He nearly followed, at least to scour the windows and try to get her attention, but the long-awaited northbound train whistled its approach. Merritt still took a step toward the southbound, but no familiar faces appeared in the windows he could see, and a moment later, its own whistle was calling out.

He blinked, shook his head, and turned to wait for the incoming train. Maybe it was his imagination. Maybe he'd just been thinking about the lady even more than he'd realized, and he'd summoned up her face on a stranger's form.

Except that it was *her* form. Not her usual way of moving, but her form. Her height, her slender figure. He would bet that had he taken that girl's arm, he'd have felt the toned muscles again.

Less of a mystery, that one, now that he'd met her brother and seen her gymnasium. He'd yet to catch her in there, but that must be the explanation for her physique.

A Beautiful Disguise

Bother. He hadn't planned on returning to Hawkhill House between his meeting here with Gaines and the Ballantines' party, but perhaps he would. Just to give Xavier the chance to tell him he'd lost his mind and was obviously too preoccupied with the oddities that were Lady Marigold Fairfax.

"Livingstone, hello!"

"Gaines!" Merritt swung around, chiding himself for yet again staring after the southbound train, looking for Marigold in one of the windows, instead of having been hunting for his colleague in the crowd debarking from the northbound. He spotted the chap easily enough, even with him out of uniform, and greeted him with a lifted hand and smile.

They exchanged how-do-you-dos, and Gaines pointed to one of the benches against the building. "I'm afraid I have only as much time as it takes the locomotive to refill its water tanks and take on a bit more fuel, so forgive me for not inquiring at length about your health. You look better, though. Yes?"

"Much improved." Merritt followed him to the bench and took a seat, barely even smiling at the claim of not asking, followed so quickly by doing just that. "But by all means, we can skip the formalities, given the circumstances. You have news concerning Ballantine?"

Gaines's face was as stony as the building behind them. "Would that I didn't—or not this particular news, at any rate. He's dead."

"What?" Merritt felt as though his breath had been snatched from his lungs, but pneumonia wasn't to blame this time. Yes, he'd known it was a possibility. It was *always* a possibility. But he'd thought it far more likely that the young man had been arrested, or even that he'd simply fallen out of communication as he chased a lead somewhere.

Gaines opened his attaché case and pulled out a photo-

196

graph. A man's form, lying on the ground. He wore a dirty and ripped suit of clothes—not his uniform—but the profile looked vaguely familiar. Cornelius Ballantine.

"It was only by chance that we could identify him before he was buried in a pauper's grave. Or, well, not quite chance. I had men out looking for him, thanks to your questions. Had they not been, we'd never have known *what* became of him, I daresay."

Merritt's throat was hot and dry. "What did happen? Were you able to piece it together?"

If anything, Gaines's face went even stonier. "I had his friends and fellow officers questioned at length. He'd been missing for weeks, but everyone knew he'd been given special tasks, so it wasn't reported. Everyone assumed he was about NID business, as he'd been several times before. He was last seen in Berlin."

"Berlin? Why?"

"No one knew."

Merritt studied the photograph in his hands, even though he didn't want to, searching it for evidence of the man's death. "When was this taken?" He was careful to keep it tilted so that none of the few passersby could see.

"Last week."

Merritt looked up again. Gaines was nodding. "I know. A long time missing to only *just* turn up dead. We can only assume he'd been detained by the German authorities, likely on charges of espionage. And we have no way of knowing what he may have told them about *our* operations."

Merritt lifted a hand to rub over his face. "Has this made it through official channels yet? Will his family be learning of it now?"

"Not yet. I'd expect news to make it here officially by next week."

"Good. I'm glad the news won't reach them today. It's his

father's birthday." Merritt let his eyes slide shut. Right now, the Ballantines were worried, yes. But they still had hope. Enough to enjoy the celebration of the patriarch's life. He wouldn't take that from them, not in a million years. They needed what sunshine they could bottle before this storm unleashed its fury upon them.

"Poor chap." Gaines sighed and handed over a manila envelope. "Here are the reports. Those copies are for you, so read them at your leisure. But do pay especial attention to the 'Other Cases' section."

That made Merritt's brows rise even as his stomach sank. "Other cases?"

"I was disturbed enough by how long Ballantine was absent without anyone questioning it that I went through all the rosters, within all the branches. Well, I started it before we knew what had happened to him, hoping that I'd find this wasn't at all unusual, and that the men usually resurfaced on their own."

"And?"

Gaines sighed, his gaze latched onto the train. "I did find others who had similarly gone silent within the last few months, across the branches, when there was no particular mission to account for it. All on the Continent, mostly in Germany."

Merritt had to force a swallow. "How many?"

"Three."

Three men, three soldiers, lost to the enemy in a time of peace. Three of them gone because of the clandestine work they'd been asked to do. His hand drew into a fist against his leg. "This would never have been allowed to happen if there were a central command keeping track of them all. We would have caught on sooner."

"You're assuming they're all connected. No doubt I made it sound that way." Gaines pursed his lips. "I'm inclined to think it too. But it needs to be proven. Only if we can prove them connected can we also discover if anyone is to blame for it."

Of course. That was reasonable, logical. "But if they are . . . There are only a few people who would have had access to all the information, across all the military branches."

Their gazes met, understanding and unadulterated fear passing between them. There were only a few such individuals, and they were all in their office—the one designated by the Crown to create this new intelligence division.

They were still months away from the official installation of what they'd dubbed MI5, and already they were facing scandal that could shut them down before they even breathed their first official breath.

They would all be investigated. Each and every one of them. And while Merritt had nothing to hide, even *he* didn't relish that process.

Gaines let his case fall closed and fastened it. "We could simply let this question drop. Let Ballantine be reported as an isolated incident. Only you and I know about the others."

Merritt had nothing to hide . . . but what if Gaines did? He swallowed. "Is that what you want to do?"

"No." The answer came fast and hard, like the tennis ball Fairfax had spiked at his head yesterday morning. Then calmer, slower, "No. I want justice for those men, if they're all lost. I want answers. I want to recover any who are able to be saved. No matter the cost."

"We're agreed." Merritt held out a hand. Gaines shook it. Their eyes met again, and he nodded. "I realize there isn't much I can do while I'm here on leave, but—"

"I'm well aware that you're still working. Perhaps in less conventional ways. That will suffice until you get a clear bill of health and return to London." He stood, case in hand, when the train let out a quick toot of its whistle. "Stay safe, Colonel Livingston. And good hunting."

"The same to you, Lieutenant Gaines."

He stood there until Gaines had boarded his train again, until it chugged out of the depot. Then Merritt slid the photo into the envelope, returned to his rented horse, and rode back to Hawkhill House. He found Xavier napping, so, rather than disturb him, he simply deposited the file in his chamber and hurried back outside.

He would go to the birthday gala. He would pray that the Lord would give him words to say to whomever he met. He would pray that, in God's gracious favor, He would find a way to breathe comfort today on this family that would be grieving so soon.

He wished he didn't know about Cornelius. Wondered if perhaps he *should* tell them. Knew he shouldn't, couldn't.

But the knowledge burned his chest more than the sickness ever had, made his lungs ache. As he handed the reins over to a stable boy forty minutes later, as he surveyed the people spilling through absolutely every inch of the estate, he wondered if maybe he should have stayed home. Read through the file. Looked at those dreaded other cases.

Instead, he started maneuvering through the crowds, his eyes looking for bright colors, bold plumes, brave flowers.

There. A familiar hat, the very one she'd worn in Hyde Park a few weeks ago with its unmistakable rainbow of feathers, paired this time with an even brighter dress of yellow-green. Proof that his mind had been playing tricks on him at the train station, because there she was. The one person he felt like talking to just now, even though he couldn't imagine telling *her* what burdened him either. Not here. Even so, it would be good to talk to her. To see if he could tease her dimples into her cheeks, even though she never smiled so fully in company.

She was moving in that way she had at the ball, skirting the edges, cutting through open spaces between groups, but never engaging with anyone. Being seen, being noted, but otherwise being ignored. Tracking her, catching up to her, proved quite a challenge here in this outdoor wonderland that the Ballantines had created. Five minutes later, he finally closed in on her by one of the many refreshment tables.

He opened his mouth, ready to hail her—and then stopped. She was reaching for a tart. His brow furrowed. One thing he'd learned after two weeks of daily visits to the Tower was that neither of the Fairfaxes *ever*, of their own will, ate sweets. Which explained why she'd seemingly wasted the assortment of them she'd had that first time they'd met, in the Hemming drawing room in London. Lady Hemming must have fixed the plate for her. She never would have chosen those things for herself.

Just as she would never reach for that fruit tart.

That was not Lady Marigold. Someone inspired by her style, perhaps? Seeking to imitate her? If so, they were imitating more than just her fashions—they were imitating her very mannerisms. He moved a step closer, his frown only deepening when he recognized the face largely hidden by the hat. "Miss Parks?"

She jolted, dropping the tart she'd been raising to her lips, and glanced up at him with wide eyes before lowering her face again. "Shh! I beg you, Sir Merritt, don't call me that. Not here."

"Don't . . . why?" His mind buzzed. Had she not been invited and so snuck in under the guise of being her friend and employer? But no, that made no sense—the Ballantines had invited everyone in the county, small and great alike. That had been the Hemmings' complaint about the event. "Where is Lady Marigold?" He kept this question quiet, at least.

She darted a look over her shoulder, as if searching for help.

Perhaps she was, and perhaps she'd found it, because when he followed her gaze, he saw Fairfax now weaving toward them.

"Marigold was feeling under the weather today," she whispered. "But she still wanted to put in an appearance for the sake of the family. So I came in her place, that's all. Only you mustn't point out that it's *me*, or that won't do any good for the Ballantines at all."

He knew he looked every bit as dubious as he felt at that explanation. "So you think to just . . . stand in for her? In her hat? And that no one will notice?"

She gave him the strangest look. "I've been here for three hours, and no one has. Until *you*." She shot it at him like an accusation—as if it wasn't more an indictment of everyone *else* than of him.

He turned to level a hard look at Fairfax as he drew near, because obviously he was in on this, too, whatever "this" was. "I'm informed that your sister isn't feeling quite the thing today, my lord."

Fairfax darted a glance from him to Miss Parks and then back again, his expression morphing through several options before landing on amused. "I didn't think you'd be here. I knew Lord Xavier wasn't planning to attend."

And so he assumed no one else would notice if Miss Parks just pretended to be Lady Marigold? Was her presence really so beneficial?

Yes. He knew it was. Weren't his cousins proof of that? They waited with bated breath for the next mention of where Lady M had been seen, what she had been wearing, and where she planned to go next. By showing up here, she'd been lending the Ballantines quite a bit of prestige.

But . . . "How did you intend to pull this one over on Miss Ballantine?"

Miss Parks chuckled. "Anytime she sets a course for me, we just let her come across *Yates* instead."

Merritt was beginning to see the humor in the situation—or would have, had he not been carrying such a cloud over his head. He sent a half smile toward the young earl. "That's dedication to the story."

"Selfless dedication. Mountains of it." Fairfax flashed him a grin. "Play along, won't you, old boy? Marigold would be distraught if this little plot of hers proved futile."

Merritt held up a hand, palm out. "I solemnly swear myself to silence. Although, I must say, if you want to truly act the part, *my lady*, you oughtn't to be eating sweets."

Miss Parks scowled at him. "No one would have thought a thing of it."

Wouldn't they? No, probably not.

"Gemma!" Fairfax's scowl looked oddly serious as he fixed it on his sister's companion. "That was sloppy of you."

She sighed and reached instead for a cucumber sandwich. "Do excuse me, gentlemen. I have been seen talking far too long to you."

Merritt watched her return to her orbiting and shook his head. Nothing from this day made any sense at all.

SIXTEEN

$\mathscr{R}$avenscleft Academy for Young Ladies was everything their adverts claimed. Marigold took in the grounds and the view of the manor house as the carriage rolled her up the drive—her and two other women who had arrived at the train station at about the same time and made their way to the driver who stood with a sign proclaiming *Ravenscleft Academy Applicants*. They were, the driver had told him, the third group to arrive already, and if they didn't have their references in order, they might as well turn right back around there and then.

Marigold had informed him that she had hers and was quite ready to begin the process. As, of course, Miss Cora Richards. She and Gemma had created the character in great detail. She had been Miss Cora Richards in her mind ever since that morning, when she'd donned the staid grey dress and pulled the utilitarian hat from her costume collection. She'd been Miss Cora Richards as she walked to the train station, as she'd purchased her ticket to Leeds, and as she'd waited for her southbound train to pull into Alnwick Station.

She'd been Miss Cora Richards still when she spotted Sir Merritt there, watching the tracks for the northbound train, though it had been a bit panicked then. What if he saw her? Recognized her? Shouted to her? How would she have explained her clothing—and her going?

But he hadn't. He'd glanced her way once, but then she'd made a quick escape onto the train, chosen a seat on the opposite side, and thanked the good Lord that it had been a short stop and they were soon pulling out.

And now there was no one to question her role. She was Miss Cora Richards, French teacher, formerly a private tutor for a family she knew well tended to be reclusive, and who lived in the south, traveling frequently into France. They were, in fact, traveling now, and would be difficult to track down for verification of the forged reference, if someone from Ravenscleft were to try to wire them today.

All she needed was today. Or rather, tonight. She had only to make it through this one day here, and then she'd find what she needed and be gone.

The carriage passed through the gates and crunched its way up the macadam drive. It was a beautiful property about ten miles outside of Leeds, filled with gardens and promenades, a labyrinth, horse paddocks—everything a young lady could need.

The place must have cost a fortune. It had been a family estate until twenty years ago, when Miss Feuerstein somehow came into possession of it and launched the academy. Marigold had done some cursory digging, but she hadn't had time to discover much. It seemed that it was still technically in the possession of the same family who had owned it for centuries. But where they were, and how Miss Feuerstein had funds enough to keep the place running, was a bit more difficult to discern.

Perhaps the family was simply swimming in wealth and kept it running themselves while they enjoyed warmer climes. They wouldn't be the first to do something like that.

The carriage pulled to a halt at the side of the house—no

front door entry for potential staff, it seemed. Which was fine by Marigold. Side and back entrances would prove far more useful anyway. She noted each door she could see, and any window with a reasonable drop too. The single piece of luggage she carried had one of Drina's silks folded neatly in the bottom, just in case she needed it.

A lady never knew when she might need to make a quick escape.

A woman—tall and angular and prim—stood outside the door with a warm-enough smile. "Good day, good day. Welcome to Ravenscleft. If you could all produce your references?"

They certainly were serious about those, weren't they? Marigold pulled hers out as her two companions did and handed them over with a smile and a small curtsy.

The woman gave each of their offerings a few seconds of attention and then nodded. "Thank you. We will be following up on these, and any position offered will be contingent on your former employers' validation of their words. But for now, please follow me." The woman turned and entered through the nearest door. "I am Miss Malcolm, and I will be conducting you to the first round of interviews. Those of you who pass will be given the chance to meet our illustrious headmistress, Miss Feuerstein, this evening. She will be conducting tomorrow's final interviews."

Marigold fell into the middle of their little line, making certain she kept the grip on her bag firm and confident, her step sure, her posture perfect. And the wince nowhere in evidence when they passed by a series of open rooms and saw girls reciting Latin, practicing their pours, and sitting in that way Genie and Lavinia both did that looked so drattedly uncomfortable.

Each step hammered it home—this place was everything their adverts claimed. Down to every horrifying, disciplined detail. The white uniform blouses, the black uniform skirts. Each girl's hair in the same uniform style, the sides tied back with a uniform pink ribbon.

It made Marigold want to sew a few more flowers onto her latest gown underway at the Tower, in self-defense.

Or in spite. Perhaps it was spite.

"This way, please." Miss Malcolm led them along a well-appointed corridor and held out a hand, indicating they should proceed into a drawing room.

Ten other women of various ages already filled it, nine sitting primly in the rows of chairs set up opposite the final woman, who stood before a wooden podium. Marigold and her two traveling companions didn't need to be told to take three of the six open chairs.

Twelve. There were twelve of them vying for those final interview spots tomorrow, and she had a feeling each and every one had been trained at a place just like this. The fact that they were applying for positions meant that they were women from respectable families, but not nobility. Would that give her an edge? That she actually *was* a lady?

Laughable. Much as Mama had tried drilling the social graces into her, Marigold simply hadn't had years enough under her gentle hand. She had instead learned far different— but no less useful—lessons from the Caesars and the other traveling entertainers.

Far *more* useful, really. She could sit as straight as every other woman on these hard wooden chairs, but she'd been trained to notice the subtle language of their movements too. Movements that told her whether they were uncomfortable, hopeful, bored, excited—cues a good performer wanted to recognize in their audience and be able to replicate and exaggerate in their roles.

Miss Malcolm pulled the twin doors shut behind them, and Marigold could imagine a *clang* of prison locks. Or at least that's what it would have felt like had she been sent here as a student and not just a spy.

The woman at the podium offered them all a smile. "*Bonjour, mademoiselles. Je suis Mademoiselle Dumas.*"

She paused, brows arched, and Marigold joined in with the other ladies—only half a second behind—with a nearly singsong "Bonjour, Mademoiselle Dumas."

Good heavens. It was like every nightmare of school she'd ever had. And they weren't even the pupils!

The woman quickly explained—in French—that she was the current French teacher but would be leaving the academy thanks to the happy occasion of her wedding next weekend. They all, naturally, interrupted with a chorus of French felicitations.

Marigold had no trouble wishing her well, given the gleam in her eyes as she shared that news. And since it meant freedom from *this*. Though to be fair, the mademoiselle sounded genuinely sorrowful to be leaving behind her beloved students and fellow teachers.

All right, so perhaps some people enjoyed places like this. Lavinia and Genie both seemed to have. And no doubt many a young woman with few other prospects in life would count themselves blessed to land a position here.

Well, Marigold could assure them that their chances were all a little better than they looked, because she was certainly no serious contender for the role.

"Now," Mlle Dumas said, still in French, "becoming a teacher here requires more than just passable French. You must also be proficient in our other subjects, as we are often called upon to assist one another. This afternoon you will undertake a series of tests to gauge your skill in the very subjects our students must learn."

Oh, leopard stripes. Had Marigold really avoided such lessons all her life only to have to walk this fire *now*? When she was a mature five and twenty? Yates would laugh stitches into his sides when she told him about it tomorrow.

"First, though, is the French, as it will be your primary class. I will meet with each of you individually to assess your fluency. In the order in which you arrived, please." She motioned to the lady in the first row, the leftmost chair, and led her into an adjoining room.

Miss Malcolm smiled from her position by the doors. "Do feel free to chat among yourselves. The housekeeper will be arriving with some refreshments for you all directly. I know many of you traveled a great distance to reach us."

This, too, would be a test, Marigold was sure. Their movements, manners, and habits would be watched every moment that they were here.

Well, she was used to that. Miss Cora Richards would just have to borrow a bit of Lady Marigold Fairfax's expertise in these situations. She smiled at the other ladies, answered questions with the information she'd come up with alongside Gemma, asked them questions in turn. Never interrupting, always complimenting. When the tea tray arrived, she stood only when invited to do so and joined the others in line. She chose only a few items from the generous offerings, all of them healthy choices, and ate without dropping a single crumb or spilling a single drop. Her cup and plate never clattered, nor did her hands shake with nerves as half of her companions' did.

As they visited, they were called one by one into that adjoining room, and Marigold had plenty of time to pray that Zelda's French didn't fail her. She *had* supplemented it over the years with an array of French literature, and she'd had cause to eavesdrop on many a French conversation in the last five years. She knew her fluency was good. Her accent she could only give to the Lord. She hadn't the ear for such things that Yates did.

"Mademoiselle Richards?"

Marigold accepted the whispers of good luck with a smile, exchanged another encouraging one with the girl just leaving the room, and slipped into the quiet antechamber. Mlle Dumas welcomed her with a smile and launched right into the test.

She'd feared she'd be asked to simply recite her conjugations—and had practiced them on the train ride just in case. But thankfully, the woman had decided on a conversation-based approach. She asked a question using complicated vocabulary, and Marigold had to reply. She then asked questions about how many years she'd been speaking French—twenty; had her teacher been a native French speaker—yes; what region had he or she been schooled in—Paris.

She was handed a written document and was asked to read it aloud, which she did with all the skills of oration the Caesars had taught her. She was then handed paper and a pen and asked to write a page on the French Revolution and its impact on European society, which she put down quickly and neatly . . . mostly recalling a lecture she'd listened in on during surveillance of a professor two years ago.

The man in question had been stepping out on his wife, but he'd been a well-versed teacher.

When that met with Mlle Dumas's approval—Marigold wasn't immediately dismissed, anyway—she was sent back out to make room for the last applicant.

Phew. Perhaps she hadn't actually passed muster, but at least that part was complete, and she'd done the best she could imagine doing.

Another instructor waited in the larger room. If she wasn't mistaken—which she wasn't—this woman had been in one of the classrooms they'd passed on the way in, schooling her pupils in posture and deportment. *Ugh.* Lavinia had taught her all those lessons when she came home for holidays, and

Marigold could put them on with the role. She simply preferred *not* to sit like a letter of the alphabet and pretend a ruler was jammed into her corset.

Perhaps it would be best to look at it all with amusement. Here she was, feeling like an utter imposter (ha!) at this academy for young ladies, when in truth she *was* a young lady. Or not-so-young lady, as the case may be. She had navigated actual ballrooms and drawing rooms and the like. She had no reason to feel anxious enough that she wanted to dart her eyes about and see what everyone else was doing.

Gemma would certainly chuckle over it all. But she would also don a proud smile when Marigold told her that it was looking over and seeing a copy of *London Ladies Journal*, open to one of G. M. Parker's columns, that made the flutter of nerves settle.

She pretended every day of her life. This was just one more stage. One more audience. One more role to play for a few hours, and then she could escape back to Northumberland and the Tower, where Peabody would squawk at her, Leonidas would roar a greeting, and Penelope would chatter a hello from Yates's shoulder. Back with her brother and dearest friends, her family. Back to morning visits from Sir Merritt and Lord Xavier.

Lionfeathers. Now her stomach was fluttering for a whole different reason.

Twilight had seized the world by the time Marigold found herself called into the headmistress's office with three other applicants. Was she about to be dismissed? If so, she had a contingency plan in place. She would ask to be let out at the village a mile away rather than the larger town with the train station, claiming to have an acquaintance there. Wait for dark, hike back to the estate, climb the stone wall that enclosed the manor house.

And now she knew which office belonged to the headmistress. Perfect. It wasn't on the ground floor, but she could scale the stone walls to the first floor easily enough. As she filed in with the others, her gaze flicked to the window. It was open at the moment, allowing in two inches of spring breeze. She daren't hope it would remain that way overnight, but if Miss Feuerstein made a habit of opening it day by day, she might not see the need to latch it at night, given that it wasn't on the ground floor. *Please, God.*

If she did close it, then Marigold would have to come in through a door and sneak up the stairs. Riskier by far. But she'd done such things many times.

"Good evening, ladies. Thank you so much for applying for the position here at Ravenscleft Academy." A woman, presumably Miss Feuerstein, had stood from her chair behind the desk, a smile upon her face.

She looked nothing like Frances Hemming; that was what Marigold noted first. Fair blond hair instead of midnight, short and round physique instead of tall and slender. She had a cheerful face—a bit unexpected of a headmistress to Marigold's way of thinking—and blue eyes that gave the impression of sizing them all up in a single glance.

Marigold could respect eyes like that. She liked to think she had a pair herself, though she usually took great pains to hide them under the brim of a hat.

Miss Feuerstein looked at each of them in turn, her smile not dimming. "The four of you have been selected as most suited to the position. Congratulations."

Gasps of pleasure from the other three, but Cora Richards wasn't given to such extravagant displays. She allowed herself only a pleased smile and a minute relaxation of her spine for exactly three seconds, before she "remembered" herself.

The headmistress would perhaps read it as her telling herself, *"You're not there yet, Cora."* For her own part, Marigold was mentally whispering a prayer of thanks that she wouldn't have to hike a mile back to the estate in the dark.

"I am pleased to offer you all a room here for the night. This evening you are invited to attend a little banquet we are hosting for our dear Mademoiselle Dumas. This will give you an opportunity to meet both students and faculty and get a sense for whether our academy will be a good fit for you. Then, in the morning, we will conclude the interview process. Do you have any questions?"

How long will this banquet last? Will you all be busy enough that I can sneak away then, or should I wait until everyone is asleep? Not that Marigold would ever voice those aloud.

Wait, she decided twenty minutes later, when she got her first glimpse of what this "little banquet" was. Apparently Ravenscleft in celebration granted far more freedom than was particularly convenient just now—there were pupils and teachers absolutely everywhere. Someone would no doubt notice her trying to slip into the headmistress's office, given that there were girls in giggling clusters all along the upstairs corridor.

Didn't they have anything better to do? Like practice their waltzes with one another in the ballroom downstairs, from which music was spilling?

Oh well. Treating it like any other gathering she had to attend, Marigold sipped her drink, nibbled her food, spoke to whomever was at hand—as was expected of Miss Cora Richards—and filed away every detail she observed.

Some of the things that struck her were purely personal. This was where Lavinia had spent two years of her life, two years when Marigold had missed her deeply, before she fell ill with the scarlet fever that had changed everything. But mostly she was noting which girls traveled together, which teachers seemed particularly aware of every movement and responded to it, who rushed to tattle about each spilled cup or dropped plate.

She definitely wanted to avoid *those* types.

She was beginning to think this farewell to Mlle Dumas would go on all night when the music went silent, a shrill whistle sounded, and sudden silence fell. Miss Feuerstein stepped to the center of the ballroom, still smiling, and said, "On behalf of all of us here at Ravenscleft Academy, we wish you all the best life has to offer, Mademoiselle Dumas. Girls?"

Three of the pupils approached, a large box balanced between them. A flushed French teacher stepped forward, her eyes dancing. She opened the box, pulling out gift after gift with profuse thanks. She gave a short speech—in English, let it be noted—and was greeted with enthusiastic applause.

The headmistress then dismissed them all, reminding them that they would still be expected to arrive at breakfast by seven o'clock, so to go straight to their nightly ablutions.

Good. Marigold followed the guide assigned to the applicants to the dormitories on the top floor. The four of them had been divided between two rooms, each with two beds. Not ideal, but her roommate seemed exhausted, so that was something.

Marigold hadn't the luxury to be tired. Not yet. She prepared for bed like all the others, bade her companion good night, and settled in to listen. To catalogue each creaking board. Each night sound. Each footstep.

Long after most of the movement ceased, she lay there still, not trusting the headmistress to have gone to bed at the same time as the others, especially given the interviews the next morning and the gala that evening. She would quite likely be taking some extra time after the others had retired to prepare for tomorrow.

A wise decision. A solid hour after the rest of the house was silent, Marigold heard soft movements from the floor below. A lowering window, a closing door, footsteps, creaking stairs. She waited another long hour and then finally, finally dared to slip from her bed, scoop up her bag, and sneak her way downstairs.

She'd already noted the loudest boards and had long ago perfected how to mitigate such noises. With her feet bare, she needn't worry about clicking heels or squeaking soles. Her senses all on high alert, she made her way through the darkened house and to the headmistress's door.

Locked? Yes, but her master key worked its wonders within a few seconds. She was soon in the quiet room, the door locked behind her again, her electric torch out of her bag and in her hand.

While she was in here before, she'd noted the filing cabinets, which she headed directly to now. She didn't honestly know where Miss Feuerstein might have information pertaining to her connections to Lady Hemming, if such a thing even existed, but she intended to search for photos, through correspondence, and in Lavinia's file.

That's where she started. With any luck, there would be a note front and center that proclaimed their relation. The file drawers were in scrupulous order—no surprise there—which made it easy to locate the folder with her friend's name on the tab. *Lady Lavinia Hemming.* Marigold plucked it out and, torch anchored between her teeth, opened it up.

A cursory glance through the neat stack within told her that the academy kept records of her marks in each class as well as on final exams. As curious as she was, Marigold wasted no time on that. She went straight for the personal records that listed her parentage, residency, and so on.

Lady Lavinia Hemming, only child of Lord Thomas Hemming and Lady Franziska Hemming née Coburg.

But . . . wait. That wasn't right. Her mother's name was Frances, not Franziska. Wasn't it? And Lavinia's maternal grandmother was Lady Vivian Moore, widow of a baronet named Daniel Moore. Marigold had met them both, before Lord Moore's death some eighteen years ago, and saw the lady every Christmas still.

There was no *Coburg* in her family tree, not to Marigold's knowledge.

But here it was, in her admission records. And unless her torchlight was playing tricks on her, that *née* had been written with a bit more force than the rest of the names.

Interesting. She didn't know exactly what it meant, but she intended to find out once she was home again.

SEVENTEEN

*Y*ou do realize, I hope, the irony of this."

Merritt pulled his gaze from the glorious morning sky with its painted clouds scuttling along the horizon in shades of rose and gold and orange, to the smirking face of Xavier. "Of what?" He hadn't been particularly irony-minded in the last thirty-six hours. Rather, he'd been burdened enough that he'd confessed the sad truth of Cornelius Ballantine to Xavier, who certainly hadn't been smirking *then*.

Oh, but he was now, as he repositioned his fedora and guided his horse around a fresh puddle from last night's rain. "Of the fact that you came here under the guise of courting a lady you had no interest in just to learn more about her father, and then went and fell in love with her eccentric friend."

"I have not *fallen in love*." That was a phrase used only by silly girls and poets, wasn't it? Perhaps he held Lady Marigold in the highest esteem after getting to know her. Perhaps thoughts of her had plagued him all of yesterday as he wondered if she was feeling any better, as he wished in every moment that he could dismiss his decision to give her time to rest and recuperate before shoving this burden of knowledge onto her shoulders. As he longed to simply be in her presence, share this weight with her, along with his concerns for the safety of Gaines and anyone else who poked this particular hive of bees.

If someone really was behind the missing agents, if it was a purposeful, treasonous action, then whoever was guilty of it would be willing to kill to protect the secret. Of that he had no doubt.

But he clung to the *if*. It could be coincidence. And there was certainly no solid evidence pointing to Hemming. It could be any one of his colleagues, and if it was one still in London, watching Gaines's every move . . . The man had a wife, two children. Far too much to lose. Merritt had been praying incessantly for them all.

Wanting to talk it over with Marigold, wanting to see the compassion in her eyes and the quick thoughts behind them didn't mean he was *in love*. It meant . . . well, it clearly indicated only . . . "Friends. That's what we are."

Xavier snorted a laugh. "Right. I can't recall you ever leaving home at the veritable crack of dawn to come and talk to *me*."

Neither could he, come to think of it. But still. "Perhaps she's more pleasant to talk to than you are."

"Which has nothing at all, I'm sure, to do with her rather attractive figure or pretty face or the way she makes your heart go pitter-patter?"

"My heart hasn't been pitter-pattering." Much. And so what if it had? Perhaps he *did* find her attractive. That also didn't equate to the stuff of poets and giggling girls.

"But you've certainly noticed her figure and face."

Merritt scowled at him. "I have fine eyesight, haven't I? So yes, I've noticed that she's not only lovely of face but of figure." Perhaps he'd even let his mind wander a few times to what it might feel like to pull her into his arms. But what was Xavier doing noticing such things? "It seems *you've* noted it as well."

218

His friend laughed. "Jealousy! Well, let me assure you that while I've noted it, it was only in passing. Far more interesting has been watching *you* note it."

His scowl only deepened. "And why is that so noteworthy? I've admired plenty of lovely ladies over the years you've known me."

"But not like this. Not someone like her."

"Someone like her?" He didn't mean to bristle. Certainly didn't mean to toss the phrase back like it was a demand for explanation.

Because of course Xavier would explain. With a grin. "I'm saying nothing against *her*. But it's *you*. You. Lieutenant Colonel Sir Merritt Livingstone, a Coldstream Guard. You with your uniforms and most boring civilian clothing in the world. You, who literally rolled your eyes at me when I suggested you come to the tailor with me a few months ago. You, seeking out the company of the most audaciously dressed young lady in London, who sets the fashion columns to buzzing with her every appearance. You *must* see the irony in *that*."

Merritt nudged his horse into a faster trot.

"Have you given any thought to how you'll afford to keep her in her frippery? She must spend a fortune on all those feathers and flowers and ribbons and lace."

That one inspired Merritt to send his friend a *you're-a-dunce* look. "Have *you* noticed the aviary of exotic birds they have at the Tower?"

Xavier opened his mouth, paused, nodded. "All right, so the feathers may be free. They may, in fact, be able to sell their abundance to London shops to subsidize the lace and sequins. Not that you've given this much thought."

"Of course not." Much. Not enough that it kept him up nights.

There were plenty of more serious things competing for *that* honor.

Xavier held up a hand in surrender, but the grin stayed glued to his face. "Fine, deny it awhile longer yet. But I know you, my friend, and never in all our years have I seen you so eager for a lady's company."

He was eager—it was particularly singular company. Had he been healthier during their first several meetings, he would have seen it at a glance. She was far more than her *frippery*, as Xavier called it.

Even so, he found himself rather looking forward to seeing what she chose for each new day. He hadn't even names for many of the colors she wore, but they were never boring.

Fairfax Tower came into view, and the horses increased their pace when they spotted it, no doubt eager for a mouthful of grass and the doting attention of Franco. Or perhaps for a visit with their exotic striped cousins, for all he knew. Merritt had nearly gotten used to seeing grazing zebras instead of ponies or thoroughbreds. He'd even almost gotten used to seeing one pull the lawn mower about.

They were arriving a good two hours earlier than usual—all the longer he'd been able to convince himself to wait. He wasn't exactly surprised, then, when Franco wasn't lingering around front as he often was, so Merritt led the way to the stables himself. He had noted that the Tower was frightfully understaffed. Their hosts had said it was because they hadn't originally planned on being here rather than in London, but he wondered if perhaps their traditional servants had objected to working alongside the Romani. Regardless, he and Xavier had no trouble putting up their own horses at the end of the stable well removed from all big cats.

"What is that noise?" Xavier asked as they stepped back out into the beautiful morning. "The squeaking?"

Merritt hadn't noticed it until that moment. "It seems to be coming from the courtyard." He paused, and his eyes went wide. "The trapeze, do you think? Perhaps the Caesars are practicing." He'd yet to see them on any of the courtyard equipment, but maybe he'd never shown up early enough.

He and Xavier exchanged grins and took off at a lope for the courtyard entryway. They slowed once they were close, approaching silently so as not to startle anyone in the middle of a precarious move, then hovered in the shadows of the arched door.

The trapezes were in motion—both of them. But it took only a glance to see that it wasn't Franco and Zelda swinging. Nor any other of the Romani.

It was Lady Marigold and Lord Fairfax himself.

For a moment, the shock of it rendered him motionless. Then the beauty overtook him, and he leaned into the arch to watch.

They were swinging in matching arcs, both of them dangling from their knees, arms outstretched. But even as he watched, their rhythms began to change, and within a few swings, they were instead at opposite ends of their arcs. Both out as far as they could go. Both in, so close they could reach out and touch. Would they attempt one of those transfers he'd seen other performers do? Surely not.

And they didn't, which had him breathing a little easier. At least until three swings later, when they were yet again in unmatched arcs. Marigold flipped herself up, somehow switched which direction she faced, and then *let go* at the apex of her swing, sending herself flipping, somersaulting through the air.

Merritt's breath held, and he couldn't bring himself to release it, even after her brother's hands had caught her and she'd joined his swing as if it were effortless, him holding her up as if she weighed no more than one of her beloved peacock feathers.

His breath gusted out. They were fluid grace, those two, and must trust each other implicitly. He couldn't imagine ever leaping into the air and just trusting someone else to be there, to catch him.

Or perhaps he could. In a way, that was what a soldier did. Leaping into battle and trusting one's brothers-in-arms to be right there at one's back.

Only sometimes they weren't. Sometimes one found oneself alone in the charge, the only one to make it through, the only one left to get others to safety.

Sometimes one found oneself knighted for one's efforts. As if that could undo the horrors.

But if Fairfax had ever dropped his sister, she didn't show any of the expected doubts now. They executed a series of flips and turns that left him breathless once again, and then Marigold swung up onto his trapeze, turning to face her own.

It had stopped swinging. What did she mean to do? He wasn't certain until he realized that a third member of the household was up on the platform attached to her trapeze. Drina, and she had pulled the bar back, was watching the duo, her head bobbing a count. With a firm nod, she sent the second trapeze swinging.

Marigold leaped, somersaulted in the air again, and caught the bar once more.

"Thunder and turf." Xavier rubbed a hand over his chest. "They've taken a decade off my life, I think."

Merritt hadn't even the wherewithal to speak. He could only nod and try to breathe again.

Xavier never had a problem finding words, though. He leaned close. "Makes you feel a bit better, doesn't it? About being trounced by him in every sport? I mean, I always thought myself rather fit, but not like *that*."

Merritt hadn't honestly looked much at Fairfax, he had to admit. But he did so now and had to breathe a laugh. He'd attributed the earl's athletic prowess to being five or six years younger than he was, but X was right. He was corded with muscles, all on display just now, given that he was wearing only a fitted shirt without sleeves and thin cotton trousers that looked a bit like pajamas.

Which then drew his attention to the fact that Lady Marigold was most certainly not in her usual attire either. She wore a black . . . thing. Like what he'd seen dancers wear, only without so much as a skirt. Fitted and brief and making it glaringly apparent that she was every bit as fit as her brother, if nowhere near so bulky.

He no doubt shouldn't stare at her but couldn't quite avert his eyes either, given that she was again climbing onto the trapeze. He wasn't about to miss whatever she did next.

Even if Xavier *was* leaning close and elbowing him in the ribs. "Going to try to tell me again that you're not particularly taken with her figure and face?"

"Xavier?"

"Hmm?"

"Stow it."

Xavier laughed, but Merritt noticed that *he* didn't look away from the swinging duo either. Part of him wanted to give his friend a good long examination to make sure he wasn't giving too much attention to Marigold's too-little clothing, but that would have required missing this part of their performance, which he wasn't willing to do.

And he was glad he hadn't. After another series of interchanges and flips and even switching bars with each other, the siblings dismounted in unison, both twirling through the air and landing in the sand below on the same beat. Feet planted, knees bent. For a second, they both seemed to be letting their balance find them again, then they straightened at the same moment, arms up in a *V*.

He and Xavier both erupted in applause and shouts, stepping out of the shadows of the arch and into the courtyard.

Only when the Fairfaxes spun toward them, clearly surprised to see them, did it occur to him to wonder if there was a reason they hadn't bragged of their acrobatic skills before now.

Earls and their sisters, after all, were not circus performers. They ought not to know how to perform on the trapeze.

But then, the Fairfaxes weren't your typical nobility. After that initial moment of gaping, they both grinned.

"Marigold!" Drina called down, tossing something from the platform that fluttered like cloth.

Marigold spun back, darted toward the falling fabric, and a moment later had the simple house dress on over her whatever-it-was.

He told himself not to regret it. To remember he was a gentleman.

Mostly he saw Fairfax jogging their way with his considerable muscles on display and quickly brought his thoughts of the man's sister into line, valuing his nose and limbs as he did.

"You're out and about early this morning," the young earl called as he neared, neither self-awareness nor protective-brother threats evident on his face. Only his usual bright smile.

It faded as he drew near and looked from one to the other. "Something's wrong."

Thoughts of the something had pummeled Merritt again the moment he mentioned their early start, but he was nevertheless a bit surprised that Fairfax noted it so quickly. Was he such an open book?

His gaze skipped, quite of its own will, over Fairfax's shoulder to where Marigold was hurrying their way. She'd had a purple scarf tied over her hair but swept it off as she moved. A long honey-brown braid unfurled itself over her shoulder and down to her waist.

He heard Aunt Josie's voice in his head, chiding one or another of the not-yet-out girls. *"Soon enough you'll be grown and will pin up your hair, and then you'll never let it down again. Never be a child again. Don't rush yourself.*"

He'd only ever seen Lady Marigold's hair down one other time. And it wasn't exactly *down* then, or now. But enough that he found himself wondering what it would look like loose.

And it was Xavier's fault that he was so distracted by her looks this morning, planting thoughts in his head as it were. Merritt shook himself and offered a tight smile. "Forgive us for intruding so early."

Marigold drew to a halt at her brother's side, those wise eyes of hers searching Merritt's face. "Something has happened. What is it?" Though before he could answer, she shook her head and nudged Fairfax in the back. "No, not out here like this. Let's go inside. Have you two had breakfast?"

He hadn't been able to think about food. "No, not yet."

"Not even a cup of tea," Xavier put in, ever helpful. And subtle.

"Well, we can't have that. Let's get some breakfast—and tea—and you can tell us what's happened."

Merritt was vaguely aware of renewed trapeze noises and caught a glimpse of Drina taking her turn on it, but he couldn't possibly think of watching that when Marigold snagged his arm and tugged him toward one of the doors that opened to the courtyard. Just tucked her arm around his as if she'd done so a thousand times. As if he wasn't still keenly aware of that small black thing she wore under the pale blue dress.

Focus, man. He cleared his throat and tried to think of something clever and kind to say, but that wouldn't be a terrible non sequitur to their true purpose in coming.

Marigold frowned up at him. "You haven't had a relapse in your health, have you? You've seemed to be improving so quickly."

"No, no, nothing like that. Although I do hope you're feeling better. I was concerned when I saw Miss Parks at the party the other day in your stead."

The strangest look fluttered over her face. He hadn't the words to describe it. A bit of surprise, a bit of pleasure, a bit of pain. And perhaps a half dozen more things besides. "Yates mentioned it. I'm back to my normal self. And sorry to have worried you. And confused you."

"I am only surprised you thought no one would notice."

And amusement. One couldn't overlook her amusement. "No one else did."

She led him into the kitchen, her brother and Xavier trailing in behind them, chatting about the weather. He'd snuck into his fair share of kitchens over the years and was no stranger to them, but he was still a bit surprised that she'd brought them in this way.

Though not nearly as surprised as he was a moment later when she pointed at the table, smooth from time and use, and said, "Sit, please. I'll have some porridge ready in just a few minutes. Yates, can you manage the tea?"

Though Merritt exchanged a confused look with Xavier, Fairfax didn't find the request odd. He moved to the stove and put on a kettle, humming a happy-sounding ditty that brought to mind big tops and circus rings.

Though it went against his every lesson in good manners, Merritt sat, despite the fact that the only lady present was *not* seated.

Xavier followed suit and voiced what Merritt couldn't bring himself to. "You cook? Both of you?"

Marigold sent them another amused look over her shoulder. "We can make do when Drina's otherwise occupied. This is a great secret, but did you know that it is in fact *not* illegal for a gentlewoman to know her way around a kitchen? Nor for an earl to make his own tea."

226

"I thought for certain I'd be arrested the first time I tried it." Fairfax reached for a tin, still grinning. "But here I still am, free as a bird."

Blast, but Merritt liked these two. The more oddities he discovered, the more he hoped they counted him a friend, as he now counted them. "And you can fly like one, too, at least when on a trapeze. Very impressive, my lord. I'd ask where you learned, but the answer is obvious."

Fairfax laughed. "We've been training on it since we were children, haven't we, sister mine?"

"Much to our mother's dismay. But it was far too much fun for us to listen to her chiding. We'd sneak out every morning before she rose. Though we certainly didn't attempt the particular routine you saw this morning when we were little. Yates hadn't the strength for it until his teen years."

If it was an insult, it rolled right off Fairfax's back. Perhaps it had rather just been a statement of fact. "We once dreamed of running off and forming our own circus troupe, you know."

Marigold shot him a look. "You needn't tell them *all* our secrets."

They were far better secrets than the one weighing Merritt down. "Now, don't listen to her, Fairfax. What were your plans? You can regale us while the porridge cooks."

He did, painting quite a picture of the five of them—the Fairfax siblings, Miss Parks and her brother, and someone called Graham, who had been their father's ward, a distant cousin. What role each would play in their show, what animals they would keep, where they would tour.

Xavier's grin was fixed to his face. "I love it. Did you have a name for your circus?"

Fairfax glanced at Marigold. The lady lobbed back an arch look. The earl cleared his throat. "Dozens of them, over the years. I personally always favored something with *royal* in it, but Marigold insisted it was overdone."

"Because it *is*." She moved to the table with a stack of bowls and set one at each of the chairs, adding spoons, honey, a pitcher of cream, and some fresh berries on subsequent trips. Finally, she brought over the porridge pot and ladled a generous serving into each bowl. Fairfax brought the filled teacups. "But instead James joined the church, and Graham studied architecture, and Yates and I had our own responsibilities."

Once it was clear Marigold actually intended to join them, Merritt sprang up and pulled a chair out for her. She gave him a warm smile of thanks and sat, then looked to her brother. "If you'll bless it, Yates?"

He did, using a familiar prayer that Merritt recited over his own meals when he was alone. Once they'd all said their amens, Marigold looked to Merritt, studying his face. "I think you'd better eat first, and then tell us. That is quite a shadow in your eyes."

He didn't want the food she'd made him to go to waste—as it may well if he just spit out the news about Cornelius Ballantine—so he nodded and spooned up a bite.

"Tell me about your family," she said between bites of her own. "You mentioned your mother is traveling. But you see your uncle and his family regularly, correct?"

The Prestons were a safe topic, so he regaled them with a few stories of his own while they ate. There never was a dull moment with five girls in the house.

But all too soon the bowls were empty, the teacups drained, and an expectant heaviness fell over them.

Merritt drew in a long breath, said a silent prayer for fortitude, and then met the gazes of each of his hosts in turn. "I have spoken to a colleague who was looking into the Ballantine business for me. He informed me the day of the birthday party that Cornelius Ballantine was found dead just a few days before."

"No." Marigold pressed a hand to her mouth, her eyes swimming with tears. "Oh, that poor family. Genie. And her parents!"

Fairfax's face had morphed into something hard and stern, all evidence of his usual cheerful self gone. "Do they know yet?"

Merritt shook his head. "I believe someone will be arriving today to tell them. I certainly don't want word getting out before they know, but with the aid Lady Marigold has already lent me, and knowing that you traveled to London on Miss Ballantine's behalf to open inquiries, my lord . . . I thought—no. I needed to tell you, that's all it is. Purely selfish on my part."

"That isn't selfishness. Quite the opposite." Marigold reached over and rested her fingers overtop his on the table. "I'm glad you told us. A death is always tragic, but in this case, when the circumstances are questionable . . . That is a heavy burden to bear." Her eyes slid shut, and she averted her face. "It will be even heavier for Genie. She knew. She knew something had happened."

"When did it happen?" Fairfax asked.

Merritt wanted to turn his hand under Marigold's. To catch her fingers with his. To hold them tight. To squeeze until some of the horror leaked out.

Instead, he held himself still and said, "About a week ago."

She would be able to do the maths as easily as he had. A week ago—just days after they heard Lord Hemming ordering Colonel May to find him first, to make sure he didn't spill the truth to the wrong sources.

It could be a coincidence, with those wrong sources finding him instead. But what if it wasn't?

EIGHTEEN

*Y*ates sat in the pew beside his sister, the sunshine from the stained-glass window sending fractured colors over the collection of friends and neighbors. Only five days ago, the last time they had been together at the nearby Ballantine estate, they'd been celebrating. Everyone in their bright spring colors, laughter trilling.

Today, those spots of filtered light were the only color. Muted greys and blacks made an ocean of visible grief. He kept his hands clasped, his head bowed, his eyes focused on the back of the pew before him.

His ears, though, he kept open. And the whispers that filled them made his chest burn on behalf of the Ballantines.

"I don't know what they'll do now," one neighbor was murmuring, two pews back. "He was everything to them. Their future. He was only in the navy, you know, to learn more about the shipping world from that side. Who will take over the business now?"

"I suppose the burden will fall on the girl. She'll simply have to marry well, someone who can be groomed."

"Poor child. She looks sick with grief."

"And she was never that fair of face to begin with."

"Hush!"

Yates curled his fingers into his leg. Genie wasn't his favorite person in the world, but she deserved better than this on the day she buried her brother. He glanced over at Marigold, who sat rigid and pale beneath her black netted hat. Nothing bold for her today, nothing flashy. She was as understated as every other mourner, and likely more mournful than most. He reached over and took her hand, gave it a squeeze.

She squeezed back, though she didn't look at him. She probably didn't dare, given the quiver in her lips. Marigold wasn't usually prone to tears, but this had hit her hard, just as it had him.

He couldn't escape the feeling that had he done his job better, faster, he could have prevented this. If he'd only stayed in London—or perhaps come home sooner—or sent Hector to the Continent earlier. If he'd done something more or something else, his neighbor wouldn't be dead now.

In the pew in front of theirs, Lady Hemming leaned close to her husband. No doubt she thought her words, the barest of murmurs, beyond anyone's ears.

She clearly hadn't counted on Yates and Marigold having trained themselves so well, or she never would have whispered, "When will you make another offer?"

Lord Hemming must have suspected the words weren't protected by the other murmurs in the chapel. He shot his wife a quick glance, far harsher than the doting looks he usually sent her way, and muttered, "Not today."

Yates's fingers flexed again. Not today—but he would. Because Mr. Ballantine was reeling from loss, no doubt wondering along with everyone else in the neighborhood what he'd do now, who would keep Ballantine Shipping going after him. He'd feel the burden of the company in addition to the loss.

He would be vulnerable. Overwhelmed. More easily pressured.

Perhaps Hemming only meant to press the advantage circumstances had given him—not flattering, but not dastardly. Or perhaps he'd had a hand in creating the circumstances. He didn't want to think it of his father's friend. He didn't want to wonder what secrets the Hemmings kept. But he had no choice now. Hemming was, according to the report Sir Merritt had sent the Imposters, one of only five or six men who had access to all the reports of the men who were missing throughout the various branches' intelligence divisions. He was one of only a handful who could be responsible.

And the last message from Cornelius had been Hemming's name, encoded for Merritt. Hemming had been the one to send Ballantine out on the mission that had ended his life—something personal, not something official. His wife lied about never leaving the country. She may have even been lying about her maiden name, if what Marigold had discovered at the finishing school could be trusted.

When people lied, it was for a reason. Not always the reason that seemed obvious, but a reason nonetheless.

He would find out why, and how deep the lies went. He would find out because the truth mattered. Because Cornelius Ballantine was dead. Because Genie was mourning. He would find out because Lavinia could just as easily be hurt by the shrapnel. Because Sir Merritt had enlisted his help. Because Hector was even now on the Continent, the telegram that arrived yesterday assuring them he was seeking answers.

He would find out because that's what he did.

The service started a few minutes later, and Yates made a point of pushing all the other thoughts and concerns aside and focusing on the vicar's words. Remembering Cornelius. Lifting his grieving family before the Lord.

He filed outside at its conclusion along with the other mourners, the pallbearers leading the way to the small family cemetery at the back of the chapel, within view of the grand Ballantine house. He stood, still and steady, as the coffin was lowered into its prepared hole and the weeping Mrs. Ballantine had to be restrained from throwing herself atop it.

But the moment it was over, he leaned over to whisper in his sister's ear—far more quietly than those other "whispers"— "I'm going to go and find Milo."

Marigold nodded. She, he knew, would find Genie. He would have to do that at some point, too, but he didn't know how to offer her comfort. He only knew how to get her answers.

While the neighbors meandered toward the house and the luncheon that would be served, Yates aimed instead for the stables. They were bursting with visiting horses and carriages, and the Hemming auto was parked outside too.

Yates waved off all the offers of help from the staff and simply moved through the building until he spotted a familiar head of curly brown hair. Once near enough, he said, "Milo."

Milo Hughes, former stable boy at Fairfax Tower, straightened and spun, smiling even as he lifted a hand in greeting. "My lord! I thought I spotted old Mercy and Grace. Haven't you got new horses yet?"

As if he could afford them. And as if Milo didn't know the situation—hence why he was now working *here* instead of *there*, while his brother Jax was working at Alnwick Abbey. "You know I can never part with old friends. Have a minute?" He motioned with his head to the nearest door.

Milo cast a look around, probably for whoever was his boss. "I suppose I can, if you make it sound convincing enough."

His old friend always did know how to have fun. After tossing him a grin first, Yates positioned anger on his face and pointed to the door. "If I'd wanted your *opinion*, boy,

I'd have asked for it. Now, I *said* to fix that blighted step you broke when you lowered it, and I expect to be obeyed! *Now!*"

Milo could have had a career on the stage if he'd fancied it more than horses. He darted from the stall he'd been working in, all but stammering, "Yes, my lord. Of course, my lord. Right away, my lord!"

Rolling his eyes, Yates called out, "Your tools, boy!" Props had never been Milo's strong suit.

"Right!" Doing a quick pivot, he darted into a tack room and emerged a moment later with a small toolbox.

Excellent. The step on the carriage really could use a bit of Milo's attention. Yates kept meaning to take a spanner to it but always forgot once they were back at the Tower and he was faced with everything else that needed doing too.

But oh, did his friend send him a look when he saw that Yates's excuse wasn't fabricated. "Haven't I told you to let me or Jax know if you need help?" he muttered. "I'd be happy enough to run over on my afternoon off and fix this so your sister doesn't break her neck."

Yates grinned, though only once he'd checked to be sure no one would see him do so. "It takes more than a broken step to trip Marigold, as well you know."

"When in her leotard, yes. But when all trussed up like a Christmas goose . . ." He crouched down and examined the half-dangling step. "This isn't what you needed though, I assume."

"If only." Yates folded his arms over his chest and kept his face in hard lines, just in case anyone happened by. "Does Ballantine still do most of his business from here, or is he in the shipyard itself most days?"

Milo drew out a spanner and tested its size. "Here, mostly, unless he needs to inspect something."

"So the last time Hemming came and made him an offer on the business, a few months ago—that happened here?"

Milo's brows lifted. "Is that what he was doing? I only knew that Hemming was in a mood when he came back out for his car and tore out of here so fast we had to rake the gravel behind him. Mr. Ballantine was downright jolly for days afterward."

That sounded about right. "I have reason to believe he'll be making another offer now—and I daresay Mr. Ballantine won't be so jolly."

"He'd come *now*? With all they've lost?" Milo gave the remaining bolt a good twist. "What a blighter. I hope another position opens here soon so Jax can get away from the Abbey."

"Glad you feel that way. Up for a little eavesdropping when he comes? I'll make it worth your while."

Milo fished around in the toolbox, coming up with a few bolts of various sizes. "I could be persuaded. For, say . . . a box of Drina's baklava."

Yates winced. That stuff was so sweet with honey he practically turned into a bee if he took a bite. "Deal. She'll be delighted to have an excuse to make it." He edged back a step, pointed an accusatory finger at him. "If I get wind of when he plans to come, I'll let you know."

Milo bent over the stair. "Yes, my lord. Right away, my lord." Quieter, he added, "Tell everyone I said hello, will you? I'll try to swing by one afternoon soon."

"See that you do. Zelda worries, you know. And thanks for the repair."

Milo breathed a laugh. "Handy excuse, right? Get back to the funeral, Yates."

He obligingly stomped off.

Marigold had been standing in the garden with Genie—flanking her on one side with Lavinia on the other—for over an hour now, but she'd yet to find time for so much as a whispered word of her own condolences. The parade of neighbors and family who had traveled down from Scotland had finally slowed to a trickle.

Poor Genie looked exhausted. Depleted. She was trying to be strong for her parents, Marigold knew, but who was then being strong for her?

She leaned close to Lavinia and whispered, "Try and get her to sit down for a while. I'll get her a plate."

Lavinia nodded and touched a hand to Genie's elbow. Marigold darted away toward the food tables, trying not to think how this occasion, draped in black crape, was such a different gathering from the one she'd missed. She could only imagine how the memories clashed in the minds of everyone present now. Indeed, they kept looking about them with sad, bewildered gazes. She knew the feeling, even having only experienced the birthday gala secondhand. Too much had changed in so short a time.

Gemma and Yates had both been bursting with tales of the extravagance and whimsy when she'd returned from Ravenscleft Academy—as well as the disturbing news that Sir Merritt had caught Gemma in her impersonation.

Disturbing . . . but in a way that sent the trapeze swinging through her stomach.

She filled a plate with a few things she hoped would tempt Genie—her favorite biscuits and cakes, a few sandwich quarters—and a cup of something that looked just as sweet and pink as the icing. Carrying it back, she noted with relief that Lavinia had managed to get Genie into a chair. Even better, she'd found one tucked out of the way, where she wouldn't be under the scrutiny of absolutely everyone here.

Marigold exchanged a tight, sad smile with the hovering Lavinia and offered the plate to their friend. "Here, Genie. Try to eat something."

"I don't want anything." Her voice was flat, empty.

A feeling Marigold well remembered from her own family's funerals. But Genie had been there for her then, both times, forcing *her* to eat and drink and remember that she yet lived, even if her parents didn't. She crouched down beside her. "I know you don't. But you still need to eat. You'll need your strength."

"Why?" Genie finally looked at her, her eyes not just grieved. They were angry. Of course they were angry—her brother hadn't just died of a fever or heart condition, he'd been stolen from her. "Why should I bother? So that my parents can marry me off to the highest bidder, the man best suited for taking over the business?"

"I'm certain they . . ." But how could she finish that? They likely *would*. They'd have to. Should she lie to give comfort, when Genie would *know* it was a lie? She sighed. "They'll not rush anyone into anything. You're all they have left. They'll want your happiness above all."

Genie's laugh was dry and scratchy. "It won't be about me. Nothing is ever about me. It will be about the Ballantine name, the Ballantine legacy, the Ballantine wealth. While *you* parade around, rubbing my nose in the fact that you don't *need* to marry some overbearing, pompous lout just because he knows how to run a business. You already have the title and the estate and the money. Precious Lady Marigold, darling of the world."

Lavinia's eyes went wide. "Genie! We all know you're distressed, but you needn't take it out on Marigold—"

"Oh, go away. Both of you. I don't need your pity. We all know you never even liked me. I was always just the one tagging along with the two of you."

"That's not true." Perhaps Genie had never been her dearest friend, but she *was* her friend. Marigold set the plate and cup down so that she could reach a hand for Genie's shoulder.

Genie knocked her hand away, eyes wild now, and kicked the plate and cup rather viciously, sending frosted cakes and that sickly pink liquid all over Marigold's skirt. "I said *leave!* Isn't it enough that you're all anyone talks about on a normal day? Must you interject yourself today, too, and make it about you?"

"I . . ." She had no idea how to respond to that. Perhaps people talked about her—but they never talked *to* her. If she sought attention, it was only to also avoid it. But it must not look that way to Genie.

Lavinia, naturally, was too quick to defend her. "How can you say such things? Can't you see that she went out of her way to choose something that wouldn't offend you?"

Genie's face had gone scarlet under her white-blond hair. "She's turned it into her own little publicity stunt, just like she always does. Haven't you heard everyone? 'Oh, look at how somber Lady Marigold is. How respectful. What a good friend, how lucky Eugenia is to have her.'"

Marigold's throat went tight. "Genie, I—"

"No." Genie surged to her feet, hands clenched into fists at her sides. "Not today. I can't stand to hear your praises sung today of all days. Because I *know* you, Marigold. You're not what they all think. This perfect friend, this doting sister. You're nothing but a costume. A mask. But you and I both know what you *really* are."

She pushed past Lavinia, running toward the house.

Marigold's cheeks stung as if she'd been slapped. She barely noticed Lavinia moving toward her, other than to wave her away. "No. Don't worry about me. Go after her, Lavinia. Perhaps she'll let you comfort her. If she needs to blame me, so be it. But she still deserves *you.*"

Lavinia gave her a long look, but she obeyed and chased after Genie.

Good. That freed Marigold to make her escape in the

opposite direction, away from all the crowds, all the eyes, all the wagging tongues.

She didn't know what they were saying, if they'd really paid any attention to her today. She didn't know if anyone had witnessed the exchange, if they saw the stains on her black dress. She didn't care. She only cared that they wouldn't see her crying.

Within a few minutes, she'd escaped the tidy lawn, the hedge of gardens, the milling neighbors, and had picked up her pace, running toward the crashing waves of the North Sea. The wind wrapped its arms around her, the gulls cried their own lament, and the spray of surf splashed its own tears up onto her face, to make hers feel not so lonely.

Except that she was so, so lonely. Nothing but a mannequin in the crowd. Lifeless, unknown. Her face could change, and no one even noticed.

And one of the few who might have, who she'd thought truly knew her, hated her. How long had those feelings been brewing, to erupt like that now? Had they ever been friends?

"Marigold?"

Had it been any other voice, even her brother's, she would have marched away, making it clear she wanted no company.

But it was Merritt. And she *did* want company—his. She just hadn't known it until she heard him say her name. Her eyes slid shut against the tears, and the breath she drew in to try to calm herself only shook her all the more, all the way to her core. "She hates me." The whisper emerged with a quaver, a quake. He probably didn't even hear her.

Or perhaps he did. He took her hand, holding it carefully between both of his, as if she were a delicate, precious thing. "No, she doesn't."

"She does. She said the most horrible things."

"Because she's grieving. It was the pain speaking, not her. She only needed someone to take it out on."

Marigold shook her head. "She couldn't have said it if she'd never thought it. She must have been building up resentments all these years, and now they've come out." Tears burned their way from her eyes, down her cheeks, scalding her. She wanted to leave them, to feel it. But she was afraid to leave them, afraid it would look like a bid for sympathy, afraid it *was*. She dashed them away with her free hand.

Merritt's thumb stroked over her knuckles, a soothing that she didn't deserve. "I suppose that much could be true. She's jealous of you; that's been clear from the moment I met her. The way she works those catty little insults into everything she says to you . . . She has hardly been a good friend."

"But she has! When my mother died, and then my father—she was there. I only wanted to be the friend to her that she'd been to me. I only—but—she doesn't—" More tears blurred her vision, and her breath wouldn't come steadily.

"Ah, sweet Marigold." He moved one of the hands from hers, and in the next moment his arm had come around her. An anchor, that was all. Just there to steady and support. "You *are* her friend. Even if she can't accept that right now. You've been nothing but a friend to her, just as you are to Lady Lavinia."

Had she? Or had it all been selfish, like Genie had said? She'd thought so many uncharitable things about her over the years, sighed at the thought of another encounter. Teased Yates about her crush on him.

The next breath she tried to draw tangled up in a sob. "N-no. Sh-she's right. I'm-I'm . . . horrible."

Now that arm pressed, pulled her half a step closer, so that she could feel the comfort of his chest even though she didn't touch it. "You're many things. But horrible isn't one of them."

She shook off the assurance, even as she wanted to latch

hold of it. She didn't deserve his comfort when she couldn't even give hers properly to someone she'd known all her life.

His thumb stroked again. "Listen to me. If I'm certain of anything, it's that everything you do is out of love for those lucky enough to be counted as your friends and family. If she can't see that, then the fault is in her eyes, not in your love."

He was right about her motivations . . . and yet that just made her aware all over again of all the things he didn't know, the secrets she kept. It *wasn't* the fault of Genie's vision. Marigold worked hard to only be seen as she wished to be seen. To hide behind that costume and mask, just like she'd accused. No one ever saw beneath it.

No one but him.

Her shoulders slumped. "Sometimes . . . sometimes I just wish . . ."

"What? What do you wish?"

That was the question, wasn't it? What *did* she wish? That she could be herself? Put aside the audacious choices? No. Not quite.

"I wish people could see me. Through it all." Because she was *there*. So long hidden, but she was there.

He shifted to face her, dropped her hand, and touched his fingers to her chin. She obeyed their command to look up, through her tears, into those shockingly blue eyes of his. There were only inches between them now. And yet a gulf. A gulf of secrets she couldn't tell him if she wanted to.

He had to see them there, as he saw everything else about her. But still he held her gaze, never shrinking back. "That's easy, then. All you have to do is lift your face and smile. Then the world couldn't help but see you. And admire you for far more than your peacock feathers."

She had to look away before his eyes swallowed her whole. At least her tears had slowed. She pulled away a few inches, sniffling, reaching for the bag dangling from her wrist.

Though upon opening it up and seeing the contents, she blustered out a breath.

"Don't tell me—that's the one thing I *know* a lady carries in her bag."

"Not this lady, it seems. I never expected to have to dry tears."

"Well. Perhaps you'll allow me to assist, just this once." He reached into his pocket and pulled out a crisp white square.

She took it and dabbed at her wet cheeks, her lips still feeling trembly. "Shouldn't you be running the other way?"

"I have five cousins who are like sisters to me. It takes more than a bout of tears to send me running."

Good. And yet it wasn't, not for him. If she were truly the sort of friend he thought her, she would push him away now, for his own good.

Not that she could convince her feet to budge. Though at least she mustered a few words. "I'm afraid I'm undeserving of your kindness, Sir Merritt. Certainly of your . . . regard."

His fair brows arched. "If you're undeserving, then how much more so is everyone else? Because I have never met another woman who has captured my . . . regard . . . as you've done."

She knotted his handkerchief around her fingers, afraid to look up past his chin. Needing to. Giving in. And she found his gaze just as blue, just as true as it had been a minute ago. Her heart raced as though she'd just flipped all the way across the gymnasium floor.

The hand that had raised her chin now cradled her cheek. The thumb that had stroked her knuckle now wiped away a tear she'd missed. The lips that had spoken such comfort now lowered toward hers.

She ought to pull away—for his own good. She ought to tell him here and now that she had no time for romance, that marriage was out of the question. She ought to just

242

blurt out that they were broke and working for their food, and that he would be wise to run fast and far in the other direction.

Instead, she pressed her lips to his.

She could have sworn she was flying through the air.

NINETEEN

Merritt had never much liked desks. He didn't like being stuck at one during his school days. He had resented being assigned to one when pneumonia had wreaked its havoc on his lungs. And he found himself thinking very ungracious thoughts about the scratched and wobbling one in his room at Hawkhill House, despite the fact that no one but himself had told him he must attend his correspondence.

It wasn't that he didn't want—need, even—to read more carefully through the letters that had arrived in the post yesterday evening. It was that he would far prefer to be riding toward Fairfax Tower right now, even if it meant enduring the continual ribbing of Xavier over the way he'd apparently been looking at Marigold since the funeral three days ago.

As if he could help it. After he'd kissed her—that one sweet, breathtaking moment when his lips had claimed hers—he'd been able to think of little but repeating the action. Preferably in a location where there weren't hundreds of neighbors just over the rise, where someone could come upon them at any moment.

Not that he'd found that opportunity yet. And he wouldn't

right now either, not until he finished making notes on the letters and writing his replies to each of them.

First, the one from Mother. It was full of her adventures with her sisters in Italy, easy to read and reply to. But then came the one from Gaines.

His investigation, he said, had been slow and painstaking because the last thing he wanted to do was draw attention to himself. Even so, Colonel May had begun to wonder at all his inquiries. Gaines had become even more secretive—and suspicious of May's suspicion. Despite that wrinkle, Gaines had learned quite a bit about the men who had vanished.

More, he had found an alarming trend. Each time a man vanished—four in total now—a mysterious amount of money had been received by the censors and, upon a sealed order, sent back out to a private address. He couldn't discern who had ordered the transfer, but the amount of money was suspicious. And consistent. And that *timing*. Each deposit had come exactly a week since the last received transmission from a man who'd gone missing.

The implications made him ill. Because it looked for all the world as though someone from the inside was literally selling out their agents to the enemy.

It couldn't be Hemming, could it? He'd tasked Ballantine with a mission that had sounded like a personal favor. Would he have sold him out to silence him after he discovered something incriminating? But then, what would his motivation have been with the others? It couldn't be the money. It was enough to tempt a military man, yes. But an earl, with an estate like his, with shipping ventures and possible dreadnought contracts? He had no need of those trifling funds.

Who, then? Who else from their list of possible suspects could be desperate enough for that money?

His stomach went a little tighter with each name he read

through. He knew the list by heart, but he read it again anyway. Each name a person. A person he knew, respected.

His eyes settled yet again on the last name on the list. Colonel May. He'd been the one to send Merritt out on leave. He was trying to shut out Gaines. He was clearly involved with whatever queries Hemming had sent Ballantine in search of . . . and he was too fond of the races, according to the report from the Imposters. Perhaps he needed the money to cover debts. Perhaps he had betrayed Hemming and Ballantine and the other missing agents for so simple a reason.

Sighing, he picked up the last missive from the Imposters, unable to escape the fact that they were discovering plenty of odd things about the Hemmings too. He didn't know how they'd uncovered that Lady Frances Hemming had once gone by the name of Franziska Coburg. Not only had they learned the fact, they'd unearthed some long-buried family records on the countess.

Before her mother had married the baronet everyone thought of as Frances's father, she'd been wed to a German count, against her family's wishes. No records could be found verifying that the couple had a daughter—not here in England, anyway—but she remained estranged from her family for a full decade. They didn't receive her into the fold again until 1872, when she returned married to Lord Moore, an eight-year-old Frances in tow.

The story they told everyone was that Lord and Lady Moore had met on holiday, had wed, had stayed in Europe all these years enjoying the Riviera. No one questioned it.

But Merritt questioned it now, as had the Imposters. Was Lady Hemming half German? Had she appeared in that photograph with, perhaps, relatives?

Being German was no crime—and if it was, half the aristocracy's blood was guilty of it. The noble families of Europe, especially those close to the monarchies, had been intermarrying for generations. And Victoria's grandchildren now sat on pretty much every throne the world over. It was a bit amusing, how alike King George, Kaiser Wilhelm, and Czar Nicholas looked. They could have been brothers, not just first cousins.

But political tides were changing rapidly, and the general populace had become increasingly wary of anyone German. Thanks to those ridiculous spy novels by William Le Queux, every civilian thought it their duty to report as suspicious every waiter and tourist with an accent.

It wasn't a good time, in short, to have those connections. And from what the Imposters had learned about Lady Hemming's grandparents, they had simply wanted to deny that first marriage had ever happened for reasons of their own, whether politics or biases or personal dislike of the count. So they rewrote their daughter's—and hence their granddaughter's—history.

A history it seemed Lord Hemming hadn't known . . . but he was looking into now, given that photograph. To what lengths would he go to keep it hidden?

Did he realize that someone else in England knew the truth of his wife's heritage—Miss Feuerstein, the headmistress of the academy to which they'd sent Lady Lavinia? Somehow Merritt doubted it.

How in blazes had the Imposters gotten into the finishing school, he wondered? Did they have a young lady on their payroll to pose as a pupil? Did they bribe someone attending or teaching there to snoop through the records? He'd accompanied his aunt and uncle to that very place to deposit Estelle several years ago, and he'd joked with his cousin that they clearly didn't mean for her to escape, given the security measures. They were actually in place to keep the girls safe—and keep unauthorized male visitors from calling—but even so.

More to the point, what *was* the connection between Feuerstein and Frances? Did they know each other? Were they friends? Cousins?

Merritt leaned back and rubbed at his eyes. What he was learning through this investigation was how blind he—and *everyone*—tended to be. Never pausing to wonder at the secrets each person held.

But they were there. They were always there. Whether it was family connections they didn't want known, debts that put them at risk of extortion or prone to corruption, mixed loyalties, or bad habits so easily exploited, it seemed every person he'd assumed he could trust had something to hide. Made a man wonder how he could ever be certain his friends were truly his friends.

He picked up the final letter that had come for him, forwarded by Uncle Preston. Jonathan. Who had, as always, written exactly what his heart most needed to hear, through some Spirit-breathed wisdom he oughtn't by rights to have had. His eyes skipped over the introductory bits and family news that he'd already read over eagerly last night and revisited the section that began at the bottom of the first page.

> As I declared my need to write to you today, Mary laughed and mused about how odd it was that we count each other as such dear friends when we met only once in person. A fortnight spent together, then so many years apart. Of course I've explained the circumstances to her before, and lamented before that had she but been there, she would understand. That going through such a thing together forged a bond that cannot be broken.
>
> But the thought has stayed with me today, and I've been musing upon it. Because it was more than the circumstances. Yes, you saved my life, my parents' lives, my

*siblings' lives. But the other soldiers we rendezvoused
with two days after your initial coming certainly helped
with that, too, yet I cannot claim the same friendship with them. It was something more than circum-
stance. It was, I think, a recognition of like minds, like
souls. Is that perhaps what friendship always is?*

*It was the same when I met Mary when we were in
England on furlough. I'd known her only three weeks
when I proposed, when she agreed to give up all she'd
ever known to come back to China with me. She has,
I am happy to say, never regretted it (or not for more
than a few minutes here and there as she struggles to
learn the way of things here, at any rate).*

*Friendship—true friendship—the kind that lasts
years and lifetimes, no matter whether the friends occupy the same physical space, is, I am convinced, a
reflection of the Divine. Perhaps even of the Trinity
itself. If God the Father and God the Son are one even
if separate, if from their love pouring out the Holy
Spirit has sprung, and if that Spirit then fills us . . . if
we are created in His image, then we must also have
that natural yearning for and ability to find true unity,
true friendship, true oneness with others.*

*Perhaps in our human frailty it is often corrupted.
But sometimes it finds its true expression. Sometimes
we find that whole and life-giving example. Sometimes
we meet our true friends, and our spirits—or perhaps
the Spirit within us—recognizes it when we do. I am
blessed to count you as one such friend.*

The words filled his mind and expanded in his chest, not
only humbling him but encouraging him. It would be so easy
to doubt everyone. Not just the Hemmings and the Mays and
the rest of his colleagues, but the Prestons. The Fairfaxes,

the Ballantines. Xavier. He *could* look on everyone around with fresh suspicion.

But he shouldn't. Because Jonathan was right. They were created in God's image, created for unity and brotherly love. *That* was what he ought to be focusing on, embracing, and celebrating. He could mourn the times and occasions when it was instead broken, yes, and he could open his eyes to it. But he mustn't ever fall into the trap of having his eyes so opened to the darkness that they failed to see the light all around him.

A tap came on his open door, and he looked away from his letters to find Xavier in the doorway, dressed in his riding clothes. And, of course, grinning. "Are you quite certain I can't tempt you into joining me on the hunt at Alnwick Abbey? It's been ages since we've had a good foxhunt together."

Merritt made a face. "Because I'm a lousy hunter, you know that. I always find myself feeling sorry for the fox."

His friend laughed. "I imagine you'd come anyway, if a certain young lady was going to be there."

"But she isn't." He'd asked yesterday, when they received the invitation from the Hemmings, but Marigold had shaken her head. She was not, she'd said, in the habit of hunting beautiful creatures for sport. Though she'd considered adding an arctic fox to their menagerie once . . .

And so he and Xavier would simply go their own ways this morning, X to the Abbey and Merritt to the Tower. Not that he could let Xavier go without a jab of his own. "And I have a feeling you wouldn't be quite so eager if it weren't for another young lady."

Xavier granted it with a tilt of his head, no embarrassment whatsoever on his face, the strange man. "You know, I've yet to tire of her company. Rather remarkable, really. Perhaps there's hope for us making something of a match, if we don't discover any deal-breaking habits in the next month or two."

He just *talked* of it, so matter-of-factly. Strange, strange man. Merritt shook his head. "You take all the fun out of teasing you."

"Exactly." Chuckling, X spun away. "I'll see you this evening."

"Have a good day." Once alone again, Merritt turned resolutely back to his correspondence and finished three of the four replies he must make, to Mother and Gaines and Mr. A. He wouldn't reply to Jonathan quite yet—better to let his thoughts stew and grow before he answered that one, since there was certainly no rush.

Once finished, he put the outgoing letters on the front table for his batman to put into the post and saddled his rented horse. A twenty-minute ride, and the increasingly familiar sight of Fairfax Tower coming into view drew a smile to his lips.

He hadn't bothered going to the front entrance since the morning he'd eaten breakfast in the kitchen. Why act like a guest when he'd been accepted as a true friend? Might as well save them all time and effort and take his horse to the stables himself.

He nearly collided with Franco, who was juggling a pile of boxes and letters, all of which he dropped when Merritt's mare sidestepped and whinnied in alarm, silly creature. Not that Franco—expert juggler that he was—dropped the stack out of anything but a desire to help with the horse, Merritt knew. The old man's hand had hold of the bridle before Merritt could tug on the reins, a series of low croons in Romani coming from his lips as he stroked the horse's nose.

Merritt smiled and dismounted. "Thanks. Let me get these out of the mud for you."

Franco smiled. "Probably should have let you handle it. You're capable. But instinct, eh?"

"I'm not offended." He gathered up the letters first, shuffling them into a neat stack to set atop the parcels. Though he had to blink when he saw the seal on one of the envelopes, which had flipped over.

A dab of black wax, with an ornate, familiar *I* stamped into it.

An *I*. Not an *F* for Fairfax. Not the red or purple wax he'd seen on their other outgoing post. Black.

"Here, I'll take those. And your mare, too, with my other hand." Franco held out his now-open arm.

Merritt handed the stack over to him, careful to keep his face blank. His churning thoughts tucked away.

An *I*. In black wax.

"Thanks," he said. Not an *F*. "Are they in the house?"

Franco shook his head. "Gymnasium."

Merritt nodded, waited for Franco to lead the horse out of the way, and strode toward the gymnasium.

An *I* in black wax. Like every single letter he'd gotten from the Imposters. In the *outgoing* post.

Though he knew Peabody was squawking and the big cats were calling to one another, he could only hear his own pulse in his ears. Though two minutes ago he'd been enjoying the morning sunshine, now he felt only shadows eclipsing it. Though he'd been looking forward to another day in the Fairfaxes' company, now he wondered who they really were.

The Imposters.

Actors, he'd thought. People able to blend into society for an hour here or there. Investigators.

He stepped into the enormous building, his eyes sweeping the space and spotting them immediately.

Marigold, on the highwire. Balancing her way across with bare feet, arms outstretched. Her brother on the mats, cart-wheeling and flipping in a series of impossible moves.

Fun, he'd thought. The skills the Caesars had trained them to do. Good exercise. Sport. Entertainment.

Skills? Where were they able to go with those skills that

252

other people couldn't? Anywhere, he'd wager. Things like walls and gates would pose little obstacle to them. Give them a long silk and he'd bet they could get down from any height, just like Drina.

The master key Marigold kept in her bag. The torch. The way Fairfax entertained them all one rainy afternoon by putting on absolutely any accent they requested and delivering lines from plays or literature in them.

Acting, yes. But they weren't actors pretending to be nobility. They were nobility pretending to be investigators. They were liars. Both of them. All of them, everyone at this blighted place.

And why? Why had they done it? Not only lying to him— they'd obviously been at this long before he came along—but to all of society?

Why? The question echoed through his mind as he watched them. It ricocheted through his impressions, his memories, his thoughts.

Then he asked it again. With his eyes actually open.

This enormous building. The theater. The stadium. All built by their father—but at what cost? The house that should have been staffed by ninety and was instead run by five—four, now that Hector had gone off to spend the summer with cousins in another circus. The earl and his sister who cooked their own food, mucked their own stalls.

Of course. His breath eased out. They were strapped. Or perhaps worse than strapped. Perhaps *broke* or even in debt. How had he not seen it before? Why had he believed their offhanded comment about sending the servants away for the summer, when no other house ever did such a thing?

Because he'd been dazzled by the feathers and sequins and flowers, that's why. He, who had thought he'd seen her so clearly, seen what others had missed, had been just as blinded by her disguise as anyone else.

Shame filled him. He had been so quick to believe the story

they'd acted out for him. Just like everyone else. He'd told himself he was different, that he saw her depths, that he knew her so well, when he'd refused to ask questions that ought to have been obvious. He'd been charmed by her disguise—her beautiful disguise. But only because he'd caught a glimpse of the girl beneath it.

The girl he now saw without the mask she both hated and loved. A girl willing to work for her dinner. Willing to sacrifice for her family. Willing to walk a tightrope every day to feed her lion and her leopard and her little brother.

Blast. What was it Jonathan had said? *Sometimes we meet our true friends, and our spirits—or perhaps the Spirit within us—recognizes it when we do.*

Merritt sank down onto the weights bench. He had no right to be angry with them. They were doing what they could to survive, to care for their family—both human and otherwise—without losing this place. And they were doing it in a way that sought answers for people, that sought truth. Hadn't he been impressed time and again with what they were able to discover? Hadn't they impressed Xavier's father with their integrity and honesty?

And wasn't it *this* that he'd come to appreciate most about the Fairfax siblings? Not the title, not the mask, not the story. *This.* The real them. The circus performers. The acrobats. The actors.

The Imposters. All along, it had been the Imposters that he'd counted as his true friends, that his soul had recognized.

His lips twitched up. He wasn't honestly certain what that said about *him*.

"Sir Merritt! A bonny day I bid ye," Fairfax called out, his accent of the morning spot-on for County Clare.

Marigold looked up, smiled, and his heart flipped just as fully as her brother had done on the mats. She hurried to the end of the rope and scurried down the ladder.

254

He turned to Fairfax, who had jogged over to him with a smile. Merritt returned it, though his own still felt a bit dazed on his lips. "You know what accent you haven't done for me in far too long? That Welsh sea captain."

Only because Merritt was watching for it so closely did he catch the momentary freeze of Fairfax's features before they shifted into confusion. "Welsh, you say? I don't recall ever doing that one. Though I have a wonderful *Cornish* sea captain in my repertoire."

Merritt met his gaze. Tried to convey in his own that he could be trusted. "You did, on our very first meeting. In the church."

Marigold had reached them by this point, and her own smile went still as glass as she caught those words. Her eyes snapped to her brother, who had pursed his lips and rocked back on his heels.

Merritt pushed to his feet. "You can drop the pretense. I collided with Franco a minute ago and saw the outgoing post."

Fairfax folded his thick arms over his chest. "That's it. I'm going to sack him." Though it was laughter in his voice, not frustration.

Marigold, however, had gone as pale as the chalk cliffs she'd told him not to visit. "Yates? What was in the post?"

Her brother sighed. "Our next update for Genie. He'd have recognized the seal, having just got one himself yesterday, and plenty before that. Well." Brightening again, Fairfax clapped his hands together. "This simplifies things. And will save on postage too. Why didn't you catch on sooner, old boy? It would have saved us a world of trouble."

He wanted to smile, but his lips just wouldn't obey that command. Not given the stricken look on Marigold's face. Was it really so horrible that he knew their secret? "I suppose it's difficult to see what one never expects. And I certainly never expected the Imposters to be peers."

"The cleverness of our name, isn't it?" Yates laughed and slapped a hand to his shoulder. "It was the one we'd first come up with for our circus. Well." Looking between Merritt and Marigold, Fairfax cleared his throat and stepped away. "I'll just, ah, go and fetch a knife to slice through this tension in case you two don't manage to fix it yourselves in the next ten minutes. Ten. Then I'm coming back if you don't make your way to the house by then."

Though he whistled as he strolled out into the sunshine, the silence within the gymnasium felt as heavy as a tombstone. What should he say? That he wasn't angry? Would that be akin to claiming he had a right to be and put her on the defensive? Should he ask why she hadn't told him? But why would she have, especially before, when they scarcely knew each other? He'd been no one. No one but an acquaintance, a client, then finally a friend. And he'd hardly seen her since that kiss, not outside of company.

But she wouldn't even look at him now. She wouldn't look at *anything*. She had her face tilted down, like she always did when she wore a hat to shield her. Her shoulders rolled back in that way that said, *"Look at my dress, not at me."* Even though she wasn't in a dress, she was in loose cotton trousers, a blouse tied over that black thing.

His chest ached, seeing her put on the mask now, here, with him. "Marigold." He wanted to reach for her, but his hands wouldn't obey. "Were . . . were you ever going to tell me?"

The real question. Not why she hadn't, because that he could understand. But had she ever meant to let him in?

Her nostrils flared, and her larynx bobbed with a hard swallow. "I never got that far in my thoughts." Her voice was barely even a whisper. "I couldn't get past that the very fact of it meant nothing could ever come of this."

"You think me so incapable of understanding? Of accepting?"

"No. Maybe. I don't know." Her eyes squeezed shut, and she turned half away from him. "How could you?"

"Because I have eyes to see you, Marigold. To see this place, all it is and all it isn't. I've only been here a month, and *I* would do anything to save it. You think I'd blame you for doing the same? There were debts, weren't there? When your father died?"

The saddest smile seized her mouth. "No. No debts. Just . . . no money left. None. He'd spent every last shilling on this, his final monument to a life devoted to frivolities." She waved at the gymnasium. "We had to let all the staff go, but that wasn't enough. He'd taken out all his father had invested, never reinvesting a pence. We needed income, and the rents were barely enough to pay for basic maintenance on the house, not enough to feed us."

"I can understand that. Your solution wasn't one I ever would have come up with, but I cannot argue with the results. I wouldn't want to."

His words didn't seem to soothe her any. If anything, they agitated her more, and she half turned away from him. "I appreciate that. But don't you see? I can't just *stop*. I can't . . . I can't choose another life now. Yates and I are a team, we need each other. We could not do half the things we do on our own, even with Gemma and Graham and the Caesars helping."

They were a trapeze act. Together, they could scale a wall twice as high, leap a gap twice as far, listen in on twice the conversations.

The implications settled heavy on his shoulders. True, he'd never given much thought to marriage, to a wife, to a family. But he'd always assumed that when he wed, his wife would do what all society wives did. She would take tea with her friends and attend aid meetings, read books and stitch samplers. She would be there when he left in the morning and there when he came home in the evening.

He winced at the thought. How very boring he'd painted his faceless future spouse. No wonder he'd never been inspired to search for her.

And no wonder she'd stopped her thoughts of them where she had. She would know those expectations even better than he did. She would know very well that it was either the Imposters or marriage.

A word neither of them had ever mentioned, obviously. Not yet. But even their few weeks' acquaintance was enough for her to know that he wasn't the type to kiss any pretty girl he found crying on a beach. It meant something. Even if he'd put no words to it, it meant something serious. She'd know that because her spirit—or the Spirit within her—had recognized his too.

"Well." He drew in a long breath, let it out. Cleared the emotion from his throat and realized idly that he hadn't coughed in two days. "There is only one solution then, as I see it."

She nodded, her chin dropping even more, well past its usual hide-me angle.

He put a hand to her shoulder and turned her around to face him. "You're simply going to have to expand your team by one."

Her brows crashed together as her face jerked up. "What?"

Merritt straightened his spine. "I admit I'll need a bit more training, but I'm a quick study. Don't expect me to learn all the acrobatics, but I have my own skills. And it would be useful for you, wouldn't it, to have someone in the War Office? And my training in the Coldstream Guards was beyond compare. I can send you references, if you like."

Was that a smile tugging at her lips? No. They were simply parting in shock. "You—you would join us? But why?"

"Because, Lady Marigold," he said, slipping a hand onto her waist and drawing her closer, "it is that or walking away

258

from you when this is all over. And that simply isn't a viable option. Unless you insist upon it."

Finally, her gaze rested on his. For a long moment she looked into his eyes, first one and then the other, as if searching for the lie. Searching for the dismissal. Searching for the insult. She wouldn't find it. It wasn't there to be found.

Her nostrils flared again. "I would never insist. Though I *will* have to have a look at those references. The Imposters don't hire just anyone, you know." There was the smile, or a foreshadow of it anyway, just beginning to win possession of her lips.

No doubt it would have, had he not interrupted it with his own lips, pressed to hers. And this time, with six minutes left in her brother's grant of time, by his estimation, he dared to draw her closer. To wrap his arms around her.

Hers came around him, too, one hand tossing his hat aside and then pressing against the back of his head, inviting him closer, deeper.

An invitation he couldn't even think to refuse.

TWENTY

Marigold's head still swam as she walked toward the house, her arm twined around Merritt's, her lips still warm from his.

He wanted her. *Her.* Wanted to be with her. Knowing who she really was, who she pretended to be, who she couldn't give up being. He knew it, and it hadn't sent him running. It had brought him more firmly into her world.

That was a revelation she would have to ponder at considerable length, as she relived the feel of his mouth, of his arms around her, of the flame in his eyes as he looked at her after he'd pulled away.

She'd never thought anyone would look at her like that. As if he found her beautiful. As if he yearned for more of her. As if he . . . but he hadn't said the word *love* yet, neither of them had. They'd only danced around it.

Which was enough for one day. Her head was already spinning. She pressed a little closer to his side, smiling up at him when he opened the door for her, wondering if it were all a dream. She'd probably walk into the drawing room and find it had morphed into a circus tent, and then turn back to find Leonidas prowling at her side instead of Merritt, the dream shifting under her feet as they did.

No, the drawing room was still very much the drawing room, and Merritt didn't change into her lion.

But the scene that greeted her was no less bizarre. Yates stood in the middle of the room, still in his exercise clothes, with a mud-spattered Lavinia and Lord Xavier, both in riding outfits, standing before him. Weren't they supposed to be on the foxhunt that Lord Hemming had planned to cheer up Mr. Ballantine? She had her doubts that the man would attend, but she'd been surprised before. Mr. Ballantine was such an avid hunter that he even carried his rifle in his car at all times "just in case some game happened by." And foxhunts—foxhunts were his favorite.

This one couldn't possibly be finished already. Hence, she supposed, the mud-spattered riding clothes.

Lavinia spun to her when they entered, her eyes as wild as the curls peeking out from beneath her hat. "Marigold! I didn't know where else to turn, and Lord Xavier said I should come to you and Yates."

"What is it?" She let go of Merritt's arm so she could rush forward and take her friend's outstretched hand. Her heart, racing a moment ago from the unexpected bliss of another of Merritt's kisses, now raced in dreaded expectation.

Something had happened. She could see it in Lavinia's eyes.

Lavinia's lips trembled. "I don't even know. Only that last night they were snapping at each other before supper—my parents, I mean. I cannot recall the last time I heard them arguing, you know how Father dotes on us both. They stopped when I came in, but I caught Mother mouth 'the old office' to Father. I—I am not proud to admit it, but I was so curious that I went and hid in the old priest hole after the meal—you remember it."

Marigold didn't let her gaze so much as flick toward Merritt. "I do."

Lavinia nodded. "They'd given up using that room after the time they found us hiding there—I think they must have feared someone would always be eavesdropping. And for good reason, I suppose, because there I was again. They didn't catch me at it this time."

Though she wanted to rush her friend along, Marigold only nodded. "Good. I'm glad of that."

"Anyway, I don't know what I expected to hear them talking about, but not what I did. They were discussing how to convince Mr. Ballantine to sell his shipping company to Father. Mother actually said, 'Apply whatever pressure you must. If losing Cornelius wasn't enough, they've another child, and I don't imagine they want to lose *her*.'" Lavinia's eyes went damp, and her fingers trembled in Marigold's. "I never thought to hear such a coldhearted sentiment from my own mother's lips!"

Neither had Marigold. She shot a look to Yates, whose lips were pressed together in a thin line. "What did your father say?"

"That he would pay Mr. Ballantine a visit tomorrow—or today, rather, now—after the hunt."

Marigold's brow creased. "Why is your mother so set on this dreadnought contract?"

"I don't know! But . . ." Lavinia dropped Marigold's hand and spun away, agitation in her every jerky movement. "She said if he didn't secure the Ballantine operations to merge with their own, then she was through with him. She said she would leave him." She lifted shaking hands to cover her face.

Leopard stripes. Marigold could scarcely catch her breath. "She can't mean it."

Her friend sank to a seat on the edge of the settee, looking paler than she had in months. "I found letters. A few months ago. I haven't said anything to them, but . . . they were disturbing. From someone named Hans, to Mother.

Full of how much he misses her, how it's been too long, how when he looks at his daughter, he sees *her*." She squeezed her eyes shut.

Marigold couldn't blame her. She had seen her fair share of horrific truths about people who were supposed to be good, who were supposed to be as lovable as they were loving, who were supposed to be *better* than such implications. "Oh, Lavinia." All she could do was sit beside her, take her hand. And finally understand why her friend had gone from calling her parents *Mama* and *Papa* to *Mother* and *Father*. Why their love was no longer her inspiration. "You needn't assume the worst. There could be an explanation—"

"Don't be naïve. I'm not." Just like that, the new Lavinia pushed aside the old, and she straightened. "What matters here is that Father knows how she has come to feel. But still, for some reason, he is set on keeping her here with him. He begged for one more chance to convince Ballantine."

Oh, there were too many questions, and Claudia had only been able to discover so much in the documents Lady Hemming had stashed away in a box underneath her stockings— the source of the family history the Imposters had sent to Merritt.

"She told him this was his last chance and said she would be spending the day with Erna, as if it was a threat."

"Erna?" Lord Xavier asked.

"Feuerstein! The headmistress at Ravenscleft Academy, who I was convinced she couldn't possibly know—but clearly she does! When I was dressing for the hunt, she breezed in as if nothing was wrong, informed me she was visiting a friend and would be home this evening, and told me to have a lovely day. Just like that." Cheeks pink, Lavinia huffed her opinion of her parents' behavior. "And Father will be going to see Mr. Ballantine as soon as he's caught the fox. Which means you need to come over and help me."

"Help you?"

"Find out who this Hans is!" she declared, as if it were obvious. "There has to be proof of it somewhere, doesn't there? Letters or documents or *something*."

"Lavinia." Marigold knew her hesitation came through in her voice. "Are you certain you want to know the truth of this?"

That didn't give her friend pause, just made her lift her chin. "Isn't the truth always worth knowing?"

Yates gave a sage nod. "I believe a wise man once said, 'The truth isn't always pretty. But I like to think it's always beautiful.'"

Lavinia's face softened a bit. "Yes. Exactly so. Who said that?"

"Me." Yates grinned, all little boy again. "Good one, isn't it? Marigold's going to embroider it on a sampler for me."

He was so ridiculous sometimes. But Lavinia snorted a laugh, her intensity seeping out in it, so it had clearly been well-placed ridiculousness. She turned back to Marigold, brows lifted. "Please? They've been coddling me ever since that dratted fever, and now I come to learn they aren't at all the happy couple I always thought them. I just want to know who my family really is. Is that so bad?"

"No." Unwise perhaps. But not bad. She sighed and looked at the three men. Yates, who looked ready to bolt from the room then and there. Lord Xavier, who was still angled toward Lavinia, clearly more concerned for her than anything. Merritt, who was looking at *her* instead of her friend, for some reason she still couldn't fathom. She nodded. "All right. Let me get dressed."

"As will I," Yates said, moving toward the door. "But I shall hasten to the Ballantines' instead. See if Milo perhaps wants a little company."

On the quest he'd assigned him already, though he didn't

264

add that bit. Even so, Lavinia would know his intention was to listen in on the conversation. She was no fool. "Good. Do hurry, Marigold. Mother granted Claudia and her maid the rest of the day off, so the family wing ought to be all but empty until Father returns."

She nodded and took off after Yates.

"Just a moment." Merritt had followed them out and caught up to them at the bottom of the staircase, his brow marred with concern. Voice low enough not to carry back into the drawing room, he said, "Before anyone makes another move, you should know what Gaines sent yesterday from London. I just sent it to you, but obviously you haven't received it yet."

Marigold listened to his quiet words as he told them about the missing men, each of whose disappearances had coincided with one of those odd deposits of money. He finished with, "I can't think that amount of money would be enough motivation for Hemming. But I don't know about Colonel May or the others."

Marigold exchanged a look with her brother and jogged up the stairs, motioning Merritt to join them.

He hesitated, glancing over his shoulder. "Upstairs? Are you certain?"

He'd never been off the ground floor, so naturally he'd surmised that upstairs was where their bedrooms were. She smiled. "Our father's study—it's our headquarters, with all our files. We may already have some information on your colleagues, if you'd like to take a look."

His face went blank. "On my colleagues. Why?"

"Not because of you." Yates backtracked to the bottom, took Merritt by the arm, and hauled him along until he came of his own will. "It's just that we've had to poke into hundreds of backgrounds and lives over the last five years. Not all of it relevant, but we kept record of all we discover anyway. It's saved us work on future cases countless times."

Minutes later, Marigold had the pleasure of watching awe wash over his face as he entered the study and Yates opened the many, many drawers full of files. "All of these are case files?"

"No. Just dossiers, mostly. The case files are over there." Yates motioned toward a mirroring wall of cupboards.

"If you're serious about joining our ranks—" She hadn't had a chance to mention it to Yates yet, but she wouldn't have put it past him to have been listening from outside the gymnasium, and he certainly didn't look surprised by the suggestion—"then you might as well acquaint yourself with our system while we get ready."

Was that panic in his eyes? No. Just surprise. "You trust me with all this?"

Obviously *she* did. But she looked to her brother. Yates's eyes had a strangely soft look to them as he regarded Merritt for a long moment. Then he nodded. "You saw the truth of my sister. I can think of no better test for joining the Imposters. Welcome aboard—and get to work." With a grin, he vanished.

Marigold edged out the door, too, before she could convince herself that one more kiss was more important than learning the secrets of the Hemmings. Yet she couldn't just leave, not yet. Not before she said, "Thank you."

His smile went questioning. "For what?"

"For seeing the truth of his sister. And not running the other way."

She would treasure the grin he sent her for all her days. "Oh, that. Well, don't think you won't be expected to return the favor. I have five female cousins who eagerly await every G. M. Parker column just to see what Lady M was wearing last, and you're going to have to meet them eventually. Brace yourself now."

She could think of nothing she'd love more. "I think I'll

survive it. I could even introduce them to G. M. Parker herself, if they'd like."

"You know her?" He frowned, and she counted a full four seconds before he rolled his eyes at himself. "Gemma Parks. G. M. Parker. I ought to have guessed it from the start."

"Ought to have, but you're so *very* slow on the uptake." With a wink, she stepped away from the door.

And ran smack into Gemma, who'd been standing there with folded arms and a hopefully playful scowl. She took Marigold by the arms and steered her toward her bedroom as she muttered, "Telling my secrets, are you?"

"Only that one." Because it wasn't really a *secret* that she was G. M. Parker. It may not be known by everyone who passed her on the streets, but she met regularly with her editors, who knew her real name. "And for good reason."

"I saw you walking in with him, arm-in-arm and cozy as could be." She didn't sound exactly happy about it.

Which made Marigold frown as she closed her bedroom door behind them. "You don't like him?"

Gemma started at the question and smoothed out a few of the frown lines from her face. "Of course I like him. And I'm the one who begged you to see that not all men are like the ones we've built cases against. I just don't want you to rush into anything and get hurt." She spun for the adjoining dressing room. "You can know someone all your life and never really *know* him after all."

Marigold sighed. "Gemma. You're not being fair to Graham—"

"Who said anything about him? We're talking about Sir Merritt." Her voice muffled by fabric and plaster, Gemma still managed to make it clear that any further mention of Graham would not be borne. "Are you going to tell me what happened with him this morning, or am I going to have to tickle it out of you as I retie your corset?"

She emerged with said underpinnings and a red-orange day dress that looked like the most marvelous sunset.

Well, Marigold knew when to pivot on the battlefield. She shrugged out of her blouse and trousers, grabbed the undergarments, and went behind the screen to peel off her leotard. She wasn't about to wear that by itself again with unrelated gentlemen apt to show up in the middle of her routine.

As she dressed, she told Gemma of the morning's events, both as related to Merritt and the Imposters, and then Lavinia's unexpected addition. Ending, of course, with their plans to go and search the house for more information while it was empty of parents and Lady Hemming's staff.

Gemma looked unconvinced by the wisdom of the plan as she brushed through Marigold's long locks. "Are you certain that's a wise idea? Any undermaid could come upon you. And Claudia already searched for her ladyship's family history and shared it with us."

Marigold snorted. "Your cousin was only looking for something to satisfy her own curiosity and prove herself right, and only among the lady's things. She wasn't looking for all we will be. And with four of us, someone can play lookout."

"Make that five of us. You're the only one of that bunch I'd trust to be lookout, but you'll do better at the actual looking. I'll come along to ward off any domestics." She coiled Marigold's hair into long ropes and began winding them around her head. "What of Yates? To the Ballantines'?"

"Yes. Not that Milo wouldn't be able to do the job in a pinch, but four ears are better than two. And since he has the advance notice—"

"Might as well put it to use." Gemma nodded and reached for the pins Marigold held up on her palm. She glanced into the mirror, her gaze meeting Marigold's there, before she got to work pinning. "Has Genie replied to the letter you sent the other day?"

Marigold pressed her lips together. It had taken her hours to compose the note, and many false starts. The balls of discarded paper were still in her rubbish bin by her little writing desk as testament. Even now, a day after she'd sent it, she wasn't convinced she'd written the right words, words that at once bared her heart but also made certain the focus wasn't on herself at all, but rather on Genie. Recognition of all she'd done for Marigold in *her* times of loss and grief. An apology for failing to be the friend she both needed and deserved.

She shook her head. "I have a feeling she won't reply. That I may not see much of her again, but for in passing."

There had been days when she'd wanted to avoid Genie. But not like this. Now she prayed morning and night to be given a chance to heal that relationship.

"She only needs a bit of time and space, I daresay." Gemma offered her a small, tight-lipped smile that said she wasn't convinced by her own assurances.

What Genie needed was an answer about her brother. And though she'd never know to credit Marigold and Yates with the finding of it, they would. Yates, as Mr. A, had written his own letter for her last night—the one Merritt had seen this morning. In it, he'd first returned the unspent fees, but then also assured her that they would not consider this case closed until they'd learned how and by whose hand her brother died and delivered any pertinent information to the authorities so that justice could be served.

Would it provide comfort or feel more like salt in the wound? She didn't know, but she prayed it was the former. That though they hadn't been able to locate Cornelius before his death, they could still find answers for her.

That even if she would never again look on Marigold as a friend, she would still accept the help of the Imposters.

TWENTY-ONE

Yates darted along the edge of the house behind Milo, who had looked mildly surprised to see him today—without baklava in his hands, anyway. It had taken only a short whisper to explain the situation, and here they were, Milo leading him through the path he'd already scoped out, steering clear of gardeners or other staff, but landing below the window of Ballantine's office, open to the spring breeze.

If this was where Hemming came to meet him, Yates would be perfectly positioned. In place, ready to set up his Akouphone and mentally record their every word. If instead they went for a walk or something . . . well, that's where Milo would be handy. He'd be back in the stables by the time Hemming showed up. He'd park his car, and then do what he could to keep an eye out for them.

"He'll meet him in there," Milo whispered now, crouching low behind a bush. "He's scarcely emerged from that room since the funeral, according to his valet. I can't imagine Hemming would convince him to do so."

Yates nodded, at once glad of the all-but-guarantee and yet sad. So very sad for Mr. Ballantine, and for his family. "Drina's still planning on making the baklava this evening. Just hadn't had a chance yet, and when Lavinia said he was coming now . . ."

Milo grinned. "All the reward and none of the risk? I'm heartbroken. Really." He clapped a quiet hand to Yates's shoulder and sidled around him. "Come back the same way when you're finished. I'll keep your horse out of sight."

"Thanks." Glad to be done with the whispering, Yates waited for Milo to disappear again and then got out one of his favorite tools—a small mirror mounted to a telescoping rod. Slowly, slowly he raised it up and out, until he had a view inside the window from within the protective leaf cover of the bush behind which he crouched.

He'd never been in Ballantine's office, but it looked as he'd expected. Dark wood shelves with more ships-in-bottles than books. A massive desk, leather chairs before it. And behind it, another massive chair, with the large, hunched figure of Mr. Ballantine upon it.

Poor chap. He looked broken. Shattered. Sitting there in pieces.

As Yates watched, a soft rapping came at the door. Three knocks. A wait. Mr. Ballantine didn't stir. Yates may have begun to wonder if he was awake, except that he was moving —one finger, sending the hand of a bronze astrolabe spinning around its face. Stopping it, sending it on again. Over and over.

The knock came again, along with a timid voice. "Mr. Ballantine? Your wife has sent luncheon."

Spin, stop. Spin, stop. Spin, stop.

Tap, tap, tap. "Mr. Ballantine? Sir, I'm going to open the door and bring in your tray."

Spin, stop. Spin, stop. Spin, stop.

The door opened, and a small maid entered, dwarfed by the size of the tray she carried. She balanced it easily enough, not even reacting when Ballantine jumped, shouting something in Gaelic, and then settled again, rubbing at his eyes. "Ah. Abigail. You should have knocked."

271

The girl just slid the tray onto his desk, curtsied, and retreated again.

Ballantine stared for a moment at the tray, but he didn't so much as lift the silver cloche. Only heaved a breath and then turned back to the astrolabe.

Spin, stop. Spin, stop. Spin, stop.

Each revolution wound the bands of sorrow a little tighter around Yates's chest. He waited a solid two minutes, but when Ballantine made no further move toward the food, he decided it was worth risking the Akouphone. He'd brought it, not certain if he'd be able to plant the microphone anywhere or not. But he was certain now that he could slip it into the corner of the window and Ballantine wouldn't notice.

He didn't want to miss a word of the exchange between the two neighbors.

It only took him a minute to get everything set up, position the headphones over his ears, and settle back down into the convenient shelter of the bush. It took considerably longer for Hemming to arrive and be shown into the chamber, but at last the earl entered, was greeted by a yet-again-startled Ballantine, and settled into one of the leather chairs.

Yates adjusted the dial on the Akouphone, now that there were voices to be heard, and checked to make certain his mirror was still inconspicuous among the leaves.

"Thank you for seeing me, Bally. I can only imagine how horrible a time you're having."

Ballantine grunted something unintelligible, but Yates didn't think the fault was with his equipment.

Hemming didn't seem put off. "I want you to know that we're here to help you in any way we can."

The next grunt carried a definite note of frustration. "What exactly do you think you can do? Can you bring my boy back to me, alive and well?"

"No." Hemming hung his head. "Would that I could."

Not the tack his wife had recommended taking—wise. But Yates thought it genuine regret, likely even guilt, in his tone. Maybe he wasn't a bad man, Hemming. He likely knew that, somehow or another, his sending Cornelius on that mission for him had resulted in his death, and he was sorry for it. "But I *can* perhaps help with the burden of business. I know it must be the last thing you want to worry with right now, yet it will be no less demanding than ever."

Silence crackled like static in Yates's ears for one second, two. Then he winced at the sudden explosion of sound as Ballantine leapt to his feet, out of Yates's view, and sent something crashing to the floor.

"You would *dare* to come here now, a week after my son was killed by some murderer's hand, and try to buy my business? My legacy? All I have left?"

"Calm yourself." Hemming's voice was both urgent yet relaxed. "And lower your voice, lest your wife and daughter hear you say such things. Would you have them think you value them less than a few ships and docks?"

Ballantine did *not* sit. "My wife and daughter know well—"

"They most certainly do *not*. Do you know what your daughter said to Lady Marigold Fairfax at the funeral? Do you? That she envied her for her freedom not to wed, because now her only purpose would be to marry whomever you chose for her—for the sake of the business. *That* is what your daughter knows. That she is nothing to you now but a marriage pawn." Hemming stood, braced his hands on the edge of the desk, and leaned in. "Is that what you want her to think? To feel? To *be*? Do you want her lashed to this place like a slave, like a—like a blighted child sacrifice, offered to the gods of shipping? How can you be so cruel?"

Yates winced—both at the truth of the situation and at Hemming's daring to put it so bluntly, for his own selfish purposes.

But maybe it wasn't *all* selfish. Maybe he did truly worry for his neighbor's family, being so keenly aware of the unseen fractures in his own. Yates wanted to believe that was at least in part his motivation.

"How dare you."

"How dare I? How dare *you* make your own daughter feel so unloved when she is in the throes of mourning the brother she adored. How dare you put her in a position to feel such things, when the expression of them cost her the only two friends she's ever known. You think Lady Marigold will ever entertain her again now? Or Lavinia, for that matter, given how Genie offended her dearest friend? Your daughter has cut her best ties to society with her rash words. She has let herself be filled with vitriol, and what man would be willing to live all his life with that, even for the gain of a shipyard?"

Yates's wince might just be permanent. Hemming had diverged fully from the truth there, and no doubt he knew it. Neither Marigold nor Lavinia would cut Genie off, and there were plenty of men who would be happy to ignore a venomous wife who brought him such an inheritance. Not to mention that Genie wouldn't be able to hold onto her anger forever. In a few days or weeks or months, the grief would overtake the anger again.

But the words clearly hit their mark. Ballantine moved back into the view of Yates's mirror and sank into his chair. "My grandfather built this shipyard. It's how he made his fortune. Our legacy."

"It's an anchor, Bally, holding you back. Keeping you grounded forever in the eyes of the peers as a man of *business*. Of trade. It's one thing for an old family to broaden their holdings, quite another for new money to come in and flaunt their wealth from a business still in their hands. You know this."

Ballantine had resorted to grunts again.

Hemming didn't retake his seat. "Sell it, and opinions will start to change. You won't be Ballantine of Ballantine Shipping anymore—you'll be Ballantine of Denwick Park. Your daughter—your daughter won't have to marry an experienced businessman. She could marry a *lord*. Young Fairfax, perhaps—hasn't she always fancied him? Think of the dowry you could send her with if you accept my offer. A handsome-enough one to earn the regard of *any* young lord. Your daughter could be a countess. A marchioness—blazes, man, perhaps even a duchess! Take this burden off her shoulders, and the sky is the limit!"

Yates let his eyes fall shut. How very clever Hemming was—appealing to the deepest hope and dream of the Ballantines. To be *more*. To claim by rights what they were accused of pretending to.

Ballantine's head rested against his hands. "I . . . I don't know. I must . . . my wife. Talk it over."

Hemming relaxed, his tone lightening again when he spoke. "Take as much time as you need. You know my offer, and you know where to find me when you're ready to take it."

A moment later, Hemming let himself out. Yates didn't dare move just yet, but he lowered the mirror, not wanting to see Mr. Ballantine crumpled on his desk, arms over his head.

And he took his headphones off too. Because it just wasn't right to listen to another man sob.

~~You do not know me. Or perhaps you do. I am Frances's husband~~

~~How long have you been corresponding with my wife that I~~

~~You say you love her. If you loved her like I do, you would have encouraged truthfulness and~~

275

~~I am not the monster she must have painted me to~~
~~be, so bigoted that I would dismiss her because of you~~
~~I have come across your longtime correspondence~~
~~with my wife. I know who you are and who she is. Let~~
~~me assure you~~

Dear Hans,

I dare to write to you with familiarity, though we
have never met. I dare because of our mutual love for
Frances. Perhaps you will think it forward, and I have
no doubt that she will be furious if she discovers that
I have initiated such contact, but it must be done. For
her sake, and for our daughter's. I fear what the reper-
cussions will be to our family if her loyalties are made
known.

I do not know what she has told you. But here is
what she has told me: nothing. All these years of marriage, and never did she indicate that her father was not
Lord Moore. Never did she hint that she had an elder
brother. Never did she even admit to having spent so
many happy years in Saxony, daughter to its leading
citizen. I have been cheated of knowing half of my
wife, and why? Because she did not trust me to love her
if I knew? Would that I could put such fears to rest, if
they are the root of this deception. Yet I fear that her
heart is more in Saxony, more with you, than it has
ever been here with me and our daughter. That I was
simply convenient.

I have told her that I know of her past, hoping she
would see that I love her anyway. Instead, she is now
angry with me for poking about. She has threatened
to leave me, to leave this life we have built together, to
leave our precious daughter.

Perhaps I am a fool. Perhaps I am worse. But I pray

*that somehow, there is a path through all this mess that
we can all live with. I pray that her love for you does
not require holding no love for me.*

*You will think me mad for suggesting this, but it is
the only thing I can conceive that may force a resolu-
tion, good sir. Will you come here to our home in Northumberland? Now, or as soon as you can manage it?
Perhaps if she sees us both at once, together, she will
realize who she is now: Lady Frances Hemming. No
longer Franziska Coburg. I will accept her history—but
please, help me convince her of our future.*

Marigold recited the last word of the letter they hadn't
dared to remove from Lord Hemming's personal sitting
room—and hadn't dared dictate within the walls of the
Abbey either. They'd all rushed back to the Tower, and
Gemma now made the last quick scribbles of shorthand on
what had begun as a clean sheet of paper in the Tower library.
Lavinia sat beside her, fingers knotted in her lap and forehead
knotted in incredulity, while Merritt and Xavier both paced
the space between the bookshelves, trying to make sense of
the words. Yates had just joined them again too.

They'd found a rubbish bin that looked much like Marigold's had after her attempt to bridge the gap between her
and Genie, overflowing with balled-up, discarded words. In
this case, words so unthinkable that the earl hadn't known
where to begin. This long, full letter had been written slop-
pily, on a scrap sheet with several crossed-out beginnings,
and had no doubt been copied over more neatly onto a piece
of the lord's stationery.

They had found no hint as to Hans's surname, no direction as to where the earl had sent the final letter, but Marigold
was already planning the note she would send to Hector.
If Saxony was where Lady Hemming had spent her first

years, that was a good place to start. That was where their Imposter-at-Large needed to go, to discover what he could about any Coburgs still in the region.

She knew they had been one of the ruling families of the kingdom of Saxony—not part of the Austrio-German empire, but still with its own independent king—for generations. If Lavinia's grandmother had married into that family, it should have pleased her parents, shouldn't it have? They must have had some particular reason for disapproving of the match. Perhaps because the count already had an heir, perhaps their politics didn't align, perhaps they'd had another match in mind. Who was to say?

But this brother. If he had been the Coburg heir, he was likely now the titled lord, sitting in the upper chamber of the Diet. Something Marigold knew only the rudiments about because she'd spent an hour looking for the name *Coburg* in a book of history of the German states and had found them listed there. Which meant he was important. Powerful. Hector ought to be able to find him easily.

"I don't understand." Lavinia didn't look at any of them, nor at the letter Gemma was now working to copy out in longhand. She looked only at the air in front of her. "If Father knows, then why is he trying to keep Mother here? How could he possibly forgive her? And why would he ask *him* to come here?"

Marigold moved to her friend's side and wove their fingers together. She had learned uncomfortable truths about her own parent five years ago—that her father had valued amusement above their future care. Much as he had loved them, much as they had loved him, he had loved himself more.

But this discovery about her mother must bring Lavinia pain on a whole different level. To realize not only that she had been lying about her heritage all these years, but that she was threatening to leave not only Lord Hemming but

Lavinia as well. How could that *not* make a daughter question her very self-worth?

The men seemed far more concerned over the question Lavinia posed aloud, rather than the ones she must be asking silently. "I cannot conceive the answer, my lady," Merritt said, his gaze finding Marigold rather than Lavinia. "He clearly adores your mother, but I cannot imagine wanting to face this Hans fellow. Perhaps we're missing something. Perhaps he knows something about Hans that we don't."

Marigold drew in a long breath. "Cornelius Ballantine must have discovered more," she said, though it felt strange to speak of that connection—a connection discovered by the Imposters—so freely with Lavinia. Merritt had already shared the bare outlines of it with her, though, when they'd found the letter and Lavinia had wondered how her father had even discovered the secrets so long buried. "Which means that your father has the information here somewhere, Lavinia."

"It means more than that." Yates raked a hand through his hair and went to look out the window, a million thoughts whirling through his eyes. "Cornelius didn't just discover this information and send it to your father. He died for it. Whoever this Hans is, we can't discount the possibility that he's a dangerous man."

Marigold's gaze tangled with Merritt's. What her brother wouldn't say aloud here in mixed company was that they knew now that Cornelius had been arrested and detained for weeks before his anonymous death. They knew he hadn't been the only field agent to die under similar circumstances in the last few months.

Which meant that if Cornelius died for this information, if Hans was somehow involved in that death, then Hans was also involved in the disappearance of the other agents.

Which meant Hans wasn't just dangerous. He was powerful.

And if Hemming's request was fulfilled, Hans would be coming *here*.

Had the earl invited a spymaster into their midst? Had he *known* it?

And if so, then one must ask a far different question: Was he really reaching out to the man so that they could confront his wife together . . . or was he writing as a spymaster himself, trying to spring a trap on his opposite number?

TWENTY-TWO

*M*erritt strode down the familiar London street toward the townhouse he was suddenly glad he hadn't let go, his eyes searching every shadow for he knew not what.

It was blighted uncomfortable, looking always over one's shoulder. "Does this ever get easier? Being constantly on one's guard?"

Beside him, Fairfax chuckled. "It becomes second nature. I'd have thought you'd know that, given that you *are* a Guard. Don't tell me you're not always on it when protecting His Majesty."

Merritt grunted and gestured toward the darkened house in a row of similar brick houses. "That's different. It doesn't carry over to my off-hours, walking along my own street."

"No? Shouldn't it?"

He'd never thought so. Yet here he was, back in London for a day to investigate his own colleagues. Walking on familiar pavement, but with Fairfax by his side instead of Xavier, who had opted to remain in Northumberland instead of spending twelve of twenty-four hours on a train. He'd ordered his batman to stay as well, wanting no more witnesses to their work here than necessary.

Fairfax nodded toward his door. "Looks like Gaines is awaiting us already."

Even with the indication, it took Merritt a few more steps and seconds of searching the shadows to pick his colleague's form from them. He led the way up the steps, fishing out his key to open the door.

As if a lock did anything to keep out those who meant to get in. It made him wonder which ones could *not* be opened by that master key.

"Thank you for coming so quickly," Gaines murmured as the three of them moved inside. "I feared I'd be undertaking this on my own and wasn't quite certain I'd be successful."

"Happily, your wire arrived in just enough time for us to catch the train." Fairfax followed Merritt into his utilitarian study and moved directly to the windows, checking the coverage of the curtains. "We ought to be safe to light a lamp without anyone noticing it, but I wouldn't recommend the electric."

Merritt grabbed an oil lamp from the shelf and lit it. Its light revealed the frown that Gaines was directing toward Fairfax. Who, granted, didn't look much like Fairfax. He'd added grey streaks to his hair with the help of powder, had pasted a bushy mustache and beard onto his face to cover its youth, and even used stage makeup to add lines around his eyes. They may not pass inspection in the full light of day—or of electricity—but they looked quite convincing by oil lamp.

He had completed the getup with an old suit at least a decade out of date, far too big around the middle, and bearing the marks of hungry moths. He'd added a bit of a stoop to his shoulders, too, which completed the image of a middle-aged man who wasn't in the best shape either physically or financially.

Remarkable, really. He'd thought so when Fairfax first

emerged from his room at the Tower in his Mr. A persona, and he'd thought it again every time he'd looked over at him during the six-hour train ride south.

Gaines finally transferred his dubious gaze from Fairfax to Merritt. "You mentioned bringing a trusted colleague. Who is it, if I may inquire?"

Fairfax held out a hand. "Mr. A of the Imposters, Ltd. Good to make your acquaintance, sir."

Remarkable indeed. He knew for a fact that Fairfax had been as well trained as the next gentleman to greet everyone with "how do you do?" and never "nice to meet you." But when in his role, he had no trouble forgetting long habit for what he'd determined fit his character better.

The flicker of surprise in Gaines's eyes said he'd heard of the Imposters. "I see. I didn't realize your firm was involved in this."

"I hired them to assist me when my health demanded the aid and have kept him apprised of the situation from our end as it unfolded—though the Top Secret elements I did not share, I assure you. He happened across certain sensitive information through his own means." Merritt motioned to the leather sofa and chairs. "Please, gentlemen. Sit. Let's hear this latest development, Gaines."

Fairfax chose the chair and lowered himself into it as if it took a bit of effort. Very much, in fact, like Franco tended to do. It also put him farther from Gaines than the sofa would. Smart. Merritt chose the end of the sofa closest to him, leaving his colleague to take the farthest seat.

Gaines sat, and apparently decided there was no use in arguing about the presence of an Imposter. He pulled out a sheet of paper and handed it to Merritt. The only thing on it was an address in Vauxhall that he'd seen several times before. "More cash has arrived, matching the other amounts I'd seen in the records. I instructed a courier to deliver it at precisely eight o'clock this evening, leaving us enough time to position ourselves and see who fetches it."

Fairfax grunted. "Been meaning to ask you about that, Livingstone. If these are truly payments for perfidy, why would they come through the War Office?"

A question that had been bothering him ever since Gaines first mentioned it. "I can only think that whomever they are going to didn't want the sender to know how to reach him directly—or else wanted it to remain off any personal records and thus thought to use the government itself to hide it."

"And we don't know who created those instructions?"

Gaines shook his head. "We'll know soon enough when we see where it goes. I daresay that amount of cash isn't going to be left long unattended. The recipient is surely the one who created the order—we'll catch him. We had better be off."

Good. Merritt was feeling far too antsy, just sitting here talking about it all.

Though his nerves didn't exactly ease as they arrived at the address in question half an hour later, hid themselves in the alleyway opposite . . . and looked with dismay at the sign hanging from the side of the building. "A blighted solicitor."

Gaines snatched his hat off his head and dashed it to the ground in frustration. "Blast. I should have swung by before now to see what it was. I thought it would be a simple matter of seeing who arrived to receive it."

Only Fairfax seemed unperturbed. In fact, a smile twitched under his false whiskers. "No need for dismay, gents. This is better. Business is shut up for the night, isn't it? We can simply let ourselves in and check their record books."

Gaines blustered. "You want us to break in? I am no thief, sir."

"There will be no breaking. No stealing. Simply . . . researching." Fairfax lifted his newly bushy eyebrows. "Or if you prefer, you can simply follow the solicitor every time he leaves this office for the indeterminate future, until such a time as he hands this envelope to someone else or takes it to a bank. Assuming you even know when he does it, which you will not, as he certainly wouldn't brandish it about on the street. He'll have it in a case. But even if you did—"

"All right, you've made your point." Gaines huffed and reclaimed his hat. "Very well. We *are* duly appointed officers of the government, are we not? Pursuing a legitimate lead on an investigation in which lives are at stake. So long as we neither break nor steal anything . . ."

Not exactly logic that would hold up in a court of law, if it came down to it. But Merritt wasn't going to argue.

Neither did Fairfax. "You have my word."

A minute later, their office courier arrived. He slid the envelope into the slot in the door and was quickly on his way.

Not that he left the street empty. It was one of those neighborhoods that mixed residences with places of business and shops, which meant that though the shops had closed their doors, residents were just returning for their evenings at home. At Fairfax's insistence, they hid themselves away until the foot traffic had slowed and omnibuses were gone for the night, then stole across the street to the door.

One bit of luck—this building was exactly halfway between the two flanking streetlights, making it the darkest section in the line. And Gaines was still in his uniform, which at least lent them an official air, if anyone did look out and see them.

Not that they would have had long to do so. Fairfax opened the door with the second key he tried, and soon they were slipping inside.

The solicitor's office consisted of four different rooms on the building's ground floor, and it didn't take long to find the one that stored the records. Happily, it was an interior chamber with no windows, so they could turn on a light without worrying that it would be seen from the street. Gaines agreed to keep watch at the front window—he seemed a bit relieved by the assignment, in truth—so Merritt and Fairfax got to work.

Slogging through the files took more time than he would have liked, but eventually he came up with something useful. "Here we are. A record of deposits made on behalf of clients for the last six months. Although . . . none of them match the amounts in our records."

"His fee."

"Pardon?"

Fairfax's sigh sounded exaggerated. "The solicitor doesn't work for free, you know, and a mere retainer wouldn't cover anything that came with risks. He'll have charged a fee. Deduct your standard ten or fifteen percent and look again."

"Right." He made the mental calculations and looked down the list again, immediately spotting the entries he needed. Though following their lines to see to whom they were sent from made him let out an incredulous breath. "No."

"What?"

"May." He lowered the book to the desk, staring without really seeing the incriminating lines. Even knowing from the Imposters' research that the colonel was in debt, he hadn't wanted to think it of him.

"Well, that's odd. Because May isn't anywhere in his client records. But Hemming is listed here as a client."

That brought Merritt's gaze up to Fairfax's. "We're missing something. We must be. I cannot get Marigold's theory out of my mind—that Hemming is trying to flush this Hans chap out, spring a trap for him. That it has very little to do with whatever history her ladyship may have with the chap and much more to do with the fellow's position, if he is

286

behind the disappearances. But what role does May really play in this, aside from errand boy?"

"Not exactly a role befitting his rank, that." Fairfax tapped a finger to his pasted-on mustache. "Obviously your friend Gaines thinks someone in the office is selling out the agents, and this record will point the finger at May. And at Hemming."

"But Hemming can't be both responsible for the agents vanishing *and* for trying to catch the man in Germany who possibly ordered their arrests and deaths." Merritt rubbed a hand over his eyes. "Both of these theories cannot be right. Either Hemming is on the side of England, or he isn't. Either May is being bribed to betray his men, or he's Hemming's ally in the search for truth. Either Hans is a powerful man in Germany, or he's just an old flame of Frances Hemming's. We need to sort out which is true."

Fairfax snapped the folder in his hands closed, reinserted it into its drawer, and slid that shut. "I don't know. But we won't untangle those threads here, with this information. We might as well slip back out."

They reported their findings to Gaines as they were walking to the tube station, and the clench of his jaw said he did jump to the only conclusion these facts on their own presented: Colonel May was betraying their men, quite possibly helped along by Hemming. "I knew it had to be someone in our office, but even so. I'd never have thought it of Colonel May. He always struck me as such an upstanding chap."

Merritt let the whole situation simmer as they walked. They *had* to be missing something, and the only thing he could think of that would make sense of it was discovering who this Hans was. If Lady Hemming knew him from her life in Saxony—in which she was the daughter of the leading citizen—it wasn't far-fetched to think him a powerful chap himself. It wouldn't be odd for him to consider England an enemy, given the current political climate.

But he was still in communication, it seemed, with Lady Hemming.

Who was still in communication, it seemed, with *him*.

A rock dropped into Merritt's stomach. They had considered at the start that Hemming might be out to cover up his wife's relation to Germany. . . . Perhaps they needed to revisit that thought, but with this new information. It may not be her bloodlines he was ashamed of, but it could well be her behavior with this Hans—and not just an *affaire de cœur*.

What if she had mentioned information at some point that compromised their intelligence operations? What if this Hans had been using her, and hence indirectly Hemming himself, to seize their agents operating in Germany?

That would certainly get the earl's attention. That would make him desperate enough to undo the actions that he would devise a mad plan like inviting the Hans fellow to come, to spring a trap like Marigold had mused. That would be so big an undertaking that he would need an ally—someone like Colonel May.

What if . . . what if that cash was *from* Hemming, to offset the risks May was taking on his behalf? There was still the timing, however—that they came in when agents went missing.

Blast. Coincidence? Not that many times.

But wait. What if Ballantine wasn't the first one Hemming had tasked with these questions? Could they *all* have been lost as a direct result of trying to discover something about Hans? If so, then maybe—just *maybe*—each failure made May jumpier, made him demand something more to keep working for Hemming. Perhaps Hemming sent the funds anonymously through the military to keep their association off the books otherwise.

It was a stretch. But thus far, he could come up with no

better explanation. He would run it by Yates after they parted ways with Gaines and see what he thought.

He glanced over at his colleague, resolve settling over him in place of the dread. Ultimately, his job was not to undo the past—he couldn't. Ultimately, his job wasn't even to find answers. Ultimately, his job was to serve his men—to make certain no more of them were lost.

He looked to Gaines as they walked. "What safeguards have you put in place for our agents?"

"I gave orders a week ago for them all to make their way back quietly to their official billets and to check in with their fellow officers daily. Anyone who does not at least send an 'all's well' telegram will be reported as missing immediately, and a few trusted men will go in search of them."

"Good. Good." It wasn't necessarily enough, but it was far better than leaving them in the field blind to this new risk.

The tube station loomed, and their pace slowed as they approached it. "I shall part from you here," Gaines said. "Sorry to have called you all the way to London for nothing."

"It wasn't for nothing. We have more information than we had this morning." Information Gaines wouldn't have gotten without Mr. A, but he wasn't about to point that out.

Gaines was a clever chap, though. He knew it as well as Merritt did. He turned to Fairfax, hand extended. "I'm glad you were here, sir. It was indeed a pleasure to make your acquaintance."

Fairfax shook, but he didn't smile, neither his usual Fairfax one, nor the Mr. A version he'd used since they boarded the train in Alnwick. "Lieutenant Gaines, if I may . . . it isn't aspirin in your wife's pill case. Not to overstep, but please. Seek help for her, for the sake of your children."

Gaines jerked away, eyes wide. But no accusations or denials spewed from his tongue. Only a choked "I suspected. I . . . thank you." And he spun, running for the ticket booth.

Merritt rubbed a hand over the back of his neck. "Isn't it dratted uncomfortable knowing so much about so many people?"

"Horribly." For once, there wasn't so much as a hint of levity in Fairfax's voice—which sounded like his own again. "Honestly, I think that's why Marigold remains unattached from most people, more than the role. She has learned to distrust."

Understandable. He certainly never would have suspected that Mrs. Gaines had any addictions. Once again, it made him wonder what else he'd missed that was right under his nose. He sighed. "Did you have a dossier on me? Before I hired you, I mean?"

"Only with the barest of facts, from our work for the duke." The grin winked out from between the whiskers. "That you were Lord Xavier's friend. Knighted. A Coldstream Guard. We knew nothing else until you hired us. I believe then our first note was 'utterly boring.'"

"It was not. Why would you note something like that?" Except he'd seen their dossiers—he knew they *did*. Which made him huff. "Well, better boring than hiding dark secrets, isn't it?"

Fairfax chuckled and started toward the tube again. "Much. You think I'd have let you near my sister otherwise? I have a deep appreciation for boring. Especially when it's combined with a strong sense of right and wrong and an abiding faith. Also necessary, let it be noted, for me to let you near my sister."

"About that." He hung back, knowing well that his companion would snap back into Mr. A as soon as they joined the small crowd of tube passengers, and there would be no more discussion of Marigold. They could talk about it at his house . . . but then there would be lights to reveal his flushed neck. "As her only male relative, I suppose we should—I should, I mean. Declare my intentions."

Fairfax wasn't going to make it easy on him. He just stood there, hands in his trouser pockets and face unreadable in the streetlight. And waited. Where were his usual helpful interjections now?

Merritt cleared his throat. "Right. They are—my intentions, I mean—honorable."

"Good to know." Or perhaps his interjections weren't helpful after all. "And they include . . . ?"

What did he *think* they included? "Well. You know. I suppose . . . courtship." Time to get to know each other properly, when all this business was settled. That would appease her brother, wouldn't it? No rush, no threat of taking her away too quickly. Time to sort it all out.

"Not good enough."

Merritt felt his brows slam down. The man hadn't objected to anything at the Tower, when Marigold had all but declared him a permanent part of their life. What could his argument be now? "I beg your pardon?"

Fairfax shook his head. "Courtships end all the time. That won't do. You know the most intimate details of our family and have come alongside us in our profession—more or less applying for a partnership share in our limited liability company. We need something far more permanent than a *courtship*, Sir Merritt."

Well of course he hadn't meant *only* courtship. Although . . . "Who said anything about applying for a partnership share? I'm wise to you, you know. You're not going to strap *me* with all the paperwork and legal filings and call it my part of the company as a junior partner."

There. Fairfax was chuckling. "Would have been a fine plan. Though the company aside, the objection stands. Courtship will not suffice. You, my good man, are going to profess your undying love, marry her, and make her happy."

Words he hadn't really even thought, much less spoken.

But words that settled like a balm on his soul and made his lips twitch into a smile. Because that's exactly what he would do. "Or what?"

Fairfax, grin going mischievous, turned back toward the tube. "Or I'll feed you to the lions."

Merritt jumped to keep stride with him. "You don't have lions. You have only one singular lion."

"All right, to the lion and the leopard and the panther. Better?"

"Much." They walked a few steps in silence, and Merritt was just beginning to congratulate himself on weathering that permission-asking with success when Fairfax looked over at him again.

"One more thing."

"What?"

Fairfax smiled. "We're having lunch tomorrow with your family before we go home. I need to do a bit of reconnaissance before my sister joins their ranks."

Heaven help him. He didn't know whether to feel sorrier for the Prestons or Fairfax.

No. On second thought, they ought to be pretty well matched.

TWENTY-THREE

nother telegram should be arriving any minute—or hour, at least. Today, surely. Marigold couldn't fathom it would be any later than today. Hector had sent one two days ago that had arrived shortly after Yates and Merritt returned, and he had promised more information soon. Waiting for it, however, had proven too much a stretch on their nerves, and they had all—she, Yates, Merritt, and Gemma—come to the gymnasium to work off their anxious energy.

What Hector had sent already had rocked all their assumptions with two little words: *Hans Coburg.* She flipped onto her hands and walked the length of the mat on her palms. Perhaps the extra blood flow to her head would make sense of everything.

"It ought to be a relief," Gemma said from above her. She had climbed up to the trapeze but was simply treating it like any garden swing—the only thing she *ever* did on it. "If Hans Coburg is *the* Hans, then her ladyship isn't guilty of infidelity. It's her brother she's been in communication with, not some old flame."

Marigold had no doubt it would be a relief to Lavinia when they sorted out a way to tell her without making it obvious that they'd been investigating her family long before she came to them with her own concerns about her mother. And from that perspective, it *was* a relief. She returned to her feet. "So why, then, can I not shake the feeling that this is even worse than the first assumption?"

"Because you're too intelligent to think it anything but a potential disaster that Hans Coburg, one of the leaders of Saxony, has been in secret communication with the wife of a man who wants to build battleships." Merritt sat on the weights bench, between repetitions at the moment. "Though at least the earl's letter makes more sense now. I couldn't quite square what I know of him with the thought of him writing to someone his wife had been romantically involved with."

Very true. But a husband writing to his wife's brother— that made perfect sense. As did the letter from Hans that Lavinia had found months ago, that said he saw Frances when he looked at his daughter. Niece and aunt could certainly bear a resemblance that would inspire an elder brother to miss his little sister.

"Hemming's motivations, though." Yates, as usual, pinpointed the exact thing that had kept them from simply being glad to receive Hector's first message upon arriving in Königsbrück, Saxony, where the Coburg family resided.

They'd had this conversation already, more or less, three times. But it seemed none of them could resist picking at the threads of mystery, hoping something new would unravel.

Gemma sighed on her swing. Merritt slid another disc onto his bar. Marigold bent over backward, planted her hands, and kicked her feet up, over, and back down.

Yates had his skipping rope in hand and had set himself a dizzying pace that didn't wind him in the slightest. "What does he know about Hans Coburg that we don't yet know? Is he a harmless aristocrat?"

"In which case Hemming is simply trying to prove to his wife that she can love both her father's family and her husband without any need for the tension she seems to have been feeling." Marigold flipped again.

"Or is he perhaps involved in Germany's intelligence machine?" Merritt, this time, posed the more bothersome question.

"In which case," Marigold finished for him, "is Hemming luring him here to spring a trap?"

It would be dangerous. Foolhardy, even. But if he thought himself trying to undo damage wrought by information his wife possibly let slip to her brother . . . it would make sense.

"He won't come though, will he?" Gemma pushed off the platform to give the trapeze a twirl. "Not if the second is true. If he isn't just an innocent brother, then there's no way he'll risk coming to the home of an earl."

"You think not? I rather think he would jump at the chance for an excuse to do on-the-ground reconnaissance, especially of shipworks. Let us not forget Lady Hemming's ultimatum to her husband—it hinged on acquiring Ballantine's operation."

Yates introduced a crisscross into his jumping. "I think he'll come. And when he does, we need a way to listen to whatever conversations are had at Alnwick Abbey."

Something in his tone made Marigold pause rather than flipping again. She'd stopped near Merritt's bench, and seeing that he made no move to begin his next round of lifts, she sat beside him so she could better frown at her brother. "What are you about, Yates?"

Yates flicked his gaze upward, toward Gemma. Was that an answer?

"Oh." *Graham.* He was the one person who had a hope of helping them sneak about the Abbey, and if Yates thought they'd need his expertise, he'd have already called him up to the Tower, despite that their cousin hadn't stepped foot on the property since December.

Merritt's brows rose. "I like to think I'm learning your private language, but I still need a bit of help. What does 'oh' mean in this case?"

"Well . . ." She too darted a glance upward, where Gemma was still twirling, though in the opposite direction now. Meeting Merritt's blue eyes again, she mouthed, "I'll tell you later." Aloud, she said, "I suppose if Hans comes, we'll simply have to sort out where they'll be when and do what we always do. We can always play fly-on-the-wall. The stone would give us plenty of purchase, or we could rappel from the crenellations. Too dangerous in daylight, but it would work at night."

Merritt blinked at her, muttering under his breath, "Rappel from the crenellations, she says."

"I don't think that will be necessary."

They all looked up at the new voice, and over to the gymnasium door, which they'd left open to the breeze. Graham strode in, a leather tube under his arm and a smile upon his lips. His gaze swept the room, darting upward at the little noise of protest Gemma made.

Yates dropped the skipping rope and looked at the utilitarian clock mounted to the wall. "Right on time. Tell me you found something. Blueprints? Or schematics or sketches or whatever they would have had in the sixteenth century?"

Graham dragged his gaze down from Gemma—who stared resolutely at the wall opposite her—and grinned at Yates. "Not exactly. But I *did* find a few drawings by Nicholas Owen for an unnamed manor house, which bears a striking resemblance to the old plans for Alnwick Abbey I've had for years. Here, I'll show you." He dropped to the floor and unrolled the parchment he pulled from the tube.

Marigold leaned close to Merritt. "Graham Wharton,

architect. We mentioned him that morning over breakfast, if you recall—he's the distant cousin who was Father's ward." At his nod of acknowledgment, she added, "The hides in Alnwick Abbey are actually what spurred his interest in architecture. They've always been a pet project of his."

"I'm going to find them all eventually," Graham said, smiling over at her. And then glancing once more up to the trapeze, "You can come down, Gem. I know you're dying of curiosity."

"I most certainly am not, Mr. Wharton."

Exasperation painted its colors over his face. "You've always been as intrigued by those hides as I have. You came with me for a solid week while I sketched the current house's floorplans."

"Did I?"

Graham growled. "We both know the moment I leave, you'll be down here looking them over—"

"Will that moment be soon?" She delivered it in a sickly-sweet voice, complete with a bat of her lashes.

"Enough!" Yates didn't often flaunt his rank, certainly not with them. But in that moment, he sounded every bit the earl, more stern than their father ever had, as he sliced a hand through the air and looked from Gemma to Graham. "We haven't time for this argument, nor for your anger with each other. People's lives are on the line. So if you aren't about to add something useful to the conversation, button your lips."

Marigold's heart swelled. Her baby brother, taking charge. She felt a bit like a mama bird watching her fledgling take flight for the first time. Saying *that* out loud would certainly not add anything useful to the conversation, so she buttoned her lips against it and leaned forward to better see the papers.

Some of them she recognized—the drawings Graham had made when he was, what, fourteen or fifteen? He'd gone over every inch of the Abbey with his measuring tape, sketchbook, and pencil. Lord Hemming had been happy to let him, encouraging him to take all the time he needed. He'd been eager to know if there were more priest holes or hides that would set Alnwick Abbey apart as a noteworthy historical landmark.

The one off the study the family had always known about, but Graham had been the one to rediscover the one off the kitchen, only the second one they had record of, based on those measurements and sketches. She had no doubt he'd have uncovered more if he hadn't gone away to school at Eton and then moved to university and been immediately hired by a firm in London.

But in addition to those familiar drawings were new ones.

Graham had turned back to them, too, and pointed to the drawing. "You'll note they don't match in general shape, but that's to be expected. What are now the north and east wings were added centuries after the Reformation. Only the central part and the west wing were built by the 1590s, so taking that into account, you can see right away how closely the shapes match."

Marigold nodded along with the others. That was clear, but also not definitive, since without the more modern wings, Alnwick Abbey looked very much like many other manor houses in England.

"But here's what convinced me these plans of Owen's are for the Abbey. See this here?" He pointed to a place on the Owen sketch that was marked as a hide. "That corresponds to that old study with the known hole. And this one," he said, tapping one in the main part of the house, "with the one I found for them in the kitchen."

Yates rocked back on his heels. "I find that convincing. So then what does it mean in terms of others?"

Graham's smile surely would have won even Gemma over, if she'd been down here to see it. "It means, my friends, that no one has to go scaling walls or rappelling from crenella-tions. Because there is a narrow escape corridor running along the entire length of the main house."

Marigold frowned. "How? There are windows on the out-side wall, and the inside walls aren't so thick."

Her old friend grinned and held up a finger. No, not just held up—*pointed* up. "Not in the walls, Marigold. In the ceiling—or under the floor, from the perspective of the up-stairs rooms. Accessible by a series of ladders that have been hidden in various rooms, connecting both upper and lower floors to the space."

"Genius. That would provide a priest with far more op-tions than the other hides."

"That old study must have been the bedroom they set aside for him. And the other one I found was off the old kitchen. But this passageway would be accessible from just about anywhere else in the main part of the house, and if you look here"—he indicated a darkened box in the drawing—"you'll see what must be another full chamber, like the known ones, connected to the passage. So, if the priest was, let's say, in the original chapel, he could move a panel to access the ladder, climb up into the passage, hide there, crawling along, while the agents of the Crown searched for him, and eventually come out here, where there would be water and food stored for him, to wait it out as long as a week."

Not in comfort—and Marigold's nose wrinkled even imagining the smell that would keep the priest company after a few days of using a chamber pot in a confined space. But it was certainly ingenious—and better than death by hanging, which was the punishment for daring to be Catholic in Elizabeth's England. "And we think they're still there? In place?"

Merritt pursed his lips. "Even if they are, what are the chances that the ladders aren't rotted through?"

To that, Graham shrugged. "The wood in the other priest holes hadn't fared too badly. Being sealed off as they are, I suppose they avoid most of the damp air. And yes, I think they're still there. The Hemming family has done very little to alter the structure of the old house, which his lordship told me time and again when I was measuring and sketching everything. Surface changes only, and they otherwise focused on building new additions."

"Well then." Yates slapped a hand to his leg and stood up. "We have only to get in and find one of the entrances, and we'll have access to all the main rooms. Invaluable part of the team as always, Graham."

Marigold looked up just in time to see Gemma's lips press tight together. Though a moment later her attention was snagged by Franco striding through the door, waving a paper in his hands. "Zelda just returned from her errands in Alnwick. Word from Hector. And she picked up a wire that had just come in for you, too, Sir Merritt."

Marigold leapt up, beating the others to Franco by a few seconds. She took the note from Hector and read the short words out loud. "'HC purchased two tickets to England. Bringing wife. Freida née von Schlieffen.'" She lowered the sheet, brows knotted. "Why does that name sound familiar?"

Merritt held his own telegram without looking at it, that muscle in his chiseled jaw ticking. "Because Count von Schlieffen was the chief of staff of the Imperial German General Staff until a few years ago. His name is still used for Germany's primary military plan to invade France."

Yates muttered something in Romani that Marigold decided to pretend she didn't understand and then said, "Perhaps they're not related."

Gemma snorted her opinion of that hope from the platform. "Quite right. Highly unlikely that one of Saxony's leading lords would marry into the family of one of the empire's leading military men, who is of an equal rank."

"Well, we can dream, can't we?"

Merritt rested a hand on Marigold's waist that probably shouldn't have made her heart flutter, given the circumstances. "We ought to assume the worst—that Coburg does have military connections. If so, then it is quite possible he is coming not for a reunion with his sister but to gather intelligence."

"How ironic. Le Queux has the whole populace suspicious of every waiter and common tourist, but it could well be a visiting count who has been gathering information from an English countess." Marigold leaned into Merritt just a bit.

Engine noises broke into the room, distant but growing louder. Franco stepped back outside, wandered away a few steps, and then hurried back in. "The Hemming car."

Graham spun back to his sketches, quickly rolling them up and putting them back into his leather tube. Gemma finally climbed down from the platform while he was distracted, aiming directly for the door.

Marigold snagged her wrist on her way by. "Gem—"

"I just remembered—I think I have some Continental magazines that may mention the Coburgs." Gemma's smile was strained, but she offered it anyway. "I collected some to see how the other European social Seasons were covered. Don't you remember? Zelda had to help me translate them all."

Another project that had been created to keep her busy last winter. "Gemma—"

"I know he's still a valuable part of the team. I know this information he brought could mean our success." She'd dropped her voice low and sent a glance toward the corner of the gymnasium where Graham was storing his sketches. "But I can't, Marigold. I can't be with him. If he's staying at the Tower, please tell me and I'll get a room in Alnwick for a night or two."

Marigold could only bluster out a sigh. "Let us know if you find anything relevant in those magazines."

As she slipped out, Merritt sighed. "Oh bother. Of all the timing."

He'd finally opened his own telegram. Marigold lifted her brows. "Bad news?"

"Just my uncle and aunt and the girls deciding that a weekend in Scotland is just the thing, thereby giving them an excuse to stop for a few hours on their way through." He met her gaze, apology in his. "They want to meet you. On Saturday. I can tell them now isn't a good time—"

"But that will make them think I don't *want* to meet them. And that couldn't be further from the truth." She smiled, even though anxiety fluttered in her chest, along with a thousand doubts.

What if they didn't like her? Or what if they *did*, but the "her" they liked was Lady M, rather than Marigold? Or what if they liked Marigold but disapproved of what they might perceive as the reckless spending of her other self? She could imagine Merritt's family warning him against a match with her, lest it bankrupt them.

And then there were the simple facts: She couldn't let them see the true state of Fairfax affairs. It would ruin all the careful work they'd done to preserve appearances so that the Imposters could work in anonymity. If she compromised that, she would compromise all of them. She would put their investigations in danger and risk all they'd built. But how could she create a relationship with his family when she couldn't show them who she really was?

Her chest went tight as she watched the Hemming auto come to a halt and Lavinia jump out. Even one of her oldest, dearest friends didn't know the truth.

Lavinia was soon bounding their way, Lord Xavier on her heels. Marigold couldn't tell if the flush in her friend's cheeks was from the sun and wind, or whatever news had brought her here.

"I don't know whether to be excited or anxious," Lavinia said by way of greeting. "I received an invitation weeks ago to attend a masquerade being thrown in celebration of a classmate's recent marriage, in Leeds. Mother had at first said I couldn't go, but Father has just insisted that I should—and it's this weekend! He says I ought to ask you to join me, and he's convinced Lord Xavier to attend as well. Claudia will come as my chaperone."

Marigold exchanged a look with Merritt, who had fisted the telegram and had a resigned look on his face. He nodded. "That's all right. I can tell them—"

"No." Perhaps she couldn't reveal everything to them, but she could still do this. She reached for Lavinia's hand. "Sorry, Vinia. Sir Merritt's family will be coming through that day."

Her friend's eyes went wide. Not with surprise—Marigold had already whispered a confession to her of their shared kisses, and she hadn't been surprised *then* either. But wide with excitement. "Oh, how thrilling! You *must* meet them instead. But perhaps you can help me plan my costume? Mother refused to order anything new. Marie Antoinette is the theme."

"Of course she will help." Yates came up to Marigold's other side and sent her a pointed look. "In fact, you should give her the full costumery studio tour, sister mine."

Was he quite serious? To show Lavinia where they made all her clothing would be tantamount to admitting that they were far from the prosperous peers they appeared to be—with no seamstresses in London or Paris or even York or Leeds.

Obviously he *was* serious, or he wouldn't have said it—

and no doubt he said it because he was, as usual, reading her mind.

And taking the decision about how much of herself she could share with those she loved best out of her hands.

She wasn't certain if she ought to be grateful or annoyed.

"That sounds intriguing." Lavinia glanced between them, obviously trying to read their body language.

Yates was on a roll with his authority-taking. "You should also know that your father likely made this decision about the ball because a visitor from Saxony will be arriving at the Abbey this weekend. Hector just let us know."

Lavinia no doubt would have wondered at Hector's quick success if the point of Yates's statement hadn't eclipsed any such trivialities. "No. Hans?" Her face washed pale.

Marigold leapt forward to put an arm around her, just in case she went faint. "It isn't quite what we thought. His name is Hans *Coburg*, it seems. Your uncle."

"My uncle." Her echo sounded weak, strained. Marigold watched the thoughts whirl through her eyes—confusion, relief, but then renewed questions. "You're certain? This is the Hans my mother has been in correspondence with?"

Yates nodded. "We asked Hector to look for the Coburg family. He found Hans Coburg just as your father's letter to him arrived, it seems. He immediately booked passage to England."

"But then . . . why has Father insisted I leave?" Even as she asked it, Lavinia pulled away, paced a few steps, and turned back. "He doesn't know if this fellow is trustworthy. If he's someone I should have any association with. He doesn't . . . he doesn't know how Mother will react to her brother's appearance, given her ultimatum to him." She stopped, her eyes sliding shut and her hands fisting at her side. "He's afraid she'll leave and doesn't want me to witness that. Though is it really better if she does so while I'm not there to say good-bye?"

Was there a "better" in such a situation? Marigold drew in a long breath. "He's protecting you as best he knows how."

"I know. But I shouldn't have to be protected like this." After granting herself one more moment of quivering lips and curled fingers, Lavinia forcibly relaxed and smiled. "At least Papa is trying. So then I'll do my part. What's this costumery studio you're going to show me?"

"Oh, that isn't something to tell. That's something to show." Marigold mirrored her friend's smile, linked their arms together, and pulled her toward the house. "Zelda!" she called the moment she crossed the threshold. "Lavinia has a masquerade to attend, and we're going to outfit her! Marie Antoinette!"

Zelda appeared at the railing, her eyes bright. "What fun! How long do we have?"

"Three days."

Those bright eyes flamed into panic. "Three—ach! What are you walking for? Run, hurry! We will need all hands, every moment. Gemma! Away from those magazines, sweet one, we need you!"

An hour later, they'd selected a few likely options to use as a base and hauled them down from the attic, into what they'd dubbed the costumery studio, which made Lavinia gasp in surprised pleasure. In here, Zelda had stored the bins and jars full of sequins and paste gems, beads and baubles that had once been in her vardo. Here they dyed and stored their feathers, designed their next attempts at haute couture, and always had a remade gown or two underway on the mannequin sized to Marigold's dimensions.

"*This* is how you acquire all your gowns?" Lavinia turned in a circle. "I ought to have known! The things I've missed these last years—and you, never telling me!"

Since she said it with a laugh, Marigold could smile in return. "Some secrets a young lady never shares with anyone."

She pulled off the sleek blue-and-green beaded creation she was working on for her next London ball and settled the voluminous old *Robe à la Française* on in its place. It was a beautiful aqua silk, thankfully without any shattering.

Though she clucked her tongue when she spotted some staining. "What do you think, Zel? Could we cover it with lace or beads?"

"Mm. Perhaps, perhaps. Gemma, put the red one on the other form. Let us see which is in the better condition, yes? And then we'll get Lady Lavinia's measurements and resize a form."

They were still debating between the two when a masculine "What in the world?" had all four of them spinning about.

The men stood in the doorway—Yates and Graham looking half bored and half amused, Lord Xavier and Merritt both with dumbfounded expressions.

Had it been just anyone from London stumbling upon her secret—that she actually made all her dresses herself, under the tutelage of an aging Gypsy—she may have flushed. But it wasn't just anyone, and so she twirled her hands through the air like a ringmaster, bowing at the waist as she did so. "Good gentlemen, allow me to present . . . the costumery studio!"

Merritt entered with his hands clasped behind his back, as if the rows of fabric might lunge from their bolts and bite him. Lord Xavier, on the other hand, came in with fascination on his face and immediately began to feel this and touch that. "Amazing. You have a whole tailor shop right here. Where did you come by it all?"

"Here and there. Now and then." Zelda gave him a grin. "I collect for many years."

Merritt had paused before a rack where several of Mama's old gowns had been draped. "These aren't new."

"Far from it. They were my mother's." She reached out, trailing her fingers down one of the richly embroidered skirts. "Father spent on her just as he did on the entertainments, you see. She was never without the newest thing, the latest fashion. More than she ever could have worn, with some only worn once or twice. We remake them. Some of them go through multiple iterations."

"Zelda is always experimenting with new dyes and bleaches." Gemma turned the red-clad mannequin around to check the back, grimacing when she saw a panel where the silk had shattered. "The aqua, then. We'll just have to cover the stain."

"We can use that lace I've been saving," Zelda offered.

Merritt turned his face toward Marigold's, somehow making the large room, with its eight occupants, feel close and private just with a glance. "Resourceful."

Since he packed approval into the word, she smiled.

TWENTY-FOUR

erritt had no reason to be in Alnwick already, it was true. His uncle's family wasn't due to arrive for another hour, and Xavier didn't exactly need him tagging along to see him and Lady Lavinia off for the masquerade ball.

What else was he to do? Pace around Hawkhill House for the next sixty minutes, wearing a path in the floorboards? Better to wear out the cobblestones of Alnwick, by his way of thinking.

Marigold would be joining him here soon, too, both to send off Lavinia and to receive Uncle Preston, Aunt Josie, and the girls. They'd dine together at the hotel, perhaps stroll about the town for a while, and then see his family back onto their train. Just a few hours. An initial introduction. No need for any of them to be nervous.

A fact that had neither stopped Marigold from all but vibrating any time they brought up the plans over the last few days nor calmed his own roiling stomach. Because what if they didn't like one another? What if Mother didn't approve, whenever she made her way home from the Continent? What if the future he'd begun to imagine dissolved into the wretched details of reality?

"You look about as happy about this impending introduction as my sister does."

Merritt spun from the bookshop window he'd been idly staring at, toward the voice that had become so familiar. Fairfax stood there alone, which made disappointment spring up inside him.

He might be anxious over the coming meeting, but the hope of seeing Marigold even a few minutes before he'd expected had been quick and fierce. Proof that his feelings for her were stronger than any nerves.

He smiled at her brother. "It's only the initial bit that has me nervous. Because it matters, you see. What they all think of each other."

Fairfax granted that with a tilt of his head. "If it makes you feel better—or perhaps it won't, I don't know—your uncle could tell just from the way you spoke of her that day in London that things were trending this direction. When you went off to the loo, he chuckled and said that it sounded as though we'd have to start chatting about dowries." He flashed a grin. "I assured him that we were ready to negotiate. The retired circus lion is on the table, and I may be able to swing a peacock or cassowary or ostrich too. He seemed to find that quite amusing."

Merritt breathed a laugh, though it quickly faded. "He would. Though I do realize . . . what with your situation . . . know that I expect nothing. And don't much care what my uncle may have to say on the matter." He was accustomed to living on his own means, and Marigold clearly was too—or rather, she was accustomed to living on repurposed dresses and the simplest of table fare. Neither of them would bring new wealth to the Preston estates if he inherited them someday, but they'd get along just fine, regardless, both before and after.

"You can't sidestep my generosity that easily. The lion is

nonnegotiable." Fairfax frowned, though, and nodded at something past Merritt's shoulder. "Isn't that Colonel May?"

Here, now? Merritt spun, nodding. Had Hemming called him up to be present for whatever plan he had in place for Coburg? He couldn't think of why else his superior would be here.

And he hadn't the chance to decide whether he wanted to be seen or not either. May was already striding his way, a hand raised. "Livingstone! You're looking well."

"Colonel May, how do you do? I didn't know you'd be coming to Northumberland."

"Nor did I, truth be told, until yesterday," May replied as they shook. He had a questioning set to his eyes and mouth, and it didn't seem to be directed at Merritt. "I received a note from Hemming inviting me up for the weekend. Only, when I just bumped into him an hour ago, he was clearly surprised. A strange misunderstanding." Though the colonel shrugged and smiled, he looked genuinely baffled by it. "I've got a room at the hotel tonight, regardless. I don't suppose you're available for dinner this evening, since we're both here?"

Blast. They'd been planning to keep the Abbey under surveillance via the secret passages beginning as soon as his family boarded their Scotland-bound train. But he had been assigned the first shift with Fairfax, which *could* mean that he'd be back in Alnwick in time for a meal, if it were a late enough one.

He certainly didn't just want to tell his superior no. "Depending on the time, perhaps so. My family is coming through and I've an engagement with Lord Fairfax here this afternoon, but my evening is free." Or at the least, Marigold would be on *her* shift, and Xavier would be gone, so what else did he have vying for his time? He'd planned on simply spending it with Fairfax at the Tower, but he had a feeling his friend would understand the change in plans.

The colonel held out a hand to Fairfax and introduced himself, ending with, "You are welcome to join us, my lord, if you're free. Perhaps at eight?"

Their shift should be well over by then. Both Merritt and Fairfax nodded, a few other pleasantries were exchanged, and they agreed to meet at the hotel dining room then.

"Very odd," Fairfax muttered after the colonel strode away. "Why would Hemming invite him and then forget? Seems sloppy. And generally unusual."

"Mm. Unusual indeed." And it yet again gave Merritt the feeling that he was missing something.

Marigold trailed a few paces behind Lady Preston and the four daughters who had made the journey with their parents, needing just a moment's reprieve from the veiled questions and awestruck gazes. They were a delightful crew—and she could tell within a few moments that Lady Preston loved Merritt like a son, which endeared her to Marigold.

But Lady Preston loved Merritt like a son, which meant that she was clearly set on making certain Marigold was deserving of him . . . and Marigold wondered a bit more with each step if perhaps she wasn't.

The sleepless night was largely to blame, she knew. She'd stayed up late with Zelda and Gemma, putting the finishing touches on Lavinia's costume, but even after she'd gone to bed, she'd lain awake hour after hour, worrying over the coming weekend. Merritt's family, the arrival of the Coburgs, the risk of doing surveillance on a place where everyone knew them . . . it all swirled about her mind in an endless loop.

She'd delivered the gown to her friend this morning at the Abbey, and Lady Hemming had wrinkled her nose at "the gaudy monstrosity." Lord Hemming, however, had praised it profusely and insisted their Lavinia would be the belle of the ball.

Perhaps she would be, if she could remember to smile. But when Marigold had ridden with her to Alnwick and left her to await her train with Claudia and Lord Xavier, her brows had once again been drawn into a frown. And her parting whisper had seared itself into Marigold's mind.

"I'm afraid, Marigold. I'm afraid I'll return and find my family has fallen to pieces. Because how can anything survive that's built on lies?"

Marigold smiled at the Preston ladies when they stopped to exclaim over a storefront, but the words still echoed. Was it enough that she'd let Merritt into her secrets? Would that ensure their foundation was solid enough to weather the future?

What if she reverted to type and began closing herself off to him? He deserved better than that—something his family would no doubt see, if they looked closely. What if they told him to abandon his court? He would listen. He *must*. He'd been loving them all his life, and she was just a new acquaintance, in all honesty. They'd exchanged no words of love.

What if Lavinia not only came home to a wrecked family, but also to a best friend with a wrecked romance? This could well be the weekend that spelled disaster for them all.

For the twentieth time that morning, she whispered a prayer for peace and strength and tried to give the worry over to the Lord. It helped that Merritt's cousins were clearly enamored with the very idea of her and were determined to like her . . . even if it *was* Lady M they adored more than Marigold.

She edged back against the building when a trio strode their way from the direction of the train station, making room for them on the pavement. They weren't locals, but as they drew near, the couple leading the way seemed vaguely familiar.

It wasn't until the third figure shifted into view though that she knew why. Miss Feuerstein. Which meant that the couple must be Hans and Freida Coburg—two of the three people from that photograph that had been hidden in the study.

Marigold's heart hammered. They'd come. She'd known they were on their way, but even so. Now there was no question. They'd *come*.

"Mademoiselle Richards!"

Marigold jolted when Miss Feuerstein halted at her side, a smile beaming from her face even as she reached for Marigold's hand.

Leopard stripes. No one—*no one* had ever recognized Marigold in her Lady M attire when she'd first met them in some other costume. Blast the woman's attention to detail! What should she do? Play oblivious? Deny knowing her?

But Miss Feuerstein gave her no time to debate anyway, as she was already saying, "How lovely to see you again! And doing well, clearly. I had no doubt that you would find a private position with all haste." The woman surveyed the flock of Prestons, her smile knowing and content. Leaning close, she whispered, "This bunch ought to keep you in work for several years."

Danielle, who had been casting shy glances at Marigold all morning but had yet to actually speak to her, had detached from her mother's side and drifted a step closer to Marigold, her curiosity clear on her face.

Miss Feuerstein simply directed her smile to the girl. "*Bonjour, mademoiselle. Comment va ton professeur de français? Apprends-tu bien?*"

How is your French teacher doing? Are you learning well? Marigold would have winced, had she dared.

Danielle merely said, "*Très bien. Merci.*"

313

"*Bien, bien.*" Directing that bright smile first at Danielle and then at Marigold, she squeezed Marigold's hand, added a whispered, "Good luck! Though a word of advice, my dear—you may want to dress a bit less flamboyantly when in the company of your employers," and then she was on her way, rushing to catch up with the couple again.

Danielle finally stepped to Marigold's side, confusion on her pretty face. "Why was that lady asking about Mademoiselle Moreaux?"

The laugh that bubbled up tasted like solace after all her worrying. "I have no idea."

"And did she call you Mademoiselle Richmond or something?"

To that, Marigold shrugged. "I think perhaps she mistook me for someone else."

The explanation seemed to appease Danielle. She nodded at something behind Marigold. "That girl is trying to get your attention too."

Marigold spun, not sure who she expected to see waving to her and hurrying around the Coburgs.

Genie.

Lionfeathers. Genie hadn't so much as acknowledged her existence since the funeral, but naturally she would find her now, here, in present company that would no doubt be shocked to hear her every complaint about Marigold.

Even so, Marigold took a few steps to meet her, glad to have the chance to see her. She bore shadows under her eyes, but she didn't look nearly so hollow as she had that day at Denwick Manor. "Genie, hello."

Genie came to a halt a step away, her gaze searching the crowd of Prestons. "Is Lavinia with you? I tried to call on her just now and was informed she wasn't at home."

Oh. It wasn't *Marigold* she'd been eager to see. Why would it be? She shook her head. "She went to Leeds for the weekend. A friend of hers from Ravenscleft has just been married recently, and they're hosting a masquerade."

Genie frowned at the group. "Who are they?"

"Sir Merritt's aunt and cousins."

At least the arch of Genie's brow didn't look cynical. If anything, simply curious. "Have they come to meet you?"

Marigold sighed and pitched her voice low as she replied, "No doubt, though they said they were just passing through on their way to Scotland. I'm terrified they're only here to find reasons to dislike me, so if you'd like to pass them your notes . . ." She said it lightly, teasingly. A test she probably shouldn't have put to her old friend.

But Genie passed it with a wince. "I shouldn't have said those things. They were cruel—and have turned around and bit me horribly. Lavinia must have recounted it all to her parents, and Lord Hemming actually had the gall to use my words against my father! To convince him to sell the shipyard to him! I'd like to have a word with her about that."

How fortunate for Lavinia then that she was gone. Marigold wouldn't wish anyone else to be on the receiving end of Genie's frustration. "I can't imagine she expected her father to do that."

"Well, he did." Thinking about it had that fury brewing in her eyes again. "And it *worked*. My father's convinced that the only way to give me the life I want and prove his love to me is to sell everything our family has ever worked for."

Marigold's heart sank. "He's taking the offer?"

"So he says. He sent a note to Lord Hemming this morning, inviting him to tour the site on Monday so they can begin official negotiations." Genie shook her head, tears crowding out the anger in her eyes. "I've been trying for days to talk reason into him, but he won't hear me."

Marigold dared to reach out and rest her fingers on Genie's arm. "I daresay he thinks he finally *has* heard you. He wants you to be happy—and didn't you say you wanted freedom to choose your own future?"

"Not at the cost of my family and our legacy." Genie huffed, but she didn't pull away from Marigold's touch. That was something. "I don't know what to do."

Marigold sighed. "I wish I had wisdom or comfort to give."

Genie's snort had the barest blush of amusement in it. "You haven't pointed out that I brought it on myself with my cruel outburst at the funeral, which is more than I deserve. I'll simply thank you for that."

"You needn't. I'm only happy to see you. I've been praying."

Genie's eyes softened. "I know. On that, I can always depend." With a sigh, she nodded toward the end of the street. "There are Sir Merritt and your brother—I'll let you go. And will try to convince myself that it's for the best that Lavinia is out of town, to save me from another outburst certain to bite me."

The Genie whose brother was still alive and well would have instead linked their arms together and demanded introductions, certainly staying long enough to flirt with *Yates*. But there was no evidence at all of the breathless social climber today. Just a young woman who had learned the cost of her own desires.

A lesson Marigold would have spared her if she could have. Lacking such magic, she could only bid her farewell, thanking God in one breath for a friendly conversation with her and asking Him in the next for more fortification.

She watched Yates and Merritt approach with Lord Preston, not missing the way Merritt's gaze flew from his aunt to her, clearly searching for evidence of how they were getting along. What would he see?

For a moment, she felt the trapeze beneath her, the momentum carrying her up and up and up—hope and joy and an unnamed love carrying her to that weightless moment that had been Merritt's second kiss. That moment when he'd seen her world and her truth and accepted it. Accepted her.

She ought to have known the downswing was coming when gravity took hold again. She was in its grasp now, her stomach continually in that knot that came of falling, falling. Of reaching out for arms that weren't there. Of wires snapping instead of swinging her up again. It had happened before in her training, both of those things—Yates not in position, the trapeze itself breaking. She knew firsthand the determination it took to trust again in both mechanics and her brother.

She wasn't sure she'd have the same fortitude in matters of the heart. There were no safety nets strung between the poles of her heart as there had been in her training. If Merritt walked away . . . If concerns of dowry or the mask she must keep at least partially in place won out over this fragile, beautiful thing they'd discovered . . . She couldn't imagine reaching out again, not knowing how it would hurt.

TWENTY-FIVE

$\mathcal{Y}$ates waited for the all-clear signal from Jax, Milo's brother, and then darted across the open space between him and the side entrance to Alnwick Abbey, Merritt a step behind. According to Graham's schematic diagram, this door would put them the closest to one of the hidden ladders. He'd have preferred waiting until darkness had fallen to sneak into the manor house, but they hadn't that luxury.

Miss Feuerstein and the Coburgs had waited at the hotel in Alnwick while they sent a note to the Hemmings, but they would be arriving any minute. And Yates was relying on the sudden flurry among the staff from unexpected overnight guests to help them sneak in. So far as they'd been able to glean, Lady Hemming hadn't yet discovered that her brother and sister-in-law were coming, and he wanted to be in position to hear what happened when she saw them.

He eased through the door, glancing about to make sure the corridor was empty before waving Merritt in behind him. Jax would remain in the carriage, waiting. Not knowing what the situation may dissolve into, they already had an exit strategy.

He heard no footsteps or voices apart from their own as

he led the way along the corridor and toward one of the seldom-used sitting rooms that should, if Graham was right, have a hidden access. His breath came a little easier when he slipped into the room. They'd gotten into the house and this room unseen before the guests arrived. The hardest part was behind them.

Or so he told himself. Though as he surveyed the wall where there ought to be a ladder but which looked for all the world like it was just a *wall*, he wondered at his own claim.

Merritt didn't waste time staring at it, just strode directly over to where the drawing said the access should be and began running his hands over every seam and bump and crack.

Yates joined him. He had the advantage of knowing what the latch for the fireplace and kitchen entrances felt like, but those were different. There, whole architectural features moved. Here? He couldn't imagine it would be quite the same.

"Ah. I think I found something." Merritt, voice barely audible, motioned him closer and pointed to a gap in the wainscoting. Scarcely noticeable, but there.

They each traced it to its opposite edges and down, pressing, pulling, trying to widen the gap. At last it began to move—with a low groan and an exhalation of stale air. That portion of the panel slid inward, into the wall, opening up a narrow space above it.

After giving it a minute to fill with fresher air, Yates ducked under the plaster portion of the wall and eyed up the opening. He would fit—but barely. "Well," he muttered to Merritt, "the size of these hides would certainly guarantee that the priests stuck to their vows of poverty and didn't overindulge at dinner."

"How is the ladder?"

Yates tested a few of the rungs fastened to the wall. The

319

wood seemed petrified, hard as stone. "Excellent. Though stay there for a moment and let me see how the closure works from this side. I have no desire to be trapped in the walls of the Abbey for the rest of my days."

At Merritt's nod, Yates fished his torch from his pocket, turned it on, and stepped fully into the opening. There was just space enough to move to the side. From there, he could see that the back of the panel had handles on it, allowing him both to push it back into place and then pull it open again. He motioned Merritt in with a grin. "Clever design. Though I'd expected nothing less from Nicholas Owen."

Had he ever met the man, he would have asked him to make his hides just a *bit* larger. Yates could climb the ladder and then crawl through the passageway that ran the length of the old house—but barely. His back bumped the ceiling, and his shoulders hadn't but an inch of space on either side.

"Perhaps if you were a bit less bulky," Merritt suggested ever so helpfully when Yates voiced his complaint.

"Would you like me to drop my sister when she's using my hands as a springboard or relying on me to catch her as she leaps from the trapeze?"

"Heavens no."

They crawled another few feet, stretched across an opening in another room, and paused, listening for signs of life below them. Nothing.

They risked no further conversation, given that another few shuffles had his ears straining toward sound from below. Someone was definitely in one of the chambers along this passage, though he didn't know which. Sound traveled a bit strangely through the tunnel, and it was two rooms later that the voices became distinct and loud enough for him to make them out and be confident that he knew where they were.

Masculine voices. He recognized Hemming's, but the other one was less familiar. Their words soon made it clear it was a servant of some kind—his lordship was giving quiet instructions on what to do when his guests arrived, and when the countess ought to be fetched. "Deliver both the guests and my wife to my study," he said.

His study? Lionfeathers. No doubt that was where Hemming would feel most comfortable and in control, but it was on the opposite side of the house. He used his torch to signal to Merritt and kept crawling, but he wasn't sure what the point was. According to Graham's diagram, only the rooms on this side of the house had access to this tunnel.

"I'm not certain how we'll listen in on the study," he whispered when his torchlight bounced off the wall ahead of them.

"Let's not discuss it this close to him. Go to the end and we'll turn around in the ladder well."

"Good plan." He continued forward, reached for the ladder, and stopped, frowning. He flashed his light to the left, and his pulse skittered. "Looks like Graham isn't as brilliant as he thought."

"What?"

"It continues! To the left, along the back wall here."

Merritt's breath caught behind him. "If it's mirrored along the other side . . ."

"Let's see, shall we?" It could well be that Nicholas Owens had simply not drawn the identical plans for the other side of the house. Or that his intention had only been this one side, but the proprietor had insisted upon having the escapes in *all* the rooms.

Whatever the reason, he was praising God for it when they turned not once but *twice*. Yes! A matching corridor along this side, stretching as far as his beam of light could show him. He counted rooms as they bypassed the ladder accesses, slowing down to ensure silence when they reached Hemming's main study.

Yates glanced down the ladder well, more than a little surprised when he saw threads of light seeping in around the door. If the cracks were so big, how had they gone unnoticed all these years?

But no—the paneling in that room was dark and thick, with deeper grooves between each board than in the other rooms. Cracks would be harder to see in it, and there was a window just off to the side, so any drafts would be blamed on that.

He climbed onto the ladder and moved silently down it. If Merritt wondered what he was about, he didn't do anything as stupid as ask, just followed him.

They both bent in the narrow space and put their eyes to either side of the cracks.

Hemming's desk was just in front of them, put out far enough from the wall that Yates's sliver of a view showed him half of a desk drawer and half of Hemming himself, seated in his fine leather chair. If Merritt's slit showed him the other half, they had decent coverage.

They sat in silence for several interminable minutes before footsteps sounded, and then Lady Hemming came into view. "You called for me?"

Hemming straightened in his chair. "Yes, thank you. Will you sit? I have a few guests coming who I'd like you to receive with me."

"Guests?" Though Yates couldn't see what seat she chose, he heard the squeak of a chair.

Hemming cleared his throat. "They should be here any minute. And it's my hope that, when faced with us all, you'll realize that there is a clear future we can live out together, my love. We don't need to steal the Ballantines' legacy from them for this dreadnought contract that I never wanted to begin with."

"What nonsense are you talking, Alfred? I've made myself

perfectly clear, haven't I? If you don't secure this contract, then I'm washing my hands of you."

"But *why*? Haven't we wealth enough, prestige enough as it is? Fran—"

"You think it *enough* that I'm just one more English countess, tucked away up here in the middle of nowhere? Not even making it to London for the last five years?"

Hemming huffed. "Lavinia was ill. You know well that I would have stayed with her myself if I wasn't needed in Parliament and for all the offices you always pushed me toward."

"She was hardly an infant. She would have been perfectly fine at home with a nurse while I came to London—"

"You are her *mother*! And pray God she never hears you say such horrid things."

Yates winced on Lavinia's behalf. He'd always thought Lady Hemming to be a rather typical aristocratic mother—not exactly the most affectionate, especially when they were all young, but she'd taken an interest in her daughter as they grew up and Lavinia became so beautiful. She had big plans for her first Season, before the fever stole that dream from them.

"She's a grown woman. She can handle the realization that I wished for a life beyond tending her up in the wilds."

Hemming sucked in a long breath. "And yet you have been pushing me toward this contract that will necessitate *more* time in Northumberland. I don't understand—ah. That must be our guests now."

Yates could just barely make out the sound of footsteps, though they grew louder over the next few seconds before the butler finally stepped inside. "Your guests have arrived, my lord. Count and Countess Coburg and Miss Feuerstein."

The chair squeaked again, and Lady Hemming's hand landed on the desk within Yates's view as she whisper-shouted, "What have you done?"

"What *you* should have done decades ago—made introductions to your family." Hemming stood, angling toward the door. "Ah, thank you so much for making the journey! Miss Feuerstein, I'm so glad you could join us too."

No matter how he positioned himself, Yates couldn't get a glimpse of the guests, but he heard their polite greetings easily enough. He had only to be patient—a moment later, a man who must be Hans Coburg passed into view, saying, "Franny! It has been too long. You are as beautiful as ever."

"Hans."

Yates frowned. Where the brother's voice had been warm and effusive, Lady Hemming's was cool and strained. From the surprise? Anger with her husband?

"Freida, what is the meaning of this?"

Yates's frown pulled even tighter. Why would she be questioning her sister-in-law about it?

"Calm down, Franziska." The voice, feminine and accented, came from closer to the room's exit.

"Calm *down*?" Lady Hemming spun into view again, facing Hemming and hence Yates. He caught a glimpse of her face—the word *irate* sprang to mind, quickly chased by *panicked*. "Why are you such a fool? I knew you were digging—sending that stupid Ballantine boy to try to discover my past. But why could you not just let it drop? You're going to ruin everything!"

"I'm trying to *save* everything—to save our family! Can't you see, Fran? I will accept you for who you are. Why you ever feared that I wouldn't—"

"Idiot man." Lady Hemming's voice vibrated. "You think I kept this from you out of *fear*? *Nein!*"

It was the German word that did it—that made it all snap into place in Yates's mind, and perhaps in Hemming's too. Because he stood, and before he braced his hands on his desk, Yates saw them tremble.

"You were not afraid I would judge you. Refuse you." Now the earl's voice was low but calm—the kind of calm soaked in sorrow. "You kept it from me because I was never anything to you but a pawn, was I?"

"Fran?" Coburg's voice, sounding as confused as Hemming's did resigned. "You always told me it was the increasing tension between our countries politics that kept you from wanting to claim our father. That your husband would never approve, and you feared if he found out, he would divorce you. When he wrote to me so earnestly, I thought we would finally have the chance to build a relationship, all of us."

"You're as much a fool as him," Lady Hemming spat. "Never concerned with anything but your own little corner of the world."

"Wait." A third feminine voice—it must be Miss Feuerstein. "All these years, when I was helping to ferry messages . . . Fran. I thought it just a sister wanting to stay in touch with her brother and his wife. But if your husband was never so opposed, then why the secrecy? Why . . . What have I been party to?"

A beat of silence—no doubt everyone was considering that question. Then Lady Hemming darted around to Hemming's side of the desk. For a moment, Yates wondered if she was going to throw herself into his arms, claim that fear he'd been ready to ascribe to her, beg for forgiveness . . . but no. She didn't reach for her husband. She reached for a drawer of his desk, which she yanked open in one swift motion.

Her hand dove in and reemerged a second later with a pistol. A chorus of shouts greeted its appearance, from absolutely everyone.

Yates couldn't see where she pointed the weapon, exactly, but from her stance, it must be leveled at Hemming.

Blast it—this wasn't at all what he'd been expecting. What should they do? Storm out? But that could increase her panic and make her do something rash.

325

"Fran, stop! What is the meaning of this?" Coburg, who from the sounds of it had rushed forward as Hemming stumbled back, out of Yates's view. "He is your *husband*!"

"He is my jailor, keeping me here when I only want to go home." Lady Hemming's chest heaved. "I married him because Freida told me it would be useful, that he was destined for great things in politics. I stayed with him all these years so that I could send her information to pass along to her uncle. But he's ruined it all, Hans. All the questions he's been asking! Sending agents to dig about in Saxony, trying to discover who I was—"

"Only so that I could assure you I knew and loved you anyway!" Hemming's shout turned to a groan. "Wait. Cornelius—you knew I'd sent him. You . . . what did you do, Fran?"

"What I had to," she barked in reply. "I gave Freida the information on his whereabouts as I'd done with the other agents you'd mentioned. So that they could be arrested and questioned."

"*Killed*, you mean." Hemming's voice shook. "You—no. You couldn't have done such a foul thing. Those innocent young men—"

"Innocent? Ha! They were *spies*, Alfred." She backed up a step, so that Yates had a perfect view of the gun as she cocked it. "But no—officially it was not *I* who did something so foul. It was Colonel May. Or so it will seem when the investigation reveals that he's been receiving money from Germany for the information."

Yates lifted his hand, trusting that Merritt would be able to see it in the scant light from the crack. She either meant to kill Hemming or use the weapon to hold him at bay while she made her escape.

Neither was acceptable. They had to act.

"What exactly are you planning to do, Fran? Kill me? You know well I'll never breathe a word of this—I can't, it would tear apart everything I've worked for. If you want to go, just *go*."

Her laugh sent a cold chill down Yates's spine. "You always did think too small, darling. I'm not just going to kill you. I'm going to use you—and my dear brother too—to start the war. Freida, I trust if you're here, you saw that May is as well?"

"I had a telegram delivered to him yesterday while we rested in London. We'll be able to lure him to whatever place you've picked out."

"Good. Hans, do be a good fellow and go with Freida."

"Why? So you can kill me too? Make it seem like a political assassination? Is that what you're planning?"

"And my own dear husband will die trying to save you, proving himself a hero. Then I, the poor widow, can see that his business dealings carry on as a tribute, and once we control England's battleship construction . . . well. I have a feeling the quality of them may suffer a bit."

"Freida?"

"It is nothing personal, Hans. It is just that you can do more for Germany dead than you have ever done for it alive. You are a hero. Now, come with me."

"Absolutely not!" Hemming shouted.

"Then Lavinia will pay the price. I have someone ready to intercept her if they don't hear from me," Lady Hemming said, voice cold. "It's your choice, Alfred. You . . . or her."

Yates couldn't quite wrap his head around the scale of what those two women had planned. But what he knew without a doubt was that if they let them leave that room, tragedy would follow. They would have to rescue Lavinia later—for now, Hans Coburg and Hemming. He looked over to Merritt, who was already bracing a hand to his side of the panel. Together, they nodded their count. One, two, *push*.

As they shoved the wall outward and both rolled out, Yates

yelled to Merritt, "Get Hemming and Coburg out of here!" Since Merritt had already earned a knighthood by getting people to safety, it seemed a logical assignment for him.

Yates made Lady Hemming his aim. He didn't know exactly what his plan was, but the first step was simply to throw his bulk at her.

They had the element of surprise on their side, that was certain. The lady spun, her pistol going off wildly—he hoped. He rammed into her, knocking them both to the ground and sending the gun clattering across the floor.

He wasn't counting on the knife she produced from somewhere and stabbed into his thigh, but it made him scream and move enough for her to slip away.

Clutching his leg, he looked up in time to see Freida Coburg pick up the gun, take aim at someone—and then crumple when another gunshot rang out, this time from near where Merritt had run toward Hemming. He didn't know which of them had taken the shot, but a moment later, Merritt and Coburg were running from the room, Hemming supported between them and Miss Feuerstein following behind.

Yates scrambled to his feet, though Lady Hemming had already taken the pistol from her fallen sister-in-law's hand and turned to level it on him. Perhaps she hadn't until that moment realized *who* had burst from the wall, because confusion mixed with the mad rage in her eyes.

Well. For all she thought she knew and had been manipulating, she hadn't bargained on the Imposters. Nor, perhaps, their skills. He dove as she fired off another round, rolling like he'd been taught and then springing up. And up more, his aim to land the balls of his feet on the desk so that he could launch himself over the chair between them.

His feet landed exactly as he'd planned . . . but then his leg screamed in pain, his knee buckled, and before he could compensate, he toppled backward.

Given the bullet that lodged in the shelf behind the desk, the fall might have saved him in that moment. But it knocked the wind out of him, his head cracked against the floor, and that split second of immobility and fog could spell disaster.

"No! Mother, stop!"

No! He tried to yell it but managed only a wheeze as he fought for air. Yates pushed himself up, begging his lungs to expand again, his spinning vision slowly coming to rest on something he shouldn't be seeing. Lavinia was supposed to be far away from all this, out of harm's way, in Leeds. Not rushing toward them as her mother rounded the desk, throwing herself atop Yates.

"Lavinia! Get out of the way!" Lady Hemming shouted.

She kept her body plastered to Yates's, covering his every vital organ with her own. "No! I don't know what this is all about, but I'll not let you hurt him!"

Little did she know that her mother had already threatened her life. Was she so heartless that she'd pull the trigger now, take them both out with one shot? *Please, God. Please spare this family that betrayal.*

War, that's what Lady Hemming had claimed she wanted. And it raged now across her face. "Lavinia, you don't know what you're doing. There is more at play here than you can know."

Lavinia's hair was in his face, her fingernails were digging into his back where she'd flung her arms around him, and she was shaking like a leaf.

He'd dreamt, once upon a time, of holding her like this—minus the knife wound to the leg, of course. It had been much less painful in his dreams.

"I know all I need to know. Mama, please. Put the gun down."

He saw the flicker move across her face at that *mama*. Saw the brief sagging of the gun. Then the lady's face hardened—

but she took a step back, strangely. "It doesn't matter. It doesn't matter what you think you know, Yates. Nothing you can say will stop the wheels of war if I can get Hans in place. Where did Sir Merritt take him?"

He eased Lavinia aside. If her mother was going to kill him for his answer, he wouldn't take her with him. "I have no idea."

Another battle waged across her face before morphing into something decided. "Have it your way. I know exactly how to bring him to heel. Your sister should be at the Tower this time of day, shouldn't she?" An evil smile curved her lips. "It's high time I pay her a visit."

TWENTY-SIX

*M*erritt prayed with every footstep, the urgency increasing as Hemming put more and more weight on him. He hadn't had a chance yet to see where the earl had been hit, but the red stain was spreading over his torso. Chest? Stomach? Side? *Lord, preserve his life. He was only trying to save his family.*

"I didn't know," Hemming wheezed out after they'd finally gained the carriage and he collapsed against the seat. "I thought . . . I never guessed. I should have."

"I am as guilty of ignorance as you, my lord." Coburg pulled the door shut behind Miss Feuerstein even as Jax spurred the horses into motion. "My wife—my sister! They got on so well that summer Fran spent with us before she came out here in England, but I never for a moment dreamed . . ."

Miss Feuerstein took her seat beside Coburg, her hand shaking. "I share the guilt too. I acted as courier for her all these years, never for a moment thinking their letters were anything but the usual correspondence of sisters-in-law."

"And I brought you here, right into their trap." Hemming winced, pressing a hand to his side.

Just his side, not his chest or stomach. That boded well.

Merritt shrugged out of his jacket—the only spare fabric he had—and balled it up, pressed it to the wound. "Here, my lord. Keep pressure on it."

Hemming blinked at him, as if only in that moment realizing who he was. Merritt could hardly blame him for that—*he* wouldn't have expected to see him burst from a wall and come to his rescue either. "Sir Merritt. What are you . . . no—more important. The other agents she mentioned. That she means to pin on May. We must discover who—"

"Already done, my lord. Gaines and I have a comprehensive list. There were three others—four, counting Ballantine."

The pain on Hemming's face looked far deeper than the physical. "My fault. I can never undo what she's done."

"You cannot, but that doesn't make it your fault. The important thing is that you are trying to stop her now. To keep this assassination those two have been planning from happening." He glanced over to Coburg, whose face was as white as his collar. "We can only change the future. We can only protect those still with us."

Hemming nodded, squeezing his eyes shut. "They must have some sort of plan in place, if they meant to force Coburg somewhere and have May there."

Merritt had no idea where either Frances or Freida were, but they soon wouldn't have any idea where *they* were either. "We have our own plan in place, my lord. They'll not find either of you, not until May and I and the constable have them in custody and have made certain your daughter is safe as well. You did well, sending her away for the weekend."

Coburg rubbed a hand over his eyes. "All my work for peace, undertaken for love of my sister and her family. This is what it's come to—I've made myself their target. 'Hero' indeed."

Miss Feuerstein reached over and covered her Hans's hand. "You have always been the best of men. Never let them make you regret that."

Silence descended for a few more fast-paced minutes, then the carriage began to slow. A glance at the window verified that it was for good reason. They were approaching the end of the grove of trees. And there, hidden from view of the Abbey but within sight of the crossroads, was the Caesars' old vardo, the zebras hitched to it.

Jax reined to a halt at the crossroads, and Merritt opened the door, jumped down, and reached a hand back into the carriage. "Time for a change of transportation."

The lady and gents filed out, Miss Feuerstein's mouth gaping when she spotted the Romani wagon. "You must be joking."

"I'm not. I can promise you, miss, that the Caesars will take the best possible care of you—and no one will ever think for a moment that you're in there. Franco will drive you to a safe place."

Franco was already striding toward them, waving an arm in welcome. "We're ready!"

"Do you have first aid supplies? Lord Hemming has been shot." Merritt kept an arm under the earl until Franco came to take over, nodding his assurances.

"Always! You are in good hands, my lord."

The sound of a car's engine broke through the day, coming from Alnwick. Merritt motioned to the vardo. "Hurry! Get in before anyone comes by."

As they ran toward the wagon, vanishing into it just before the car came into view, Merritt strode a few more steps along the road, craning for the first glimpse of who it was.

Though he knew, generally speaking. There were only two automobiles in the neighborhood, and Hemming's couldn't be coming from that direction. It had to be a Ballantine. He would wave them down, suggest they return to Alnwick, or better still, to Denwick Manor.

It was Genie at the wheel, and she looked none too happy

when he stepped into the lane and forced her to a stop. "Do get out of my way, Sir Merritt. I mean to have a word with Lord Hemming."

He shook his head. "He's not at home."

"Oh, I know. I just saw his car from the rise back there, taking the turn toward Fairfax Tower."

"What?" No. It must be the lady behind the wheel—and he didn't know what that meant for Fairfax. How had she gotten away from him? *Lord, no. Please. Let him be well!*

Then the implication hit home. The only one at the Tower was Marigold. The Caesars were all here in the vardo, and Graham Wharton had returned to the room he'd let at the hotel to rest up before his shift at the Abbey. Marigold, there alone . . . and an armed madwoman bent on assassination. She must know exactly what could inspire him to give up Coburg and her husband.

The woman he loved.

He yanked open the passenger side door and jumped in. "What are you waiting for? Drive!"

Marigold stroked her fingers through Leonidas's mane, her other hand rubbing at the velvet of his nose. She sat on the floor in his stall, her back against the wall, his enormous head in her lap. In her mind, that sleepy rumble in his chest was a purr, even though she knew that, by definition, big cats did not purr. They roared. Something, Hector had said, about a bone in their throat that was fused in the big cats and not in the small cats.

It didn't matter. He was purring at heart, and it did hers good. "What do you think, old friend?" she said, smiling at the lazy flick of his ear. "Do you think I made a good enough impression? Can we really make this work, or will I ruin everything? I keep hearing Lavinia in my head, saying nothing built on lies can last. And yet . . . we *do* know the truth of each other, don't we? Even if no one else does." She sighed and lowered her head to rest on his. "No one else in all the world has ever made me think that maybe there's something more to life than this."

And *this* had to stay part of her life. Always. But maybe . . . maybe more could come alongside. Maybe they could find a way to live out truth under the secrets. It was what Merritt would have to do anyway, wasn't it, given his position? Sometimes it was just a strange part of life.

Secrets, preserved so that lives could be. Truth, lived out behind a mask.

An engine cut through the peace of the day, making Leonidas's ears twitch, his head lift, and igniting a whole chorus of questions from the rest of the menagerie.

"Lionfeathers." It must be Genie, and here she was in her exercise clothes, with hay and who knew what else on the seat of her trousers. Smelling most assuredly of the stables, which Genie despised on a good day.

This was not a good day. Perhaps she'd been civil this morning, but she'd never *actually* said she thought the words she'd thrown at Marigold were untrue, had she? Only that she regretted saying them because they'd come back to bite her. In the moment, it had been apology enough. But the more she'd pondered it, the less convinced she was that Genie really meant to mend fences.

And the more Marigold wondered if it would be unspeakably rude to just hide out here with the animals and let Genie think her not at home. She'd knock at the front door of the house, no one would answer, and though she may peek into the gymnasium or theater, she'd never come in here.

Only, the footsteps on the gravel didn't sound quite like Genie's. And they headed straight for the open stable door at the far end, the end closest to the house. The end where the horses lived, when Grace and Mercy were at home. "Marigold!"

Lady Hemming? Here? She pushed to her feet, making it just outside the stall door before Lady Hemming stepped into the stable, the afternoon sun silhouetting her—and the gun she held. "Ah, there you are. Come with me, my dear."

This couldn't be good. "My lady! How—"

Lady Hemming raised the weapon. "I did not come to have a conversation. Your darling Sir Merritt has something I need, and you're going to ensure he returns it. Now come here, or I will start shooting these stupid animals."

"What?" What exactly had happened at the Abbey? Nothing good, clearly. Marigold couldn't hope to piece it all together just now, but obviously the lady meant to use her as a hostage. A bargaining chip.

Marigold's fingers curled into a fist. *No.* Never. She wouldn't let herself be used that way. Spinning, she ran, bolting out the door, praying madly with every pounding step that she wouldn't make good on the threat to the animals.

"I don't mean to hurt you—but I will if I must. If you don't want to be leverage, you can be punishment." Footsteps pounded behind her. "I've found that a broken man can be quite pliable. I daresay if your beloved and your brother see your lifeless form, they'll lose all will to fight."

A shot rang out. Marigold heard something whiz by her ear, strike the stone of the wall before her, and her gaze darted around the possibilities. The gate into the courtyard was locked. The back door to the house wasn't, but only because it stuck so badly and took three good yanks to get it to budge.

She didn't have three good yanks of time. But she must get into the house, to the old hunting pieces of Father's. The courtyard door—or better still, she could vault right onto the upstairs balcony and enter directly into his old bedroom, where they were stored.

Into the courtyard, then. Dodging and weaving to avoid the next bullet, she rounded the corner, knowing it would buy her a few precious seconds when she wasn't in Lady Hemming's line of sight.

A few precious seconds when she could grab the silk hanging over the side, scale the wall with five well-trained steps, and pull herself up onto the top of the stones.

"Idiot girl! Why could you never be a proper young lady?"

She would shoot again—and she did—but Marigold had already leapt into the air. Her fingers caught the edge of the trapeze platform a moment later, and she pulled herself up, careful to keep herself bent at the waist, so she remained out Lady Hemming's line of sight.

She was running, somewhere out there. The courtyard gate and its rotting wood and rusted lock probably wouldn't deter her for long.

Marigold didn't need long. Unhooking Yates's trapeze from its rest, she turned ninety degrees from their usual swing, aiming for the house instead of the opposite pole.

Even as she swung out, she eyed the distance between her and the balcony, her and the wall. Zelda had done this maneuver once, to present Mama with flowers as she lay dying in bed, trying to bring a smile to her face. But she'd nearly crashed into the courtyard wall behind her, had barely made the connection with the balcony. And Zelda was four inches taller than Marigold.

She hadn't been nearly as desperate, though. That would just have to bridge the gap. Swinging her body with all her strength, she sent herself forward, back, forward again. Close. Two more swings and—

The earth shook. No, the air. No—her wires! Was the

angle damaging the pole? It was creaking and groaning, twisting. Falling.

She was falling, a scream tearing from her lips. She tried to scramble up the trapeze's ropes, but they were slack, giving her no purchase.

As she crashed to the ground, she saw Lady Hemming, the guidewire stakes in her hands. It hadn't been the torque of the off angle. It had been *her*.

Marigold knew how to take a fall, how to roll. Even so, her head struck the sand, a roar filling her ears, making them ring as she rolled over and again. Her vision went grey. Black. *No.* She could die if she didn't cling to wakefulness. She forced her eyes open again, forced herself up onto her elbows. She had fallen before. She had gotten up. She would get up now.

Just in time to see a blur of tawny muscle take form. To realize that the roar wasn't in her head, it was in the air all about them, coming from the throat of her lion, who leaped on Lady Hemming as if he were a mighty hunter of the plains and not a tired old creature who lived his life in a stable.

Lady Hemming shouted something. Her gun fired.

"No!" Though her head thundered and her body screamed, Marigold scrambled toward them, crawling more than walking, falling more than standing. "Leonidas!"

Lady Hemming was screaming. Leonidas was growling, snarling, roaring again.

Blood. She saw blood, and a sob caught in her throat. "Leonidas!" She'd shot him! Shot her old lion because he'd tried to come to her rescue.

Not tried—*had*.

But the blood wasn't the lion's. As she finally made it to them and draped an arm over his back, she saw that he had the countess's arm in his teeth, and it was the woman's thrashing making the spatters.

"Leonidas, release! I said *release*!" She put her arms around

338

his neck, knowing she had to get through to him before the taste of blood overtook his training. Knowing that if he killed a person—a countess—no matter why, they'd take him from her. They'd kill him.

He'd gone for the arm, not the throat, Marigold realized. Leonidas was acting on what he'd been taught for his "King of the Forest" act, when the Caesars had pretended to attack each other. Not on instinct. No doubt if the lady hadn't fought against him, he wouldn't even have drawn blood. Perhaps a lion couldn't be tamed, but hers was trained.

Marigold pulled on his neck, and he released Lady Hemming's arm, peeled his lips back in one more vicious, scripted snarl, and then sat back on his haunches.

Marigold kept her arms around his neck, afraid to let go.

Lady Hemming staggered to her feet, blood dripping from her right arm. The gun now in her left. She raised it.

A shot rang out, but from behind Marigold, not before her. From a rifle, not a pistol. She jumped but had to focus on holding Leonidas steady, crooning nonsense to him, so it was another moment before she could crane her head around.

Genie stood there, her father's hunting rifle—the one he kept in his car just in case some game happened by—in her hands.

Merritt came charging in, sliding to his knees beside her, his arms coming around both her and Leonidas. "Marigold! Thank God."

Yes. Yes, that was what she had to do. And would, just as soon as she had words. For now, she sagged against his chest.

He held her so tightly against him that it shored up all the sagging places inside. The hand he plunged into her hair shook so badly that it steadied her. The lips he pressed to her temple broke in a sob that healed her.

"I thought I'd lost you. I cannot lose you."

"I'm all right." She anchored his hand in her hair with

one of her own, let her eyes slide closed. "What happened? Where's Yates?"

"I just spotted him at the bottom of the road as we pulled up." Still he trembled, still he shook. "I don't know anything else. Nothing—except that I love you."

"Merritt." They were the most beautiful words, words that brought tears to her eyes, words that sent her heart's trapeze soaring again. "I love you too."

And with one arm still around her lion, she kissed him.

TWENTY-SEVEN

hough it wasn't cold enough to really need a fire, they'd lit one anyway. They'd needed the cheerful crackle, the dance of light, the added warmth. The night had been long already, but Merritt knew none of them were ready for sleep. His own mind was still trying to sort through the afternoon and evening—the interviews with the constable, with Colonel May, with Coburg and Lord Hemming. It kept replaying for him—every word he'd said, every word he'd heard.

Every moment that could have gone so differently. He had his arm around Marigold so that she didn't get any ideas about leaving his side, and though there were probably a thousand rules of society that forbade them from sitting so on the sofa in her drawing room, no one said anything.

Not Xavier, who had accompanied Lavinia back again when she insisted she'd changed her mind about going to the ball at the first stop. He had then returned to Hawkhill House, never guessing he would "miss out on all the fun."

Not Gemma, who was bent over her paper, pen scratching furiously.

Not Graham, who was correcting his blueprints of the

Abbey—probably just for something to keep his hands busy, given the looks he kept darting at Gemma.

And not Yates, who had declared himself an invalid, insisting that meant that someone should wait on him hand and foot—even though the doctor had patched up his leg and assured him he'd be right as rain soon enough.

Merritt let his eyes slide shut and breathed in the scent of Marigold's hair—soap and flowers, sunshine and hay . . . and a little whiff of lion. That beautiful, blessed lion. *He* deserved a knighthood, without a doubt.

"All right." Gemma stood up, waving her paper in the air. "I have it drafted. Anyone up for a listen?"

He didn't exactly *want* to hear the article that would be printed about the day's events. He'd already helped the constable and Colonel May craft the story. But he nodded along with the rest.

Gemma brushed a stray curl away from her face. She looked exhausted, but her voice didn't shake as she began, "'A tragic accident has sent Northumberland into deep mourning today at the untimely death of one of its beloved own, the Honorable Lady Frances Hemming. It was at four o'clock on the evening of Friday last that a passing horseman noticed a prostrate form along the seaside cliff between Alnwick and Denwick. Upon investigation, the visitor to the area, Lieutenant Colonel Sir Merritt Livingstone, was distressed to see the familiar face of her ladyship. After rushing to her aid, he reported finding her ladyship already expired from this world. Upon consulting her physician, it became known to her family that the countess had been recently diagnosed with a serious heart condition, which is suspected to be the cause of her demise; she succumbed to her illness during one of her seaside walks that she loved so well.'"

Merritt drew in a long breath at the recitation. It was the only story the public would ever know. Colonel May had been quick to insist that they could not have the truth come out. It was not only a matter of national security—it would be a blight on MI5 before it ever even received its official charter.

Better, May had said, to seal the truth away under a Top Secret stamp. To spare Miss Ballantine the pain of lengthy official questioning by the local constabulary. To preserve the dignity of the Hemming name for the sake of the distraught Lord Hemming and Lady Lavinia.

She wasn't here now, neither she nor her father. They had clung to each other upon their reunion, had wept over the sad truth of who Lady Hemming had chosen to be. They had wept, too, with Hans Coburg, who would bury his sister here tomorrow and then escort his wife's body home, his own cover story in place.

None of them would ever contradict the official story, he knew. For the sake of the country and that Top Secret stamp, yes—and because the pain of that truth hit too hard to ever want to speak of it. Lord Hemming had told him and May that he intended to resign from his various appointments. That he and Lavinia would stay here in the healing quiet of Northumberland until . . . until they could bear to leave it. Lavinia had sent a curt note to Lord Xavier, thanking him for his court but disinviting him from any future calls in light of their family's mourning.

Xavier, though distressed at the tragic events he'd gotten only the barest version of, hadn't seemed alarmed at being cut out of Lavinia's life. He had simply shrugged and said, "If it's meant to be, it'll find a way."

He was most definitely *not* in love with her. If he were, he'd feel like Merritt did at the thought of months or years without Marigold by his side. As though his lungs hadn't enough air. As if his side was absent the security of his weapon. As if his soul was missing a vital piece of itself.

She looked up at him as Gemma kept reading, and she smiled. Her movements had been stiff all evening, and she reported ample bruising where she'd landed in the sand. He wasn't entirely convinced there was nothing else wrong. He wouldn't put it past her to hide a broken rib or two—not that *he* would ever do such a thing, ahem.

"I'm fine," she whispered, obviously reading his thoughts. "Stiff and sore, but fine."

"Mm. No doubt you'll be at some ball or another tomorrow, right?"

She winced at the thought and shook her head. "Heavens no. Not quite ready for that. Honestly, even the thought of the rest of the Season doesn't bear thinking about right now. Perhaps Lady M needs to take a bit of a holiday and sit this year out too."

"Oh no."

Her gaze flew back to his and tangled there. "Don't tell me *you* are eager for the Season, Sir Merritt."

"I don't give a fig about the Season." He smiled, feeling the light of it down to his bones. Down to his soul, and the place in it that was hers. "But Lady M and her assistants have a new dress to design."

Confusion knit her brows. "We have?"

"Oh yes—the most audacious wedding gown to be seen in a generation, I'm sure."

That light seemed to leap to her eyes and kindle there. "Does she?"

He leaned close, ignoring everyone else in the room. "I certainly hope so. That is, if she'll have me. I don't have a lion to offer her, but my heart is hers for the taking."

She smiled and lifted a hand to his cheek. "I already have the lion—but you. You are just what I've been missing."

AUTHOR'S NOTE

*I*t started, hilariously enough, as a dream. I woke up one morning with a lingering idea about a group called the Imposters—Edwardian investigators of the elite. I knew there were siblings . . . and that one of them was a fashion-forward young lady. The dream had involved them spying on aristocrats at a ball. As I fleshed the idea out over the course of a year or two, it grew to involve circuses and acrobats, theater troupes and Romani vardos. And it was so . . . much . . . *fun.*

Of course, part of the story of my aristocratic investigators also required a plot for them to investigate, and that took a bit more work! Research for me generally involves starting with a question and then following rabbit trails until I happen upon something that screams, "This is it!" In this case, it came when my research taught me that MI5 was in its conception in 1909, and that it was quite a task to combine the forces of the various branches of military and police intelligence into one centralized organization.

Up until then, England's intelligence game was sporadic, disorganized, and not nearly as sophisticated as that of Germany or Russia or the United States. The novels of William

Le Queux had lit a spy mania in the mind of the general populace, but they were pure fancy, based on nothing but the author's imagination. His tales proved so popular, however, that many people came to believe he had insider information and that there really were German spies abounding in England in the early 1900s.

Even more fascinating, though, was when I learned that a high-ranking German official had been selling out his own agents to the Russians in exchange for money, in this same era. That was what inspired my plot for the Hemmings; I borrowed much of this real-life German tragedy and applied the situation to my English lady, stopping her before she could achieve her warmongering goals. Her historical German counterpart, Colonel Alfred Redl, was in the pay of the Russians from 1903–1913. Shortly after he resigned his office in the intelligence division, his successor saw the next incoming payment to him, followed it, and was shocked to see who the recipient was. He promptly arrested Redl, who was then left in a hotel room with a loaded gun and unspoken expectation. He killed himself rather than bring shame upon his family and country, leaving a note that read, "Passion and levity have destroyed me. I pay with my life for my sins. Pray for me."

Another happy coincidence for my story was the rise of haute couture during this period; 1909 was in fact the year that Coco Chanel opened her first boutique in Paris! While I'm not the sort of fashionista who will don outrageous clothing, I have a love for it that is purely intellectual, and my daughter and I have been known to binge-watch fashion shows when the guys in the family are otherwise engaged. I had so much fun giving Marigold a love for high fashion, even if it's a begrudging love at times.

As always, I need to extend my thanks to my family; my critique partner/best friend, Stephanie Morrill; my agent,

Steve Laube; the amazing team at Bethany House; and the wonderfully supportive ladies of my Patrons & Peers group, who cheered me on and prayed me through the writing and revising of this one in a season when I was exhausted with health issues. I don't know where I'd be or what my writing would look like without the love and support of each and every one of you!

I hope you enjoyed my circus-loving aristocrats, my noble-spirited hero, and the colorful cast of characters . . . because you will be seeing more of them as the adventures of the Imposters continue. Graham and Gemma and Yates have their stories to tell, and the menagerie and Romani family will be playing their parts too.

For a peek into the Imposters' world, some of Lady M's budget-friendly fashion tips, a look inside her unusual handbag, and some secrets of the spy trade, be sure to visit RoseannaMWhite.com/Imposters.

DISCUSSION QUESTIONS

1. Lady Marigold Fairfax has created a persona that society sees and identifies as her, even though it hides much of her true self. How do you think we do the same thing today in the world of social media, and even in person?
2. Sir Merritt both knows the value of a team and hates to have to ask for help. Do you have trouble admitting when you need to call for backup? Or do you seek out a team as your first step?
3. Yates is still coming into his own in terms of responsibilities, given that he is now the earl but is also the little brother. How do you think his relationship with his sister has shaped him? What do you think he'd have chosen to do with his life if responsibility and duty weren't an issue?
4. If you could learn any of the skills Marigold and Yates have picked up from their circus friends, which one would it be? Would you make friends with big cats or other circus animals if you could?

5. Who was your favorite character and why? Your least favorite?

6. Lavinia observes that when her heart was weak, she was weak. Have you ever been in a position where your physical well-being (or lack thereof) shapes your whole life, or have you known anyone who has? How did you or they cope with those limitations?

7. Sir Merritt's friend Jonathan observes that sometimes true friends recognize each other quickly, seeing that "kindred spirit," or perhaps the Holy Spirit, in another. Do you have any friends with whom you formed fast bonds and whose friendship has remained strong for years? What is it, do you think, that knit you together?

8. Sir Merritt is one of the only people to ever truly see Marigold, and his clear vision of her helped her to better see herself. How do the people you love best help you to understand yourself better? What did you think of the progression of the characters' relationship?

9. Were you surprised by the revelation about the Hemmings? How do you think Lady Hemming kept her loyalties secret so long? Have you heard of any true stories about such things?

10. Book two in THE IMPOSTERS, *A Noble Scheme*, will be about Gemma and Graham. What do you think is the cause of their animosity?

*Keep reading for more exciting romance and intrigue
from Roseanna White in book two of*

THE IMPOSTERS

A NOBLE SCHEME

Available Spring 2024

*Gemma Parks and Graham Wharton may both be members
England's most elite private investigation firm, but they've
barely spoken in a year, and Gemma intends to keep it that
way . . . until a case involving a kidnapped boy mistaken
for his aristocratic cousin forces her hand. She and Graham
are the logical investigators, yet can she withstand days in
his company without succumbing to the pain of the past?
Graham, for his part, is determined to use the time not just
to rescue the missing boy but also to win back the heart of
the only woman he's ever loved. Can even the noblest of
schemes restore a heart so completely shattered?*

ONE

Gemma

4 December 1909
Fairfax Tower, near Alnwick, Northumberland

he Wedding of the Decade. That's what Gemma would call it when she wrote her column for *London Ladies Journal.* Or maybe "of the century"? Was it too presumptuous to call it that when the century was only nine years old?

Oh, it hardly mattered. G. M. Parker wasn't known for her unbiased view of society and history; she was known for her clever turns of phrase and descriptions of exclusive events. She was known, mostly, for always "intuiting" where the fashion icon she'd dubbed Lady M would show up, and for writing every detail of her latest haute couture ensemble.

Gemma sipped her punch, smiling at Lady M now. It was really a wonder that no one had yet suspected that she did in fact know every place Lady Marigold Fairfax—now Livingstone, as of an hour ago—would show up, because she helped plan her schedule.

And occasionally showed up in her place, decked out in her audacious and ostentatious frippery, head tilted down so no one thought to look at the face beneath the hat or mask or headpiece. All so that Marigold would have an alibi while she did Imposters work, usually spying on the very people who lapped up news about her like overeager puppies.

Covering this wedding would be a true coup for G. M. Parker, though, in the eyes of society. The engagement between Lady Marigold Fairfax and Lieutenant Colonel Sir Merritt Livingstone had been unexpected, and instead of a lavish London ceremony, they had opted for a small, private event here in the bride's home parish. They had exchanged their vows at the humble local cathedral and invited their very select list of guests back to Fairfax Tower for a private reception. No more than sixty people were in attendance. No one would expect G. M. Parker to be one of them.

Little did they know that Gemma Parks and Lady Marigold Fairfax had been inseparable companions all their lives. Gemma had grown up in the halls of Fairfax Tower as surely as the heirs had, her father managing the estates as best as the late Lord Fairfax would allow, what with bleeding money on amusements and entertainments as he did.

Back then, neither Gemma nor Marigold nor her brother Yates, and neither Gemma's brother James nor the Fairfaxes' distant cousin Graham, had any idea that the circuses and theater troupes, the acrobats and musicians were costing what should have been saved for their own futures. They knew only that their childhood was enchanted and magical and endlessly fun.

She slid her punch cup, still half full, onto a table. Perhaps ten-year-old Gemma couldn't be expected to know such realities. But twenty-five-year-old Gemma had learned long ago that nothing in life was truly all roses and birdsong. Nothing was enchanted moments and golden memories. They were illusions, those. No more substantial than theater costumes. No more real than stage smoke. No more lasting than a two-dimensional set.

Every happy ending was a tragedy's beginning. It was all a matter of what story one chose to tell. And though her society column focused on things sparkling and well designed, on colors and cuts and styles, on liaisons and courtships and rivalries, she never penned a single word without counting the lies and illusions.

Lady M's masterpiece of a wedding gown, over which everyone would argue about its origin—Paris, Milan, New York?—was a perfect example. *She* knew very well it came from the attic right here at Fairfax Tower. A gown soaked in vinegar until the silk whitened again. Seams ripped out and resewn. Discolored lace removed, beading added by the Romani seamstress who had learned her trade in the circus.

The result was undeniably gorgeous. And today—unlike most days—the extravagant gown had no hope of outshining its wearer. Today, Marigold was beaming with joy. Overflowing with happiness. Today, nothing could eclipse the beauty of the face she usually hid.

Gemma's heart squeezed tight as she watched her best friend waltz with her new husband. Sir Merritt was a good man, worthy of this remarkable family, worthy of their secrets. He loved Marigold. He loved the Tower. He even loved the investigative work they did anonymously as the Imposters and had joined their ranks. She was happy for her friend. She wished her every joy.

She just knew that it wouldn't last. Not this moment, not this bubble of light and laughter. Storms would come. Pain. Loss. Arguments. Hurt feelings. Rough patches. Hunger.

Judgment. She *wished* only good things for her friend—but she didn't believe them possible.

That wasn't the world they lived in. Her brother, vicar that he was, would remind them all that it was because they lived in a fallen world. That sin had stained all of creation. And no doubt he was right.

It would stain this too, eventually. It would steal happiness. It would tarnish every golden moment.

And she was depressing herself at her best friend's wedding ball, which proved what a wretch she was. She ought to have focused on what wording she would use to describe the wedding guests rather than wax darkly poetic. Best to leave the poetry to Yates, the current Lord Fairfax and Marigold's little brother.

"Has anyone told you today how beautiful you look?"

The voice brought a tempest of reactions swirling through her, like it always did. First the old one—the pleasure, the thrill. The recognition of *Graham*. The boy she'd grown up loving. Fury chased the thrill away—fury and fear and something even darker that she refused to look at. She clenched her jaw and sidestepped those warm words whispered in her ear.

Don't even look at him, she commanded herself, even as she swung around to face him.

More conflicting emotions rose, because no matter how much she dreaded seeing him, she loved seeing him. Loved looking at him, as she'd always done. That wave of dark hair, the eyes so deep a brown they were nearly black, sparking always with intelligence. The lips so well shaped that any woman would be jealous of them, the ones that had kissed her countless times.

No. Those days were over. Had been for nearly a year now. She made herself lift her chin and put another step of crucial space between them before her arms forgot that their place was no longer looped around his.

She would be civil, though. It was Marigold's wedding day, after all, and he loved her like a sister, the same as Gemma did. The last thing the bride needed was two of her guests making a scene that stole the attention. So, she pasted a small smile on her face and pretended he was a stranger. A random guest she'd never met before, one who would flatter any lady before he asked her dance. "I believe all compliments ought to be directed to the bride today, sir."

He'd always known, somehow, every story she told herself. His eyes flashed now as he rejected this one. "I promise you, Gem, if you call me *sir* one more time, I'm going to remind you of how well you know me, right here in front of everyone."

She faced the dance floor again, keeping her chin at that angle that said *Keep your distance.* "My apologies, Mr. Wharton. If it's a lack of respect you want, I can certainly oblige."

"Gemma." He'd always had a way of growling her name— and she'd done all manner of things to provoke him into doing it over the years, just to hear the rumble. "Please. If only for tonight, can't you remember the good things? It's Marigold's wedding day."

And her friend, as she danced with her groom, looked blissfully happy. She wasn't thinking today about how they'd all scrimped and saved to pull off this modest celebration; how the entire staff of five and the two noble siblings had worked their fingers to the bone over the last month, getting the Tower ready to receive guests. How they'd patched and hammered and plastered over all the evidence of an estate on the brink of bankruptcy so that no one would know. No one would see beyond the shimmer and the shine. No one would realize that all the waiters and maids were actors and acrobats and Romani who had gathered here for the day to help one of their favorites celebrate her new start.

Imposters indeed. That's what they all were.

But they were happy Imposters. Focused on the beautiful, focused on the future. Gemma used to be too, back when she thought the future would always have sunshine to chase away the storms, rather than always have clouds to cover the sun. It was a lesson too hard learned to forget even for an evening.

The best she could give him was to focus on the neutral. "Did you and Yates have time yet to work through the new project?"

His sigh was as blustery as the December wind blowing in from the North Sea. "Not yet. We decided it could wait until Marigold and Sir Merritt left for their honeymoon."

And that seemed to exhaust *that* topic. The new investigation they'd been hired to do promised to be complicated and would take several months. It wasn't exactly urgent, as it involved background searches on players in a business deal still six months from being finalized, but it came with a hefty enough stipend that they'd actually been able to afford the food for all these wedding guests. Still, they didn't have a plan of action worked out, and didn't need to quite yet.

A perfect job for the season, from the point of view of the Fairfax siblings, with this wedding and honeymoon to plan. Not so perfect for Gemma, who was as desperate for distractions as a fish was for water.

She cleared her throat and wished her punch cup hadn't been gathered up by a passing waiter already. Casting her gaze around for something else to talk about, she focused on the gleaming chandeliers. "We got the ballroom looking splendid again, don't you think? Like it was when their father was still alive and hosting events every week."

Graham didn't look up or out, though. His gaze was still firmly latched onto her profile. She could feel it searing into her cheek like a brand. "Did you do something different with your hair?"

Lionfeathers. He always noticed every detail. Every new

style she tried, every new ribbon. It was one of the things she'd always loved about him. He made her feel noticed and appreciated and cherished in a world so shiny with faux glitter that a steward's daughter ought to have been ignored. "We were going to try the style on Marigold, but her hair was too long for it, and she ran away when I got out the shears." She smiled—at the memory, not at *him*.

He had to have known what elicited it, but still he drew closer, boxing her in against the side table. "It suits you. Everything suits you, but this . . ." He actually reached up and traced the tips of his fingers along the sweep of hair that went from temple to nape. "Beautiful."

Her breath froze in her lungs. Half of her wanted to bat his hand away, and half of her wanted to lean into it, and the war that raged between the parts was what made her turn her head so she didn't have to look at him. "You should go."

"Gem—"

"Please." Her voice broke on the words, her eyes sliding shut against a sudden burning that she fended off with a deep, quick breath. It was perhaps the most vulnerable word she'd uttered to him in months. Usually she hid behind acid and ice just to keep him at bay.

Because this was what happened if she didn't. He slid too close, reminded her too quickly of what once had been, made her want to remember all the wrong things. Happiness and hope and love songs.

That wasn't real. What was real was broken hearts and despair and dirges.

"Darling, please. It's been nearly a year—"

She couldn't have said which of his words brought the fury rushing back, filling her veins and pushing her past him in one sweeping step. The endearment? The plea? The reminder of those full twelve pages of the calendar that had flipped by since the world came to a screeching, shattering halt?

Definitely that. "You think I don't know how long it's been?" She hissed the words when she wanted to shout them, clenched her fist when she wanted to pound it into his chest. "You think I haven't counted every month, every week, every day, every hour?"

His face shifted from earnest and pleading to cold and hard as the granite he favored in his work. "You think I haven't too? If you would talk to me—"

"Why? You never listen. Had you listened a year ago—"

"You think I don't know that?" Somehow he managed to whisper his own shout, but the muted volume certainly didn't mute the fire in his words. "You think I haven't replayed that conversation in my head over and over? You think I haven't regretted it every single minute of every single day?"

Of course he did. But that was the thing—regret changed nothing. Sorrow changed nothing. A million apologies couldn't undo the damage his arrogance and pride had caused.

And if she didn't escape this ballroom right this minute, she'd ruin her best friend's wedding ball with a fit of weeping that was sure to garner the attention she wanted to avoid at all costs. With a shake of her head, she stormed away—out of the conversation, out of his presence, out of the ballroom.

She didn't stop until she'd stormed directly out into the courtyard. They'd taken the trapeze down for the wedding so that Merritt's family and friends wouldn't wonder at it. Gemma had never had the skill on it that Marigold and Yates had, but she could have done with swinging from the bar and letting the wind chase away the tears. Let it ruin her hair and replace the feel of Graham's fingertips on it. Let the rush of gravity and air pull her out of her head and away from the memories always lingering right below the surface.

Another rush of wind as the borrowed car spun out of control. Another squeak—not of guidewires, but of body panels.

No. *No.* The memories had gotten even heavier as the weather cooled again, and when her foot crunched through the layer of ice on top of a puddle last week, she'd very nearly shattered too. But she wouldn't let herself fall into that. Not here. Not now. Not while *he* was right inside, when he might chase her out here.

"Gemma?"

She sniffed, telling herself her nose was running from the cold air and not from the tears burning the back of her eyes. She pasted on a smile and turned back to the door from which she'd run. The happy friend. The well-wisher. *Imposter.*

"The bride shouldn't be sneaking away from her own wedding ball, Marigold. Get back inside."

She didn't, of course. She came to Gemma's side instead, not even shivering in her gown of silk and lace, though Gemma was, she suddenly realized, quaking more than she ought to be from mere cold.

Marigold draped a shawl, colorless in the moonlight, over Gemma's shoulders. "We should have had the wedding in November. Or January."

"Don't be ridiculous." Marigold had always wanted a December wedding, filled with holly and ivy, yew and laurel and the promise of eternity . . . before she'd given up on the idea of marriage when her father died. When Merritt reignited those dreams, they'd breathed life again into her old imaginings.

Her friend frowned. "I told you December was a bad idea."

"I wanted the distraction." And it had worked as long as Graham was safely in London while Gemma and Marigold and Yates were all here. She could ignore the gap his absence left, fill it with busyness and plans and laughter. She could write extra columns and pen a few stories she'd never show anyone and read novels until her eyes went blurry and crossed and there was no room left in her head for reality.

Sighing, Marigold slid an arm around Gemma's waist and pulled her tight, resting her forehead on hers. They were the same height. The same size, had the same general figure. They'd learned to walk in the same way, had studied the same posture. They had worked for years to be interchangeable whenever life called for it.

But never before had it been clearer that they weren't. There stood Marigold in her breathtaking wedding gown, the future spread out before her, filling her with warmth and light.

And here was Gemma in the shadows, nothing but her words to keep her company, a lifetime of winter waiting.

"Come inside, Gem," her friend whispered after a long moment of frozen silence. "You'll turn to ice out here."

She let Marigold pull her inside. But she didn't know why she bothered.

She'd turned to ice almost a year ago, and there was no fire on earth strong enough to thaw her again.

Roseanna M. White is a bestselling, Christy Award–winning author who has long claimed that words are the air she breathes. When not writing fiction, she's homeschooling her two kids, editing, designing book covers, and pretending her house will clean itself. Roseanna is the author of a slew of historical novels that span several continents and thousands of years. Spies and war and mayhem always seem to find their way into her books . . . to offset her real life, which is blessedly ordinary. You can learn more about her and her stories at roseannamwhite.com.

Sign Up for Roseanna's Newsletter

Keep up to date with Roseanna's latest news on book releases and events by signing up for her email list at the link below.

FOLLOW ROSEANNA ON SOCIAL MEDIA

Roseanna M. White   @roseannamwhite   @roseannamwhite

RoseannaMWhite.com

More from Roseanna M. White

During WWII, when special agent Sterling Bertrand is washed ashore at Evie Farrow's inn, her life is turned upside down. As Evie and Sterling work together to track down a German agent, they unravel mysteries that go back to WWI. The ripples from the past are still rocking their lives, and it seems yesterday's tides may sweep them into danger today.

Yesterday's Tides

Fleeing to the beautiful Isles of Scilly, Lady Elizabeth Sinclair stumbles upon dangerous secrets left behind by her cottage's former occupant and agrees to help the missing girl's brother, Oliver Tremayne, find his sister. As the two work together, they uncover ancient legends, pirate wrecks, betrayal, and the most mysterious phenomenon of all: love.

The Nature of a Lady
THE SECRETS OF THE ISLES #1

When Beth Tremayne stumbles across an old map, she pursues the excitement she's always craved. But her only way to piece together the clues is through Lord Sheridan—a man she insists stole a prized possession. As they follow the various leads, they uncover a story of piratical adventure, but the true treasure is the one they discover in each other.

To Treasure an Heiress
THE SECRETS OF THE ISLES #2

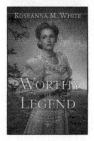

After uncovering a diary that leads to a secret artifact, Lady Emily Scofield and Bram Sinclair must piece together the mystifying legends while dodging a team of archaeologists. In a race against time, they must decide what makes a hero. Is it fighting valiantly to claim the treasure or sacrificing everything in the name of selfless love?

Worthy of Legend
THE SECRETS OF THE ISLES #3

BETHANYHOUSE

Bethany House Fiction   @bethanyhousefiction   @bethany_house   @bethanyhousefiction

 Free exclusive resources for your book group at bethanyhouseopenbook.com

 Sign up for our fiction newsletter today at bethanyhouse.com